PRAISE FOR THE DRUID'S TUNE

"From Iron Age Ireland to modern-day Vancouver, the author takes readers on a wild ride fueled by love, revenge, and ecstasy . . . a tall, sexy drink of satisfaction."

—JP MCLEAN. SUPERNATURAL THRILLER AUTHOR

"Great characters that are incredibly well-built. A depth of emotional description that will surprise you. Drama, lots of drama. A connection with Nature that will have you looking around with new eyes. Great erotic scenes of intimacy, many of which aren't even 'sexual' per se."

—JULIO CARLOS, SCRIBBLE'S WORTH

"This story reads like a journey, and one with exactly the kinds of people you'd want to be on an epic adventure with—complex, intriguing, and with enough nuance and contradiction to, like the plot itself, add a frisson of unpredictability at interesting moments."

—JUNIPER GREER-ASHE

"a dangerous world where engaging characters could easily lose their lives to vampires, while losing their hearts to love."

—ROXY BOROUGHS, AUTHOR OF *WOLFEN TIME*

"Beautifully written . . . suspenseful and steamy."
—SIONNACH WINTERGREEN, QUEER FANTASY/CRIME AUTHOR

THE DRUID'S TUNE

THE MAN IN BLACK 5

HARPER CARR

Blue Haven Press, Vancouver, Canada

http:bluehavenpress.com

ISBN: 978-1-998738-08-3 Paperback
ISBN: 978-1-998738-09-0 Electronic Book

Book Design: Wendy Hawkin, Blue Haven Press
Cover Image: Mythology Art
Developmental Edit: Donna Tunney
Revisions & Copy Edit: Wendy Hawkin

Cataloguing in Publication Information is available from Library and Archives Canada.

Dedicated to my dad,
who gave me music and poetry,
the quest for spirituality,
and enough emotional issues
to write this series forevermore.

Poetry. And it was at that age . . . Poetry arrived
in search of me. I don't know, I don't know where
it came from, from winter or a river.
I don't know how or when,
no they were not voices, they were not
words, nor silence,
but from a street I was summoned,
from the branches of night,
abruptly from the others,
among violent fires
or returning alone,
there I was without a face
and it touched me.

La Poesía. Y fue a esa edad . . . Llegó la poesía
a buscarme. No sé, no sé de dónde
salió, de invierno o río.
No sé cómo ni cuándo,
no, no eran voces, no eran
palabras, ni silencio,
pero desde una calle me llamaba,
desde las ramas de la noche,
de pronto entre los otros,
entre fuegos violentos
o regresando solo,
allí estaba sin rostro
y me tocaba.

—Pablo Neruda, 1904-1973, Chilean poet and
diplomat, and winner of the 1971 Nobel Prize in
Literature. From *Selected Poems,* 1949

1

Once Upon a Time

A spray of saltwater soaked them all. Diego had risen from the sea in the guise of a thunderbird. Thrusting its muscular legs through the yacht's broken skylight, talons reaching and grasping, it attacked. They scrambled back. But as Estrada turned, the creature caught him by the shoulders. His scream pierced Michael's heart. He knew that feeling—the squeezing and breaking of bone and flesh.

Clutching Estrada, the vampire hauled him up through the jagged glass. His feet were off the ground. In a breath, he'd be gone. Michael sprung, and clinging to Estrada's back, he pulled at the curved talons embedded beneath his clavicle. Though his hands were flayed by the vampire's claws, still he pulled and pulled. Estrada's bones snapped. And then they were both free falling.

But suddenly, the bloody claws punctured Michael's chest. Screaming, he stared down. Saw Estrada hit the deck. Saw his friends drag him off. And then Michael was in the sky, being buffeted by the night wind as the creature carried him up and up.

Then, as if in sudden recognition of its mistake, the vampire somersaulted and careened down. Michael's face hit the surface of a concrete sea. Breath caught. Pain surged. Beating its thunderous wings, the creature dragged him through the waves. Gasping. Broken-faced. Drowning.

And then he was under, and salt water filled his lungs.

2

Co. Offaly, Ireland

"How much farther to this *Lolly* place?" Estrada swiped the sweat from his forehead with the back of his hand. After enduring weeks of frigid rain in Iron Age Ireland, its modern counterpart felt like Jamaica in July. His ass ached from bouncing through the countryside on a sweaty gray horse, and his gut was as hollow as the volcano beneath Croghan Hill. He stared at the hind end of Sorcha's round brown pony and waited.

Sorcha raised her left hand without turning back and showed him two fingers. He snarled. *Two more hours?* Raising his hand, he flipped his middle finger. He had to believe the sassy archaeologist who'd gotten them into this mess could get them out. Ireland was Sorcha's territory, and she claimed to know people in the next county who could stable their horses and lend them enough cash to get home. Cernunnos, the ancient Horned God, had sent them back through the wormhole with no means to traverse the twenty-first century. No credit cards, no cash, no drivers license. Not even a piece of I.D.

He glanced over his shoulder at Conall, who rode behind him on his white stallion, head bowed, lost in his own tuneful world. The bard had ripped the sleeves off his pale homespun shirt and tied a hank of linen around his forehead like a headband. Conall was a living piece of history, a stunning Druid bard flown forward in time, still clutching his blood-slick iron sword. He'd popped through the wormhole with them at the last second—no doubt because Estrada had expressed a desire to bring him back to the contemporary world. Another gift from Cernunnos. Estrada would rather be hoisting beers with Conall than bouncing along on this wide-backed Irish draught horse, but as Robert Frost once said, they had miles to go before they could drink themselves to sleep.

Finally, as the three friends left the pasture behind and trotted single file down the narrow country road, Estrada breathed in hope. The square stucco homes inched closer together. Then he saw a gas station and a sign written in Irish Gaelic he didn't dare pronounce. Late afternoon shadows climbed stone garden walls, whispering the promise of a cool evening. As he licked his dry lips, his stomach growled.

"How do they feel about buskers here?" Estrada asked. Perhaps the bard could play his pipes, or he could whip up a few magical sleights-of-hand, if they could find an audience. Sorcha just shook her head.

As he listened to the rhythmic clip clop of the horses' unshod hooves, his thighs ached for his Harley. He raked his fingernails through the loose hair that dusted the back of his damp neck. When they passed a shop with a giant Red Bull image in the window, he snorted. What he wouldn't give for a cold shot of sweet caffeine. But the lights were out, and a CLOSED sign dangled cockeyed in the window. The silent village was eerily vacant. Where were all the people? Holed up inside with fans or air conditioners away from this oppressive heat?

As they crossed the old stone bridge, his throat felt too parched even to swallow. Still, the rippling river sang her siren song, and he gazed down, remembering another bridge like this—a bridge he'd crossed in a vision when he'd traveled to the Underworld to rescue Michael's fractured soul. That moment seemed long ago, and yet; it hadn't happened yet. Wouldn't happen if he succeeded in his task.

Foreknowledge was the best gift Cernunnos had ever given him. Today was June 21st, and he knew the vampires wouldn't strike until August 1st—the eve of his daughter's first birthday. He squeezed his fist and pounded his breast. He had just over five weeks to annihilate Diego and his vampire horde. Five weeks to foil the abduction of his child. Five weeks to save Michael.

I must save Michael.

Estrada had arrived at the far side of the bridge when he realized he'd been so caught up in his revery, he'd forgotten about the others. He could see Sorcha up ahead and hear the rushing water beneath the bridge, but the steady clip-clop of Conall's horse's hooves had stopped.

He stared over his shoulder and searched the road behind him, but the bard was gone.

A rush of adrenalin raced up his legs, and he tugged the leather reins across his horse's neck and spun her with the force of his thighs and heels, just in time to catch the white flash of Capall's tail as the stallion disappeared down the abutment.

"Conall," he shouted. Urging his horse into a trot, Estrada bounced over the single lane bridge and down the steep trail to the stream below.

"Conall," he yelled again, panic clutching his gut. The bard's blood-stained clothes lay in a heap.

When his gray mare saw Conall's white stallion belly-deep in the stream, she headed down the bank. Estrada leapt off and doffed his leather boots, waded into the cool water and stared upstream, then followed the current down.

He gasped. Conall floated face down, arms outstretched, his shoulder blades and the slick curves of his ass the only pale parts showing above the coppery water.

"Conall," he screamed. *Please don't tell me you've given up after all this.* "Raise your head, man. Breathe."

When the bard didn't move, Estrada waded closer, caught his shoulders with both hands, and yanked. Conall's body turned, his head flew back, and he blinked. Estrada crushed him to his chest. "What're you doing, man? I thought you were—"

"Why?" Conall stepped back, his brown eyes wide. "Why would you think that?"

"You lost Ruairí and your home, and I can't imagine what it must be like to see your beautiful Ireland purged for peat." The flat black striations bothered Estrada, and he was used to environmental destruction. Conall was not. Pre-industrial Ireland was virginal. Pristine.

"Aye. My heart breaks for all those things." Conall grasped Estrada's face in both hands. "But I'm alive, and I have you and Sorcha. This is still my Ériú, and Ruairí walks with the goddess."

Estrada grasped Conall's bearded jaw with both palms and held him. He had no words. But their eyes locked, and he knew his friend spoke the truth. For this moment, at least, Conall had surpassed his grief and there were only the two of them standing under the bridge, hip deep in water.

Leaning in, Estrada pulled Conall's jaw closer until their lips brushed, and he breathed Conall's breath and tasted the silty stream on his skin. His body fired with their first kiss, one he'd waited days and nights to feel. It was only the bard's grief for Ruairí that had held Estrada's desire at bay. His hands slid down Conall's cool naked back and drew him in. Their mouths formed promises. When Conall's hand slid down Estrada's wet leather breeches, he groaned.

"*Jaysus, Mary, and Joseph.* I thought I'd lost you two, and here yous are, making out under the feckin bridge like a couple of horny trolls."

Estrada ignored Sorcha and continued to savor Conall's kiss. Eyes closed, tongues teased, thighs pulsed, fingers caressed. He wanted more. They both wanted more.

"Alright then, lads. You stay here and have at her. I suppose we all need a little recreation after what we've been through. I'll be down at the Village Green enjoying the free solstice barbecue."

The kiss ended abruptly as Estrada and Conall turned to face Sorcha, who stood on the bank behind them with her hands on her hips. "Free barbecue, you say?" Estrada waded closer with the bard in tow.

"Aye. Burgers and pints. All you can eat and drink. Music too. It's put on by the village to celebrate Summer Solstice. No cash required, and I've just secured us an invitation."

Conall squinted. "Burgers and pints?"

"Trust me," Estrada said. "You'll love it. But we can't go like this."

"Aye, you'd best dry off and—" Before she could finish, Estrada stumbled out of the stream, threw an arm around Sorcha, and yanked her into the water. She screamed and sank below the surface, then popped up grinning, and pressed back her wet red hair. "Ah lads, it does feel grand."

Conall splashed her and the two of them played like kids as Estrada stripped off his wet shirt and leather breeches and hung them on a bush. Then he staggered back into the current and slipped underwater. The stream wasn't deep, not even over his head, but he emptied his lungs and sank to the bottom. Sitting as stoic as Houdini, he felt his body and spirit infuse with the healing power of the water. Running his hands over the accumulated sweat and dust, he scrubbed his face and hair, arms, and chest, then let the river do the rest.

When he burst through the surface, he could feel the gods and goddesses of old all around him, cheering him on. *You can do this. You'll find a way.* And when he stepped from that silty stream, Estrada felt like a man reborn. A thirsty, hungry man.

"Where's this barbecue?" he said.

"Same way we were heading." Sorcha grasped the bard's hand. "Come on, Conall. I want to see your face when you bite into your first burger in this millennium."

3

Heads turned as the motley trio rode onto the trimmed green grass, their spirited horses revived by the stream. Tall Scots pines bordered a square of verdant parkland fringed by oak, ash, and hazel trees. Yellow fringed flags fluttered from tall, leafy branches and crisscrossed over their heads. Barbecues belched smoke laced with the scent of charred beef. People sat eating and conversing in lawn chairs, while children played chase or frolicked to the band in front of the wooden stage. Others, clutching large plastic cups, queued in front of a table stacked with vats and ladles.

Is that beer? Estrada leapt off his horse and tied it loosely to a shrub as Sorcha and Conall had done. The mare lowered her head to graze the rich grass.

"Beer," he shouted, and shambled over to join the queue. His thighs weren't quite right after hours on that broad-backed nag, but after a few pints he figured he might forget.

If it hadn't been Summer Solstice, Estrada might have got some strange looks, dressed as he was in wet leather breeches, boots, and a dirty linen shirt. But today, many were in costume. Some resembled faeries and elves—thanks to the power of Tolkien, no doubt—others, gods and goddesses. There were even Vikings.

I like this village, Estrada thought, as he sniffed the scent of incense and cannabis mingling on the wind.

He dipped a ladle into the dark brown vat labeled Guinness and filled three large plastic cups. Then he scanned the crowd for Conall and Sorcha. He shook his head when he discovered her flirting with a tall, fair-haired man in front of a barbecue, burger in hand. Even after their experience with Kai Roskilde in Scotland, Sorcha still had a penchant for blond, burly Vikings.

Then he spotted Conall. Crouching before the stage, the bard gazed intently at the band, no doubt fascinated by the plethora of instruments and sounds. The musicians were all pros—acoustic base and guitar players, a raucous fiddler, another pumping some exotic bagged instrument while using his rapid-fire fingers to create a melody. While still another blew a high-pitched tin whistle with enough zeal to rouse the fey.

Estrada strolled through the crowd, carefully minding the sloshing red plastic cups and offered one to the bard.

Conall sat back and squeezed the cup curiously until Estrada stopped him from busting it, then threw back his head and downed the whole pint. Estrada handed him another and hunkered down on the grass beside him.

After draining his pint, Estrada glanced at Conall's rapt face. The bard had unbound his long brown hair, and it glittered with gold streaks as it dried in the sunlight. Freckles dotted his cheeks above a wolfish nose. As he watched the band, his eyes, a deep caramel shade, sparkled with intensity.

Estrada reached over with one hand and ran his fingers down the bard's cheek into his fine beard. "You're beautiful, man." When Conall's lip quivered, Estrada caught his jaw in his hand, leaned forward, and brushed his lips gently with his own.

The bard drew back, perhaps fearing the impropriety. Homosexuality was esteemed in Iron Age Ireland but not expressed publicly from what Estrada had seen.

"It's cool, man. No one here cares if we kiss. Look around." There were several amorous couples in the crowd of varying genders, and no one gave them a second look. It was a solstice celebration and that meant merriment in all its guises.

"That's not it," Conall said. "I just . . ."

"Just what?"

He shrugged. "I'm not good at it. I'd never done it until—"

"Wait. What? Are you saying that kiss back in the stream was your first? Ever?" Estrada squinted at Conall's nod, then shook his head.

Conall smiled shyly. "Was it alright?"

"Alright? That kiss left me spun, man." He brushed Conall's lips with his thumb. "I can't understand how you, looking as you do, have never been kissed." Estrada had seen plenty of kissing in Iron Age Croghan. The ancient Irish weren't sexually repressed by any means. Had Conall really been so hung up on Ruairí, his straight best friend, that he'd never had other relationships or experiences?

When Conall dropped his head and averted his gaze, Estrada remembered a drunken conversation they'd had back in Croghan on the night of Ruairí's inauguration. Conall had alluded to being in a sexual liaison not of his choosing. Had there been no tenderness? Was he forced, used, raped, abused?

"Look, friend. Talk or don't talk. But know I'm here for you, and I'll listen." He elbowed the bard. "I might even teach you some kissing tricks." One way to get past a bad sexual experience was with words. Another was by making love to someone who cared.

When Conall's shoulders eased down, Estrada leaned in and kissed him again, gently, lovingly, savoring the yeasty taste of their slow, hungry mouths. Chugged on an empty stomach, the beer had gone straight to his head and roused his desire. He laid Conall back on the grass, fingers straying down the bard's neck inside his linen shirt, stroking his firm pecs. Conall's breath quickened, and his body rose. With gentle lips, Estrada explored his neck and the hollow of his collarbone, then crept up to catch his full mouth again.

Their bodies pulsed to the beat of the music. Pulling back, Estrada gazed into the bard's bright eyes and watched his pupils dilate with desire. He brushed Conall's lips with a finger. "Want more? Wanna take a walk in the woods?"

Conall squeezed against him and exhaled. "Aye. Aye, let's walk."

"How about we walk over there and get some burgers, boys?" Sorcha's voice was loud. Annoyed. She gestured to the smoking barbecue and glared at Estrada.

He glared back. Was she jealous? She'd kissed him herself in Scotland and tried her damnedest to get him into bed. His first impulse was to tell her to mind her own business. But Conall had already risen, so he let it go. Estrada grasped his hand and the two men wandered through the crowd toward the barbecue. He left the bard standing in the queue, and motioned Sorcha away.

"You've changed, woman. When we met in Scotland, you were open to whatever suited you. Now you're judging me." He stared at Sorcha as her green eyes flared gold.

"I'm not judging you." She stepped back, but held her ground, then rolled those eyes, and he knew he'd have to fight to win this, whatever it was.

"You're acting like my fucking mother." He crossed his arms over his chest. Needed another beer. Needed several.

"It's not *you* I'm concerned about."

"He's fine," Estrada said, gesturing with his chin to Conall. "A consenting adult who knows what he wants."

"Oh, aye. He wants you. There's no doubt about that."

"Then what's your problem?"

She poked his chest with her finger. "Have you forgotten about your man, Michael Stryker, alive and waiting for you on the other side of the sea? I thought you were in love with *him*."

Estrada scoffed. "The Sorcha I once knew was open to love in all its guises."

"This isn't about *me*."

"Look. Michael and I are loose. No rules. No judgment. We do what we want. We always have."

"And what about Conall? How's himself going to feel when you and Michael Stryker reunite? Are you going to take him to bed with you?"

"If that's what he wants."

"For feck's sake, Estrada. Conall's just crossed through time after seeing the man he loved his whole life tortured and executed. The man is heartbroken. Vulnerable. Grieving. Even if he doesn't know it." She narrowed her eyes. "I don't want to see him hurt again."

Estrada shrugged. "What are you saying?"

"I'm saying you need to think with your head and your heart and not just that." She pointed to his crotch.

"You think it wouldn't help Conall to be loved for the man he is? Christ, he'd never even been kissed until today. He's never been able to be himself openly or choose his lover."

"And that's you, I gather."

"It's consensual, and the attraction's mutual, yeah."

Sorcha snorted.

"Look. I know that Conall's grieving, and I know someone hurt him in the past, but making love with a man he's chosen could help him heal."

"Aye. Well, mind you don't hurt him again. I love that man like a brother, and if any harm comes to him from you, I'll feckin kill you myself."

S orcha scowled at the bricks of black peat stacked across the front pasture of Sullivan Stables like a frontline of British soldiers. The Bog of Allen, Ireland's largest peatland, surrounded Lullymore, but she hadn't expected to find mining here, on *this* land. The Vivian Sullivan who'd been her best friend at the University of Galway, would never have compromised her horses' pasture for the cash to be made from fossil fuel.

In fact, the two of them had met at a student-activist group organized by Vivian to protest open pit mining. Vivian had compared it to the degradation of the Amazonian rain forests, and they'd garnered plenty of support with their demonstrations. Viv had always said that to create true and lasting change, you had to be prepared to die for your cause, or at least get arrested. Once, the Garda Síochána had hauled them in when they'd danced, draped in greenery and nothing else, encircled by smoldering blocks of peat. Her mother was out on a dig in Greece, so Sorcha spent the night in jail because there was no one to bail her out. Vivian spent the night because Mrs. Sullivan told them to teach her a lesson. She was that kind of bitch.

Sorcha chewed her bottom lip and considered her options. If Estrada wasn't so desperate to get home and save his family, she'd wheel her pony around right now and ride back to the solstice celebration where she'd left him and Conall too wasted to walk. She'd volunteered to go ahead and promised to return, preferably with a truck and trailer. She knew Estrada was sick of riding and was betting on her old friendship with Vivian to get them out of this mess. But now she wasn't so sure. Her fluttering gut told her something was off.

Rowan pawed the grass with an unshod hoof, bored with standing idly on the verge. What to do. Night was falling. She had no money for a bed and breakfast and knew no one else in the area. She could try to ride back to the lads, but both she and the pony were exhausted. When she loosened the reins, Rowan made the decision for her, and walked on.

At the end of the driveway, she saw a huge white FOR SALE sign hammered into the ground and tugged on the reins. *Jaysus.* How could Vivian sell Sullivan Stables? It was all she'd ever wanted. Peat was one thing. This was something else. What had happened to her old friend? There was only one way to find out.

She took a deep breath, gave her pony a kick, and they plodded up the lane toward the estate. Shadowed by old leafy trees, this part of the farm looked much the same as she remembered, but an eerie stillness hung over it like a shroud. After almost a decade, Sorcha didn't know how she'd be received, but her curiosity trumped her trepidation.

She rang the doorbell and waited, hoping that Vivian wouldn't peek out, see her standing there and refuse to answer. Images flashed through her mind of their last day together. Then the red oak door opened and Franya wavered before her. Wearing nothing but a sheer white silk slip, she held a martini glass between her lacquered fingers. Her hair was chopped short, spiked, and dyed bright mahogany, a shade that contrasted with her pallid skin.

Franya squeezed her huge hazel eyes shut, then blinked as if seeing a ghost.

"Foxy?"

The sound of her pet name spoken in Franya's sultry voice brought everything racing back and left Sorcha speechless. She chided herself. She should have been prepared for this. She knew Franya would be here. Knew Vivian and Franya had married three years ago, after Mrs. Sullivan died. She'd seen the story in the *Irish Times*, "Gay Childhood Sweethearts Marry in Kildare." Vivian was society and it'd been big news for the small community. What Sorcha wasn't prepared for was the rush of feelings. Attraction. Repulsion. Desire. Her mouth went dry, her cheeks red. She licked her lips and scolded herself for standing mute as an eejit.

"It *is* you, Foxy. My, my." Franya's words slurred as her elfin eyes flashed. "It's been donkey's years."

"Nine." Sorcha spit out a fact. Franya was unaltered, as alluring as ever.

"Well, come in." Her head swayed, exposing her thin pale neck, and Sorcha wavered between wanting to kiss it and wring it.

"I have a pony." Sorcha gestured to Rowan, who stood grazing on the front lawn with her weathered leather reins dragging on the ground. Then wanted to smack herself in the head. *I have a pony? Jaysus, how old am I? Ten?*

Franya glanced out the door and back again. "Oh, so you do." She downed the last dregs of her martini and set the glass on a table in the entryway. "I'll call Declan to deal with it, shall I?" She said *deal with it* as if Rowan were some pest needing extermination.

Sorcha huffed. "Where's Vivian?" She needed to speak to someone sane, and Vivian had been her friend much longer than Franya had been her lover.

Franya's eyes glazed, and she stumbled backward, swaying like a willow caught in the wind.

Sorcha stood rooted to the threshold and stared at the teetering woman she'd once passionately loved as the ugly scene came flooding back. She could still see the look of wide-eyed surprise on their flushed faces when she'd returned home early from a dig one afternoon and caught Vivian and Franya in bed together. Best friend and lover, naked and sweating, and her flat wafting the scent of love.

She could have forgiven a one-night stand or entertained the notion of a triad had they invited her to join. But they hadn't. When the women admitted they'd had a secret sexual liaison since high school, Sorcha's understanding of the situation didn't ease her pain. They'd claimed that Mrs. Sullivan would disown and disinherit Vivian if she found out, and that's why they'd hidden their relationship. Sorcha had met the stuck-up matriarch and could understand their fear, but why keep that secret from her?

Their betrayal was the deal-breaker. Sorcha had suffered through her last year at uni, depressed and alone, then signed on for every archaeology dig she could find that was not in Ireland. And she'd never come back. She couldn't bear to run into them. Yet now, she stood on their doorstep with her hand out. Had she gone feckin mad?

A dark-haired stranger pushed past her just as Franya hit the floor. He scooped the slender woman up in his arms and carried her into the sitting room. Sorcha froze. Bewildered. Heart-pounding. Franya was obviously inebriated, but what had triggered her fall? Sorcha's sudden appearance or the mention of Vivian?

After laying Franya on a chaise, the man covered her with a throw. "There now," he said with a clipped Cork accent.

Sorcha crossed her arms over her chest and the two of them stood staring awkwardly at the dishy drunk for several seconds. The tableau would have made a decent paparazzi photo.

"Is she alright?" Sorcha asked at last.

"Oh, aye."

"Is Vivian here? I've just arrived and, honestly, I'm in a bit of a bind."

"Friends, were you then?"

Were? Sorcha froze, heart wailing in her chest, then she found her words. "Aye, we were all friends at uni."

He approached and offered his hand. "Declan Doyle. Stable manager." When she clasped it, she noted he was as sexy as Killian Jones, the fairytale Captain Hook.

"Well, Sorcha, I hate to tell you this, but . . ." When he paused, a shiver rippled up her arms. Something was off in this house. She could feel it. "Ms. Sullivan died three months back. Horse hit the jump." Sorcha stepped back and held a fist to her mouth as a bitter bile rose in her gut. Declan exhaled, then added. "It was fast." He gestured to Franya. "But this one, she's sufferin' still."

"*Jaysus.*" The news, and the ease with which Declan delivered it, left Sorcha feeling faint. She leaned against the frame of the open door and took a breath. Equestrian accidents happened, of course. Fifteen-hundred pounds of horse could inflict calamitous damage, through a kick, a twist, a refusal, or a tumble, especially to a novice rider. But Vivian was no novice.

Wringing her hands, she glanced up the staircase, remembering Vivian's butter yellow bedroom papered in blue ribbons. Horses were her life. She didn't just compete and win. She was a teacher who'd ridden her whole life. How could such a thing happen to her? It seemed impossible.

"Ms. Rousseau will be up and at it tomorrow." Declan ambled toward the door, and Sorcha followed, mind scrambling. "Stayin' nearby, are you?"

"No, I . . . No."

"You look knackered, and you've had a shock. Perhaps you should stay the night."

"Oh, I don't know." The house felt empty without Vivian, and the idea of Franya rousing her in the night in that silk slip caused sundry sensations—some she ached to feel again, others she was desperate to forget.

"If you're uneasy here in the big house, I've got a decent pull-out."

Sorcha glanced at Franya, stretched out on the chaise like a Hollywood actress, and wondered what might have happened if she hadn't caught them that day. After her time in Iron Age Ireland, the one thing she knew for certain was that one action affected another. How long might her mad affair with Franya have lasted had Fate not played her hand?

She flinched when Declan spoke. "Your pony looks knackered too. How about we stable her for the night? I'll make you a cuppa, and you can decide where you'd like to bed down." When his dark eyes flickered, Sorcha wavered between running to and running from the sexy stableman. Anything was better than staring at Franya and remembering what the woman could do to her with one flick of a finger.

"Ah, I'd love a cuppa." There was no way she was going to get anywhere tonight with her plan to borrow some cash and a vehicle. And Declan was right. Both she and Rowan were exhausted. Neither had slept since escaping Ana and her prehistoric posse. What harm could it do to spend the night?

She followed him out the door and closed it behind her. Tomorrow, she'd steel herself and speak with Franya. Keep it business. A loan for an old friend. Nothing more.

Outside, Declan picked up Rowan's reins. "She's a sweet wee thing. Reminds me of a Connemara pony."

"Oh, aye. She has that look about her."

"They're a native breed. A mix. Wild Scandinavian ponies brought here by the Vikings bred with Spanish Andalusian horses in the fourteenth century."

"Is that right?" She rubbed Rowan's velvet nose.

"Aye. This one. She's a stunner. More Scandinavian than Spanish, I reckon. Closer to a Shetland."

A stunner? Perhaps Declan was more enamored of horses than people. He seemed different with the pony, gentler, and more interested in Rowan than in herself.

Sorcha breathed a sigh of relief. The madness was passing. It was just the shock of seeing her ex again and hearing about Vivian. Touching the pony brought her back to the present moment and her mission to get them out of the Midlands.

"Aye. Sweet she is, and clever, I wager. What's her name?"

"Rowan." She was a native breed, alright. A twenty-two-hundred-year-old time-traveling Croghan pony.

Sorcha followed him into the stable and watched silently as he found the pony a clean stall, doled out grain, and filled a pail with fresh water. Beside herself with pleasure, Rowan nickered.

"My cottage is just here." Declan gestured to a small gray stone bungalow sheltered by oak and ash trees, quite separate from the rest of the farm. The long shadows of early evening had stretched into dusk and a crescent moon rose above a late-flowering crabapple tree. As her muscles relaxed, Sorcha yawned.

Declan walked ahead, then shoved open a weathered door that led into a rustic living room. A gentleman, he waited for her to enter. Despite the heat of the day, it felt cool inside. The comforting scents of horse, leather, coffee, and burnt applewood defined the cottage as much as the man.

"I'll get your tea. Milk and sugar?"

"Aye. That'll be grand." She was achin' for a cuppa. Hadn't missed it in Croghan but now that he'd mentioned it, she was salivating.

Hands folded across her chest, she wandered toward a wide stone hearth and glanced at the framed photographs on the mantle. An older couple smiling. His parents, she assumed. The same couple earlier, seated outside an RV with three small children. One had to be pre-pubescent Declan, wide-eyed and bucktoothed, his hair a messy, black mop.

His bedroom door was open and spying the cozy double bed framed in forest green fabric and plumped with white cotton pillows, she yawned again. How long had it been since she'd slept in a proper bed with quilt and pillows? There'd been that platform of skins at the fort and then that horrible spider-infested, dirt-floored hovel when she'd been banished. Ah, but Ruairí had made that hut feel like a palace. She rubbed her belly and sighed. They'd made a baby there—a baby that longed to sleep in a real bed as much as she did.

She turned when she heard the clatter of dishes. Declan had put a tray on the coffee table in front of the couch.

"I found a few biscuits. Not too stale, I hope."

Sorcha smiled and lowered herself into a cozy corner of the soft brown leather couch. Seeing two white mugs, she reached for the teapot and poured for both.

"Have you been working here long?" she asked. He seemed comfortable but there weren't many personal items, at least not on display.

"Well." He scratched the dark stubble on his chin as he calculated. "It'll be five years this summer."

Five years? Suddenly, she had a million questions. *Are you close? Why peat mining? Why is the estate for sale? Is there financial trouble? What's really going on with Franya?* Rather than ask, Sorcha sipped her tea, nibbled on a digestive biscuit, and made polite conversation.

"God, I remember these. We practically lived on them at uni."

"I have a confession, Sorcha." His eyebrows rose. "I recognized you right off. We all got hammered last New Year's Eve, and Ms. Sullivan pulled out the photo albums. She missed those days."

She tried not to question why he'd held that back until now. People were funny. But the knowledge eased her mind. Declan knew she wasn't a stranger, and that's why he'd invited her to stay. There was nothing sinister about it.

"Ms. Sullivan and Ms. Rousseau. Why not Vivian and Franya?"

Declan shrugged. "It never seemed right. They're my bosses, like."

Sorcha nodded, finished her tea, and yawned again.

He gestured to the bedroom door. "Take my room tonight. I'll be fine here on the couch, and you look like you could use a solid night's sleep."

Indeed, she could.

"We've been sleeping rough the last few days. It started out as a lark, you know, riding and sleeping out in the pasture under the stars. Then someone stole our packs while we were bathing in the stream. We lost everything—phones, ID, credit cards, the works."

"*Jaysus.* What morons."

"Aye. We enjoyed a solstice celebration tonight. It was great craic, but the fellas got into the black stuff. I knew we were close to Lullymore, so thought I'd ride ahead and see if Vivian could . . ." Her voice faded. Viv was dead. She still couldn't believe it.

His lips flattened as he nodded. "Ms. Rousseau's usually fit by noon—"

"Noon?" Sorcha blurted the word and Declan raised his eyebrows.

"If you need to crack on, I can hook up the trailer and take you to gather up your mates and their ponies first thing. Most of the stock's at pasture and I'm up by six."

Sorcha considered. She'd need to get back to Estrada and Conall well before noon. Estrada was eager to collect Magus Dubh in Scotland and arrange their flights home. And she needed to return to her camp at Kilmartin Glen. She'd been missing several weeks.

She glanced at the clock. It was half-ten. No wonder she was shattered.

"If you could help me get the fellas and their horses back here, that'd be grand."

"It would be my pleasure." Declan smiled and nodded once. "There's plenty of hot water, so help yourself to a shower. I'll put the coffee on in the morning. And Sorcha, don't fret. Old bonds hold firm."

Crawling between those cool cotton sheets after a hot shower was the best thing Sorcha had felt since the last night she'd spent with Ruairí. As soon as she thought of him, her throat tightened, and the tears came again. It had been a fast and furious affair. For a moment, he'd been the center of her world, and then he was gone.

She must have fallen asleep crying because the next thing she knew, she breathed in coffee and opened her eyes to a gray haze. Sorcha patted her belly as she did every morning.

"Good morning, Ronan, my little love."

But as she stood, she felt suddenly queasy and had to race for the bathroom.

5

Estrada awoke, travel-worn and bleary, with the dregs of last night's beer still simmering in his cells. He laid in the grass with his eyes closed, listening to the drowsy sounds of night—the soft hoot of an owl, the sough of Conall's breath as he slept beside him and, in the distance, burbling water. When he opened his eyes, constellations flickered like faerie lights etched in indigo glass, and memories of Primrose filled his mind. Her big Elfin eyes and tricksy smile. He'd loved her, and then she was gone. Sacrificed herself for him and joined her ancestors in Faerie. He called out to her in his mind, hoping she might come this once since they were back in Ireland. Then, knowing that rarely worked, he relented and stared up at the waning moon.

In her third quarter, she cast a gray haze over the woodland. It must be three or four, the witching hour—which struck him as funny, him being a witch and this being the hour. Better still, it wasn't quite dawn, which meant there was time to greet the sun on this languid solstice morning.

He leaned up on one arm and glanced around. Last night's revelers had left the village green, though the tables, barbecues, and wooden stage still stood silhouetted against the somber sky. Perhaps the people would return to watch the sunrise.

He'd fallen asleep watching Conall perform on the stage. The last band was an Irish traditional group with a bodhrán player, two fiddlers, and a guitarist. Conall had taken his wooden pipes from their worn leather case and jammed with them. The five pipes of varying lengths were bound, and Conall played the melody by blowing through different mouthpieces. It was more complex than modern-day flutes or recorders with one mouthpiece and finger holes that allowed for varying tones. His ancient pipes were an instant curiosity, and the amazed musicians kept him playing the whole set.

After the break, they offered him a guitar and Conall blew them all away. He'd learned to strum and pick just by watching the other guitarist. Estrada couldn't wait to get him on stage at Club Pegasus with his mouth edging a mic.

The owl hooted again, tugging him from his thoughts, and he searched the trees and hedgerows behind the stage, trying to place it. Finally, he rose and padded across the damp lawn. When he heard it a third time, he glanced up into the branches, only to be startled by twin tangerine eyes that stared back at him, unblinking. He backed off then, not wanting to disturb it, or get morose with thoughts of owls being harbingers of death and it staring at him as if that death could be his own, or worse, someone he loved.

After discreetly relieving himself of the evening's beer, he went in search of something to slake his thirst. The horses huddled under the trees—Conall's white stallion standing guard over his gray mare, who drowsed with one hoof tucked up. There were no predators here, but how was Capall to know? What must it be like for the horses to have traveled through time? The sights, sounds, and scents had dimmed and changed. Prehistoric Ireland was so much more vibrant, the colors vivid, the woods thrumming with every manner of insect and bird, the waters abundant with trout so unafraid, Sorcha had plucked them out of the lake with her hands.

As he padded back across the lawn, the burbling water beckoned, and he followed. Stone steps led down into a grotto rimmed by mosses and ferns. A small plaque revealed that this was one of Ireland's holy wells dedicated to "Saint Brigid the Triple Goddess, Patron of Poets, Healing, and Smithcraft." Having recently befriended a blacksmith in Iron Age Ireland, Estrada knew why smithies warranted their own patron saint.

Water flowed from a fissure into a rock basin. Reaching out, he cupped his hands and sipped, tasting raw earth and pilgrims' prayers, the spirits of weary travelers like himself, teeming with dreams, and not much else.

Falling to his knees, he bowed his head to the sacred spirit of the holy well, and offered prayers of gratitude, for he'd returned from the past unscathed. Then he asked for blessings. If the gods would gift him as they'd done before, he might just pull off the Herculean quest that lay before him.

The sacred water song deepened until his ears rang with its roar. He felt adrift from his limbs, as if enthralled by some somnambulistic spell. His body sank like stone into the earth and tears fell. It seemed he'd been fighting monsters forever, and he knew another battle lay ahead that would take everything he had, and more.

He'd fallen into a meditative state praying but flinched when he felt warm hands upon his shoulders. Then Conall's breath tickled his ear with hope.

"Today, we rise. Tomorrow, we triumph."

Estrada leaned back, enjoying the sensation of Conall's knees pressing into his shoulder blades as the bard wrung the knots from his neck.

"The Goddess of the Land is strong here," Conall said. "I feel her in all her power."

"Yes, this is one of the holy wells dedicated to Brigid. Do you know her?"

"Brigid is de Danann, daughter of the Dagda and patron of bards. To rise in such a place on Midsummer and drink from her holy well is a blessing and good omen." He cupped his hands and sipped.

Conall knelt beside Estrada and the two men stayed silently praying in that holy shrine, surrounded by votive offerings and mementoes of believers come before, until the gray veil of night lifted. Then the bard took a small, stoppered horn from the purse at his belt and filled it with holy water.

"Come. Greet the dawn." He rose and held out a hand to Estrada, who grasped it and climbed from the well, feeling energy surge from the earth through the soles of his bare, leathered feet.

"I wish I had my ritual tools," Estrada lamented. He felt naked, with nothing to raise the power. Every solstice for years had been Hollystone Coven, theater and drama, the playing of the gods and the dancing of the magic.

"You have this," the bard said, backhanding him across the chest. "The Sun God needs nothing but devotion."

So, Estrada followed the bard and did as he did.

After prostrating himself on the dewy ground, he rose slowly with the sun as it crested the horizon. He felt its power coursing through his veins and asked for courage and strength.

And then he saw the ravens.

Leaping up, he stood staring as a chill ratcheted up his thighs.

"What is it, brother?"

Estrada shook his head to topple the terror. "Ravens. Diego told me they stalked me for months."

"These are just scavengers." Conall bent over, picked up a smooth stone and rolled it between his fingers as Estrada might play a coin. "But if you need proof, I will bring one down so you can see for yourself."

"No." Estrada had killed too many ravens and would only destroy those he knew for certain were vampires.

"Come then. Leave the ravens to their scavenging. We have work to do."

Estrada followed, wondering what was coming next.

Conall walked into the glade where stood an enormous oak tree Estrada had somehow missed during his stupor the night before. It was tall, old, and wizened, its trunk several feet in diameter and perfectly formed like trees he'd only imagined. Conall embraced the trunk with wide arms, touching his forehead and chest to the gray, furrowed bark. For several moments, he stayed that way, head and heart attuned to the tree, and then he turned his face and put an ear to its skin, listening.

Magus Dubh had told Estrada that Druids had a special relationship with trees. He remembered the story of Crann Bethadh, the Tree of Life, he'd told Lucy at her first birthday party—a party that hadn't happened yet. There was something so natural and loving in Conall's intimacy with the ancient oak, Estrada felt like a voyeur.

He turned away and sat on the ground with his head in his hands. Sorcha was right in her threat. Conall was vulnerable and innocent, and he must do nothing to change that—no matter how pleasurable it would be to deepen those kisses. They were already touching each other as naturally as lovers.

"Come," Conall said, yanking him back. "We must cut the mistletoe."

"Mistletoe?" Estrada repeated. The only mistletoe he knew was a little plastic ball of leaves and white berries people hung over thresholds at Christmas so they could kiss beneath it. They needed no catalyst for their kisses.

Conall pointed to the massive balls of blossoming greenery that hung from the gnarly branches of the old oak. "There," he said.

"How are you going to cut that?" The tree had to be eighty feet tall, and the balls hung from branches protruding from its thick trunk.

"With this," Conall said, pulling his iron dagger from the sheath he wore on his belt.

"Really."

"I cannot refuse," he said, as if the tree had made a personal request.

"But how?"

Conall sheathed his knife, then took a run and launched himself at the oak tree. Skittering up the trunk using bare feet and hands, he made it to the first heavy branch and gripped it with his brawny arms. Then he shinnied up the trunk like an acrobat, using the knotted limbs for leverage, until he arrived at one from which hung an orb of mistletoe. Inching across the branch on his belly, he used his arms to pull and toes to push. When it sagged under his weight, the bard laughed. The threat of falling was part of the thrill. He hacked away the stems that bound it to the oak, and the bundle of blossoming vines tumbled from the sky.

As Estrada dodged to avoid it, he breathed in its citrusy scent. Many of the blossoms had died, leaving small embryonic berries, not yet the iconic white they would become by winter.

"Do you have your dagger?" Conall shouted.

"Yes." Estrada gestured to the knife that hung in its sheath from his belt.

"Come, join me."

Estrada stared at the wide trunk of the oak. He'd never tried a stunt like this. What if he failed? Conall had climbed the thick tree trunk like an elf. But how could he say no?

"Alright. Here I come." He took one deep breath and ran at the tree. Feet scrambling, his hands connected with the first big branch. Clinging with his fingers, he swung his body until he could get one leg up and hook his foot overtop the branch. He hoisted up the rest of him and lay face down with his arms and feet hugging the wood like some pathetic caterpillar. He could hear Conall cackling high above him.

"So glad I amuse you."

"When you finish fucking the tree, come up," the bard said, between snorts.

Estrada inched his way back to the trunk, where he was relieved to discover the branches were much closer together, then climbed rather nimbly to where Conall balanced above him. His chest swelled with pride. "Now what?"

Conall's smile faded. "The mistletoe has sunk roots into the oak and is feeding from her."

Like a vampire, Estrada thought.

"We must cut away the roots, as close as we can, without harming the tree."

The two men worked away in silence, hacking through the sinewy roots and tossing down leafy spheres. As Estrada took out his vampire angst on the parasitic plant, he recalled some sacred association between Druids and mistletoe.

"What do you use the mistletoe for?"

"I have no use for it, though we sometimes steeped a bitter tea to use in sacrifice."

Estrada glanced at Conall, confused, but relieved the bard wasn't envisioning a ritual killing. "If you have no use for it, why are we harvesting it?"

"She asked me to save her from this leech that steals her essence. The task befits this sacred day."

"The oak spoke to you." He wasn't surprised. Dylan could talk to stones and Sorcha saw visions when she touched metal. Why shouldn't Conall talk to trees?

"What are you boys up to now?"

Estrada glanced down, then felt dizzy and swayed. Sorcha was suddenly standing below them amongst the scattered balls of mistletoe.

He focused on Conall to gain his equilibrium. "Is the tree good now?"

"Aye, we've cut away the worst of it and she breathes easier."

Estrada closed his eyes. In the stillness, he could feel the rise and fall of the oak tree's breath. When he opened them, he saw her aura blooming several feet out and shimmering like a rainbow.

"Blessings," he said, "and thanks to you both." This was the best solstice morning he could have had an ocean away from Hollystone and his family.

"We brought coffee," Sorcha shouted.

Conall cocked his head curiously. "Coffee?"

"We'll be right there." Estrada stared down at fifty feet of thick gray trunk and wished he was in his aerial silks rather than about to free fall.

"Just wait," Sorcha said. "Declan's gone to get rope from the truck. The last thing we need is for you to break a leg."

Estrada felt his face flush, but caught the proffered rope, swung it over a thick branch, and used it to rappel down the trunk. Conall stood above him chuckling, then dropped the rope to the ground at Estrada's feet and scampered down as confidently as an arborist. Indeed, the Druid bard was a tree surgeon among other things.

S orcha watched Conall's bravado wane as Declan prepared to load the Iron Age horses into the trailer. The dark-haired stranger appeared to be managing the bard more than the horses. Everything was a novel experience for Conall—even the coffee, which he'd called "vile swill" though he'd chugged most of it. They'd laughed, but Sorcha realized his stress would only amplify as he navigated their world. And she had worries of her own. She'd thought a quick visit to Vivian Sullivan might be the answer to their current dilemma, but now she wasn't so sure.

All they really needed was a place to leave the horses and enough cash to get them to Dublin. Her old grad student, Rook, had discovered he had more of a talent for forgery than archaeology. He could produce high-quality identification, passports even, and they'd need them to cross the border into the U.K. Once they had ID, she and Estrada could access their own bank accounts and get on with it. Since she'd left in the middle of the night with Cernunnos, her documents, mobile, and credit cards were at her archaeology camp in Scotland. At least, she hoped that one of her team had secured them when they'd discovered her missing.

It should have been simple. But it wasn't.

She turned to Estrada, who was refilling his steaming coffee cup from the thermos Declan had thoughtfully provided. "Come on. We should talk while they . . ." She gestured to the horses, who each had their heads stuck in a twenty-first century oat bucket. Conall seemed calmer as he stroked and sang to his white stallion.

"Nothing happened," Estrada muttered, as he turned and stepped away.

She touched his arm. "I apologize for sticking my nose into your love life. I was just concerned."

"No apology necessary. I agree with you. Conall's innocent and dealing with enough novelty without me adding to his angst." Estrada raked his fingers through his tangled hair and smoothed back the waves. "You look after the people you love, Sorcha, and you don't play games. Those are two things I admire about you."

"Besides these?" she said, shoving out her chest.

"Yes, besides your gorgeous Irish breasts."

They both chuckled, remembering the moment they'd met at Kilmartin Glen, and she'd taunted him into touching one. She'd always hoped for more, but the time had never been right for them. Still, their flirting eased the tension.

"Aye, well." She glanced over her shoulder at Declan. "There's a bit of a game needs playin' to remedy our current situation. And there's a story."

"Of course, there is."

"I just found out that my friend, Vivian, died last spring in an equestrian accident, and her widow . . . Let's just say, Franya and I have a complicated past. There's no need for me to replay the whole tragic melodrama that transpired between the three of us at uni, but you should know that Franya is my ex-girlfriend, and she seems to have an alcohol problem. Things could get difficult."

Estrada pursed his lips. "How difficult? Like she might not lend us the money to get out of here?"

Sorcha shrugged. "I don't know. I haven't asked yet. She passed out last night with a gin martini in her hand. Declan was gracious enough to look after her, and then lend me his shower and his bed."

"Oh. I thought you looked different." Estrada winked, then pulled a handful of Sorcha's long red hair to his face and breathed it in. "Smell better too."

"Ha ha. Declan's a decent man. I'm sure he'll do the same for you and Conall. I told him we'd been on a horse camping adventure until someone nicked all our stuff while we were swimming."

Estrada pulled his lips flat and sniffed. "I can work with that. What's our strategy?"

"Best-case scenario? Leave the horses here and borrow a vehicle and enough cash to get us into Dublin. My mate can set us up with passports, and from there we can drive to Glasgow. We'll have to cross the border from Northern Ireland into the UK, and they'll want to see papers aboard the ferry."

Estrada scowled. "They don't much like me in Scotland."

"They should have given you a medal for solving the murder of that journalist." She huffed. "Don't fret. I'll drive, and you can travel under an assumed name. Something sexy and Spanish like . . ." She patted his leather pants. "El Cuero. Andreas El Cuero."

Estrada snorted. "Andreas the Hide? You're going to name me after my leathers?"

She wriggled her brows. "Maybe my Spanish is rusty, but it works, yah?

One horse nickered, and they both turned. Conall eyed the rig warily.

"Come on," Estrada said. "Let's see if we can calm him down."

The bard stood firmly rooted to the ground, clinging to his stallion's halter.

"What do you call him?" Declan asked.

"Capall."

"Horse? That's simple enough. I'd like to take Capall first. I'm betting the mare will follow."

Conall didn't move.

"Unless you'd prefer to walk him into the trailer yourself."

Estrada came around and held his dusky mare by the halter. "He'll be fine, man. Declan here knows what he's doing."

Conall took the stallion by the side of the halter and stepped up into the trailer. Capall stepped up beside him, and Conall urged him on.

"There's a halter clip at the front," Declan said.

Estrada stepped up into the trailer too and secured the stallion to the clip while Conall sang to him in Irish.

"See," Estrada said. "Capall doesn't mind. You're more nervous than he is."

Declan passed up a bucket of oats. "Here. Put this in the trough. It'll keep him busy while we load the mare.

Estrada caught Conall's arm, and the bard turned reluctantly. "They'll be fine. Trust me."

Once they'd cleared the trailer, Declan led the mare in, left her with a bucket of oats, and fastened her clip.

Sorcha was relieved how easily the horses had taken to being loaded into the trailer. She hoped they'd stay as settled when the vehicle moved.

Conall was another story.

"I cannot get in that thing." They'd only advanced as far as the chariot in his time.

"It's called a Land Rover, and it's the fastest way to Lullymore." Sorcha tried cajoling the bard, but he stood stiffly with his hands crossed over his chest.

Finally, Estrada swung in and whispered something in his ear.

Conall snorted and climbed into the back seat beside Estrada. Sorcha wondered what the sexy magician had promised the bard. She climbed into the passenger seat and Declan started the engine. But when Estrada tried to belt Conall in, he panicked.

"If something happens, this will keep you from flying out on the road and getting hurt," Estrada said.

"No," Conall said, and refused to belt up.

Sorcha had forgotten what it was like to be frightened by new gadgetry. And, for Conall, everything was new.

"Just buckle it up behind him so it doesn't scream all the way home," Declan said.

"Conall's not from around here." Sorcha wondered what Declan must think of a man who refused to get into a vehicle or buckle up. "More of a cowboy. Likes the open range."

Estrada did as instructed. Declan nodded and put the Land Rover into gear. They pulled away slowly.

"Come here." Estrada caught Conall's jaw with his palm. "I don't make promises I can't keep."

Sorcha turned to face forward when she saw what bribery Estrada had used to get Conall into the back seat. It was nothing she hadn't used herself, and Declan seemed oblivious to the two men making out behind him.

After a while, they stopped kissing but remained anchored in each other's arms. "Just breathe, man," Estrada said.

Sorcha couldn't imagine what it would take to get the bard buckled into a seat on an airplane. "Conall's a brilliant musician," she said, nodding to the radio.

"Right so." Declan reached over and turned it on. Once the music started, Conall closed his eyes and fell into a kind of rhythmic stupor.

They drove on in silence for several minutes with the windows wide open, bathing in the fresh air and the oldies. When "She Wolf" came on, Sorcha leaned over and turned it up. Shakira's voice and moves had amazed them at uni. Franya and Sorcha had made "She Wolf" their song and made out to it for months. Her mind drifted back to Franya, and she nibbled her nail, imagining the woman's lips.

When the commercial interrupted, Declan turned the radio down and laughed. "Ms. Rousseau blasts that song whenever she's in the mood to dance."

"Really."

"Oh yeah. Sometimes, she plays it over and over. When the windows are open, I can hear it all the way to my place."

"Huh."

Commercials done, he cranked up the tunes.

Franya Rousseau was once Sorcha's one and only. The woman she'd hoped to spend the rest of her life with. But they hadn't spoken since the day she'd caught her with Vivian. When Sorcha had walked in, all she saw was Viv's enraptured face. She didn't know who was moving beneath the sheets, giving her friend such intense pleasure. And then Franya appeared, and Sorcha gasped. She thought either her heart would break, or she'd break both their heads. Sanity prevailed, and she'd left shattered.

She glanced at the two men cuddling in the back seat. When Michael Stryker came on the scene, what would happen to Conall? Already, she could see he was falling in love with Estrada. Part of her chided: *It's none of your business.* But another part kept imagining Conall walking in one night to find Estrada gasping with pleasure and Michael Stryker's face popping out from beneath the sheets.

7

Estrada was as sober as he'd ever been when he called Michael from Sullivan Stables at eight o'clock on Monday morning. Michael was not. Though, fortunately, he answered the phone. Probably because he didn't recognize the number. Michael dealt in the highest quality *erotigens* and had a web of handlers who constantly bought and dumped burner phones. And he hated to miss business.

"Michael?"

There was a long pause followed by a deep breath, in and out. And then, "What the fuck, Estrada."

Things rarely went well when Michael called him by his legal surname.

"It's good to hear your voice."

"Is it." Michael's tone dripped with sarcasm. He hated being left behind, and Estrada didn't know when or under what circumstances he'd left.

"What time is it there, amigo?" Estrada hoped to ease his way in.

Michael cleared his throat. "Time you fucked off. No, wait. You already did that."

Estrada rubbed the scruffy beard on his aching jaw. This was going to be harder than he thought. He heard voices in the background, distant coughing, and closer, the sound of clinking glass. He quickly did the math. Vancouver was eight hours behind, so it must be Sunday midnight. Pegasus closed at eleven p.m. Michael had brought people home to party, and they were just getting started. Any moment now, someone would be dragging him off to the bedroom or the bath.

"I'm sorry, man. I'll explain everything when I get home, but right now, I need your help."

"Of course, you do."

"Come on, Mandragora." A gravelly voice. Deep. Sultry. Close to the phone. A stranger he didn't recognize. Male or female, he couldn't tell. "We need our director." And insistent too.

"Please, amigo. Talk to me. It's important."

He heard a gasp, and then a moan. "I'll be right there, darling." Michael sniffed. He'd had his silver spoons out. "It seems *everyone* needs me. What is it *you* need?"

"My wallet. Do you know where it is?"

Michael scoffed. "Perhaps where you left it when you disappeared a month ago?"

Estrada's head hit the wall. "A month? I've been gone a month?"

He'd been in Iron Age Ireland about that long but didn't understand that was how time travel worked. Maybe it didn't. Maybe that was just how Cernunnos worked. And then it hit him. *If I've really been gone an entire month, Sensara will kill me.*

"What happened when I left?" He needed some context for this disappearance.

He heard the familiar rasp of Michael's silver zippo, the long inhale, and the deep click as he closed the lid. "What do you mean, what happened?" Michael exhaled. "Weren't you there?"

Estrada paused, wishing he could ease some of his own stress with a snort or a smoke. A joint would be an absolute godsend right now. But begging would have to suffice.

"Just tell me what you remember, man. It's important."

"It can't be *that* important if—"

"Michael," he snapped, then lowered his voice. "Please."

"Fine. It was Sunday morning. We were drinking espresso at your place, and you were getting ready to drive out to the lake to spend a couple of days with Lucy. There was a knock at the door. You said you'd get it and *poof.* You vanished and never returned." He scoffed. "Didn't even close the door. I haven't seen or heard from you since."

"*Jesus.* I get why you're pissed."

He must have been more than pissed. He must have been worried sick. Likely thought he'd been abducted by some of the shadier types that frequented the club.

"I'm sorry, amigo. I'll explain everything when I get home."

Estrada's mind raced. How did Cernunnos do it? Was he such a powerful god, he could change a person's perceptions? Their memories? A month ago, would have been May 24th, and he'd spent every Sunday, Monday, and Tuesday with Sensara and the baby since she'd been born the previous summer. Did Cernunnos implant the same memory in Sensara? If he did, and Estrada suddenly didn't turn up or answer his phone for an entire month, she'd be frantic. She'd assume he was in trouble. Or dead. *Did she call the police? Report me missing?* She'd called the cops when the vampires abducted Lucy. *Jesus Christ.*

"Did Sensara call you?" he asked.

"Only about a dozen times. She still doesn't believe that I know nothing of your whereabouts."

Estrada sighed. "Did she call the cops?"

"I don't know. You'll have to ask her. That's if she ever speaks to you again."

"*Fuck*." Estrada could hear laughter in the background. Corks popping. Hoots and cheers. They were doing the champagne fountain and calling for Michael.

"Can you please do me one favor?"

Silence.

"Come on, man."

Dare he tell Michael he'd gone back to Ireland? Both times Estrada had gone abroad, he'd nearly died, and Michael had flown across the ocean to be with him. If he knew he was in Ireland again—

"One moment, Jazz. Estrada's about to tell me where the hell he is."

Manipulative and telepathic.

"Michael, please. I can't get home without my stuff. I need my driver's license, credit cards, cell phone, and passport."

"Border-hopping, are we?"

Estrada ignored the question. "Can you please go to my flat and get my stuff? Will you do that for me?"

"Where. Are. You?"

Estrada breathed deeply. "Ireland, alright? I'm in Ireland. But as soon as I get my stuff, I'll be on a plane back home."

"What the fuck, man? The last time you went to Ireland, that madman tried to kill you. And Primrose . . ."

Estrada sighed. "I know. I know. But Sorcha needed help, and I had to—"

"Sorcha? That crazy archaeologist? She nearly got you killed in Scotland."

"Look. I promise to explain everything when I get home. I just can't *get* home without my stuff."

Michael let out a heavy sigh and coughed. "I suppose we can take a drive over there tomorrow."

"Thank you, amigo." He didn't dare ask who he was bringing with him.

"Mandragora, we're waiting for you." There was that voice again.

"I'm coming, darling," he answered, and then someone turned up the tunes.

For a moment, Estrada wished he was there with them, snorting, smoking, and drinking his way into one more mad, sexy stupor.

"Michael. Listen. Put everything in an envelope and send it by courier. I'll text you an address from this number. So, watch for it, please. It's a life and death situation." Perhaps that sounded melodramatic, but it was the truth, and this seemed a safer plan than boarding a transatlantic flight with a forged passport.

Estrada heard Michael light another cigarette and take a swallow from his drink. And then the phone went dead.

He leaned back against the wall. It was eight a.m. and felt like midnight. The last time he'd left Michael alone in Vancouver, he'd taken up with one of Diego's pimps and ended up at Le Château des Vampires—an act that had spawned this current crisis. He just prayed Michael was staying off the blood.

Estrada heard a strange noise and looked up to see Conall scratching at the edge of the glass panes on Declan's wooden door. With his other hand, he held a steaming mug. Estrada couldn't help but smile. Everything was a first for Conall.

"I thought you didn't like coffee."

Conall grinned. "This is called chai tea latte. Try it."

Estrada sipped. "Cinnamon is my favorite spice. I'm glad you like it too." He loved sharing the bard's discoveries.

"Declan said we could share it when we took our shower."

"Did he say shower or showers?" Perhaps Sorcha was right about Declan. So far, he'd been nothing but magnanimous. "Where is Declan?"

"With Sorcha, tending the horses."

Estrada had already started looking for the bathroom. If there was one thing he missed in Iron Age Ireland, it was a hot shower. And it would be Conall's first.

"Come on. It's here in his bedroom."

Conall stopped wide-eyed and stared at the soft quilted bed and pillows ensconced in the forest green frame.

"Shower first. Then you can try the bed," Estrada said. He turned on the hot water and shut the door. "While you're in there, I'm going to ask Declan if he can lend us some clothes. I'm sick of wearing wet cowhide."

Conall set the latte down on the bedside table, opened the bathroom door, and stuck his head in.

Estrada grinned. "Go on. You can go first."

Conall's eyes widened as he ran a hand through the steam. "Water coming from the sky. Where is the fire?"

"Uh, in the other room. The hot water is piped in."

Seeming to accept that explanation, Conall tugged the linen shirt off over his head and dropped it on the floor. A ripped warrior, his flesh was etched with scars and freshly bruised from battle.

"What do I do?" he asked.

"Just stand under the hot water, and let it wash over you like a waterfall. Maybe use a little soap here and there, you know."

Conall had climbed out of his leather breeches by now. He glanced down at the "here and there" Estrada gestured to with his eyes. Then he took Estrada's cheeks in both hands and set his beautiful mouth against his lips. What could he do but sink into the bard's cinnamon kiss? Then Conall backed him up against the shower and kissed him inside. Hot water rained down on their heads as the kiss deepened. Estrada shut the door.

Conall pulled off Estrada's wet linen shirt, loosed his breeches, and jerked them down. Estrada stepped out of them and kicked them into a corner. *God, the hot water felt incredible. And Conall's mouth. And Conall's hands.*

Estrada had to slow them down. Be gentle. Talk about things before— *Oh, hell.*

He grabbed the shampoo, opened the cap, and squeezed some into his palm. It was thick, the color of a Pacific forest, and smelled of cedar and spice. He spread it in both hands and ran it through the bard's hair.

"That smells incredible," Conall said.

"Agreed. Turn around and lean back." The bard's fine hair fell in waves halfway down his back. Estrada ran his fingernails along Conall's scalp as he massaged his head. The bard moaned. When his hair was done, Estrada proceeded to wash the rest of him—beard, face and neck, shoulder blades, pecs, pits, and biceps. But before he could finish, Conall turned and shoved him up against the opposite wall.

"My turn," he growled.

The kisses continued as the bard shampooed Estrada's hair and washed him with avid tenderness. When his hands slid down, Estrada didn't stop him, just took some of the soft lather from Conall's hands and exchanged the favor. Breath caught. Eyes rolled. They both gasped and groaned. And that was enough. For now.

After, Estrada tied a towel around his waist and Conall did the same. The thought of climbing back into those grungy clothes was sobering.

"I wish he had some spare toothbrushes." Estrada squirted some minty green toothpaste on his finger and massaged his teeth and gums.

Conall watched curiously as he took a mouthful of water, swirled it around, and spit.

"How do you clean your teeth?" Estrada asked.

Conall raised his brows in confusion, then opened his lips to reveal two lines of lovely, cream-colored teeth.

"I gotta say, for a caveman, you have excellent teeth. Not that I'm judging."

Conall sniffed the toothpaste and turned up his nose. Then he squirted some of the shampoo in his hand, ran a finger through it, and rubbed it on his gums and teeth.

Estrada grimaced, but Conall seemed to love the taste of the cedar shampoo. Perhaps it was his tree thing.

Estrada shushed him when he heard voices in the other room. Sorcha and Declan were in the kitchen. He poked his head out the bedroom door. "Hey man. Do you have a couple of extra pairs of jeans we could borrow? These pants can walk on their own."

Declan chuckled. "You're lucky. Saturdays I do laundry." He walked by Estrada and opened an immaculately organized closet. The man's neurotic neatness reminded him of Michael. One shelf housed several pairs of identical pale blue jeans. "T-shirts. Boxers. Jeans. I can't guarantee they'll fit but help yourself."

Estrada touched his shoulder. "Thanks, man. Oh, and one more thing. I hate to ask, but do you have an electric shaver we could borrow?" He ran a hand through his beard. "Mine is bad, but I've never seen this guy's face and I'd like to, if he'll let me shave off his beard."

Conall narrowed his eyes.

Declan produced an electric shaver, as well as a razor. "For that extra closeness," he said. "Help yourself to whatever else you might need." He opened a drawer containing personal items. "And don't forget the aftershave." It had the same label as the shampoo—cedar spice.

Conall watched as Estrada shaved off the heavy, dark hair that grew down his cheeks and chin. "I don't mind a little stubble, but this is ridiculous." When the hair was gone, he lathered his face and shaved with the razor until his skin was smooth. "Hope I didn't dull the blade." When he splashed on a little aftershave, Conall sneezed.

"You're right. It's too much," he said, and washed it off. "Now, your turn."

Conall sat on the toilet and nervously chewed his lips. "When's the last time you shaved?" Ruairí shaved the sides of his head, so Estrada knew they had the technology, plus he'd seen men in Iron Age Ireland with smooth faces.

"Never."

"Never? Why not?" Estrada pursed his lips and waited.

Conall shrugged.

"Is it a bard thing? I don't want to shave your beard off if it's some cultural thing."

"It's not." Conall grabbed the long, straight hair below his chin and twisted it.

"Then why have you never shaved? Is it a secret?"

"A secret?"

"Something you've told nobody except maybe Ruairí. I know you told him everything."

"Shave it off, and then I'll tell you."

"Alright. But if you don't, I'll just keep shaving." He winked and glanced down the copper hair on Conall's chest to the bulging towel.

Estrada ran his hand through the bard's fine, chestnut locks, pushed them back from his face and bound them with an elastic band. Then he wound another band around Conall's beard just below his chin. Pulling the hair taut, he cut through it with scissors. Then he turned on the shaver and began. After one pass with the electric shaver, he lathered

Conall's face and ran the razor gingerly over his pale skin. When he was done, he applied a steaming facecloth.

"Now. Tell me about your beard."

Conall answered from beneath the warm cloth. "The others grew beards very young but mine took years to appear."

"They teased you." Estrada knew how cruel kids could be.

"Aye. When it finally grew, the hair was wispy and straight. They called me . . . goat boy."

Estrada was glad the cloth covered Conall's eyes, so he couldn't see him grin. Even now, his beard was as long and fine as his hair. "I wanted to shave it off but was afraid the gods would be offended, and it would never grow back."

"And now?"

"Now, I fear nothing." Conall plucked off the cloth and stood up. Leaning in, he rubbed his smooth cheek against Estrada's.

"That feels good, man."

"This will feel better." His hands slid down Estrada's body as he dropped to his knees.

"Whoa, man. As much as I'd like to take *this* to a whole other level, we need to talk first."

Conall looked up, his pale cheeks gleaming. "So, talk."

"Come on," Estrada said, hoisting him up. "Let's get dressed and eat some breakfast. We'll go donate your beard to the birds and talk about things."

"When you want me, I want you. If you want someone else, I'll still want you. But I won't stop you from wanting or having someone else. Love and desire are infinite. Is that enough talk?"

"It's a hell of a start." Estrada pulled Conall tight against his chest. "Why do you have to be so goddamned perfect?"

8

Sorcha had spent the morning feeling queasy and hanging around the horses to avoid the big house where Franya slept. Declan had taken Estrada and Conall shopping in Kildare. It was now almost one, and the moment was coming. She perched on a patio chair patterned with buttercups just outside the kitchen. Vivian had undoubtedly chosen the bright yellow umbrella that shaded her from the direct sun.

If only Viv were here now. Sorcha felt time ticking in her bones, and the longer she fretted over confronting Franya, the more anxious she became about her current situation. Perhaps *confront* wasn't the right word or the right tactic. She was in no position to confront Franya or delve into their past. Beggars could not be choosers, as her mother had reminded her frequently.

To complicate things, Estrada had told Michael Stryker to fetch his wallet and passport and have them couriered to Lullymore, which meant they'd have to stay longer.

"Four to seven days minimum," Sorcha had pointed out. "No matter how much you pay. We're not in a teen movie." Though lately it'd seemed that way. Estrada had been aglow since the lads had their morning shower, and Conall hadn't stopped singing.

"Don't worry. By the time we get back from Glasgow with Dubh, my stuff should be here. I'll use your fake passport for the ferry to Scotland, but I want my actual documents when I board that plane to Canada. Immigration has never treated me kindly, and I'd rather not take a chance on Andreas El Cuero getting busted for fraud with my daughter's life hanging in the balance."

Sorcha couldn't argue with that kind of logic.

"Besides, the more time I spend in Vancouver, the more Diego's ravens will stalk me. Right now, I'm trusting they don't know where I am." He'd glanced around as if bloodthirsty corvids might swoop out of the sky at any moment.

It was half one when Franya finally opened the back door and strolled outside barefoot with a steaming cup of black coffee in her hand. She'd changed into a sleeveless white jumpsuit with spaghetti straps that revealed just how thin she'd become. Her clavicle protruded in two horizontal lines like an emaciated ballerina and reminded Sorcha of Franya's childhood stories of brutal workouts, ballet competitions, brawls with her mother, and starvation diets.

Feeling like a cow, Sorcha stared at the floor.

"You're *really* here, Foxy. I thought I was dreaming."

At the sound of her nickname—one that Franya had given her after discovering that more than the hair on her head was bright red—Sorcha's chest tightened.

"Aye. I'm here. My friends and I were on a horse-riding holiday in Offaly when someone nicked our stuff."

Franya scoffed. "I don't believe *you* volunteered to ride a horse. You hate horses as much as I do."

As Franya set her coffee cup down on the patio table, Sorcha noticed she wasn't wearing a wedding ring, and thought it odd.

"People change." Sorcha tugged nervously at the strapless red linen sundress that hugged her breasts. It was once the skirt she'd worn as Queen of Croghan, but she'd altered it when they landed here in the heat. Sweat drizzled down her cleavage. "I've been wearing *this* for days. The bastards took everything we had while we were swimming. I was hoping you could help us out." She paused, and then added, "For old times' sake."

Franya tilted her head and batted those enormous hazel eyes, and for a moment, time stopped.

Sorcha breathed in Franya's floral scent and teetered.

"God, I've missed you." Leaning forward, Franya brushed her fingertips along Sorcha's knuckles. "Of course, I'll help. It's the least I can do to make up for—"

"Let's not talk about that," Sorcha said, letting go a breath. "The past is the past."

"But it's not past, is it? Because you're here now and you're obviously still hurt."

Sorcha didn't know what to say to that.

As perceptive as ever, Franya strolled toward the kitchen. "Where are my manners? You must be thirsty."

Before she could reply, the woman disappeared. Sorcha stood and swiped at the sweat as she stared at the forested hills. How could Franya sell this place? It was all Vivian ever wanted. She used to say, "Sullivan Stables is a repository of my childhood. I buried all the animals I loved and lost in that ground." But where did they bury her? She remembered Vivian once pointing out a small family cemetery atop a hill. Dare she ask? No, she'd see for herself. The less they spoke of Vivian, the better.

"I noticed you have the place up for sale," Sorcha said, as Franya appeared balancing a tray containing a pot of coffee and a pitcher of iced lemonade, along with cups and glasses.

"Oh, that." Franya set it down in front of her. "The contract's just about up."

"So, you're not selling?"

"Coffee or lemonade?" Franya smiled sweetly, and Sorcha wanted to smack her. She'd forgotten what it was like to have a conversation with the woman. An endless barrage of unanswered questions and diversions. Franya was a skilled litigator.

Sorcha filled a glass with lemonade.

"I saw you on the news last year, talking about that Egyptian jeweled collar you discovered in Scotland. You've done well, Foxy. PhD now?"

"Aye, and you?"

"Corporate law." Franya slipped into a chair, crossed her never-ending legs, and sipped her coffee. "I'm on hiatus at the moment."

"I'm sorry about . . ." Sorcha couldn't say Vivian's name out loud.

"Why do people say they're sorry when someone dies? It's not like you could do anything about it."

"Well, you lost your wife, and I lost a friend. Those are things to feel sorry about." Sorcha picked up her lemonade.

They sat in silence for some time, sipping their drinks and avoiding each other's eyes.

Rather than diminish over the years, Sorcha's feelings for Franya had intensified. Perhaps it was unrequited love. The one who got away. Whatever it was, her desire for the tall, lithe woman shook her to the core and left her tongue-tied.

She was relieved when she heard the rumble of the Land Rover in the driveway. "They're back," Sorcha said, and stood.

"You and Vivian are about the same size. Help yourself to her clothes."

"Oh." Sorcha didn't know why that felt awkward, but it did.

"And stay as long as you like."

"Thank you, but I'm hoping to leave tomorrow if you can lend us some cash and a vehicle." There. She'd said it.

Franya finished her coffee and stood as the men walked around the corner of the patio.

Sorcha saw something pass between Declan and Franya. It was just a glance, but it left her curious. She introduced the lads, then Franya insisted on giving them all a house tour so they could see their rooms. Franya showed Sorcha to the yellow room that adjoined her own via a shared bathroom. Vivian's childhood bedroom. Estrada and Conall had separate rooms; but of course, that wouldn't stop them.

Before they went downstairs, Sorcha excused herself. She couldn't keep her eyes open. The stress of being near Franya again after all this time was taking its toll. She walked into the butter yellow room. Someone had stripped her blue ribbons from the walls and left only pin holes. She was more surprised when she opened the closet door. Blouses and skirts in varying shades of yellow and turquoise half-filled the rod. The other half housed Vivian's riding wardrobe. Had they been sleeping apart? Sorcha's lip trembled when she saw Viv's worn leather boots jammed in a back corner. Poor Vivian. For a moment, she'd had it all. The horse farm she'd always wanted. The woman she loved. And then . . .

Sorcha laid down on the bed and cried into the pillow. The turquoise pillow. The pillow that was Vivian's.

9

Estrada and Conall wandered through the back pasture, admiring the horses and leafy trees, the verdant beauty that was Ireland. They'd spent the bulk of the day practicing knife-throwing at a rotting stump they'd rigged up as a bullseye. Estrada's skills were sharp because of his stage act, but Conall's fighting prowess was with an Iron Age sword. It may come in handy when they faced off with the vampires, but knife-throwing was not his purview. When he pulled the iron dagger from his belt in hand-to-hand combat, he was close enough to jam it in a gut in such a way that it found its mark. Conall was a to-the-death fighter, but he'd never fought the undead. A knife to the heart did nothing to stop an alacritous streak of teeth and torment. At close range, they'd have him. Estrada taught the bard how to hold the sharp tip between his fingers and snap his wrist, so the blade turned in midair and could pierce the brain between those undead eyes.

The sun was leaning west now and not a cloud marred the azure sky. They followed the hedge rows, tramping through thick grass where bees and butterflies meandered between the buttercups. Estrada tugged off his pale blue T-shirt so he could feel the sun's heat on his bare skin. Lullymore was a little piece of paradise.

Conall hummed some intricate tune with leaps and trills, using his voice in ways Estrada had never heard.

"We gotta get you into a recording studio, man. You're gonna be a rock star."

"What does a rock star do?"

"Party and travel the world, play and sing for millions of people at concerts, make videos, get photographed and chased by paparazzi." Estrada grinned. "Oh, and they make shitloads of money."

"I don't understand, but I think I'd rather not be a rock star."

Estrada wasn't surprised. The bard was an Introvert who kept to himself unless he'd been into the ale. "Yeah? What would you rather be?"

"Do I have to *be* something? Can I not just sing and play music?"

They wandered down a soft hill to where a stream cut through the pasture and elegant ferns swept the banks.

"You can be and do whatever you want. You're starting a whole new life in a whole new world. I'm kinda jealous."

"Why? Can't you start a new life?"

Estrada dropped his T-shirt and hunkered down on the riverbank, rolled up his pale blue jeans, and dipped his bare feet in the water. He'd rather strip off and lay in the slow rush of current but was feeling too amorous to control what would inevitably occur. "Not really. I have a past waiting for me on the other side of the ocean. Family. Friends. A career." He leaned back on his hands. "Not to mention this crazy-ass vampire who wants to make me his boy toy."

Conall laid back in the grass with his hands behind his head and closed his eyes. "We won't let that happen."

"Diego won't go down easily. Do you have vampires in your culture?"

"Perhaps. You've shown me how to destroy them. Tell me more about them."

"They're sometimes called the undead because they're immortal. They stay youthful and beautiful forever by drinking human blood." When Zion had turned Michael, he'd become young and virile. For a moment, that thrilling vampire blood had seduced Estrada too. It was like no drug he'd ever experienced.

"Diego was after me, but Michael jumped between us. He sacrificed himself to save me."

"So, that's why you must change the future."

"Yes, and because he's my best friend. My partner." He saw Conall's face tense, but it needed to be said. "Diego bit Michael last year and gave him the virus. He's not the same man he once was. He's sick and getting sicker." Estrada clenched his jaw.

"What does the virus do?"

"It's slowly turning him into a vampire. He craves human blood." Estrada feared Michael had found a source for vampire blood, and that was accelerating his transformation.

Conall growled his understanding, but Estrada wondered how the bard really felt about his relationship with Michael and the quest they were on because of him.

Estrada swallowed. "You could die or become a vampire if you come with me. You should know the risk."

"A warrior takes risks every day. At Croghan, I was a warrior for my clan. Here, I am a warrior for you."

"I don't want you to risk your life for me."

"My life. My risk. My choice."

"But if something happened to you—"

Conall sat up and squeezed the back of Estrada's neck to stop his thought. "In my culture, we have a creature much like your vampire. We call her the Leannán Sidhe."

Lee-a-non Shee. Estrada silently repeated the words. "Is it a type of faerie?" he asked, remembering that the Sidhe were immortal beings like ancestral ghosts who lived in a parallel universe. The Irish called them faeries. Primrose had become one of them when she died. He'd seen it with his own eyes, and for a time, he'd crossed over with her, though the memory was as vague as a dream.

Conall kneeled behind him, massaging his neck and shoulders. "The Leannán Sidhe is a beautiful faerie who gives her magical creativity to poets and musicians. Then, when they fall in love with her, she abandons them, and they ache for her until they go mad. They can neither eat nor sleep, and eventually they die."

"Lovesick. I'm glad this faerie hasn't come for you."

"A bard must be vigilant." He walked his strong fingers up and down Estrada's spine. "When her lovers die, she drags their bodies back to her lair and drains their blood into her cauldron of inspiration."

"*Jesus.* What does she do with the blood?"

"Drinks it? Bathes in it to keep her youth and beauty?" Conall tumbled onto the grass, rolled onto his side, and propped his head up with his hand. "Though I've never met the Leannán Sidhe, I wonder if Sorcha's friend is not someone to watch."

"Who? Franya? Why do you say that?"

"When we came around the back of the house, the trees whispered, 'Beware.'"

A shiver raced up Estrada's arms. "She's a lawyer, and I'm always wary of lawyers, but she's Sorcha's ex-girlfriend."

"Trees don't lie," Conall said.

"Indeed. Next time you talk with the trees, ask for more information. We need details."

Estrada pulled his feet from the stream. He didn't need the trees to warn him about Franya. The moment he met her; his gut tensed. But she'd agreed to lend them cash and the SUV, so they'd soon be gone. Sorcha could manage her in the meantime.

He glanced at Conall, who was drowsing on his back in the sun. How perfect it would be to make love to him here in this peaceful valley where, for a moment, they were safe and alone and both eager to plunge into whatever bubbled between them.

But his conscience responded harshly, and a spell emerged in one long breath.

"No harm must come to him from me, but only good. So mote it be."

Estrada's flesh tingled as the incantation reverberated through the ethers and he exhaled deeply. *There. It's done.* Whatever happened between them now could only be in the bard's best interest.

"Did you speak?" the bard whispered.

A tangerine butterfly flitted between them, landed in Conall's hair, and spread her black and white tipped wings. "You have a new friend. She must like the scent of Declan's cedar shampoo." Leaning over, Estrada picked up a lock of Conall's hair and breathed it in. "I like it myself."

Conall grasped his shoulder. "Lie with me, friend, and feel the throbbing heartbeat of the goddess all around us. Rare are these moments on the battlefield. We must claim them when we can."

10

When Estrada climbed into bed that night, he sank into the mattress like a straight man might settle into a buxom woman. One thing he could say for Franya was that she was generous. She'd opened her liquor cabinet when they'd gathered in her plush living room, toasting anything and everything well into the night. Franya preferred gin, but when she caught him gazing longingly at an uncracked bottle of tequila, she offered it to him, along with a crystal glass. Several shots later—he'd lost track as quantity didn't seem to count in this house—he sauntered into his room and nose-planted in the bed.

How long had it been since he'd slept in a proper bed? Those weeks of sleeping rough in Ireland vanished as he relished the luxury of Egyptian cotton. The window was open, and the curtains fluttered with the night breeze and a frog serenade. He'd hoped to pass out, but sleep eluded him. He should have known better. Tequila often fired his intellect and sent him riding a train of thoughts that solved the world's problems but disappeared by morning.

Tonight, his thoughts drifted back to Michael and their early morning conversation. His memory of the months before Summer Solstice was clear. Michael had been sick. He'd been slipping further and further into a vampire-induced stupor since last summer when Diego ripped a piece of flesh from his neck and infected him with the virus. Michael didn't know that Estrada knew anything about what had transpired out there on that island, but during their sojourn up the Pacific coast, he'd discovered the truth. They'd spent those months together, dallying here and there when the mood struck them, but were, more or less, partners.

Estrada now knew the vampire virus that percolated in Michael's veins reproduced rapidly during sex. The orgy that he'd orchestrated hours earlier was something different; something that hadn't happened at Summer Solstice. Estrada had gone to the ritual at Buntzen Lake that night, but when he'd returned the next day, Michael was in a semi-stupor, not from partying, but because he felt sick. That meant one thing.

While he'd been away in Iron Age Ireland, Michael had been consuming vampire blood—enough that it had caused a personality shift. The man he'd spoken to this morning, the man orchestrating the orgy, wasn't Michael. It was his alter ego, Mandragora. And as much as Mandragora could be entertaining, he was as "mad, bad, and dangerous" as the man he believed himself to be—a reincarnated Lord Byron.

Estrada was wondering how this might affect his quest to destroy the vampires when his door opened and closed, and he heard someone pad across the room. The bed dipped slightly. Without opening his eyes, Estrada knew it was Conall. He'd spent enough time with the bard to know his seductive scent. He could even feel his energy. The bard burned warm.

His first impulse was to reach over and draw him in. But he knew if he did that—given his current inebriated state—there'd be no stopping. And a drunken tumble, no matter how good it felt, would have lasting repercussions. So, he lay there, watching his breath, and pretended to be asleep.

Then it occurred to him that Conall may have never slept alone in his life. At Croghan, the nobles all shared a longhouse. The odd partition divided it, but they bedded down together on raised platforms padded with sheepskins and furs. What would it be like to be sent to a vacant room if you'd never spent a night alone in your life? Terrifying? Lonely?

Conall's hand came out of the dark and settled on Estrada's bare chest. The feeling of that palm against his heart felt better than any sexual act ever could. He lifted his hand and covered the bard's, and a few minutes later, he heard deep, steady, breathing. Conall had drifted off to sleep.

Their day may come, but with Mandragora on the prowl, Estrada would need to stay vigilant. One thing he knew for certain was that he didn't want him anywhere near Conall in his current state. If he thought Estrada was sleeping with the bard, he'd want him too. Sharing was Mandragora's prerogative. Estrada squeezed Conall's hand. He wouldn't allow that.

11

Finally free, and fueled by cash and hope, the trio cruised into Dublin on Monday morning in the Land Rover. Sorcha turned up the tunes and drove while Conall rode shotgun. The bard sat rigid, hands folded in his lap, staring through the windscreen as vehicles shot along the M4 like bullets from a machine gun. He'd never be the same. Estrada dozed in the back seat; his eyes hidden behind a new pair of shades. Sorcha didn't ask what had kept him up all night. She'd been awake and ruminating herself.

At her first opportunity, she pulled into a shop and purchased a cheap mobile. She'd rung Rook the previous evening from Lullymore and made plans to meet at College Park, an expanse of manicured lawn on the grounds of Trinity College. His call. She knew his rookery was somewhere on Pearse Street, and that's all she needed to know.

They pecked each other's cheeks, *faire la bise*. Rook was thinner and grungier than he'd been at uni, but just as fastidious. His blue-black hair flew wild, and stubble etched his long, hooked nose. When he stared, his dark eyes pierced your soul. Rook was not a man to feck with and never negotiated, but Sorcha was an old mate, and this, they both honored. After tacking a plain sheet of bristle board onto a tree, he produced a mobile, and took their photographs one by one, deadpan as required. Sorcha collected the requisite information—date and place of birth. Conall didn't know his date of birth, a situation that didn't faze Rook.

"Samhain is the witch's new year," Estrada said. "Let's make your birthday October 31st. What do you think?"

Conall shrugged. "I don't know Samhain."

"That would make him a Scorpio," Sorcha said. "It fits."

"Why?" Conall asked.

Sorcha grinned. "Ah, well, Scorpios are the sexy, silent type. They don't take shite from anyone, and they sting when provoked."

"That most definitely fits," Estrada said. "Let's say he's turning twenty-eight this Samhain."

"You think I sting?" The bard tensed and thrust out his chest.

"I *know* you sting," Estrada said, and pursed his lips.

Sorcha knew it too. She didn't fancy bringing up how he'd decapitated the Crow Queen before he rode through the wormhole or the hard slap he'd given Estrada when he'd discovered he'd gone to the blacksmith's home without him. "Isn't it strange how our personalities match our astrological signs," she said.

Conall narrowed his eyes and they moved on.

Estrada made Andreas El Cuero a twenty-nine-year-old Spaniard born in Barcelona and assured her that August 6th was his actual birthday.

"Ah, fantastic. We're both Leos turning thirty this summer. Whatever continent we're on, promise me we'll have a hell of a party." She did a little dance, but Estrada grimaced. Then she remembered the vampire had stolen his child only a few days before. She hoped like hell, Michael Stryker hadn't been killed on Estrada's birthday. What a tragic memory that would hold. But this was not the time and place for such talks.

Rook said he'd need two hours, so Sorcha suggested they reconvene at the *Beanhive*. Between their chocolate art and chai tea lattes, she knew this trendy café would delight Conall.

It was just ten a.m. when Rook peeled off on his bicycle and Sorcha turned to the boys. "The National Museum is free to browse." She pointed to the Neoclassical structure across the street with its marble columns. "In an hour or less, himself could see the evolution of his country over the last few thousand years. I'm headed that way myself." Conall was silently shell-shocked, but she knew Estrada could manage him. She'd given them a share of the borrowed cash. "And if the city's too much, St. Stephen's Green is just there." She pointed down Kildare Street. Conall seemed to need regular doses of nature.

When they parted ways, Sorcha crossed Leinster Street and headed down Kildare past the National Library to the museum, sidestepping the ever-present summer tourists who crammed this part of town. She had one thing on her mind.

Sorcha had been in her teens the first time she saw Ruairí Mac Nia's mummified torso at the National Museum of Archaeology. Her mother took her after hours for a special viewing with colleagues. Old Croghan Man's body had just arrived, and the team was delirious about their latest bog body.

Even wearing gloves, when Sorcha had secretly touched the copper mounts on his braided armband, a vision of his beautiful face flashed through her mind. In that moment, she'd decided to become an archaeologist so she could learn about her ancestors. She'd never forgotten that vision, and when he came to life in Iron Age Ireland, she couldn't help but fall in love with him. Now she carried his child.

Her skin tingled as she tiptoed into the Kingship and Sacrifice exhibit. She walked directly to the glass case that housed his leathered torso and arms with those fists and manicured nails. Staring at Ruairí's curled fingers, she remembered his tender caresses.

Employees ambled about checking the Iron Age exhibits, while she perched on a bench, eyes closed, heart pounding, wanting privacy. This was the closest she'd ever come to finding him again. She'd considered begging Cernunnos to send her back to ancient Croghan one more time so she could try again to rescue him, but in her heart, she knew it was futile. Fate was fate because it couldn't be changed. She'd learned that the hard way. Her one comfort was in remembering what he'd said when she'd warned him what was to befall him. "To be sacrificed and reborn with the Goddess is the greatest honor." And her Ruairí was the most honorable man she'd ever met.

Alone at last, Sorcha stood beside the leathered remains of her man. "Ruairí my love," she said. "I don't know if you're here or if you walk beside the goddess or if you've been reborn, but I need to tell you some things. I'm sorry I couldn't save you. I wanted more than anything to either stay there with you or bring you home with me. I love you, Ruairí, and I always will." She wiped the tears that drizzled down her cheeks.

"Ronan is here with me." She touched her belly. "I'm going to tell him all about you. How brave you were, and how honorable and handsome. How you killed that arsehole, Bres, and became the rightful king. How you sacrificed yourself for your people." She sniffed and brushed her nose with a fist. "Conall's here too, and you should know, he avenged your death. Took that bitch's head clean off just before he rode through the wormhole into our time."

A young couple wandered in, and Sorcha hushed up and waited as they explored the exhibits. When they left at last, she leaned in and placed her palms against the cool glass.

"Ruairí, I met an old friend, and last night we stayed up all night talking. I was mad for her at uni, and well, there's something bubbling between us still. I know you won't mind. Her touch brings me comfort."

She flinched as a shadow fell across the glass.

"Sorry. I didn't mean to startle you," Estrada said.

"Where's Conall?" When she'd talked of seeing Ruairí's body, the bard had been adamant about not seeing it. Sorcha didn't want to subject him to something that would give him nightmares.

"He discovered the musical instruments. Loves the harps."

"Aw, bless him." She squinted. "He left his pipes in the car, yeah?"

"He did."

"Good. We best not let anyone here see *those* pipes. They'd be after them to study."

Estrada shook his head as he draped his arm over her shoulders. "Listen, I didn't mean to disturb you. I just thought you might need a friend."

"Always."

She laid her head against his shoulder and the two stood together in silence for several moments.

"So, this is . . ." Estrada said at last.

"Aye."

"*God.* His armband's still—"

"Full of his power." She squeezed her eyes shut to hold back the tears. "I never asked where he got it."

They stood, swaying, sniffling, and staring at Ruairí's mummified torso.

"Do you feel him here?" Sorcha asked at last. "You know, hovering around his body?" She glanced around the room. "I'd hoped for a sign or something."

"This is wrong." They both stiffened at the sound of Conall's voice. "This is why the land weeps black tears. His body should have been burned so his spirit could fly to the Sun, or at least left buried with the Goddess to whom he gave his life." When Conall wept, both Estrada and Sorcha reached out and drew him in.

If they weren't holding her up, Sorcha would have sunk to the floor like a stone.

A family walked in, saw the emotional scene playing out, turned, and disappeared.

"We should feck off," she whispered.

Conall wiped his face and turned away, refusing to look at Ruairí's flattened leather torso. Estrada put his arms around both their shoulders and they wandered. Sometimes, Conall would stop and silently touch the glass, brows furrowed. These were the artifacts of his time. The swords. The shields. What memories they must hold for him.

When he stopped before the reconstructed bust of Clonycavan man, he squinted. Then he glanced down at the deflated body laid out in the glass case with its flattened nose and wild orange hair.

"I saw him once," he said.

Sorcha stepped back. "Really? Where?"

"At Tara. The High King invited our clan." Conall's eyes narrowed. "This man was there. I remember his hair."

"And his name?"

Conall shook his head. "His uncle was a king."

"He was killed much the same way as Ruairí and buried in a bog near Clonycavan in County Meath."

Conall growled. "It is wrong to imprison our people in glass boxes."

"I know it's hard for you to see." Sorcha had heard this argument before. It was one conflict she'd had to confront as an archaeologist whose job it was to dig up the past, bones and all.

Indigenous People, the world over, wanted their ancestors left alone or their bones and ceremonial regalia returned. Now, gazing into Conall's eyes, she understood and could no longer ignore it.

12

Estrada felt exhausted by the time they'd made the ferry crossing into Scotland, and all he'd done was slouch in the back seat all day. Perhaps it was the stress of traveling under an assumed name. Or perhaps he was just feeling the weight of what lay ahead.

Darkness fell as Sorcha wove the Land Rover through the busy Glasgow streets. He was relieved she was driving and rubbed his empty belly to calm his anxiety. He couldn't wait to meet Magus Dubh again. After the adventure they'd shared on the Northwest Coast, he'd come to love the dark priest.

Dubh was a half-fey dwarf, all tattooed in blue symbols, a wise and powerful Druid with a heart as deep as the ocean. He'd proclaimed himself Lucy's godfather, driven the yacht up the Pacific coast, and fought beside him. Together, they'd found a cure for Vampire. Dubh wouldn't remember any of it since it hadn't happened yet, but Estrada would never forget.

Sorcha backed the Land Rover into an open spot and shut off the engine, while Estrada searched the shadowy street for the blue door that opened into Dubh's antiquities shop.

"Where is it?" he asked.

"There." When she opened the car door and slid out, Estrada and Conall did likewise. The side street bustled, despite it being a Monday night. There was no buzzer, just a small brass plate that said, "The Blue Door" and an antiquated brass door knocker with a leering Green Man that reminded him of Cernunnos. Estrada grasped the handle below the beard and gave it several hard raps, then stood back listening.

"His light's out. I don't think he's in," Sorcha said.

"He has to be." The notion of Dubh not being at his shop hadn't occurred to Estrada. He had it all planned. They'd meet up. He'd tell Dubh what he needed, and the wee man would pack a bag and join them on their quest. Feeling a pang in his gut, Estrada stepped up and slammed the door with his fist. "Dubh. Are you in there?"

"Easy man. He's probably just out for a pint."

"Can you call him?"

Sorcha shook her head. "No phone that I know of."

"*Fuck.* What are we supposed to do now?"

"There's a pub around the corner. Perhaps he's there, and if not, the barkeep might know where he is. It's where he takes most of his meals."

Estrada felt his muscles tense as they headed for the pub.

From the outside, the Pineapple Express didn't look like much—old brown brick lit by floodlights, a picture window crowned by a black banner hand-painted with a row of pineapples that matched the gold-painted front door. But as he opened it and stepped inside, Estrada's mouth watered. He scanned the room, searching for Dubh. The bar stools were all occupied, but Sorcha found them an empty snug in the corner.

"I've met the barman before. I'll have a wee chat with him and bring you both back a pint. Or do you want something more?"

Conall rubbed his belly. "Burgers and pints."

Estrada chuckled. Conall was fast assuming contemporary life. "I could eat," he said, and glanced at the chalkboard that hung against a side bar. Beside it was another hand-printed sign that read "Gents."

"I'll find out if they're still serving," Sorcha said, and sashayed off to charm the barman.

"The men's room is just there," Estrada said, pointing it out to Conall, who was newly enamored of toilets. "One of us should stay here and save the table. Do you want to go first?"

Conall rose and sauntered through the pub. He'd been silent all day in the car and Estrada assumed he was still brooding over the bog bodies that had been dug from the earth. And perhaps missing Ruairí.

Estrada surveyed the room again, hoping Dubh would appear from some shadowy corner. Then his gaze landed on Sorcha and the barman. A shiver rushed up his thighs and hit him in the gut. Dark-skinned with long dreadlocked hair, the barman looked enough like Zion to be his twin. All he lacked were the black tear-drop tattoos beneath his eyes.

Estrada flexed and squeezed his fists, remembering when that bastard had come to their yacht with Michael. He'd begged Michael not to let the vampire take him, but with ball-busting bravado, Zion said, "I've already taken him. Many times." It was a death blow. Michael was in thrall to the creature who'd made him young again by feeding him with sex and vampire blood, the most powerful drugs imaginable.

Vampire had transformed Michael back into the man Estrada had first met years before at the grand opening of Pegasus. An epic version of Castlevania's "Bloody Tears" blasted through the room that night, while lights flashed across the throbbing dance floor. Like lightning bolts, they struck in time with the dramatic music.

Michael wore a burgundy tux and tails with black silk cape. His glowing amber eyes were thickly lined with kohl. Honey-blond hair parted down the center, hung straight to his armpits, and his blood-red mouth gleamed in the spotlights. He was spectacular.

Their eyes met. Then Michael glided toward him, extended his hand, and clutched his shoulder. "Welcome. I'm Mandragora." He raised a scarlet lip to expose a fang.

"Dance," Estrada said. It wasn't a question. His heart pounded as he backed Michael onto the dance floor, the scent of him scalding his soul.

When one of the Greek boys appeared balancing a tray of shots, Michael took two. He held one to Estrada's lips. "Drink," he said.

Estrada opened his mouth and tilted back his head to chug the shot from Michael's fingertips. He didn't know about the E, not then.

"And another," Michael said.

As Estrada drank, Michael's fingertips brushed his neck, sending blood rushing through his body. Though craving men all his life, he'd met no one he'd desired enough to take beyond a kiss or caress. Until now.

Michael dropped the empty shot glasses on the tray and fanned the boy away.

As they danced, Estrada breathed in Michael's essence, lusty shivers coursing through his body. And something else. The first traces surprised him, and his heart fluttered. When he closed his eyes and sank against Michael's hard muscles, the hallucinations deepened.

He leaned back and stared into those deep amber eyes. "What did you—?"

"Like the blood clots? It's my special blend." Michael's black manicured nails brushed Estrada's stubbly cheek. "Relax, compadre. I'll take care of you." Then Michael's scarlet lips closed over Estrada's mouth. Their extraordinary kisses deepened as they cruised the dance floor in a sybaritic cloud.

Michael's hands grasped Estrada's hips and pulled him up hard, shaking him awake. "'The great object of life is Sensation—to feel that we exist.'" The man was a poet, a virtuoso.

Opening a door off the dance floor, Michael steered him down the hall and into a dressing room. The table mirrors glowed with lightbulbs. A black leather couch and ottoman stood against one wall and before it perched a glass-topped coffee table dusted with white powder. The designs in a thick Persian rug in the corner quavered in ocher and gold.

Michael locked the door with a click. Catching Estrada by the shoulders, he shoved him up against the wall and grazed his neck with his fangs. Even then, Michael had wanted Vampire beyond all else.

He tugged Estrada's black T-shirt off over his head, unbuckled his belt, and unzipped his jeans.

"Whoa, slow down. I'm gonna—"

Michael's laugh silenced him. "Then come, and come again, and again. We have all night."

"But I want to remember everything. I want—"

"Wait. Am I your first?"

For a moment, it embarrassed Estrada to admit he'd never bedded a man except in his dreams. Hands and lips didn't count. He nodded once.

Michael stood back and appraised him. "Do you trust me, compadre?"

"I do."

"Then come." Michael spread a thick towel over the rug. "Lay here."

Michael raised Estrada's arms above his head, bound his wrists with a leather thong, and tethered it to a metal ring in the wall. He ran his fingers down Estrada's neck and chest and then his tongue. Coming to Estrada's jeans, he tugged them down and tossed them aside. "You are exquisite, compadre."

Never taking his eyes from Estrada's, Michael stood to remove his tuxedo, and then clipped his black silk cape back around his naked shoulders. Estrada trembled when he picked up a bottle of oil and set it down within reach. Spreading Estrada's legs, Michael knelt between them and laid on top of him. Connected breath to breath and skin to skin, the silky cape covered them like a pair of wicked wings.

Leaning forward, Michael plied him with tender kisses. Estrada's orgasm was so swift, he sobbed, but Michael only laughed.

"How much do you want me, compadre? Will you open your body and soul to me? Let me crawl inside your skin and show you pleasure you've never known?" His hot breath fanned Estrada's cheek. "Will you let me turn you inside out?"

"Yes." The word slipped from his lips between kisses and ragged breaths.

13

"Dubh's away for a few days." Sorcha set two pints on the table and hunkered down beside Estrada.

"*Fuck.*" Estrada cracked his knuckles, and Sorcha rolled her eyes. How could she be so composed? A gnawing sensation in his gut told him things were off. Could she not feel it?

Conall returned, picked up one pint, and shoved the other in front of Estrada.

"The barman says he left Saturday," she continued. "Apparently, his aunt took sick, so he went to see her."

"Where?" Estrada growled.

"Inner Hebrides. That's all he knows."

"And there's no way to contact him?"

Sorcha shook her head. "I think we should get a hotel room tonight and head to Argyll tomorrow. Remember, we still have to see Dylan's grandfather and pick up my things in Kilmartin Glen. The Wee Pict might be back by the time we return."

Conall raised his eyebrows. "The Wee Pict?"

"The Picts were one of the first tribes here in Scotland," Sorcha said. "Dubh's mother's a Pict and his father's de Danann."

"He has power then." Conall looked impressed.

"Aye. You're finally going to meet someone who's actually fey." Like Ruairí, Conall was sure that she and Estrada were fey when they'd met. Their tattoos were proof.

"What if he's not back?" Estrada broke out in a sweat despite the air conditioning.

"Then we'll leave him a note and go on without him."

Scowling, Estrada picked up the pint. "But I need him." His body was still reeling with sexual energy and the memory of Michael. He would not allow Michael to die.

Sorcha raised her hands in surrender. She had no quick fix. "Didn't you tell me Dubh came to Lucy's birthday party?"

"Yes, but that's not until August, and I need him now."

14

The three of them shared a hotel room that night with two double beds. Estrada rolled onto his side and kept his distance from Conall. His memory of his first experience with Michael was too fresh, too visceral, too potent, and he wanted to hold it as long as he could.

In the morning, Conall caught Estrada just as they were about to climb into the Land Rover. "You've changed," he said accusingly. The dark circles under his eyes revealed his lack of sleep.

"I'm sorry, but I'm human, and these vampires have Michael in their thrall." He shook his head and left it at that.

"You haven't been the same since you spoke to him."

Estrada exhaled loudly. "Michael's changing faster than I expected, which means we're running out of time." He clenched his fists. "*Fuck.* I keep trying to make things right and they keep going wrong." Caught on the edge of despair, he'd no magic to turn things around.

Conall clutched Estrada's fist and brought it to his lips. "When you rise above the water, there's comfort in the sun."

Estrada huffed. He couldn't always discern the bard's cryptic lines. "I'm still that grieving man caught beneath the waves. Is that what you mean?"

As Sorcha started the car, Conall opened the front door. "I mean only that you are not alone. Your kisses gave me comfort."

That last line stung. In an effort *not to* hurt Conall, Estrada had done that very thing.

"Wait." Estrada drew Conall to his chest, held the bard's jaw in his hands, and gave him a long, soft kiss. "You're right, man. I shouldn't close off like I do. We're in this together and our kisses give me comfort, too."

The problem was, he wanted more. He wanted Michael.

15

The three-hour drive to Kilmartin Glen felt like the beginning of a summer adventure for Sorcha, rather than the end. As they drove north, the sun rose across forested peaks to the east, blanketing the Land Rover in newfound hope. Estrada rode shotgun, still brooding over Dubh's absence, but she was elated to be back in Argyll.

At Clachan, the A83 veered south, and they cruised the spectacular shore of Loch Fyne all the way into Lochgilphead. At the T-juncture, she stopped the car.

"Right or left?"

Estrada glanced up at the sign and scowled. "Lochgilphead. I remember this place. Dylan was in jail here."

"Aye, for a while, until they moved him to Greenock. South is Tarbert and Dylan's granddad. North is Kilmartin Glen. Where should we go first?"

"If we're this close, let's check on your camp," Estrada said. "Did you leave a large crew there?"

"No. Truth is, Meritaten's broad collar was my big find. When I went on the lecture tour, most of the diggers left. There were only a handful of us by Beltane. A few students might have shown up since then, but I don't expect to see too many hands. Diggers who are looking for summer experiences prefer an active site with an archaeologist who's there to teach them."

Sorcha parked off the A816 and they walked through the farmer's fields toward the place where she'd left her camp. As they crested the hill and gazed down into the valley, the creek glistened in the sunlight, but the field was empty except for a flock of sheep cavorting among the stones.

Sorcha held a hand to her heart. "*Feck.* They've gone."

"Where? And what about your stuff?"

Unperturbed by Sorcha's latest problem, Conall laid on the grass and gazed up at the cloudless sky. "The Goddess thrives here. Can you feel the land buzz beneath us?"

Estrada pulled his lips into a frown, and Sorcha touched his tense forearm. "I'm sorry. I'm a feckin eejit. I should have called this morning from Glasgow." She shook her head and pulled out her mobile. "I really didn't think they'd leave."

She punched in the number and counted the rings as she stared down into the empty valley. Just as she was about to hang up, someone answered.

"Emma?"

"Sorcha? My god. Where have you been? We've been so worried."

"I left in a rush. Family emergency. I should have called before now."

"So, you're safe. Where are you?"

"Actually, I'm standing atop the hill, looking down on an empty field. I expect it was you who packed up my stuff?"

"Aye. Everything's safely stowed. We waited a month, and several hands got offers for summer work, so . . ."

"No bother, Emma, but I need my personal items."

"Oh, aye. Your lock box is here in my bedroom."

"Tarbert, is it?"

"Aye, at my ma's place."

"We'll be there in half an hour. Text the address to this mobile, will ya?"

"Aye, and I'll put on the kettle."

16

"Mind if I drive?" Estrada said. "I think I can manage even though the wheel's on the wrong side and everyone's driving in the wrong lane."

"That instills confidence," Sorcha said, sarcastically, tossed him the keys, and climbed into the back seat. "Emma texted me her address. We'll need to stop there first to pick up my stuff."

Conall's eyes widened when he heard a British voice on the GPS, giving driving instructions as they pulled into the fishing village.

Estrada wasn't sure what to expect. Last summer, he'd stayed here with Dermot McBride while he worked to get Dylan out of jail. His granddad was a wonderful old guy, and Estrada didn't quite know how to tell him his grandson had stayed in Iron Age Ireland, and he'd never see him again. But he'd made a promise to Dylan he intended to keep.

He dropped Sorcha off at Emma's and drove up Pier Road with Conall. After pulling into the car park across from Piper's Dream, he got out and looked up the driveway at the gray brick house with its stone steps. He remembered sitting on those steps drinking coffee with Dermot just about a year ago.

The first thing he noticed was that the sign was gone.

Two kids were playing with a remote-control car on the sidewalk. Estrada glanced at Conall to gauge his reaction, but the bard just shook his head. He'd become accustomed to seeing things that made no sense at all.

"My ma's at the shops," a young pig-tailed girl said as they walked up the path.

"You live here?" Estrada asked.

She nodded her head vigorously.

"I'm looking for Mr. McBride."

She shrugged and yelled at her friend, who'd crashed the car into a tree.

Conall touched Estrada's arm. "What should we do?"

"Wait and see if her mom knows anything about Dylan's granddad. I can't just drive away without knowing what happened."

They sat on a stone bench overlooking the harbor and watched the white boats bob and dip on the slow waves. One day, he could imagine himself living in a place like this, where time went in and out with the tides. But this was not that day.

Estrada turned to Conall. "Something's been bothering me since we came back through the wormhole."

"Tell me."

"Cernunnos kept warning us not to change history. But what if Dylan's decision to stay in Croghan changed everything? What if he doesn't exist? What if his grandfather doesn't exist?"

Conall thought for a moment. "But Dylan *did* exist. He came to Croghan with you. I met him."

"That's true, but he would have died after that, after we left. And, if he died two thousand years ago, how could he have been here last summer working with Sorcha in

Kilmartin Glen? And if he wasn't here and didn't get arrested for murder, how do I know Sorcha?" Estrada felt a sharp pain in his chest and raised a hand to rub it. "God, I feel like I'm having a heart attack."

Conall put his arm around Estrada's shoulder and drew him in. "The gods present us with many mysteries but also bestow blessings."

Estrada took a few deep breaths, then stood and stared up at the house. Right now, he felt trapped in a rabbit hole of infinite possibilities, and he was terrified which tunnel to take. His churning gut told him that something was horribly wrong.

"Time is not a straight line with an arrowhead that points in one direction." Conall traced a spiral on the palm of his hand. "We are here and here and here, and we slip through time and space."

"I know. I know. The Between. I'm about to test that theory."

An older model red SUV pulled in beside the Land Rover, and a woman got out and started unloading grocery bags.

"Hello," Estrada said. "Sorry to bother you. We're looking for Dermot McBride."

She glanced back blankly.

"I stayed here with him last summer." He watched her face closely to see if she remembered the name McBride.

"Ach now, I think you've got the wrong house. These old fisherman's cottages look much alike."

The dizziness caught Estrada by surprise, and he swayed. Was it really happening? If Dylan never existed, what else had changed? He felt Conall's powerful arm around him. It was all that held him from falling down that rabbit hole again.

"Did you ever hear of Dylan McBride? He lived in Tarbert and was arrested for murder last summer." Estrada had to know how bad this really was.

"Murder, you say. I don't think I'd have missed something like that. I watch all the true crime shows, you know?" She pursed her lips, then shook her head. "No, I can't say as I know a McBride. We moved here six years ago. Inherited the cottage from my uncle."

"Mom," the young girl shouted from across the road.

"Can we help you with your bags?" Though he heard Conall's voice, Estrada was in a daze.

"Ach, no. I'll manage with Becca's help." She turned to Estrada. "Maybe ask at the post office. They'll have a better sense of who's come and gone."

Estrada nodded, then climbed into the driver's seat of the Land Rover and slammed his hands against the wheel. He stared out over Loch Fyne and tried to decide his next move. Conall got in and sat silently, waiting. He loved that about the bard.

"I can't think about time travel anymore. It fucks with my head. I have to go with my gut."

Conall touched Estrada's hand. "And what does your gut say?"

"Bring Dylan back from Croghan. Conjure Cernunnos here at the Ballymeanoch Stones where I first met him and convince him to take me back. There are too many threads connecting Dylan's life to mine. I can't risk anything else going wrong."

17

Sorcha and Emma were sitting in front of the white-washed house on deck chairs when they drove up. She hugged the young, blonde woman, picked up two duffle bags, and tossed them into the back seat.

"Hey Estrada." As Emma flashed him a flirtatious smile, she flushed.

He vaguely remembered meeting her at Kilmartin Glen when he'd first come to talk to Sorcha about Dylan's predicament. It seemed like eons ago.

"Make sure you call me when you need an extra pair of hands," Emma reminded Sorcha.

"You're first on my list, and thanks again for taking such good care of my stuff. I'll be up with a horse trailer to get the tent and clear out your shed as soon as I can."

Sorcha crawled into the back seat of the Land Rover and clutched the canvas backpack on her lap. "Right so. It feels good to hold my stuff. If we leave now, we'll be back in Glasgow by suppertime."

"We've had a change of plan," Estrada said, as he backed out of the driveway.

Sorcha was still arguing with him when he pulled off the A816 into the car park.

"Look. I have to do this. I can't risk anything else going wrong. Please just trust me, Sorcha."

"Cernunnos and I didn't part pals," she said.

Estrada turned off the key and opened the car door. "You don't have to come. I can do this alone. Wait here, and I'll be back as soon as I can with Dylan."

Conall was already getting out of the car. "I'm coming. Where you go, I go."

Estrada leaned over the hood. "What if you coming through the wormhole into this time was another mistake? What if you were meant to stay in Croghan?"

Head held high; the bard stared into Estrada's eyes. "My destiny is with you."

"Does Cernunnos know that?" This from Sorcha, who'd climbed out of the back seat and stood with her hands on her hips.

"I really think you should wait here, Sorcha. You can't risk getting stranded back in Croghan."

"Neither can you."

"But *I'm* not pregnant."

"Point taken." Sorcha threw her arms around Estrada. "Remember to be explicit with Cernunnos. He must take you back to a time *after* Ana is dead. If you go before . . . Well, you know what a bitch she is." She sniffed back tears. "And go to a place close to the blacksmith's house. Get in and out as quickly as you can, with no complications."

He scoffed. "Right. No complications."

18

"Without my ritual tools, I feel useless." As the two men walked past Dunchraigaig Cairn, Estrada glanced into the dark, narrow void. This was where they'd found the body of that Glasgow journalist Dylan had been accused of murdering last summer. He wondered again what his life would have been like if that event had never occurred.

Would he have met Sorcha O'Hallorhan? And if he'd never worked with the archaeologist to free Dylan from prison, would he be walking here with Conall today? Or waiting for Magus Dubh to come home so he could save Michael from himself? All the events of his life seemed connected by a fragile spider's web that could easily break if one frail thread collapsed or stuck to another during a harsh wind or had never been spun at all. And Dylan was one of those threads. A loyal friend who'd chosen to stay in the past because he'd fallen in love with the blacksmith's daughter.

"You are many things, but useless isn't one of them." Conall's hand slipped inside his as they walked, and Estrada felt his strength double with that of the bard's.

In this new world, Conall wore a cloak of innocence and Estrada was so determined to protect him, he sometimes forgot that the bard was a warrior. "I've killed thirty-three men in my life," he'd said after they rode through the wormhole. "Today, I killed three. And her." He'd taken the head of Ana, the Crow Queen who'd tortured and executed Ruairí Mac Nia. Conall was a soldier but also the gentlest and most sensitive of men. And that's why he needed protecting.

"Your rituals may flatter the Horned God, but he will come without them," Conall continued. "He will come because you call him with a pure heart." As they turned down the grassy avenue and the Standing Stones appeared, the bard chuckled. "But just to be safe, I will summon him with my song." He stroked the leather bag slung over his shoulder that housed his pipes.

"You know, Cernunnos is a lusty fertility god."

"Aye, and I long to meet him."

"What if you crossed through the worm hole accidentally and he demands you return to your own time?"

Conall huffed. "I am not afraid. Are you?"

Estrada squeezed his hand. "My only fear is that one day the Horned God won't answer my call."

Long afternoon shadows stretched across the pasture beneath the two parallel lines of Standing Stones. Conall laid his hand on one stone in the line of four and traced the cup and ring marks with his fingers. Then he put his ear to the stone and listened. "There are such stones in my land. Do you hear? They are singing."

"That's gotta be a good sign." Conall's attunement to nature amazed Estrada. He leaned back against one of the center stones and though he couldn't hear their song, their strength and the sun's warmth relaxed his mind. "I'm going to cast a circle around us. If you're sure you want to do this, come stand beside me."

Conall joined him, then removed his pipes from their leather case and played a melodious lament that sent rushes up Estrada's limbs. He grounded himself and began to breathe slow, deep, even breaths. In and out. In and out. As he watched his breath, he felt the Earth's heat rise through the soles of his feet. He drew the energy up his legs and through his chakras, then passed it down his arms into his hands. As he raised his right hand, he felt the first fiery sparks dapple his palms. He held up his pointer finger and smiled as a flame burst from the tip. This fire magic had taken him by surprise in Croghan, and he loved being able to summon it. Was it a gift from Cernunnos? Perhaps. The Horned God loved fire and seemed to love him too.

As he swept his arm in a slow circular motion, he drew a large flaming circle around them. Conall continued to play as Estrada spoke the sacred chant.

"I conjure this circle as sacred space.
I conjure containment within this place.
Thrice do I conjure the sacred divine.
Powerful goodness and mystery mine
From the east to the west,
From the south to the north
I cast this circle and call magic forth."
The dancing flames filled him with courage.

"I call on the Ancient Horned God, Cernunnos." He repeated this three times, then ended with, "I need you, man. Please come."

Though rooted to the ground, Estrada felt his spirit expand within the circle. And when the Horned God appeared, it was instantaneous. No fire or spectacle, as was his usual style. He was just there, as if he'd been waiting for his summons, faint at first, and then as solid as human flesh.

Conall paused his playing and watched Cernunnos prance about on his cloven hooves, his body naked save a scant hide skin askew his hips that showed the hard length of his sex. His shoulders were broad, his chest a mass of muscles. As always, Estrada grew mesmerized by the full rack of antlers atop his head and those dark-lined, deep brown eyes. It surprised him to realize how much he'd missed these moments with Cernunnos.

"Shaman. You call upon me, again."

"Yes. I need your help. I must return to Iron Age Croghan. I need—"

"Did I *not* just bring you back?" The god scoffed. "Do you think I am an Uber?"

Estrada snorted a laugh. Cernunnos spent more time wandering around this modern world than he was prepared to admit.

"You are the most powerful god I know, but I think we made a mistake when we—"

"*A* mistake?" It was the god's turn to snort. "To which mistake do you refer?" He pranced around Conall, inhaling and rolling his eyes, acting as if he were enamored by the bard but also indicating that he may be the mistake.

When Estrada saw Conall tense, he sent him a look that said, *just breathe and stay calm.* He needed the god's full attention and his blessing.

"Dylan McBride." Estrada wanted to shift the god's focus from Conall. "He stayed in Croghan, and now I can find no trace of him or his family here in Tarbert, where his grandfather lived all his life."

Cernunnos grunted. "Did I not warn you about changing history?"

"You did, but—"

"Now do you understand that all sentient beings are interconnected in this web. That you cannot remove one without changing the dynamic of the whole?"

Estrada didn't need that reminder. "But if Dylan comes back—"

"How many times do you think you can slip between the veils correcting your mistakes?"

"Just this once. After that, I won't ask again." Estrada crossed his arms over his chest and leaned back against the warm stone. He hated having to beg but would do whatever was necessary. "Please, Cernunnos, take me back. I'll convince Dylan to return with me and we'll make things right."

The god sashayed forward and laid his head upon Estrada's shoulder. His dark purple lips fell into a pout. As he tilted his handsome face to stare into Estrada's eyes, the magician felt a burst of heat through his core as hot as the fire surrounding them. "What do you offer in recompense?" he said, his voice rasping like sand over rock.

Right. The Horned God always wanted something in return. That's how Sorcha had ended up in Iron Age Ireland with him and this whole thing started.

"A kiss?" Once, they'd shared a kiss like no other. Perhaps that would be enough to placate the god.

Cernunnos scoffed. "Kisses are crumbs to my hungry heart. I will come for you, and I will have my loaf."

Estrada stiffened. When he'd come for Sorcha at Beltane, they'd spent three days and nights together.

"*If* you choose to give it." With one claw, Cernunnos turned Estrada's face. "I am here, not to take from you, shaman, but to give." As a pulsing finger caressed his lips and ran down his stubbled chin, Estrada couldn't help but become aroused.

"If I need you again, will you come? I'm going after Diego—"

The god stepped back, eyes narrowing. "Bah. That vampire is nothing to me."

"But he's something to me. Diego can best me. He's stronger and faster."

"Shaman." His voice thundered. "Still, you doubt your power."

"But will you come if I need you?" The intensity of this massive ask made his fingers tremble.

"If you call, I will come. I will *always* come." One corner of his lip pulled up into a grin. "And we will discuss the state of your bakery then." The god collapsed on the grass in a fit of laughter.

Estrada released a long-held breath and felt his body relax. "I'm so glad I amuse you, Cernunnos."

"You do more than amuse me." The god huffed a low growl. "For years, I have watched you play me in your rituals. I am flattered by your devotion."

Estrada cleared his throat and glanced at Conall, who still hadn't spoken a word. They needed to get moving before some farmer wandered into the sheep pasture with his border collie. "Can you take us to a specific time and place in Croghan?"

"Think, and it will be so."

"We must arrive after Ana is dead, but not so long after that Dylan has a family. I couldn't separate him from his children. That wouldn't be right." Estrada closed his eyes and imagined himself in the forest behind the blacksmith's home.

When he opened them again, Cernunnos stood before him. His antlers were gone, and nut-brown hair framed his angular face in waves. He rested his palms on Estrada's shoulders, then leaned forward until their foreheads touched. The breath from his lips tickled as he spoke, and Estrada inhaled the faint aroma of cinnamon.

Estrada stepped back, blinked, and blinked again. The stones and pasture had disappeared, and they stood in a verdant forest in a cool rain as fine as mist. He looked around bewildered. "Where's Conall?"

"I brought us to Croghan as you requested." He'd lost his godly guise and wore the same leather breeches, linen shirt, and long coat that Estrada wore—though his coat was royal purple, and Estrada's scarlet as before. A black woolen cloak hung from his shoulders. "The bard awaits your return. And I am here to ensure you make no more mistakes."

As he rubbed the stubble on his chin, Estrada heard rushing water, and knew intrinsically it was the stream that ran through the ravine behind the blacksmith's home. "It's this way," he said, getting his bearings.

When they walked around the corner of the barn, he was surprised to see the yard full of people laughing, eating, and talking. And his heart swelled to see such happiness after the trauma they'd experienced here. He saw Manus carrying one boy on his shoulders at the same time as the blacksmith saw him. Manus waved, then came to meet him.

"You've returned to us. We prayed you would."

"Why the party?" Estrada asked.

The blacksmith's eyes narrowed in confusion. "Dylan and Mara wed this morning. Is that not why you're here?"

Estrada glanced at Cernunnos to gauge his reaction, but the god stood poker-faced. How was he going to talk Dylan into leaving now? He didn't have a problem bringing Mara into the future, but surely Cernunnos would consider that another mistake.

"Where is Dylan? We must congratulate him."

As if he sensed their presence, Dylan looked up from where he stood amid the crowd and seeing Estrada, ran to him and threw his arms around him. "You came. I was thinking of you, and you came. When we got married this morning, I kept thinking, Estrada should be here as my best man, and now here you are."

Magic was as simple as it was complex. "Congratulations, man."

"But that's not why you're here, is it? I can see it in your eyes and—" Dylan turned and stared at Cernunnos. "Is that who I think it is?"

"Indeed, it is. Can we talk alone?"

The music started, and Cernunnos danced off through the crowd, flirting with everyone who seemed unattached and some who didn't.

"If he's here, this can't be good," Dylan said as the two men wandered down by the stream.

"Yeah. Well. I went to Tarbert this morning like I said I would."

"Oh, aye. Was my granddad upset? I thought he'd understand. He always told me stories about our McBride ancestors, about how we fought the English. He loves history and—"

"He wasn't there. Another family lives in his house and they'd never heard of the McBrides."

"Ach, you must have gone to the wrong house."

"Dylan, listen. I lived at Piper's Dream with your granddad last summer. I know the place."

Dylan sat down hard on a boulder beside the river. "But how can that be?"

"We fucked up, man. The woman said she's lived there for six years. She'd never heard of the McBrides. She knew nothing about your arrest, and in a village the size of Tarbert—"

"Everyone knew." Dylan grasped his jaw and shook his head.

"Somehow, you staying here has affected everything there. It's like you and your grandfather never existed. I don't know how this time-travel thing works, but if you stay here . . ."

"What are you saying? You want me to go back? I can't, man. Mara and I are bound. I can't leave her. I won't." Dylan pressed his temples. "We don't exist?"

Estrada took a deep breath. "Look. I know you just got married but—"

"But nothing." Dylan stood and planted his feet on the ground, hands on hips. He'd gone into warrior mode. "Don't make me choose between you and her. If you do, I'll never forgive you."

When Estrada reached out and grasped Dylan's shoulder, he felt his body tremble from the inside out. He decided to try a different tack.

"Let me tell you the whole story." Estrada cleared his throat. "Conall came through the wormhole with me and Sorcha. He's waiting for me back at the Ballymeanoch Stones."

Dylan stood up straighter. "What—? What did Cernunnos say about that? Surely that'll change history."

"He hasn't said anything." *Yet,* Estrada thought. "And, as you once said, that rule is pretty much fucked."

Dylan's snort eased the tension. "What were you doing at Ballymeanoch?"

"We went to Sorcha's camp and then to see your granddad. That's when I found out. Dylan, please. If you don't come back, I'm afraid other things will go wrong. Some already have. When we went to Glasgow to get Dubh, he wasn't there. Things are off kilter. And without your brain, I'll never figure out how to take down Diego."

"The vampire? But we already destroyed that bastard."

"No. Cernunnos took us back through the wormhole on Summer Solstice. Michael is still alive. I have a chance to stop it all. Lucy's abduction. The murders. Michael's sacrifice."

"What? No way." Dylan crashed down hard in the grass. "So, Cernunnos told you not to change history and then set you up to change it. What kind of game is he playing?"

Estrada shrugged. "I don't know. He's a god. He does what he wants. But Dylan. He gave me a second chance. And now I've got less than five weeks to destroy Diego and his horde."

"You're going after him, aren't you?"

"They're murderers, Dylan. Pure evil. And you know Diego's been stalking me all year. If I don't come for him, he'll come for me. This is a preemptive strike."

Dylan grasped his bearded jaw with both hands. "Ach, this is crazy."

"Not any crazier than what happened out there on the coast or what happened here." Estrada crouched beside Dylan. "I need you, man. Will you please come home?" He held his breath.

"Aye, I'll come. But not without Mara. It's both of us or neither." He dropped his gaze to the ground and mumbled. "That's if she'll come. If she doesn't want to leave, I won't force her. And like I said—"

Estrada stood and sighed, then clasped Dylan's hand, and pulled him to his feet.

"She'll come. She married you, didn't she?" Dylan blushed. "But what are you going to tell Manus and the Missus?"

"The truth?"

"Maybe not the *whole* truth. I'd leave out Cernunnos and the vampires and focus on medical advancements and opportunities for Mara and their grandchildren." The tips of Dylan's ears turned beet red, and he glanced up at the clouds. "Conall understands the future as just another stop on the spiral of Between. Maybe use that terminology." Estrada sniffed. "You know what? I trust you. Just go with your heart."

19

Estrada wandered off into the forest with Cernunnos while Dylan and Mara said their goodbyes amid tears and hugs.

"I thought he would be harder to convince," Estrada said, and sunk down on a huge old nurse log. Rain as faint as mist gently stippled the stream. He could understand why Dylan wanted to stay here in this simple life filled with love, family, and meaningful work.

"The threat of non-existence puts everything into perspective, does it not?" Cernunnos said.

"I suppose it does." Estrada half-listened. He wondered if he'd ever lead a life like that. He loved being a magician and high priest. And he loved Lucy and Sensara and his Hollystone family.

Crouching at the edge of the stream, he washed his hands, then cupped them and took a long drink of clear, rich water. Perhaps he should be counting his blessings, rather than yearning for something that may or may not exist.

He felt Cernunnos move behind him. "For thousands of years, I've seen men be born and die, and be reborn again.

That is the way of it. To be, to exist is what drives you mortals."

"And what about Mara? Is it a mistake to bring her into the future?" Estrada stared into the god's deep brown eyes.

"The mistake is in thinking I could deny you anything."

Estrada felt a rush of blood stain his cheeks. And that was an entirely new feeling for him.

20

When they arrived back at the Standing Stones, Conall was seated on the ground with his back against the center stone. He sprung up when he saw Estrada and crushed him to his chest. "I was trying to imagine what I'd do if you never returned, and all I could see was darkness as deep and black as the void beneath Croghan Hill."

"I hope you never have to experience that again."

Estrada turned to thank Cernunnos, but the Horned God had disappeared. Surely, that meant they'd corrected their mistake and things would flow smoothly from here on in.

As Dylan and Mara walked down the avenue of stones, Estrada could hear him telling her about what had happened here. How he'd been arrested for murder, and how Estrada had caught the actual killer, and got him released from prison. How he'd saved his life.

"It's going to be alright," Dylan said. "This is my home. I grew up here and my grandfather lives just down the road. You have a family here now too."

Let's hope, Estrada thought. *After all this, let's hope Dermot's living at Piper's Dream and everything is exactly as it should be.*

As he followed Dylan toward the car park, he turned to see if the Horned God had reappeared.

"Don't worry. Cernunnos is never far from you. His love is strong." Conall punched his arm. "I just hope, one day, you share a loaf with me."

21

Sorcha found Estrada leaning against the stone ruins of Tarbert Castle later that evening. For a long while, they stood silently watching the sun descend, as nobles and kings had done for centuries on this hill.

"A beautiful end to a long, hectic day," she said at last. She was exhausted. After they'd all piled into the Land Rover in Kilmartin Glen, Estrada had driven to Tarbert with Conall beside him. She'd climbed into the back seat with Dylan and Mara. No one spoke, and the silence was palpable. Perhaps they feared, as did she, that Dermot McBride wouldn't be living at Piper's Dream, and they'd wrenched the newlyweds from the past for nothing.

Estrada parked and they all piled out. Dylan took a deep breath and exhaled, then charged up the stone steps. He tried the door and finding it locked, turned to them with a look of pure terror on his face. He turned back and began to pound on the oak door calling out, "Granddad. Granddad," in a thunderous voice. Mara stood so stiffly beside Sorcha; she'd grasped the girl's hand. By then, they'd all climbed the steps and stood together on the stone landing.

"Easy, man," Estrada had said. "It looks different than it did this afternoon. Take a breath."

But Dylan, pale-faced and red-cheeked, continued to pound and yell for his grandfather. It was enough to wake the dead or at least inspire a visit from the police.

Suddenly, from across the driveway, they heard a deep, raspy voice. "Can't a man share a wee dram with his neighbor of seventy-nine years without a stramash?"

"It's nae a stramash, Granddad. Not till you pass the bottle." Dylan leapt off the steps and tackled the sweet old man.

Since then, a kitchen party had been ramping up.

But Sorcha had stopped drinking to be a ma, and watching others get off their head didn't interest her. Especially when Conall had joined them in blowing the feck out of bagpipes. It was enough to rouse the clans. So, she'd left to search for Estrada, who'd disappeared himself soon after they'd arrived. And, despite Dylan's protests, Mara went for a stroll around the harbor. Though new to this world, she didn't seem to fear a thing, including her new husband. Sorcha felt for her though. It was the poor girl's wedding night.

"Dylan's so grateful to see his granddad, he's forgotten about his new wife. I'll be having a wee talk with him."

"He's a married man now and not your concern. Let them work it out. It was a rough day, and we all deserve a break." Estrada scowled. "I should be home with my daughter, not standing on some hill in Scotland."

Sorcha said nothing, knowing better than to antagonize him when he was in one of his black moods.

"I know what you're thinking," he said, "We should have left right away. But if we had, Dylan and his grandfather wouldn't exist."

"Aye, that's true."

"I needed Dylan, and now he's here. And if we stay another day or two, my stuff will arrive, and we might end up with Dubh as well."

Estrada was fretting something fierce. "Don't eat the head off me. You made the right decision. So, what the feck?"

"Just because it's right doesn't mean I have to like it. I'm sure the king who once lived here made tough decisions all the time." He ran his fingers over the gray stone and glanced up at the ruined tower house.

"I'm sure he did. Ships anchored below and this isthmus connected the east and west lochs." She glanced out over the sea and its myriad islands. It would have been a stunning presence in the twelfth century when fortified by Robert the Bruce. "So, what's the story?" She knew his mind was never idle, even when he was romancing the bard.

Estrada cracked his knuckles, and the sound made her cringe. "A boot camp of sorts."

"Boot camp? Push-ups and sit-ups and all that military shite?"

He laughed. "The barkeep told me this trail runs for miles. Back home, I work out every day." He wrung his shoulders and swung his arms. "I've been idle too long."

"So?"

"So, I'm going to run this trail at first light. See how far I can get. Maybe sleep out under the stars tomorrow night."

"*Holy feck.* Didn't you get enough of that in Croghan?" She wasn't ready to give up an actual bed to run hills and sleep on hard, damp ground.

"You don't know Diego." His eyes blazed. "I saw things."

Ah. It *was* boot camp. He was preparing for war.

"Will one day suffice? I'd like to drive back Thursday morning and miss the weekend ferry traffic."

Estrada nodded. "Hopefully by then, Dubh will be back, and we can pick him up on the way."

"And if he's not?"

He threw up his hands. "If he's not, we go without him. I must see for myself what Michael's into." He sniffed and she detected some dried tears. "And I miss my daughter."

"Thursday it is." Sorcha yawned. "If the lads get hammered and pass out, I might get some sleep. If I do, I'll join you for a bit. I wouldn't mind a tramp in the hills."

"How about, I go down and grab some pillows and blankets, and we crash here tonight under the stars? What do you say?"

"Feck, why not? I've slept rough on digs around the world. How can I pass up a night in the ruins of Tarbert Castle with Andreas El Cuero? The man in the black leather pants."

22

Estrada saw the white van pulling up in front of Sullivan Stables and bolted out the door. *Yes.* The parcel was for him and labeled Vancouver. Crushing it to his chest, he tore upstairs to open it where he could be alone. Truthfully, in his present state, Estrada wasn't sure Michael could pull it off, and he'd been preparing to fly as Andreas El Cuero. But he had, and Estrada held the proof in his hands.

He was further shocked when he pulled his cell phone from the wrapping and discovered Michael had remembered to pack the charger. He turned it on and smiled as the screen lit up. After plugging it in, he stretched out on the bed, remembering those tense days on the yacht when they'd sailed up the coast to rescue Lucy from the vampires. *"In a world gone mad, I'd choose you,"* Michael had said one night. And later, when he'd returned as a vampire and tried to seduce Estrada into joining him in that life, Michael had fallen to his knees and made an eerie proposal. *"I promise to love you forever, to never forsake you, to give you everything you've ever wanted."* Estrada had so wanted to say yes.

But Vampire was no romance, as he'd witnessed on Diego's island, and in reality, both Michael and Estrada enjoyed multiple partners, disparaged monogamy, and had never talked of love before the threat of loss galvanized some latent longing, they held for each other.

He stared at the phone, remembering their first night together as he unzipped his jeans, testosterone surging through his core. It was just before noon. If he called now, he might just catch Michael before he dropped off to sleep. Michael was a sexual virtuoso, and Estrada wanted him. The sound of his voice would be enough.

"Amigo?" In the second of silence, Estrada imagined Michael sprawled drowsily across the black silk sheets, naked and pliant. He touched the speaker to free his hands. "I'm sorry to wake you, man. I just wanted to tell you that my stuff arrived."

"Estrada?" The voice was deep and sultry.

He sat up, face flushed, and suddenly slick with sweat. "Who's this?"

A long exhale. A sniff. Then, "Jazz."

Man or woman? Perhaps both? Perhaps neither? He couldn't tell. Another second of silence as they blindly appraised each other across the miles. Then Jazz sniffed again, and he imagined a scattering of white powder on a sharpened fingernail.

"Estrada, is that you? Did everything arrive alright? I packed carefully."

He growled. Had this-this *Jazz* been in his flat? Touching his things? *Fuck.* Had Michael been there at all or had he just sent his envoy?

"Now you have your stuff, I assume you'll be returning?" The question resembled a complaint.

Estrada squeezed his fist and stared at the taut knuckles that ached to punch this faceless threat. "Where's Michael?" He cleared his throat as he stood. "You know what, Jazz?

Never mind." He hit the red button and flung his phone across the room. *"Fuck."* He zipped up his jeans.

Why was he surprised? Michael abhorred sleeping alone and with the vampire virus percolating in his bloodstream, he'd be seducing anyone who would indulge his blood-sucking fantasy.

Jazz could be one of Diego's spies. As ravens they flew, and as men they walked, in darkness and in light. One of them, Leopold Blosch, had boarded Estrada's yacht, and they'd spent the night casually drinking and flirting. There was no way to tell Diego's ravens from ordinary men until they transformed or bit you.

He knew how the pleasure-seeking virus worked. Leopold had called it an aphrodisiac, and Estrada had experienced its potency himself. Michael had teased him with a drop of his own vampire blood that sent Estrada reeling. The virus feasted on nutrients, so the stronger that blood surged, the faster it replicated. If Jazz was a vampire, as Estrada suspected, they were feeding Michael's addiction. Like the parasitic mistletoe he and Conall had cut from the oak tree, he must eradicate the virus, along with the vampires.

Grimacing, Estrada rubbed the tight muscles in the back of his neck, then his fingers strayed to the scars on either side of his neck.

Where the fuck was Magus Dubh? The sooner he could get Michael away from Jazz and pump Dubh's fey blood into his system, the better.

He flinched with the knock on his bedroom door.

"Come in," he called, voice surly.

Sorcha popped her head in. "Hey, gorgeous. Got a minute?"

"As many as you need." Estrada exhaled, smoothed his wrinkled T-shirt over his jeans, and perched on the bed.

"We need to talk."

"That sounds ominous." He took a deep breath, laid down, and patted the space beside him.

"Only slightly."

Sorcha sprawled beside him, and they both stared up at the ceiling.

"How's the bump?" he said, touching her belly.

"He's grand. Still making me heave every morning though." She glanced down and stroked her breasts, which were decidedly bigger, if that could be possible.

She was nervous, building up to something she'd rather not say, and he wondered what it could be.

"What's the craic, Sorcha?" he asked, stealing one of her lines.

"I saw the delivery van. Did you get your stuff?"

"I did," he said, and held the parcel upside down. His passport, drivers license, and wallet fell out.

She cleared her throat. "Grand. I found a nonstop Dublin-Vancouver flight that departs early tomorrow morning from Dublin. Dubh might not return for a week or more, and I know you're eager to get home."

"Perfect." There was no point waiting here any longer. Estrada's best option now was to get back to the coven and prepare for war. The Wee Pict would turn up, eventually.

"I booked three seats."

"Three?" Estrada leaned up on his elbow and stared at her with raised brows. Five of them were now staying at Sullivan Stables thanks to Franya's generosity.

"This morning, Dylan and I talked about this vampire. He told me about his penchant for female blood. I believe he used the word *fodder*." She punched his arm. "Why didn't you tell me?"

He snorted. "If I'd told you not to come, you'd be standing at the front of the line waving your boarding pass."

She turned onto her side and faced him. "Am I really that—?"

"Spirited? Stubborn? Strong-willed?"

"Let's leave it at that."

She laid her head on Estrada's bare chest, and he ran his fingers through her silky red hair. As sassy as she was, Sorcha exerted a calming influence on him. "I hope Ronan's a ginger kid with hair like yours."

"Aye, me too. With my hair and his father's stature, no one will dare feck with him."

Estrada laughed. Ruairí had been six foot six, a dashing warrior who'd never surrendered to anyone or anything including his executioner.

"So, who's staying and who's going?"

"I'm staying here," she said, her voice suddenly as soft as her hair. "I feel like I've been given a second chance with Franya."

Estrada knew if he warned Sorcha about Franya, he'd drive her right into the woman's arms. And what evidence did he have that Franya couldn't be trusted? Only Conall's cryptic comment: *"The trees said beware."* It was better to let Sorcha draw her own conclusions. She obviously had unfinished business with her ex.

"Alright. Go on."

Sorcha took a deep breath and sighed. "Franya invited Mara to stay here too, and Dylan thinks it's a grand idea."

"Huh. So, you and Mara are going to stay here in Lullymore while Dylan, Conall, and I go off fighting vampires across the sea. Is that it?"

"Aye, but you know I'll come if you need me."

"I know you will." Estrada gathered her up and drew her into a hug. "Dylan's right." He could understand why he wouldn't want either of the loves of his life anywhere near Diego's lair. "We saw things on that island you'd never want to see. Dubh called it the 'Island of Sinners'. Diego has an S&M party room that he uses to attract boaters to the island. Then he uses them for—"

"Fodder," she said.

"Yep."

"It must have scared the hell out of Dylan if he's prepared to leave his new wife here."

"Indeed, and he trusts you enough to leave her in your care."

"Aye, right."

"Diego's spent two hundred years perfecting his evil vampire schtick. Which is why we're going after him. And for the record, I'm glad you won't be anywhere near it."

Sorcha sat up and swung her legs over the side of the bed, so her back was to him.

Reaching up, he squeezed her shoulder. "So, I'm curious. How long's it been since you and Franya . . .?"

Sorcha turned and backhanded him. "Ah, you're after details now, are you?"

Estrada laughed. "There's nothing sexier than two women in the throes of passion."

"Except maybe two men."

She leaned back against his chest and cleared her throat. "I haven't seen Franya for nine years, but it feels like no time has passed at all. It's still electric, you know?"

"Indeed. I am a fan of sexual energy. Why did you break up?"

Sorcha scowled and sat up stiffly, bracing her back against the headboard. "I caught her in bed with my best friend, Vivian."

"Vivian Sullivan? Late owner of this lovely home and stables?"

"The same."

Estrada pursed his lips. "I'd have crawled in with them."

"I would have too, if they'd invited me."

"Ah, I see. Betrayal's a bitch." He sat up too, then leaned over and kissed her on the forehead. "Can you do me one favor"

"Aye, sure. I mean, probably."

"Take it slow with her."

"This from the man who's had his tongue down Conall's throat for days."

"Hey, that's all that's been down Conall's throat. We're moving slow and, you know, there's something about holding off that makes everything more intense."

"Anticipation." Sorcha's eyes blazed.

"Indeed."

"I know exactly what you mean."

23

As the plane cruised over the Atlantic, Estrada considered his next move. Conall lounged beside him in the window seat, belt unbuckled, eyes closed. He'd survived takeoff with little more than a long gasp, though he'd nearly broken Estrada's fingers with his squeeze. After a few beers he'd fallen asleep. Dylan sat behind them reading some journal article on vampire archaeology that he'd printed back in Lullymore. Occasionally, he'd lean forward and spew some interesting fact.

"Vampires are as old as humanity. They used to place the severed head on top of the legs to prevent them from rising from the grave."

While Dylan discovered new ways to dispatch vampires, Estrada made a mental list of all the weaponry he could get his hands on.

Once they were back in Vancouver, he knew black raven eyes would follow him everywhere. Anything he did, he had to assume, would get back to Diego. If they were to surprise the vampires before their planned abduction attempt on August 1st, he'd need to be stealthy. More than stealthy. Every action must be veiled. He'd need to be a ghost.

He flipped through photos of Lucy and Sensara on his phone. For days, he'd procrastinated about calling Sensara, but now he had no choice. He'd need to convince the women to take Lucy and secretly leave the house on Hawk's Claw Lane. That too, must be a covert operation beyond the reach of raven eyes. He couldn't imagine anywhere completely safe for them to go but getting out of there was a start. It was the only way to prevent the vampires from abducting Lucy from her bed, the way they had on Lughnasadh. The question was: How could they leave without arousing suspicion or being tailed by the ravens?

With Sensara, it was safer to tell the truth about everything. Well, maybe not everything. But definitely things he couldn't explain any other way, like the existence of Conall. One look at the handsome bard and Sensara wouldn't just be smitten, she'd know he wasn't from around here. Who knew what her psychic powers would pick up?

Perhaps, if he appeared with both Dylan and Conall, Sensara would keep her temper in check. Perhaps not, if he'd really been missing a month as Michael claimed.

24

Estrada's skin prickled as he walked down the hall toward his Commercial Drive flat. He motioned for Conall to wait. Dylan had gone directly to his university digs and now Estrada wished he hadn't. In the same second, he realized he didn't have a key, then saw that his door was unlocked. The hair on the back of his neck rose as he kicked it wide. Edging inside, fists up in fighting stance, he surveyed the room. The air smelled stale. Perhaps he had been gone a whole month. Nothing seemed out of place, but something was off. He leaned out into the hall and motioned for Conall to join him.

The bard's face was a maze of emotion as he stepped through the threshold. Surprise. Excitement. But also dread. He gestured to Estrada. They'd had to leave their knives behind in Lullymore, and he wanted a weapon. Conall felt the threat too. An unseen presence lingered in the ethers.

Estrada nodded once and eased into the kitchen, where he grasped a cleaver and butcher knife from the block. He handed the knife to the bard, who hefted it for weight and drew it through the air. "Shadows," he mouthed. Estrada had seen them too. Someone had been here, not just grabbing his phone and ID, but searching. For what, he couldn't imagine. Whoever it was had taken their time and put their foul fingers everywhere. His desk and shelves were a maze of greasy fingermarks.

The men searched the flat, peering into dark corners, cupboards, and closets. Estrada left Conall in the kitchen while he searched the bedroom, his clothes closet, and bathroom—even ripping wide the shower curtain. Estrada's eyes and senses were primed for listening devices. Diego was a sixteenth century Luddite who still burned candles in his woodsy palace, but that didn't mean some of his newer soldiers weren't hackers or surveillance experts. If he were Diego, he'd assemble an army with diverse skills and talents.

Finally, assured that no one was there; at least in their physical form, Estrada sighed and joined Conall in the living room.

The bard concurred. "There is no one here now."

"Jazz." Estrada ground his teeth. "I must do something about Jazz."

Now, more than ever, he assumed that Jazz was one of Diego's moles. Maybe a vampire; maybe not. Christophe, the tricksy boy toy who'd lured Michael to Le Château was human. His job was to find handsome young men to be turned into vampires and sucked into the fold. Diego called them his sons, his Salvadors—saviors who symbolized the son he'd lost at sea in the late 1700s.

Leopold Blosch, who'd been kidnapped and forcibly turned, had told Estrada there were several teenaged boys being force-fed blood and held prisoner at Le Château for Diego's amusement. It was Estrada's intention to destroy them all. Obliterate the monsters from the face of the planet. But first, he needed to detox his home.

He opened wide all the windows to let in the afternoon breeze. Then he grasped a bundle of dried white sage from a carved wooden box. After lighting the wand, he fanned the smoke over himself and Conall with an eagle feather. As he set about smudging the shadowy imprints left by the intruder, Conall followed, and explored his flat.

"I did not imagine your home would look like this."

"Well, while you're snooping, grab a rag from under the kitchen sink, and do a little dusting, eh."

Conall ignored his sarcasm, intent as he was on analyzing Estrada's personality via his possessions. At least, that's what Estrada presumed he was doing.

"You often wear black, but there's so much color here." Only the nobles could wear colored cloth in ancient Croghan. Conall had been wearing a pink woolen cloak when they'd first met on the road, and Ruairí's aquamarine cloak was as striking as the man.

"I travel frequently and bring home treasures that speak to me." The white walls were decorated with hanging rugs, paintings, Indigenous art, and artifacts. Hand-woven baskets and Pueblo pottery adorned simple floating shelves. "I did an extensive gig in Albuquerque a few years ago, and during the day, I explored New Mexico. Once, I drove into the desert and found myself on the Navajo Reservation. I saw a woman weaving beneath a shelter of sticks outside her hogan. She reminded me so much of *mi abuela*, I stopped to talk to her." Estrada pointed to the large rug in a corner by the window. It was an intricate sand painting in shades of black, white, and scarlet. "She'd just finished weaving this rug and I couldn't take my eyes off it."

"So, you traded for it."

"Yes. Sand paintings are used for healing and when I sit in its center to meditate, my whole body tingles. I come away feeling healed of whatever has thrown me out of balance.

Sometimes, I fall asleep there. One night I dreamed I was running through the desert like *el lobo*. The wolf."

"Tell me of this desert."

"Vast. Hot. Dry. The light creates colors like you've never seen before. One day we'll go. The turquoise pieces come from New Mexico too." He pointed to a glass-encased bookcase and a shelf of raw turquoise rocks. "Come on, I'll show you the rest." Estrada talked as he continued to smudge the hall closets. And then they walked into his bedroom.

Conall stood back amazed. "The only thing I've ever seen this color was Ruairí's cloak."

A distressed barn door stained a soft turquoise hung across the walk-in closet. More patterned rugs hung on the walls and covered the polished hardwood floor. An aqua quilt and Navajo throw pillows covered his bed.

Stepping closer, Conall ran his fingers over the carved trees in the wooden headboard. "Exquisite," he said. "Like you."

Estrada felt his cheeks flush. If they stayed here any longer, they'd be tumbling naked in a turquoise cotton sea. "I made decent money at that gig, and spent all of it and more, before I left the state."

Satisfied that the smudge had cleansed the negative energy, he wandered back into the living room. Conall followed.

"Can I make you a chai tea?"

The bard nodded.

Estrada put the kettle on to boil and when he returned, he found Conall chatting with a tall saguaro cactus.

"Everything alright?" he asked.

"She needs more light," Conall said somberly, "and she's thirsty."

"Of course she is. I haven't watered her in a month." The only plants Estrada could maintain with his schedule were his cacti. He loved them, and they went with his decor, though he'd never tried talking to them. "Would you be comfortable over here?" Estrada asked the cactus as he hefted it and moved it to the south-facing window near his rustic dining room table. Beside it stood an old stereo and a stack of vinyl albums.

"Aye. She likes it there," Conall said.

"How are the others?"

Conall hovered over a large pot of barrel cacti and a beautiful plant called Old Lady, probably because of the tiny white hairs atop her head.

"They're all thirsty, and they want you to know they prefer rainwater. The water you are using is caustic."

"I'll bear that in mind." As the kettle whistled, Estrada walked back into the kitchen to make tea. "Relax, man. *Mi casa es su casa.*"

"Hmmm?"

"My home is your home."

"I'd like that," Conall said.

He'd invited the bard to stay but was concerned about taking their liaison further. He feared triggering something from Conall's past. Moreover, Estrada was feeling protective. He'd soon be meeting Michael and didn't want him anywhere near the bard.

When he returned with a tea tray, Conall was staring at the glass bookcase.

"See anything there you'd like to read?"

"Read?"

It suddenly struck Estrada that, although the bard understood conversational English, he was illiterate. "When we want to record words, we use these symbols." He held up a small pink paperback. "This says *Love Poems*, and this, Pablo Neruda. One is written in English and the other in Spanish. That's how I first read Neruda's work years ago and fell in love with it. His work is vivid and passionate. I can read it to you if you like."

"Why must you record the words? Can you not remember them?" Conall picked up his cup, smelled the aromatic steam, and sipped.

Estrada had read somewhere that bards studied passages for years to commit them to memory. Like Wicca, everything came in threes. Triads. But that was when the world was much smaller and simpler. "There are too many words and too many stories to remember them all. Books contain thousands of years of knowledge. We have entire buildings called libraries dedicated to words, and people can borrow almost any book they want. We read stories for pleasure the way you might sing or tell tales. If you like, I can teach you."

"Is this something everyone here can do?"

"Pretty much. We learn as children." Wary to wade into a serious discussion about literacy in the contemporary world, Estrada decided to change the subject. Time was ticking.

They were four weeks away from Lughnasadh. He'd prioritized a mental list and Leopold Blosch was number one. The chef had only been a vampire for about a month before Estrada met him, which meant he'd be heading into Diego's ambush any moment now, if he hadn't already left on his fateful cruise.

When he finished his tea, Estrada opened his closet door. "Here. Try this on." It was a pale gray leather jacket as soft as butter.

Conall flashed his caramel eyes as Estrada held out the jacket, and the bard slipped his arms into the silken sleeves. "Beautiful," he breathed.

"*You're* beautiful." Estrada tugged Conall's long chestnut hair out from beneath the collar and turned him, so they faced each other. He gazed into the bard's eyes and watched his pupils dilate as he pulled his hips tightly against his own. "I want you. You know that, right?"

"I feel your need. Do you feel mine?" His lips caught Estrada's, and they crashed against the closet door. Conall's hands were on him, squeezing, stroking. Then he spun Estrada around, shoved his chest up against the wall and mouthed his shoulder.

"*Fuck.*" Estrada gasped. He felt the hard edge of Conall's teeth against his skin, and with it came a startling vision of Leopold on The Wheel, just as *he* had been. But being drained by Zion while the others watched and cheered.

"Wait, man. Wait. Leopold. We must save Leopold."

The moment broke wide, and Conall yelled, *"Fuck!"* in a torrent of frustration.

Estrada couldn't control his laughter though the bard's face was a maze of sighs and bared teeth. "I'm sorry, but you've learned exactly the right word to use in a moment like this."

Conall pounded his fist against the door.

"We'll have our time," Estrada promised. "But we must catch Leopold Blosch before he boards that boat. Vampire is a fate worse than death."

Conall growled. "The Leannán Shee."

Estrada slipped on his black leather jacket, then grabbed two helmets and his keys from the turquoise dish beside the door. He handed one helmet to Conall. "Come on, man. I want to introduce you to my horse."

25

Estrada drove his Harley downtown in a pseudo-dream wearing the bard's energy like a cloak. It had been too long since he'd wrapped his thighs around his Fat Boy and cruised the Vancouver streets with the sea breeze caressing his face. That wasn't all being caressed. Conall's arms encircled his waist, his hands low and grasping Estrada's taut jeans. By the time he pulled up to Ecos on Robson and turned off the bike, Estrada's teeth were aching.

He turned to Conall. "You bastard. I'll get you for that."

The bard grinned. "That was the point."

This was the first time Estrada had been inside Leopold's vegetarian bistro. It was located in the trendy part of downtown, just off Robson, yet the atmosphere was pure and earthy. Sunshine beamed through the picture window. He could feel Blosch's energy all over it, from the gray, white, and wood decor to the myriad plants that hung and sprung and wound their way between the tables in a raucous green flowering tangle. The way Conall cocked his head, Estrada assumed he was already communicating with them. *If I was a plant, I wouldn't mind living here,* he thought. Patrons crowded the white marble bar watching sous chefs prepare their dishes. The bistro smelled as fresh and spicy as Blosch himself.

When the cheerful server came to take their order, Estrada asked for Leopold and was told the boss was busy in the kitchen. He took a business card from his inside jacket pocket. It was black with a white-winged horse logo on one side along with the Pegasus website, phone number and address, and his name in white caps on the other. Nigel's creation.

"We'll be staying for dinner," he said, handing her the card. "Please tell Blosch we'd like to see him." His appetite had fired now he knew Blosch was still in town.

Estrada picked up the menu card and squinted at Conall. "I'd read it to you, but after what you did to me on the way down here, I'm going to order for us both. I hope you like mashed Brussels sprouts."

The bard didn't smile. Rather, he picked up his own menu and glanced at the pictures. He pointed at the Santa Fe salad and sweet potato fries. "This and this," he said. Then he tucked the card in his jacket pocket.

Estrada was delighted to see a full bar. When the server returned, he ordered two Santa Fe salads and fries, along with twin margaritas.

Blosch brought the food himself along with a side of his famous guacamole and homemade taco chips baked with hot peppers and smokey goat cheese. His long platinum hair was caught up in a bun, his tanned face smooth-shaven, his cedar green eyes bright and curious. A look passed between him and Conall that evoked a soft growl from Estrada. He doused the burning sensation in his chest with a gulp of tequila and tried to settle into business.

He understood the lure of Leopold. Estrada was just a kid when *Brokeback Mountain* premiered in Los Angeles. He'd snuck into a theater and watched the whole thing with his mouth hanging open. Here was his fantasy come to life on the big screen in the guise of this young god, Heath Ledger. Add long, straight, platinum hair, and you'd create a man almost as hot as Blosch.

All three men appraised each other for several long seconds.

"I gather you've heard of Pegasus," Estrada said. He knew Blosch had. They'd talked about the club and more the night they'd got drunk on the yacht.

"Yes, of course. It's a pleasure to meet you." As he held out his hand, Blosch's inquisitive mouth widened to a smile. "I've seen your marquis. Magician, yes?"

Estrada nodded. He'd been recognized from that marquis many times before. *Those were the days*, he thought wistfully. Then, he was young and fresh and fully free. A hungry wolf who thrived on pleasure. With black hair hanging halfway down his back, he'd become the co-star of Michael's sensual parties. People clamored for invitations, and there were only two rules. Everyone who took part was a consenting adult, and no one got hurt. Blosch had never come. Estrada would have remembered.

He squeezed Blosch's hand as he shook it. "This is my friend, Conall Ceol."

Again, that spark passed between them like a smoldering ember begging for a burst of wind. Blosch took Conall's hand, held it in both of his, and leaned forward.

Estrada cleared his throat. "I have something to tell you which you won't believe, but please hear me out before you throw me out."

"Go on," Leopold said. "I'm intrigued."

"I understand that your financial manager—I believe his name is Lorne Wiseman—has invited you to travel by yacht up the strait to an exclusive establishment in the Broughton Archipelago."

Leopold's face turned to ash, and he drew back. "How do you know—?"

"It doesn't matter how I know. Just tell Wiseman that it's a trap. You cannot go."

"What kind of trap?"

"The worst kind. A death trap." Estrada drained the rest of his cocktail and signaled to the server to bring another.

Blosch's eyes narrowed. "How do you know my business?"

"Because I know you."

"We've never met."

"Actually, we have."

"Perhaps you should leave." Leopold tried to stare him down, but Estrada kept right on talking.

"Le Château des Vampires is a front designed to imprison desirable young men. If you go there, you'll be enslaved."

"What do you mean? They're into human trafficking?"

"Something like that." Estrada rubbed his dry hands together. "Wiseman will be murdered."

Leopold scoffed. "Murdered. I don't believe it. If that were true, the RCMP would shut them down."

Estrada let that one go. He didn't want to lie and lose his credibility.

But Blosch was caught. "Lorne said to keep it hush-hush. How could you possibly know about our trip?"

"Because you and I have talked together at length. In fact, we got pleasantly drunk one night on a yacht when I was headed to Le Château myself. We shared stories."

"What stories?" The scowl returned as the food arrived.

Conall's eyes widened. "This is beautiful," he said, softening what was building into a colossal argument.

"Thank you," Leopold said.

Conall scooped up the guacamole, beans, corn, and salty feta, as if he'd been eating tacos all his life.

"You told me," Estrada said, "that you'd never been in a relationship. You wanted a restaurant, so all your time and energy went into creating it. This place. Ecos. Your vegetarian bistro."

"That could be an assumption," Blosch said.

"You also told me you worked as a bartender for our competitor, Forbidden, in order to put yourself through college."

Leopold wiped his hands on his white pants and crossed his arms over his chest. "Anything else?"

"You went to Pegasus once and tried the blood clots."

"Have you come here to mock me? Blackmail me? What exactly do you want?"

"To save your life." He stared into Blosch's dark green eyes. "Because once you saved mine." Estrada sat back and gauged Leopold's response.

The chef's eyes widened, and he grew still. He glanced at Conall, who nodded as if to say, *Listen to him. He's telling the truth.*

"When are you supposed to go?" Estrada said.

"Tomorrow morning." Leopold blinked.

"Le Château des Vampires is real. If you board that yacht and go there, they'll turn you into one of them." Leopold made a strange sound of disbelief. "You'll have no choice. You can't fight them, and you can't escape. You'll hate them and you'll hate yourself." Estrada took a breath. "Because you'll trade one of your friends for your freedom."

"What friend?"

"Nora Barnes."

"Nora?"

"She comes here with her husband, Joe. They have a young child named Zachary. Sometimes they bring their neighbor, Nigel Stryker. He's the man who bought Pegasus for his grandson, Michael."

"I know who Stryker is. He's been here with them." Blosch sniffed. He was starting to believe. "But this is crazy. How can you know this?"

"Call me psychic." Estrada cocked his head, then shook it. "Actually, that's bullshit. I'm not psychic. I'm just getting a little drunk because talking about these fuckers disturbs me." He gulped down the second margarita. "The truth is, I know about the vampires because they stole my baby as an act of revenge for something Michael Stryker did. Your friend, Nora, nursed her until we could rescue her. She's a good woman, and I don't want anything bad to happen to her." Estrada wiped his mouth. "They were about to turn me into a vampire too, when *you* saved my life."

"I saved your life."

"Uh-huh."

"But how can you know all this?"

"I just do."

"Vampires." Blosch scowled. "And I would never do anything to hurt Nora."

"Look, these vampires play games. Telling them about Nora was a way to barter for your freedom, and they promised not to harm her. They're cunning and deceitful." Estrada scraped up some of the food and shoved it in his mouth. But it had lost its allure. All he wanted to do now was belt back margaritas.

Leopold sat stunned into silence.

"You don't have to believe me, but the bottom line is this: Don't get on that fucking yacht."

Leopold turned to Conall, who had both hands in his tacos. "Are you part of this?"

The bard swallowed and wiped his mouth with a fist. "Estrada doesn't lie."

Leopold stood speechless staring from one man to the other. Then, he took a deep breath, and signaled the server. "Bring another round of drinks. On the house."

26

The house was sadly silent since the lads left. Sorcha had driven Estrada, Conall, and Dylan to Dublin airport, said quick goodbyes, and sped home in the Land Rover with a glassy-eyed Mara huddled in the passenger seat. *Home*. It was funny how she was already thinking of Lullymore as home. Sorcha didn't know how to help the girl, so turned up the tunes and left her to emote. Grief was grief. And a new bride sending her husband into battle must feel it as it was. Whether Mara understood the word vampire didn't matter. She knew about war and accepted that this was a life-or-death quest from which Dylan might not return.

Now, Sorcha stood alone in the kitchen listening to the sounds of Sunday morning: the steady thrum of a steaming kettle, birdsong from the patio, and the ticking of an annoying grandfather clock in the dining room. It was early, so early, the rest of the house still slept. As she leaned against the counter, she stared out the window, captivated by the sunlight breaking over the eastern pasture.

She flinched when she heard Franya's breathy voice against her ear. "I've missed you, Foxy." Tall and slender, the woman leaned down, lips brushing Sorcha's neck. A lacquered fingernail caught her tank and teased it from her shoulder. The shift from touch to kiss sent a quiver inside, and Sorcha leaned back into the source of this unexpected pleasure. As fingertips found her tender breasts, she gasped. She'd wanted this so many nights, imagined it just like this. Though she never dreamed it would happen.

Turning, she sought Franya's moist lips with her own. A kiss could be a deal breaker or incite a riot. This one needed the feckin IRA. Nine years vanished in a fervent flash. Pressing with her pelvis, she danced Franya back until they were braced by the bar. Then, grasping Franya's white silk nightdress by the lacy hem, she slipped it off over her head. Her pearly skin was as perfect as ever, smooth and unblemished, her burgundy hair messed with sleep, her body as lithe and pliant as a young willow. Dropping to her knees, Sorcha pursued the source of Franya's pleasure.

"You're like a great marmalade cat with a dish of cream," Franya said, running her fingernails through Sorcha's curls. A twist of tongue, and swooning, she arched her back.

In the periphery, Sorcha spied a shadow in the shade of the patio doors and, assuming it was Declan, she took it up a notch. *What will you do?* she thought. *Watch, run, or ask to join us?*

Reaching up with her left hand, she played a pulsing nipple as her fingers moved in ways she knew would tip Franya over the edge. And with a stifled scream, it did.

Franya pulled her up, pupils wide, mouth searching, hips pressing, wanting more. Sorcha closed her eyes to the feral urgency of Franya's kiss. "Your turn, Foxy."

"Not now," Sorcha said. "Mara's gonna walk in here any minute looking for her morning chocolate." With a quick glance, she noted Declan had gone.

"I'm sure she's seen two women make love."

"I somehow doubt that."

The kettle whistled and Sorcha turned away, lips turned up in a grin. *Two women making love.*

Finally, after years estranged, it had begun again.

27

A few mornings later, Sorcha invited Mara to come for a walk with her in the back fields. Franya had slipped into her bed, twice since their kitchen tryst. It was always in the wee hours when she tasted of gin, but that didn't affect her skill in the sack. Sex with Franya was feral—a way to heal, not only their brutal breakup but from the horrific experience of watching the man she loved be tortured and executed. Sorcha wanted to be held, and they'd end up spooning until she slipped out in need of coffee.

She wanted to tell Mara about this new liaison before the girl caught them in a embarrassing situation. Mara knew Sorcha was pregnant with Ruairí's child, and she was concerned the girl might judge her for having an affair with someone else so soon after his death.

As they wandered through the pasture, the morning sun reflected off the winding stream below. The green field swayed with white daisies, purple clover, and masses of yellow buttercups, juxtaposed with the fluttering of dappled orange butterfly wings, and the mad darting of bees. For a moment, walking alongside Mara in the verdant pasture, she felt as if she were back in Croghan near the Manus farm.

"Do two women ever fall in love or have sex in Croghan?" Sorcha knew the men did; at least, Conall had confessed to being sexually harassed by King Adamair, and she'd read that homosexuality was esteemed in ancient Celtic society. But men could often get away with things women could not.

Mara was quiet for a moment. She'd been picking a fistful of meadow buttercups and now held them to Sorcha's chin. The gesture seemed so youthful and innocent, Sorcha was embarrassed that she'd brought up the question of sex only seconds before. Sometimes, she forgot Mara was only fourteen and from an ancient culture.

"Is my chin yellow?" Sorcha asked.

"Aye. Very."

"That must mean I like butter, yeah?"

"You love it," Mara said. She held the bouquet of buttercups up beside Sorcha's face. "They look lovely with your red hair. I wish my hair was the color of yours."

Mara's waist-length hair was a tangle of dark toffee, bronze, and sand, her complexion peachy, her brown eyes flecked with gold. In a word, the girl was stunning. She'd pinned up the sides in braids that wound around her head, while the back blew loose in the wind.

"Why, thank you, my dear. You're sweet to say so, but you're perfection just as you are."

Mara blushed as easily as her new husband and continued plucking wildflowers. Sorcha assumed she'd ignored the question out of embarrassment and decided to drop it.

Then casually, Mara said, "When girls are young, we explore each other's bodies."

There seemed no shame or awkwardness at all. "Aye?" Was this exploration a timeless act of puberty?

"Some girls stay with girls as they get older, and others go off with boys. Some girls like boys and girls. Some girls are boys. Some boys are girls. Some are both."

"Really. So, is that how you learned about sex?"

"That, and by watching the animals. They didn't seem to enjoy it nearly as much as we did." She giggled. "Although Capall is enjoying frolicking with those mares in the back pasture."

"Is that so? Will there be some young Croghan foals born soon?" Conall's stallion was as much a stud as his owner, though the bard seemed oblivious to his own sex appeal.

"Perhaps next summer. I'd love a horse of my own." Mara glanced at the horses grazing near the stream so longingly, Sorcha determined to speak to Dylan about getting her a horse.

"Why don't you ride Estrada's gray mare? I'm sure she could use the exercise." She knew the girl was a skilled equestrian and tracker. She'd grown up with horses and led Dylan and Estrada through the bush to their hideout beside the lake of gillaroo. To Sorcha's relief, the stable manager hadn't mentioned her affair with Franya and was as congenial as ever.

"That's how the boys learn about sex too," Mara said, circling back to their conversation. "At least, I've heard my brothers carrying on with their friends. They're none too quiet about it. But it's natural, so no-one says anything—unless we're trying to sleep." She laughed so hard she snorted, and that set Sorcha laughing too.

Two thousand years and nothing's changed, Sorcha thought. She and her friends had stroked each other's breasts in Galway, just for the sheer thrill of it, and tickled other places too. By the time she went to uni, Sorcha was more enamored of girls than boys, and questioning her sexual identity. Then she met Franya—the woman of her dreams—and declared herself a lesbian. It was nothing new to her. Sorcha's mother had always been vocal about her sexual identity.

When the sweat dripped in her eyes, Sorcha wiped her forehead with the back of her hand, then pulled a handkerchief from the pocket of her khakis. She folded it neatly and tied it around her head.

Ruairí and Conall had built a wattle and daub hut beside the lake to escape being bullied by Fearghas and Bres, and maybe to have some time alone. Sorcha figured there might have been a little rub and tug going on in that hut when those two were young; at least she hoped, for Conall's sake, there was. He'd been mad for Ruairí his whole life; something that must have been desperately hard for him when Ruairí took up with Ana. Sorcha knew all too well the pain of unrequited love.

"Years ago, Franya and I had a sexual relationship when we were both in our late teens," she said. "We met at university while I was studying archaeology."

Mara brightened. "Were you in love?"

"Oh, aye. Smitten." *At least I was,* she thought.

"And did you wed Franya?" The girl had just arrived and didn't know the history of Sullivan Stables or what or who had come before.

"No, we broke up years ago, and hadn't seen each other until I arrived a few days ago."

"But why?" Mara seemed genuinely interested in her tragic romance; enough so that Sorcha decided to tell her the truth.

In some ways, Mara reminded Sorcha of Ruairí—a quiet nature that masked an inner strength—and she'd grown fond of her. Also, something in their shared Croghan dialect produced a lilting lift to their phrasing different from a modern-day Midlands accent. It wasn't enough to garner questions, but could make an observant person wonder where she'd come from. That's why Sorcha had had Rook create a passport for Mara Manus McBride that said she was eighteen years old and hailed from some remote island in the Scottish Hebrides. There was less chance of running into someone who might know better.

Sorcha laid down in the grass and gazed up at the wispy cirrus clouds scattered through the pale blue sky. "One day, I came home from a dig and found Franya having sex with my best friend, Vivian." Sorcha patted the ground. "This is Vivian's land. She and Franya eventually wed. Then Vivian died last spring."

"Oh, I'm sorry. But why did it bother you they were having sex?" Mara said innocently. "In Croghan, people have sex with whoever they want, and no one minds."

I minded, Sorcha thought. *I minded when Ruairí wed me AND Ana because she was Goddess of the Land. And I really minded when I had to witness their public fertility rites with everyone else at the fort.* Even now, the thought of it made her want to wring Ana's pale pretty neck, though the woman was dust and her neck had been clearly severed by Conall's sword.

"Well, it's different here. When you're married or in a serious relationship, there's an expectation that you'll only have sex with that one person whom you love. We call it being monogamous. Faithful. People feel hurt and betrayed if they catch their lover with someone else, and many couples break up because of it."

"Oh." Mara was quiet for so long after that, Sorcha grew worried. Was the girl considering having sex with someone else while Dylan was away in Vancouver? Hopefully not Declan. The stable manager was young and handsome but surely, he wouldn't proposition Mara knowing she and Dylan had just married.

"Did you talk with Dylan about seeing other people?"

"Oh no. Dylan doesn't talk about sex. His ears turn red." She giggled, then rolled her eyes. "He wanted to wait until after our hand-fast, but then we ended up coming here." She sighed. "We slept at his grandfather's house that night and he was too drunk and embarrassed to do it."

"*Jaysus*. When did you finally—?"

"Not until our first night here."

"Ah, and now he's gone. I'm sorry, Mara. You're entitled to a decent honeymoon."

I'm going to have a talk with that lad, Sorcha thought. *I don't care what Estrada says. I taught him better than that. When we had sex, his face turned red, but it was from exertion, not embarrassment.* Sorcha knew she'd taken Dylan's virginity, but she'd given him an education in return. Feeling it was inappropriate to tell Mara she'd had sex with her husband, she kept that nugget to herself.

"But you wouldn't have sex with someone else while Dylan was away, would you? Especially now that you know about being faithful to your partner."

"Since the day I met Dylan, I've wanted no other," Mara said.

Relieved, Sorcha turned on her side. She was about to rise when she realized she hadn't mentioned her current situation with Franya, not that she knew enough to even define what it was.

"That's lovely, Mara." Sorcha cleared her throat. "Since Franya and I met again, we've started having sex." *Jaysus, how awkward was that.*

"Oh, I know," Mara said, and then she giggled. "Sometimes, you two are louder than my brothers."

28

Saturday Night on The Drive

Estrada veered off Commercial Drive and cruised slowly down the back alley on his Harley. He was still half drunk, the salty-sweet taste of margaritas taunting his tongue. But he'd done what he set out to do. If Leopold Blosch boarded Wiseman's yacht tomorrow morning, his fate was his own. At least, he'd been warned.

He left the bike running while the bard slipped off, then pulled in close and used his key to open the padlock on the pseudo-garage. It wasn't terribly secure; just a steel lock that several residents had keys to fit. But he'd never had a problem in this part of town. A cosmopolitan community, just north of East 1st Avenue, it was a hip, yet friendly, neighborhood.

As he pulled into the garage and shut off the engine, a sudden feeling of dread caught at his gut, and the bitter tequila blew back up his throat. He wrenched off his helmet, walked outside, and spit. His guts were churning, and not from Leopold's spicy food. Estrada might not be a psychic like Sensara, but his intense physicality was often his barometer.

Conall waited outside wearing a wide grin. He'd removed his helmet and was raking his fingers through his long hair.

Under the streetlight, his cheeks above the stubbled beard were ruddy, his brown eyes as fluid and fuming as the sea. A red mist surrounded him, revealing just how much the man radiated heat.

"I gather you like my horse." When Estrada tweaked his cheek, Conall grabbed his hand and pulled it to his mouth. One finger slipped into its warmth and the bard breathed it in through pursed lips.

"I like everything about you." He dropped his helmet to the cement and pulled Estrada close. Grasping his jaw with both hands, Conall covered his mouth with fiery kisses. "I especially like that you just saved that man's life."

"Maybe I did. Maybe I didn't." He ran his thumb over Conall's lips. "And warning a man of imminent danger doesn't make me a fucking hero. It was the right thing to do."

But the clatter of steel on concrete caught Estrada by surprise, and he flinched and turned. The lot was empty, but skaters were coming—the chaotic rasp and clunk of metal wheels emerging from the darkness as they tricked their way up the back alley. They were heading north. Likely to Britannia, where the old tennis courts, with their moveable obstacles and graffitied cement abutments, stayed lit until ten p.m.

Sometimes, Estrada smoked a joint and sauntered up that way to wander around the park and watch the kids perform on his off nights. He'd skated as a kid in Los Angeles. It was exhilarating and allowed him to manage his drug runs in triple time—which meant more money in his pocket.

As the two men ventured into the alley, he glanced up at his flat. That feeling of uneasiness clung to his muscles like wet leather. The lights were on, just as he'd left them, and a golden glow spilled out over his balcony into the night. Still, something was wrong. He leaned against Conall as they walked, feeling comfort in his closeness.

The first skaters whizzed by, giving the men adequate space, and tricking as they went. He nodded to the pair who cruised on, smacking tails to the pavement in a tandem ollie. He elbowed Conall, wanting him to watch. Like him, they adored an audience. The next kid came on slow and solitary, pulling a chain of well-executed one-eighties.

Conall's laughter lightened Estrada's mood and set him smiling too. "How do they do that?"

"Practice, and lots of mistakes. Falling and getting back up. Doing it over and over and not being afraid to get hurt or look bad. Lots of war wounds. I've seen some poorly landed flips end with broken bones. But there's a sense of freedom."

"Warriors on wheels. I want to try."

Focused on Conall's alacrity, and hoping to shift his own dismal mood, Estrada didn't notice the last skater until he was right behind him. The kid came up quick and bashed him hard in the back of his right shoulder—the one he frequently dislocated. Yowling, he grabbed it and swayed, desperate to keep it in the socket. The pain burst from his mouth. *Fucking. Fuck. Fuck.*

Conall caught him before he hit the pavement, chanting a healthy string of old Irish curses.

When he righted himself, Estrada turned to see who'd hit him. That check was no accident.

The kid was lean and dressed all in black, long hair flying behind him like a pirate flag. He braked under the streetlight and turned. Cheeks bleached white against his dark hoodie, he glared with narrow almond eyes, black and bold.

Eliseo.

"You little fucker," Estrada yelled, and pulled the knife lodged in his boot. But it was too late. The kid vanished into the night.

"Come on." Grabbing Conall's arm, Estrada pulled him as he ran. "Get inside. Now."

"What is it? Do you know him?"

"I can't believe the balls on these bastards." Estrada stomped down the hallway and up the stairs. "Next time, I'll shove my knife right through his fucking brain." He shook it in the air.

"Who *was* that?"

Estrada bolted the door when they were both inside, then searched his flat again. He glanced at the open windows with their flimsy screens and shuddered. In the lore, vampires couldn't enter someone's home unless invited. But what if these vampires didn't need an invitation?

Pretty much everything he'd read in books or seen in movies was wrong. Garlic or crosses didn't bother Diego's tribe. Christ, Diego wore a bishop's robe and cross around his neck. They'd traveled under a cloudy sky by day. They didn't sleep in coffins in the nest, but lounged in hammocks hung in a tree. Rather than bats, they transformed into ravens, while Diego took the shape of a pterosaur. And when Leopold was still a vampire, Estrada had seen his reflection in the bathroom mirror. Only two things matched the lore. They were strong and fast, and reveled in the killing. *"Sport. Sport. Sport."* He remembered their frenzied chanting the day Michael ripped apart a man with just his nails and teeth.

As he glanced at the open windows, the hair on his arms tingled. What if it hadn't been Jazz who'd searched his flat, but Eliseo? Or Zion? Or all three of them?

He twisted the top off a bottle of tequila and took a long swig. "I haven't told you much about these vampires. It's time I did."

Conall was pacing, his exhilaration edged by terror.

Estrada salted two rims, poured tequila in each glass, and slipped in a piece of lime. Then he perched in a corner of the leather couch and motioned for Conall to join him.

"Here," he said. "You're gonna need this."

Conall took the drink and gulped. Then the bard grabbed the bottle and topped up both their glasses.

Estrada pulled out his phone. "One second."

Sensara had left several texts before she gave up a week ago. For all his bravado, the priestess scared the hell out of him and he'd been avoiding her. Now he had no choice. He typed:

SORRY I WENT AWOL. CALL A COVEN. NOON TOMORROW. THE HOUSE. I'LL EXPLAIN EVERYTHING. I PROMISE.

He pressed send, hoping that might calm her down before they arrived. Then he texted Dylan:

JUST SAW ELISEO IN THE BACK ALLEY. FUCKER HIT ME. COVEN TOMORROW NOON. THE HOUSE. MUST WARN THE OTHERS.

He looked at Conall. "They're playing more games than they did before."

Did vampire eyes follow his every move? How could he plan a surprise attack while under surveillance? And then a troubling thought. Had Eliseo followed him to Ecos? And how good was his hearing? Had that little prick listened to his conversation with Leopold? If he did, they were fully fucked.

"Who was that boy?" Conall sat straight, hyper-vigilant, tension deepening lines around his eyes.

"His name is Eliseo. He's thirteen going on two hundred and fifty. And he's a cold-blooded killer."

"Why is he after you?"

"That was a message. Eliseo is the first vampire Diego created to replace his human son." Estrada swallowed half his tequila and wiped his mouth. "It was Eliseo who stole my baby from her crib on the eve of her first birthday. We chased after them. But when we finally made it into Diego's nest, they were waiting for us. Diego had his vampires bind me to an iron wheel and gave me to Eliseo who—" Estrada pushed back the hair from his neck. "See these marks?"

Conall stared and nodded.

"These are from Eliseo's teeth. He bled me. I still remember the shock of those canines piercing my flesh. I was on the cusp of death. Diego would have turned me into one of them if it hadn't been for Leopold—"

"Leopold?"

"Yes. He doesn't know it, but Leopold jammed a knife through Eliseo's brain and dusted him. Then he carried me out of there and saved us all. That's why I couldn't let him get on that yacht and go to Diego's nest." Estrada pushed back the hair on the other side of his neck. "See these marks?" Conall nodded. "I let Leopold drink from me while my blood was still tainted with Dubh's fey blood. He'd refused to eat, and he was starving. That's how we found the cure."

"You cured Leopold? But why doesn't he remember?"

"There's nothing *to* remember. None of this has happened yet."

"But you know a cure?"

"Yes. That's why I need Magus Dubh. He *is* the cure."

Conall fell forward into Estrada's arms and pressed his cheek against his chest. "You triumphed once, and you will do so again. The gods are with you."

One at least, Estrada thought. *The best one.*

They stayed like that a long while, sheltering in silence, tequila shimmering in their veins.

"Estrada?"

"Hmmm." He was dozing. After all the chaos, he just wanted to rest here in his home with his arms around the bard.

"If we were to die tonight, there is one thing I would regret."

"We're not gonna die tonight, Conall."

"But if we did—"

Estrada closed his mouth with kisses. He wanted nothing but flesh on flesh. Breath on breath. The heat of his touch.

They rose from the couch, wrestling with leather and zippers and denim, until clothing fell away and there was nothing between them but Estrada's trepidation.

Conall's comment echoed in his conscience. *"What if you don't like who is fucking you?"* Of course, the bard liked him but what if sex triggered something that brought up old wounds? Estrada wanted everything to be perfect their first time. He wanted to be gentle and kind and heal him from whatever abuse he'd endured.

But Conall shoved him up against the window and the cold, damp glass chilled his naked back.

"Do you like it rough?" Estrada whispered.

"I don't know." The bard's eyes widened. "That's how . . ." His voice faded.

"Look. I don't want to hurt you."

"The only way you can hurt me is to push me away again. I want you. Don't you see?"

They grappled like wrestlers. Then, pulling free of Conall's hold, Estrada grabbed a towel from a kitchen hook and spread it over the sand painting. "Lie here," he said, touching a finger to the bard's swollen lips. "Anyone can have sex. I want to make love. Go slow and mean it."

When he turned on the stereo, the needle fell with a soft static pop onto the vinyl. Then, Otis Redding blasted through the speakers, and he saw Conall's face melt into the beats, the horns, and that soulful voice curling through the air, so raw and honest. Redding sang of the pain of love, that agony that just won't disappear until consummated.

Laying down beside the bard, he ran his fingers over the hard curves and ragged scars on his chest. Then leaning over, he kissed his nipples, knowing what it meant in their culture. Respect. Allegiance. With his mouth, he played them hard.

Conall groaned, then pushed Estrada down and hovered over him. They were equals. Neither more dominant than the other. As the bard's lips slid down Estrada's belly, he abandoned all thought of trying to control this desire between them. What had been halted so many nights could not be stopped. He gasped when the bard's mouth took hold, then fell back, and sank into the blues, his body vibrating until he could wait no longer.

When Estrada felt Conall's breath against his ear, he opened his eyes to his beautiful face. They laid on their sides, kissing and touching, riding the beats to another level. When their eyes met like two dark stars, they stared into each others' souls for an entire song. "Stand by Me." And Estrada knew they would stand by each other. No matter what came tomorrow, they'd always have tonight.

"I've never . . ." Conall whispered, his teeth scraping his bottom lip nervously.

"Never been inside a man?" Conall's eyes confessed. Estrada kissed his belly and took him gently in his mouth. Then glanced up, curious. "And this? Is this your first too?"

The bard groaned in reply.

He listened for the ragged breaths that signaled he was on the edge, then pulled away and rolled onto his hands and knees. He felt Conall's heat behind him, damp skin touching his skin, the hairs on Conall's legs teasing the backs of his thighs, hands gripping his hips.

And then a sound in the second of silence between tracks.

"What was that?" Estrada cocked his head, his body stiffening. "Listen."

Tap. Tap. Tap. He glanced at the window. The shades were up, and silvery moonlight flooded the room. *Tap. Tap. Tap.*

"There." A raven. Indigo wings splayed against the glass. Beak banging. Watching them with shiny black eyes. Wanting to be let in. Wanting to join them.

Estrada leapt up so fast, the needle jumped and slid, static screeching through the speakers.

"Goddamn you," he screamed.

But the raven was gone, and they were left alone in their anguish.

29

THE HOUSE ON HAWK'S CLAW LANE

As Estrada and Conall pulled into the gravel drive beside The House on Hawk's Claw Lane, Estrada recognized the vehicles parked in the gravel driveway and felt a pang of awesome familiarity. Despite all, this was his family.

Dylan slouched against Sylvia's CRV, dressed in his Sunday khakis and a forest green boy scout shirt, button-down pockets and all. Clean shaven and rosy-cheeked, he'd had his auburn hair buzzed military short again. He looked ready for an archaeology dig. If he'd come ready to hunt vampires, he'd be wearing his warrior kilt.

"It's good to see you, man." Estrada extended his hand and Dylan shook it, then muffled the hug. "Are they here?"

Dylan glanced up into the trees where several large black corvids carried on. "I honestly can't tell a real raven from a fake."

"Assume the worst." Estrada was still reeling from the incidents yesterday. "These fuckers have eyes on us." He glanced at Conall, and the bard stared down. "After that skater shit I told you about, a raven banged its beak on my window last night." *At a most inopportune time,* he thought, but didn't say. Conall was disappointed enough. Crushed. Though not normally affected by performance anxiety, the thought of being watched by the vampires sickened Estrada and turned the entire night into a bust.

He could imagine Eliseo flying back to his father. "He's having sex with another man, Padrino." And Diego's reply. "Bring this man to me."

Conall was in as much danger as he was. So, he wore the unease, not knowing what else to do. And felt like a shit. He'd offered himself and taken it back within seconds.

"It had to be Eliseo." Estrada wrung his hands. "Why is that little prick suddenly so ballsy?"

Dylan bounced on his toes. "Between us, we'll sort it out." His mouth pulled sideways. He didn't have all his usual answers. He'd been missing a month too, and had left his new teenage bride back in Ireland with the woman who took his virginity.

"Did you tell Sylvia about Croghan?" Dr. Sylvia Black was a professor of Celtic Studies and would be fascinated by their story. She'd introduced Dylan to Hollystone when he arrived at the university on the mountain, knowing no one. Taken him in like a foster mother. More importantly, she was their matriarch, and Estrada needed her as his ally.

"Some. She's excited about meeting a real Druid bard." He elbowed Conall. "Be careful, man. She might drag you along on her lecture tour."

"So, she believes you." That was good. If Sylvia was on their side, she could sway the others. Not that there should be sides. But there could be. Daphne and Raine lived here with Sensara and the three women made a formidable triad. You didn't piss off the women unless you were ready for a brawl, and disappearing for a month without a word of explanation was incendiary. Daphne had been his champion in the past, but he didn't know where she currently stood.

When he knocked on the door, it opened, and the first thing he heard was Lucy's loud, agonized wails. Like a knife, they cut and twisted his guts. He pushed inside and followed the sound, past Remington Steele, the wriggling black lab that ran circles round his feet. He found Sensara in the kitchen, jiggling Lucy up and down and walking in circles of her own. The energy was chaotic and all he wanted to do was hold his child. But was she sick? Scared? Hurt?

He dashed in, hand poised to grab the knife from his boot. "What's happening?"

"Nothing."

"Then why's she screaming?" The wailing was painful. Like nothing he'd ever heard before. Clearly, *something* was happening.

"Teething."

"Teething?" He took a step back. "Is this normal?"

"If you were here, you'd know." Sensara's comment cut the air in a way his knife never could.

He braced himself, then dug in. "Did you give her something?"

"Of course I *gave her something*." The last three words spoken with derision. She thought he was questioning her skill as a mother when all he wanted to do was take away his baby's pain. When Sensara stamped her foot, he stepped back again. She was fuming, ready to explode, and he didn't know if it was his absence or Lucy's pain that was the fuse. Either way, he feared to see it ignite.

He held out his hands. "Here. Let me take her." He wanted to help.

Sensara rolled her eyes. "You think you can stroll in here after disappearing for an entire month, take *my* child, and make it all fucking better?"

Should she be talking like that in front of the baby? Wouldn't Lucy remember? Years later, he could imagine her turning to him and saying, "Hey Daddy. Did you come to make it all fucking better?"

Lucy's shrieks quelled into sobs. Turning, she saw Estrada and, for a second, there was silence.

He raised his hands and exhaled. "Hola Lucita. How's my girl?"

She touched one small chubby hand to her rosy cheek and burst out screaming again.

"See." Sensara's verdict resounded through the house.

Hearing the melodic piping of a flute, they all turned. Conall had taken his pipes from his leather sack and stood in the kitchen doorway playing a slow, breathy lullaby. The sound spiraled in Estrada's ears and sent shivers down his arms.

Lucy stopped crying, and Sensara exhaled as the child melted in her arms.

Estrada waited as they all stood caught in the bard's song, then he took another chance. "Come on. Give her to me. You need a break." The black dog laying by his feet, gazed up imploringly, wanting his belly rubbed.

Sensara balked out of principle, then handed him his daughter. The chubby skin on Lucy's arms and legs was soft as silk. Two tiny ponytails tied with pink ribbons stood on each side of her head like miniature horns.

He brushed his lips against her soft cheek. "*Mi hija bonita.* I've missed you." He rocked her in his arms as she stared at Conall. Like a character in a video, he'd mesmerized them all with his magic flute. As the collective tension dissipated, Conall continued to play. And when at last he paused for a breath, he smiled, and Lucy reached out to him.

Estrada turned to Sensara, seeking permission. Dare he give the baby to Conall? Or would she be destroyed by that? Pacified by a stranger rather than her own mother. Sensara's eyes were filled with tears. But of what? Exhaustion? Exasperation? Relief?

Sylvia decided for him. "Let's adjourn to the living room." In her long golden sundress with her burgundy hair piled atop her head, Sylvia could be the Goddess of Sovereignty. He wondered if she held such sway over her students. She turned to Conall. "Would you mind terribly if I examined your pipes?"

Always the gentleman, the bard smiled. "Not at all, Lady." He held out his elbow for Sylvia to clutch, and they stepped downstairs into the sunken living room together.

Lucy had fallen asleep in Estrada's arms.

Sensara gestured for him to follow her upstairs with the baby. Was she planning to leave her alone in her bedroom while they met? That was far too dangerous. Especially, after Eliseo's little game last night. Estrada nudged her with his elbow and shook his head. Then, gestured with his chin to the living room. He wanted Lucy where he could see her. Understanding, Sensara plumped up the cot in the corner.

"Move it to the center of the circle," he said. Sensara cocked her head, then did as he asked. He laid the baby down and kissed her soft cheek.

As Sensara turned, he grasped her shoulder. "I know how pissed you are, and I deserve it. But I need you to trust me. This is bigger than us." Her lip trembled and gathering her in his arms, he held her.

Sensara buried her face in his chest and sobbed. "I thought something happened to you. I thought you were—" Stepping back, she pounded him hard. "Never do that again."

"I know. I know. I'm here now. And we're gonna get through this together. I love you, Sara, and I love Lucy. I'm gonna keep you safe."

Her eyes wrinkled as his words registered. "Safe. Why? Are we in danger?"

He kissed her lightly on the lips. "Come, my high priestess. Let's call the coven."

Sensara cast the circle around all of them without questioning Conall's presence in the group. Perhaps, Sylvia had already told her who he was and how he'd come to be here. Estrada was just relieved she'd accepted the bard and Hollystone Coven could meet as one. There was power in their unity. They sat on the living room floor. Daphne and Raine. Sylvia and Dylan. Conall. Sensara, and him, creating a protective ring around Lucy who slept in the center.

"I don't know where to begin," Estrada said, "but I'd like to pass a bottle of blessed wine among us if our high priestess has no objection." The sharing of libations was key to their ceremonies, but he really just needed a drink.

They all perked up when Sensara nodded.

He pulled a bottle of Merlot from the bag behind his back, twisted off the cap, and took a healthy swig. "What I have to say has not been said before, and I beg your patience as I grope for the right words." He turned to the bard, who sat to his right. "First, I'd like to introduce my good friend, Conall Ceol. As you already witnessed, Conall is a master musician, a bard, in the original sense of the word. Conall and I and Dylan,"—he turned to nod at Dylan who sat to his left—"met a few weeks ago in Ireland."

"Iron Age Ireland," Dylan said.

There was a collective gasp from all except Sylvia, who grinned conspiratorially.

"As some of you know, when Dylan was arrested for murder in Scotland last year, I conjured the old Celtic gods to help us find the true killer. Our friend, Sorcha, was with us then. The Horned God, Cernunnos, wanted recompense, so Sorcha went with him to Iron Age Ireland last Beltane—"

"You're kidding, right?" This from Raine. Daphne sent her a look and she let it go.

Estrada continued. "When Dylan realized Sorcha was trapped there, and in danger, he flew to L.A. We summoned Cernunnos and demanded he take us there."

"Seriously? Ancient gods and time-travel?" Raine again. She was the newest in the coven and the love of Daphne's life, but she was a journalist and the most pragmatic of them all.

"Suspend disbelief," Sylvia said, "and let Estrada and Dylan finish their story."

Estrada nodded. "So, that was where we met Conall." A quick glance into each other's eyes, and he felt Sensara's envy blast him from across the circle. The bonds between the two men couldn't be hidden from the high priestess. He and Sensara were co-parenting but hadn't been lovers since Lucy's conception. Though he loved her, he could never give her what she wanted—a monogamous husband-wife relationship. He knew because he'd tried.

Estrada cleared his throat. "We ended up trapped there ourselves until a few days ago, when we escaped through a wormhole and landed back in modern Ireland with nothing but the clothes on our backs." He stared into Sensara's eyes. "That's why I couldn't call. We had no cash, no cards, no ID."

Sensara blinked. Lucy stirred. And everyone took a collective breath.

"And there's more." Estrada turned to Dylan. "Could you explain the time-travel thing? I still can't get my head around it."

"Aye, sure." Dylan sniffed. "When I landed at LAX, and asked Estrada to help me rescue Sorcha, it was Autumn Equinox. *Next* Autumn Equinox, I mean. Approximately three months from now."

The twisted brows among them showed their confusion.

"What the hell," Raine said. "Are we in a sci-fi novel?"

"Actually, it's more of a fantasy," Estrada said.

"It's neither," Sylvia said. "We are simply enacting a myth. For most Indigenous cultures, including the Celts, time is not linear but circular."

Conall drew a spiral on his palm and said, "The Between."

"So, you're saying you went to the future and the past?" Sensara asked.

"Not exactly. Rather than bring us back to the time we left, Cernunnos brought us back early. It was his gift to Estrada." Dylan raised his hands. "The gist of it is this: Between where we are now and where we were when we left mid-September, a shitload of crazy happened that we hope to divert." There were more furled brows as Dylan turned to Estrada. "Do you want to talk about the . . . ?"

"Yeah, sure. I don't really know how to explain this, so I'm just going to say it." Estrada took another dramatic swig of wine, as the near-empty bottle had made it back around to him. He took a deep breath. "There's a heinous vampire named Diego—"

"Vampire? What the hell?"

"I know, Raine. I had a similar reaction when I first heard about Diego myself. Last summer when I was in Scotland, Michael—"

"Michael Stryker?" Sensara shook her head. "Why am I not surprised?"

Estrada sighed and continued. "Michael got into trouble with Diego, and the vampire is seeking vengeance by coming after me." There, he'd said it.

The room was silent.

"So, you're being hunted by a vampire." Sensara's eyes were wider than he'd ever seen them.

"An evil vampire who plans to abduct our daughter from her crib on August 1st."

"What?" Sensara's shock resounded in a surge of whispers as all eyes landed on the cot in the center of the circle.

"But why?" This from Daphne, who stared anxiously with a hand drawn across her mouth.

"Because he knows I'll go after her, which of course, I do. We all do."

Dylan spoke up. "So, in order to stop that from happening, we intend to launch a preemptive strike and take out all the vampires."

"Correct." Estrada exhaled. "Questions?"

"Oh great. Q & A." Raine smirked. "So, you're saying there are *actual vampires?* Here and now."

"Indeed. Diego built a party palace in the Broughton Archipelago. He advertises to rich Americans, who arrive by yacht. That's how he finances his establishment and keeps them all fed."

"Now, *there's* a story." Raine's eyes lit up. "I'm in."

"But why's he coming after you?" Sensara said. "I don't understand."

"Revenge."

"For something Michael did."

"Yes." Sensara despised Michael and this would put another nail in his coffin. Bad analogy. "But what's critical is stopping them from taking Lucy. We've now got four weeks. They've been watching us for months, and they're watching us now. Conall and I saw one of them skateboarding outside my flat yesterday afternoon."

"Skateboarding?" Raine giggled.

While Daphne gasped. "In the daylight?"

"Yes. These creatures are unlike the vampires of myth, which makes them enigmatic and hard to predict." He pulled the knife from his boot and stroked the blunt edge. "But I know how to kill them."

"And how to cure them," Dylan said.

"What?" Sensara reached out her hand. She wanted the wine, which said reams about her state of mind. She rarely drank, and never in the afternoon.

Estrada uncorked a second bottle and handed it to her. "Vampire is a virus that replicates in the bloodstream. We can cure it." For now, he'd leave it at that.

"Alright," Sylvia said. "What I understand is this. The vampires plan to abduct Lucy on August 1st. You're intent on destroying them before they can do that, and you need our help."

"Exactly. Rather than debate whether vampires exist, I ask you to please accept what we've said as true, and help us destroy these bastards before they attack us."

"But how?" Daphne said. "Wooden stake through the heart?"

"Knife through the brain," Dylan said. "Estrada took out dozens with his knives. We never tried the legendary stake."

"And fire," Estrada said. "They will burn."

"Is that it?" Raine threw up her hands.

"That's how we fought them before. And we won."

Sensara sat up straight. "You're thinking as men. Human men."

"We *are* human men."

"We're more than human. We're Wiccans and Druids." Sensara gave a royal nod to Conall that made Estrada's heart swell.

"We're connected to the Earth." Her palm swept through the air toward Dylan and Daphne.

"We're storytellers with technological expertise and research skills." A nod to Raine.

"We're wise women and repositories of myth." She smiled at Sylvia.

"We're dreamers and mystics. Magicians and shapeshifters. And we have conjured the gods." She stared into Estrada's eyes.

"Some we even know intimately," Dylan quipped. Estrada flipped him the finger and a collective snort cut the solemn mood.

"Some of us have traveled through time," Sensara continued. "We honor the elements and meld their energy with our own."

"As always, our high priestess illuminates what's hidden by shadows." Estrada raised his palms to salute her. "At Ballymeanoch, I made my finger a flaming wand to cast the circle and call Cernunnos. I've created fire before. We all have. That's how we destroyed Diego on the yacht. But that was amid chaos, and this, I manifested with my will."

"We all have talents and skills," Daphne said.

Sylvia nodded. "Some we may not even be acquainted with as yet."

"Dylan talks to stones and Conall talks to trees." Estrada felt great pride in his friends' abilities. "I suggest we sit with this and reconvene in seven days' time."

"Do we *have* seven days?" Raine asked.

"Yes, if we're careful. We must behave as if we don't know any of this. If they catch on, they might strike without warning, and we need time to prepare."

In the collective stillness, Estrada could hear the amplified beating of their hearts. "Oh, and one last thing. These vampires can shapeshift into ravens."

Fourteen eyes stared through the French doors at a forest of fluttering feathers.

30

Estrada leaned against the bleached cedar deck and watched a raucous pair of ravens careen through the tall Douglas firs that bordered the backyard at Hawk's Claw Lane. After the coven's solemn meeting, they were pretending to be friends enjoying a normal Sunday afternoon, just in case those ravens really were vampires spying for Diego. Like Dylan, Estrada couldn't tell the difference.

He'd cranked up the barbecue. Dylan had just taken a steaming bowl of baked potatoes into the dining room where Sensara was setting the table with wine, cheese, butter, and heaps of dressed greens. Daphne's excitement about roasting the first cobs of Valley corn was contagious. She'd treated him the same way she always had as he'd helped her grill the vegetables. For the moment, all seemed forgiven. Even Sensara had let her guard down and accepted his late return without an argument. Having Dylan back up his story about time-travel to Iron Age Ireland had turned the tide. And it didn't hurt to bring a living Druid bard home either, as proof of his quest and his favor with the Horned God.

He glanced at Conall and Sylvia, who sipped lemonade together under the shade of an ash tree. Sylvia chatted away in her soft Welsh accent, as animated as ever, while Conall sat quietly attentive, simply listening. Estrada couldn't catch her words, but the musical lilt of her phrasing calmed him. It was good to see Conall smile and make new friends. He'd discovered that the bard was an introvert who expressed himself through his music rather than casual conversation. But a passionate understanding of Celtic culture seemed to have drawn him and Sylvia together. Dylan shared a similar bond with the professor.

Conall's soft pink lips widened as he laughed, and Estrada imagined cradling that firm jaw in his palms and kissing him with all the passion he'd had that day in the river. He'd never been anxious about having sex with anyone. It had come to him as naturally as performing tricks. But after his botched attempt last night, he was hesitant to try again. Mortified, actually. After that bloody raven, which had to have been Eliseo, tapped at his window, he'd lost the urge and couldn't get it back. Something that embarrassing had never happened to him before. Conall had fallen asleep on the rug and stayed there all night, while he'd crawled into bed, alone and brooding.

Even now he fretted. The blow to his manhood was one thing but Eliseo had seen him with Conall, and that put the bard at risk. Diego wouldn't hesitate to use him as he'd used Lucy, especially if he thought he cared for the man. A new dilemma had surfaced. Should he put distance between them or keep the bard tight to his chest? Which strategy would keep his friend safe?

Daphne leaned in, interrupting his thoughts. "I have news," she whispered, promising a secret, and he turned, intrigued. Her deep brown eyes shone with an innocence he'd lost long ago, and Estrada envied her. Daphne had yet to know the ache of betrayal or the weight of making a decision that affected everyone you loved in different ways.

Where the edge of her bare arm touched his, Estrada felt a soft trembling. The woman was busting out of her skin over something.

"Well, tell me." He hoped it was juicy. He needed a break from the never-ending tension surrounding the vampires.

"We've decided to have a baby. Me and Raine." Her impulsive giggle gave him pause, and he laughed himself.

"Really." He caught her in his arms and hugged her. "Which one of you is gonna be the baby momma?"

She patted her belly. "Me. It's my idea so I get to experience *pregnancy*." Her eyes widened, and she whispered the word as if it were a magical incantation. He could only hope that, for her sake, it was.

One of the bartenders at Pegasus had been trying to get pregnant for years using IVF. They'd mortgaged their condo to the max to pay for it, and so far, nothing. Twice, they'd broken up because of the stress. Cerise said it was the only thing they talked about anymore, and their talk always escalated into a fight. She still called it *The Pregnancy,* but for her, it had lost its allure.

Estrada touched Daphne's shoulder. "Listen gorgeous, if you need a sperm donor . . ."

"You'd do that for us?" He saw the fine hairs on her arms rise.

"Of course. And you've seen my work. I've got good genes, and I work for free. As many shots as you need."

"Oh God." She rolled her eyes. "Stop talking."

"You know we'd make beautiful babies," he teased. "Just look at her." They turned and stared through the French doors where Lucy danced on square chubby toes. He'd missed her first steps while he was away, and now suddenly she was dancing. Missing firsts was one problem with being a sometimes father who traveled. He felt an ache in his chest and shifted to release it.

Daphne threw her arms around his shoulders and hugged him. And that did the trick. "You're the best. And I love that our kids would grow up together as siblings. Let me talk to Raine."

Estrada picked up the barbecue tongs and clicked them together three times. Daphne was like a sister to him, and he delighted in playing with her. "Don't you women use cooking utensils to . . .?"

Her eyebrows rose. "Are you thinking turkey baster?"

"Unless you want me to—" He nodded to his crotch.

She smacked his arm. "God, no. You're like my brother."

When Estrada's phone buzzed, he pulled it from his back pocket and stared at the screen. *Michael.* His smile vanished as he turned and sauntered down the steps. He answered in the driveway, far enough away that no one could hear his conversation.

"Hey."

"Compadre? If you've got your phone, I assume the parcel arrived."

Is Jazz playing games with Michael or is Michael playing games with me?

"Yeah, man. Thanks for coming through for me so fast." Estrada could play games too.

"Why wouldn't I?" Michael sighed. "I ache to see you."

Estrada had walked as far as his Harley. He swung a leg over and bounced on the padded seat.

In the pause, Michael whispered, "I found one of your old black tanks in the couch cushions and I've been sniffing it. How crazy is that?"

"Not crazy." He'd slept with one of his first lover's scarves for years after her murder.

"I want you, compadre." Michael's voice shook. "I need you."

"Are you alright?"

"How can I be? Without you, I'm half a man. Less than half. Just a mere shade. And it's been so long."

Michael was in one of his melancholy moods. After a white powder high, he awoke in The Pool of Black Bile, which he claimed flowed from The Bog of Eternal Stench. Forever a Bowie fan, Michael often watched *Labyrinth* when he was wasted.

"Come to me, compadre. I yearn for you. This morning, I dreamt of our first time together. Do you remember how glorious it was? How I kissed every inch of you, and plied you with oil, slowly and gently until you begged me to—"

"Easy, man. I'm out at the house with Lucy." Estrada's jeans strained against the leather seat. He took a deep breath and exhaled to gain some control. He'd never had an impotency problem where Michael was concerned. But what kind of weird coincidence was this? He'd just daydreamed of that same experience.

"You're that close?" Michael's breath quickened.

"I am. Are you alone?"

"Completely and utterly."

"Stay that way." Estrada padded into the house still clutching his phone, picked up his leather jacket, and slipped it in the inside pocket. When Lucy danced over, he swept her up for a kiss. "Daddy has to run an errand, but he'll be back soon."

"Now?" Sensara frowned. "We're just about to eat."

Through the French doors, he spied Conall and Sylvia climbing the stairs to the back deck.

He nodded to Dylan. "Keep an eye on him."

Daphne opened her mouth to speak, then caught herself and glanced away. Perhaps she'd seen Michael's name flash across the screen and knew where he was headed. She'd been standing right beside him. Perhaps she'd keep it to herself. Perhaps not. Either way, Michael needed him and he needed

Michael; at least, he needed to know if he could trust Michael and there was only one way to find out.

31

As he rode his Harley through the forested hills, Estrada felt an unexpected ripple of freedom. The open road was the best high imaginable. Better than Ecstasy. Even better than vampire blood. The rush lightened his mood, and the promise of time alone with Michael sent a titillating surge through his limbs.

As much as he liked the bard, he was feeling claustrophobic. They'd been together 24-7 since Ruairí's inauguration, except for a brief time when Conall had stayed at the fort to fight Ana's army. Estrada hadn't had a moment to himself, even to shower. And for a man like Estrada, who needed his freedom, that felt confining.

He justified the abandonment in his mind. And yes, if he was being honest, this was abandonment. But goddamn it. Conall didn't need a babysitter. He was a grown man. A warrior who'd killed . . . What? Thirty-three men and more? A charming musician with a compassionate heart, Conall was quite capable of making new friends. He'd done so this afternoon. As he coasted down the ocean-side highway, Estrada told himself the ache in the pit of his stomach was only hunger, and dismissing it, he eased off the throttle, squeezed the clutch, and shifted into third.

By the time he pulled into the Stryker's driveway, he was feeling like his old self. He was relieved to see no vehicles besides Crimson, Michael's red BMW. He pulled off his helmet and ran his fingers through his hair as he glanced up at the turreted tower where he'd discovered Michael's grandfather, badly broken by Zion. Nigel Stryker was next on his list to warn about the vampires. He'd need to take his mistress somewhere safe, and soon. Ruby Carvello had been the first casualty.

Finding the door unlocked, Estrada stepped inside, removed his boots, and unzipped his jacket. The old wooden stairs creaked under his weight as he climbed. There was no sneaking into this house and under the circumstances, that was something he could appreciate.

Michael opened the door before he reached the top. With his wet hair slicked back off his face, his cheekbones were razor-sharp, the hollows deep shadows. His green eyes were lined in kohl. He'd just showered and shaved, and his skin wafted rum-soaked spice, a scent akin to cinnamon on Estrada's list of aphrodisiacs. His eyes slid down Michael's pale chest to the tight leather jeans, perfectly molded to accentuate every curve.

One long look, and Michael shoved him up against the wall. "Cedar, sweat, and Harley. God, I've missed you."

They stayed that way for several seconds, skin to skin, Michael's face buried in his neck, replenishing lost moments of intimacy, and offering anything and everything to get them back.

"Are you going to invite me in or . . .?" Estrada grinned.

"I remember nights we never made it in."

"As do I, but it was a long ride and I left in a rush."

"Ah. So it's a toilet you need and not me at all." Michael's green eyes flashed as he held the door open for him to enter. No contacts and no fangs. Just pure boy-next-door Michael.

As Estrada walked in, he assessed the front room. No mirrors or white powder, just several fat joints lined up on the coffee table, he couldn't wait to roll across his lips. Two bottles of Pahlmeyer Merlot stood breathing on the bar. "Isn't that the prize wine Nigel brought back from the Napa Valley?"

Michael winked. "He won't mind. Be quick, compadre."

While in the bathroom, Estrada searched the shelves, though he wasn't sure what he was looking for. Perhaps some sign of Diego or Jazz or proof of Michael's blood addiction or his connection to the vampires. But all he found was the usual paraphernalia and nothing seemed out of place. No matter how wasted Michael got, his obsessive-compulsive personality kept his world in order.

Back in the living room, Michael handed him a smoking joint, and he sucked it in and held it. The inhale triggered a coughing fit. It'd been too long since he'd imbibed. When Michael laughed, one more layer slipped from his defense.

Michael held a crystal goblet of the dark, earthy merlot to Estrada's lips, and he sipped. "Damn. Nigel sure knows his wine. That's mellow as fuck." He accepted the wine glass from Michael's hand.

"As is this." Michael inhaled the weed and blew the smoke through Estrada's pursed lips.

The more he relaxed, the more he recalled. There was a moment on the yacht when Michael had almost convinced him to join him in Vampire. "We can stay young forever," he'd said, and slicing his skin with a fang, he'd given Estrada his first taste of vampire blood. It was the most intense high he'd ever felt.

He wanted to know if Michael was cutting himself now and sharing that high with someone like Jazz. He could just ask.

But Michael had kept silent about Diego for the entire year before the vampires attacked. And as much as he loved him, Estrada couldn't trust him. There were too many shadows and too many holes.

"It's strange you dreamed of our first time, amigo. I did too, just the other morning."

Michael's pale skin flushed as he drew the back of his knuckles down Estrada's cheek and neck. "Was it ever better than that first time? I think not."

"Perhaps it could be."

"How so, compadre?"

"If I give to you what you gave to me that night."

Michael bit his lip as he considered what was being offered. As much as he loved to direct the show, Estrada knew he feared the loss of control and rarely let himself be bound. Now that Estrada knew how horribly he'd been abused when he was a boy, he understood why. He wished he could talk to Michael about it, but knew he never could. Michael's shame was deep, hidden beneath a Byronic veneer that could never be cracked. All he could do was love him.

His lips brushed Michael's earlobe. Then, plucking a scarf from a hook by the door, he held out his hand. "Will you trust me, amigo? Let me make up for being away so long."

The scar on Michael's neck grew red and hard under Estrada's lips, blood rushing to fill it. There were tiny cuts along the inside of Michael's wrists and inner thighs. Estrada probed one with his tongue and felt the ecstatic rush of Vampire careen through his body. Michael was indeed turning, and others were feeding from him. The seduction of the blood kicked Estrada over the edge, and he ripped the ties from Michael's wrists as they plunged towards ecstasy.

After, they laid in each other's arms, sipping the wine and laughing over moments long gone. Estrada felt lethargic, so sated he could sleep the day away.

"What's this?" Michael touched the two round holes left by Eliseo along his carotid artery.

"An old childhood scar."

"Why have I never seen it?"

"Perhaps your eyes were focused elsewhere."

Michael tilted Estrada's face to the opposite side where Leopold's teeth had left their mark. "And this? Is it also from childhood?"

Estrada stroked the scar on Michael's neck left by Diego. "We all bear scars. They make us the men we are today."

"I love you," Michael whispered. "Remember that no matter what happens."

This declaration of love was something new as well. They'd never talked of love or voiced such tender feelings.

"What's going to happen, amigo?"

"Who can say in this mad, bad, dangerous world?" Michael brushed his lips with a fingertip. "Just know that I choose you, compadre. Now and forever."

Estrada's phone rang and seeing Dylan's name flash across the screen, he broke the moment and answered. Michael stood and sauntered into the bathroom.

"Where are you, man?" Dylan's voice throbbed.

"Why? What's wrong?"

"It's Conall. He's gone."

"What do you mean, gone?"

"Disappeared. We thought maybe he'd gone for a walk but we've searched and searched. We can't find him anywhere."

32

"**I** told you to fucking watch him." On the long drive back to Buntzen Lake from Vancouver, all Estrada could think about were the vampires. He kept seeing Eliseo's snarling face in the alleyway and Zion's arrogant sneer when he turned up on their yacht with Michael. Estrada tried to shake the image of fangs sinking into Conall's neck. If they thought that abducting the bard would send him running right into Diego's trap, they were right. He'd take all his anger and thrust a knife through Diego's fucking brain.

"I had to piss." Dylan held up his fingers. "I left him alone for five minutes." The tips of his ears burned red.

Sylvia's chin jutted in her defense of Dylan. "Conall is a grown man, Estrada. A Druid warrior. He's not a child who needs minding."

"A grown man who's vampire bait. A man who knows no one, has no money, and next to no sense of this world and its pitfalls. He can't even read English." He remembered how vulnerable he'd felt when he landed back in Ireland with nothing but a horse. At least, he'd been with friends. "How long's he been gone?"

"Three hours," Dylan said. "We'd just finished lunch."

"Jesus, fuck, Dylan." Estrada scowled.

"Don't blame Dylan. It's not his fault," Sylvia said.

No, it's my fault, Estrada thought. *I know it, and they know it. I left him.*

The night of Ruairí's inauguration at Croghan Hill, they'd got deliciously drunk. Estrada said he was worried about Dylan as no one from the blacksmith's house had come to the inauguration. He needed to check if they were alright. "I'll come with you," Conall had said, but then he'd passed out. So Estrada left him sleeping and went on his own. When Conall saw him later, the first thing he did was slap him hard across the face. He was furious that Estrada had left without him.

What if the bard was so angry at being left again that he'd gone off somewhere on his own? Estrada rubbed his burning eyes with his palms. "Goddamn it. Where the fuck is he?" He glanced around the living room at their somber faces. Sylvia sat rigid in the velvet armchair. Daphne and Raine slouched on the couch. Too wired to sit, Dylan leaned against the French doors, arms crossed over his chest, eyes averting his gaze.

Sensara took Estrada's arm and hauled him into the room. "You're vibrating, and you know as well as I do, reptilian brain cannot process. It only reacts." She handed him a glass of wine and sat down on the rug with her back to the couch.

"You know him best, Estrada," Daphne said. "Do you think he might have gone somewhere on his own?"

Was she reading his mind? Estrada set the wineglass on the coffee table and hunkered down beside Sensara. "Where would he go?" His head pounded. He rubbed his temples and the back of his neck. It was as tight as a Harley tire. He licked his dry lips. He was dehydrated. Hung over. But that craving for water brought sudden inspiration. "He likes to swim."

Estrada remembered watching Conall swimming in the lake at Croghan, his long arms breaking the surface in the moonlight. It was Beltane. When he'd sauntered toward him naked and dripping, Estrada had wanted him. Perhaps if they'd made love then, Conall would be with him now instead of out there alone in the world with vengeful vampires.

"We searched around the lake already," Sensara's lips flattened, and he knew she was thinking that if Conall had been gone for three hours, he may have drowned.

"It's a large lake surrounded by a massive forest," Raine said. "If he's a decent swimmer, he could have swum to the other side and gotten lost. We should fan out and check again. Call Search and Rescue."

"Check the woods, yes, but no cops." There was no way he was getting the police involved. "What would we say? Our friend from Iron Age Ireland went missing. He may have been abducted by vampires?"

Daphne giggled. "I'm sorry, but it sounds ridiculous when you put it like that."

"Maybe so, but what about those fucking ravens?" Estrada had been thinking about them since he'd heard the news of Conall's disappearance but feared to speak the words, in case saying it made it so.

"Ravens couldn't abduct a grown man." Sensara said.

"But they're not ravens. They're vampires. And they carried you from the upper window of a lodge all the way to Diego's island. Flew with you in their talons."

"Oh god." Daphne hung her head, the smile gone from her face.

"It's true," Dylan said. "They're quick and strong, and if they think Conall is important to Estrada, they might have taken him as bait."

"Yeah, that's why they took Lucy. And you." Estrada touched Sensara's knee. She raised her fist and pumped the air.

"If that were the case, wouldn't Conall have cried out? Or fought them?" Sylvia searched their faces. "We were right here, clearing the table and stacking the dishes. The French doors were open, and we heard nothing."

"*Fuck.* Have you got some pain killers?" Estrada rubbed his temples. His head was exploding.

Sensara walked into the hall and grabbed her purse, then tossed him a bottle of pills. Rather than swallow them with wine, he padded into the kitchen and filled a beer stein with water. Between the wine, smoke, sex, and that tiny taste of Michael's blood, his brain was demanding sleep. But how could he sleep now? How could he ever sleep again?

Goddamn it. Why did I leave him without a word? It was a completely thoughtless and selfish move.

They sat in silence for several minutes while Estrada hung his head over the kitchen sink. Guilty. Defeated.

"Did he say anything after I left?" Estrada asked at last. He splashed water on his face, needing to resuscitate his ragged brain.

"Conall's a deeply spiritual and introspective man," Sylvia said. "He takes everything in but says very little."

"He expresses himself through his music. When he played those pipes . . ." A piper himself, Dylan was impressed with the bard's talent.

Estrada glanced at Daphne. "Did you tell him where I went?"

"Where *did* you go?" Sensara asked.

Estrada glared at her.

"It's a fair question and relevant to this discussion. If you two are in a relationship, and you suddenly left—"

"I didn't," Daphne interjected.

"Conall didn't seem bothered." Dylan shrugged. "We sat out back for the longest time. Neither of us talking. Me thinking about Mara back in Ireland and him staring at the trees. I think he was communicating with them in a very sacred way."

"He can hear their voices. Christ, he talked to my cacti. Apparently, they need rainwater, rather than tap water."

"That's beautiful," Daphne said. "And yes, tap water contains pathogens that are harmful to plants."

"Unless he's gone into the woods to hermit, I can't think of any other place he could be. He knows no one but me. Has no phone. And no other friends."

"*Is* he a hermit?" Daphne glanced at Sylvia. "You talked to him the longest today, Syl. Do you think he might have gone into the woods to be alone with his gods?"

Sylvia raised her hands. She didn't know. She'd done all the talking.

But Estrada remembered their time at the lake near Croghan. "That's a possibility. He once lived in a hut like a hermit." When they were collecting deadfalls, he'd offered Estrada space in that hut. Conall had loved him even then. Estrada's eyes filled with tears. "What have I done?"

"Easy man," Dylan padded his shoulder. "This is all conjecture."

"What if he wandered into the forest to talk to the trees and the vampires took him from there?" Sensara asked.

Estrada took a step back. "If he was in the woods, you wouldn't have seen or heard him if he struggled. Right?" He glanced at Sylvia, who shook her head.

"Let's assume that Conall wandered into the woods and the vampires took that opportunity to abduct him. How would we know? Will they send a message?"

"Good question, Raine. How did you know they'd taken Lucy?" Sensara reached out her hand as if to summon him toward her. But Estrada didn't want to go. Not with the answer burning on his lips.

The roses, he thought. They'd left a red rose on Ruby Carvello's corpse, on Nora Barnes' windowsill, and in Lucy's crib. Michael had been the connecting cord. And Michael had been with him today when Conall had disappeared.

What did that mean? Estrada's brain hurt but kept spinning. Michael had been more expressive than usual. He'd relinquished control, and what had he said? *I love you no matter what happens.* Did Michael know what was going to happen? Had the vampires tasked him with keeping Estrada occupied while they abducted Conall? *Fuck.*

"Estrada?" Sensara called him back. "How did you know?"

"Know what?" He shook his head, trying to erase the question whose answer would only break his heart.

"How did you know they'd kidnapped Lucy?"

Estrada sighed. "If they've taken him, they'll get a message to us. All we can do is wait."

33

B ut no message came. Estrada spent the next three nights at the house praying that Conall would return. He tried to think like him. An introspective man, Estrada rarely knew what the bard was thinking unless he asked a direct question. He realized that, although they'd been together for weeks, he knew very little about the man. He knew Conall had been in love with his best friend, Ruairí, and that love was unrequited. He knew he'd been victimized by a man whom he hated. And he knew the bard was an incredibly talented musician who just wanted to play and sing for the pure joy of it.

His pipes were missing, and that gave Estrada hope. Maybe the trees had beckoned, and he'd gone into the woods to pray as a Druid might. Perhaps, in his culture, it was acceptable to disappear from time to time to be with the gods. Everything else the nobles did together at Croghan—all of them eating, sleeping, and playing in one big house. When they needed time alone, it was logical, they'd wander off for a while. Hadn't Estrada done the same thing? Left without a word?

34

On Tuesday morning, Estrada called Nigel and arranged to meet. Michael texted several times. Estrada replied, though he still wondered if Michael was involved somehow in Conall's disappearance; after all, they were together when the bard went missing. If he was involved, Michael could be the messenger.

When Sensara taught her weekly psychic development class in Port Moody that evening, he looked after Lucy. She arrived home beaming.

"What's up?" Estrada was out on the upstairs balcony, watching the stars, and praying. He loved The House on Hawk's Claw Lane, and this was his favorite lair.

"I saw Conall in my meditation tonight."

Estrada's heart thumped. "Where?"

"Perhaps in a greenhouse or garden center. He was surrounded by plants and there was classical music playing."

"Here in Port Moody?"

"I couldn't tell, but he was happy. I don't think he's been kidnapped. That's why we've heard nothing." Sensara threw her arms around Estrada and hugged him, and he swallowed hard to ease the tightening in his throat.

"He left me." The words came out in a choke. To hide his burning eyes, he buried his face in her shoulder.

He tried to imagine what it must have been like for Conall to arrive in this new world with nothing, but all he could think about was his own shame. Conall wanted to be his lover and Estrada couldn't even give him that. Then he'd disappeared without a word and gone back to Michael.

"Were you two in a relationship?"

"No." Estrada sniffed. "I mean, maybe he wanted . . ."

"And you?"

"I don't know what I want, Sara. I never fucking do." He broke then and fell into her lap weeping.

35

LULLYMORE, CO. KILDARE, IRELAND

"Come on," Sorcha said. "Let's grab a coffee and go tramping again. I've got something on my mind I'd like to run by you."

Mara nodded and rubbed her eyes. She'd been up since dawn and looked like she hadn't slept. Perhaps she was fretting over Dylan. Franya had returned to her old habit of drinking into the wee hours and slipping in and out of Sorcha's bed just before she crashed. The sex was electric, and since she wasn't ready for a full-on relationship so soon after losing Ruairí, she'd accepted the arrangement. It left her plenty of time to think, which is what she needed.

As they walked by the barn, Mara stopped to talk to the horses.

Declan, who was cleaning the stables, leaned on his shovel, and glanced over. "Going for a ride?"

"Oh, could we?" Mara's eyes sparkled.

"Sure. The gray mare would suit you just fine." He nodded to Sorcha. "Your wee pony could use some exercise too."

Mara waved off the saddle but Sorcha was glad to have some padding between herself and Rowan. For a chubby pony, she had one heck of a hard backbone.

As they walked the horses up the path and through the field of yellow flowers, Sorcha swept her hand through the air. "This is what I want to talk to you about."

Mara glanced around.

"These yellow flowers. You remember the lake of red trout where Ruairí and Conall built their hut? You brought the lads out there from your dad's place."

"Oh aye, it was beautiful and there were so many *giolla rua.*"

Sorcha's mind drifted back to the night she'd fished out one of the red trout and they'd cooked it over the wood fire in the hut. That night they'd made love for the first time. She raised a hand and touched her heart. She'd do anything to be with Ruairí again. She'd even considered begging Cernunnos to take her back to that night in the hut. Knowing how it would end, perhaps she could change things.

Oh, but who was she kidding? Trying to change Ruairí's fate was likely the reason he was dead. Her intrusion into their lives had altered history and sparked changes for all of them. Good and bad. She wondered how history would continue to change now that Mara and Conall were here in their world. Sorcha's hand slipped to her belly. And what would Ruairí's son bring to this world? Would he have gifts like his father?

Shaking free of her thoughts, she turned to Mara. "Did you know Ruairí had visions?"

"Oh aye, he was a seer. One of the best in the land."

"When we were at the lake, Ruairí told me he had a vision of me. I was wearing my khakis and standing in a field of yellow flowers."

Mara squinted, confused.

Sorcha pointed to her pants. "These are khakis. They're the most comfortable piece of clothing I own. I wear them on digs for days and days. Sometimes I sleep in them."

Mara nodded. "Farmer breeches."

"Aye. Well, after we were here the other day, I started thinking about Ruairí's vision." They stopped at the crest of the hill and gazed down into the streambed. "He said I'd find something I'd lost."

"Have you lost something?"

"Nothing besides Ruairí. But I've been wondering if this field could be a raised bog that's built up over a lake. Our lake. The lake of gillaroo." Sorcha's throat tightened, and she coughed. "'Whatever you've lost will not be lost forever.' That's what he said that day."

"I feel like Ruairí's here when you speak his words like that." Mara narrowed her eyes. "But what makes you think this is the place?"

"Geography. There to the southeast, are the Wicklow Mountains. When Criofan banished me, Ruairí and I rode east, and I remember seeing them. It took us about as long to ride to the hut as it took me to ride here from Croghan last week. Seven or eight hours. We passed a border into what he called lake territory watched over by the Goddess." Talking about him did make it seem like he still existed. Maybe she was just trying to keep his memory alive, but Sorcha had a hunch, and her hunches usually paid off.

She stared down at the flowers. "This meadow buttercup likes alluvial soil—that's the soil of flood plains or riverbeds—and it grows on peat. This could easily have been a lake in 200 BCE."

"So, we could be standing where Ruairí and Conall built their secret hut all those years ago?"

"We could, and I'd like to prove it."

Narrowing her eyes, Mara frowned. "How would you do that?"

"Dig it up. That's what we archaeologists do."

Mara surveyed the vast field of yellow flowers.

"Not the whole thing. I'll do a field-walk. Use a metal detector and see what lies beneath the surface."

Rowan pawed the ground with her hoof. "Come on," Sorcha said. "Race you to the stream."

It was no contest for Mara on the gray mare. They slid off their horses and set them to graze while they dipped their feet in the water.

"Won't everything be rotted away?" Mara asked.

"Not at all. Raised peat bogs are made from layers and layers of sphagnum moss and other plants. Acid in the layers preserves whatever else is in there. We've found all kinds of things buried in the peat—butter, pieces of leather boots and belts, bones."

Mara's eyes lit up. "Would we find the bones of *giolla rua*?"

"Possibly." Sorcha didn't want to tell her about Ruairí's torso, not yet. Mara didn't witness his execution, and Sorcha would rather not inspire that nightmare. The girl wasn't sleeping well as it was. One day, she'd take her to the National Museum in Dublin. Mara deserved to see how her country evolved over the last two thousand years.

"What else could we find?"

"They found a bronze sword blade at Lullymore Bog about twenty years ago. There could be knives, cups, even jewelry. That's why I'd like to use a metal detector. Imagine if we found my gold pins?" She'd lost them in the lake. "I'll need to get Franya's permission first and then apply for an excavation license." The excitement of a dig always raised Sorcha's spirits until there was nothing else she could think about. "I'm a professional archaeologist and I can fund it myself, so the application should go through without a hitch."

"Can I help you? Do the digging, I mean?"

"Of course, you can. I'd love to teach you about archaeology."

"When can we start?" Mara was catching the bug and Sorcha was thrilled.

"If Franya agrees, I'll put together the application right away and email it. We have to give them three weeks to respond but I might dig a few test holes."

Mara grew suddenly pale and pensive.

"What's the matter?"

"I was just thinking. After Donella became Goddess of the Land, Dylan visited the fort. When he returned, he told me he'd taken what he could of Ruairí's body and buried it near the lake where they'd built their hut. They'd already offered his torso to the goddess and that could not be moved."

"He told you that?" Here Sorcha was, afraid to tell Mara about Ruairí's execution, and Dylan had told her everything. Sorcha had asked Dylan to bury Ruairí's remains near the hut, and was pleased he had, but why hadn't he told her?

"Don't worry," she said. "When we're digging, we'll be mindful of that." After what Conall had said in the museum about leaving their ancestors to rest with the Goddess of the Land, Sorcha had changed her view. It had never mattered before, but it certainly did now. Everything they unearthed and catalogued was the property of the state and would end up in the National Museum. But if they found Ruairí's remains, she'd leave them where Dylan had buried them and tell no one.

"Shall we explore the property some more?"

"Sure." Mara stood and rolled down her pant legs.

She was wearing an old pair of Franya's jeans and one of her white T-shirts. Tall and slim like Franya, the girl had long, shapely legs. By the time she was fully grown, Mara would likely be six feet tall. Taller than Dylan, not that he'd mind.

"What's up there on that hilltop," Mara said, gesturing farther east than either of them had gone before.

"You've got keen eyesight. That'll serve us well on the dig. Let's go look."

As they crested the grassy hill, Sorcha made out tombstones and crosses. *Sullivan Cemetery.* Vivian had once told her they'd buried her ancestors on the property, but Sorcha had never seen it.

"Let's leave the horses here in the shade and walk." She wasn't keen to disturb the graves, but she was curious. A recent grave was strewn with dead flowers. "This must be . . ." Her voice faded as she read the etching on the small granite stone.

Vivian Rose Sullivan
March 12, 1990 - March 18, 2020

"She'd just celebrated her thirtieth birthday," Sorcha mused. It was simple and frugal, just the facts, no other words or sentiments, which struck her as odd, but then, Franya was never one for poetry.

Mara went off gathering buttercups while Sorcha squatted beside Vivian's grave. "I don't know what to say, Viv. Had I arrived even four months ago, we could have put things right. I want you to know that I forgive you. I was hurt for a long time, but that's all in the past now. I hope you're at peace, and I hope you don't mind if I do a little digging on your land. This is a special place, as you always said, and I'll respect that."

Mara held out a bouquet of yellow flowers.

"Thanks love. She'll like these. Yellow and blue were her favorite colors, and look, here she is resting under a turquoise sky surrounded by buttercups."

As they turned to mount the horses, Sorcha glanced at Mara. "Let's not mention the cemetery to Franya. I don't want to upset her by talking about Vivian. She hasn't mentioned her, and I think it's best we keep it that way."

Mara nodded. "We never speak of the dead. That can bring them back and they must go on to their next experience."

"But you just mentioned Ruairí."

Mara looked suddenly guilty. "I shouldn't have, but I thought you should know."

36

By the time Sorcha and Mara had groomed the horses and left them to graze in the pasture, it was mid-afternoon. They'd just finished eating egg salad sandwiches when Franya sashayed through the front door in a sleek gray pencil skirt, skinny high heels, and a crisp white tailored shirt. In big sunglasses and carrying a burgundy leather bag, she wafted movie star.

Sorcha felt immediately shabby in her khakis. "Wow," she said, and bit her lip. It was the first time she'd seen Franya venture out of the house since their arrival a week before.

"You look like a queen," Mara said, obviously impressed. Then, perhaps noticing something eerie in the air, she vanished.

"I've secured a new position," Franya said, as she deposited a paper bag of clinking bottles on the counter. "Rosemary Ryan & Company, Solicitors." She pulled a bottle of Dingle gin from her bag and reached for her mixing glass. "I believe this calls for a drink."

Sorcha had watched Franya build enough martinis over the last few days to know that everything called for a drink.

"Congratulations. Sounds prestigious." She licked her lips. "I didn't know you were looking for work."

Franya opened the refrigerator and grasped a bottle of dry vermouth, along with some artisan brine and stuffed green olives. "Rose is an old friend. When she called asking if I could help her team, I couldn't very well refuse. Besides, the entire staff are women and the money's extraordinary."

"Sláinte," Sorcha said, raising her cup of tea.

Franya filled the glass with ice cubes and cracked the cap on the Dingle gin. It looked like more than her usual two and a half ounces, but Sorcha wasn't measuring. Half an ounce each of vermouth and olive brine followed. Franya danced to some silent tune in her head as she gave the concoction a shake and strained it into her chilled martini glass.

Sorcha wondered if Shakira would make an appearance tonight. A little "She Wolf" might really get the party rocking. After skewering two stuffed olives, Franya dropped them in.

"I'm glad you're pregnant, Foxy, but on a night like this, I wish we could celebrate together like we did in the old days." She patted Sorcha's cheek and then took a decent gulp from her martini.

"Aye." Sorcha ran her nails through her hair and fluffed it out. "I have some news of my own, and I'd like to talk a little business before the party starts."

"Do tell."

"If you're of a mind to keep Sullivan Stables, I know a way to do it."

"Go on." Franya sat on a kitchen stool and crossed her legs at the knee.

"I think there might be treasure buried in your back pasture." Sorcha watched Franya's eyes widen.

"Treasure, you say?"

"Aye. With your consent, I'd like to apply for a license to dig in the field by the stream. It could be an Iron Age site. And if it is, the property can't be sold."

"Interesting." Franya stroked her chin. "What sort of treasure?" She'd always looked at Sorcha's archaeology career with disdain.

"Bronze artifacts. Perhaps even gold jewelry."

"Really. Like the Egyptian collar you found in Scotland?"

"Possibly." Sorcha wasn't about to tell her that nothing recovered from the dig would result in personal financial gain. She needed her signature on the application.

"And what makes you think Sullivan Stables might be sitting on this gold?" She leaned forward, her eyes as big as doubloons.

"I could show you if I had a topographical map of the Midlands."

"I can find one," Franya said. "But lay it out for me first."

The litigator had arisen.

37

FRIDAY NIGHT AT CLUB PEGASUS

With the immediate threat to Conall mitigated, Estrada tried to suppress his jangly feelings by focusing on the annihilation of the vampires. As soon as Nigel had heard he was back in town, he'd requested Estrada perform his Friday night show. Nigel was like a father to him, Pegasus was home, and the patrons had been asking for him. But as he cruised to the goth club on his Harley, his mind ran ragged.

No matter what personal conflicts bubbled between them, he trusted Sensara's psychic visions. If she said Conall was safe and happy, Estrada believed her. Still, he missed the bard, and fluctuated between bouts of anger and fear, frustration and rejection. Though he tried to ignore his feelings, deep down he longed to see Conall, and hoped his impulsive decision to run back to Michael hadn't cost him this precious relationship.

He had to accept that the bard had disappeared for his own reasons. Rather than being abducted, he'd simply walked away. When Estrada tried to put himself in Conall's shoes and analyze his decision, he found himself at a loss. How could he understand a man from a culture so different from his own? When he was with Conall, he saw only their similarities. Both wanted a trusted friend, and of course, the physical attraction was uncanny. But being apart made him realize how different they truly were.

Beyond the introvert-extrovert thing, Conall had literally just stepped out of Iron Age Ireland. He was political—a member of the inner circle of high-powered Druids who controlled everything at Tuatha Croghan. He was a warrior who'd killed many men—likely taken heads, as that was the Celtic custom—and was as adept with sword and knife as he was with pipes and lyre. But Estrada didn't know the nuances of Conall's culture, his personal preferences, or the intricacies of the bard's personality. Despite the time they'd spent together, they hadn't really talked, and he regretted that now.

As he cruised past the marquis, he glanced up. A banner advertising "THE LEGENDARY ESTRADA—BACK BY POPULAR DEMAND" crossed his photograph, and another sign, "SOLD OUT" was stretched across that. A sheen of sweat broke out on his forehead as that frenetic feeling returned.

Before the business with the vampires had railroaded his life, he'd rehearsed a new act with Dell, one of the sentinels who were their version of bouncers. Tonight would be his first public performance. It was complex, and he was out-of-shape, despite bouncing on the old gray mare and his mountain run in Tarbert. He hoped he could pull it off, especially since he was expecting to be watched by sundry, hungry eyes.

As he entered the club, he saw Michael sashay through the crowd in full vampire persona. He was playing with the patrons, greeting them by dragging his fake fangs across their necks and offering blood clots of Ecstasy to his favorites.

Estrada had noticed Michael's pattern years ago. When he was depressed, as he'd been last Sunday, he was docile, poetic, loving, harmless, and needy. Melancholy Michael. That's why Estrada had run to him without reservation. But when he turned manic, Mandragora arose, and anything could happen. And though he was sure of Michael's love, he wasn't so sure about Mandragora. The man who caught his eye now across the crowd, and raised his caped arms in salute, was the latter. The shift had been abrupt, and Estrada didn't know what had triggered it.

The club was packed. The room vibrating. The stage perfect. Torchlight with intermittent mist. Black silhouetted tree branches shifting with the beats. Dangling mirrors. An epic soundscape intended to move the audience from tender pathos to paroxysm and back again through three new theatrical sequences.

Estrada had always longed to fly and had been incorporating magic into aerial silks for the past year, off-stage. Apart from the moment he'd shifted into the body of a raven and flown over Hope, being suspended in silks was the closest he'd come to the euphoria of flight. And he loved it.

He prepared in the dressing room. Gelled his hair and slicked it back into a bun. Smudged kohl an inch around his eyes. Gulped two glasses of red wine, then painted his lips that same shade. If there were vampires in the audience tonight, he wanted them transfixed. He attached the concealed raven wings to his arms, and after approving himself in the full-length mirror, he exited.

He crossed behind the wine velvet drape and climbed barefoot into the fly tower. A small microphone in the pocket of his black flexile jeans allowed him to communicate with Dell, who worked light and sound in the house and his assistant in the wings who operated the silks. After being lifted into the tower, he set up his first position. Then he began to breathe. *Inhale. Exhale—da DA da DA da DA.* His thrumming heart slowed as he focused.

"Ready," he said, and slowly the scarlet silks lowered. The spotlight blazed and "The Legendary Estrada" appeared, standing on his hands, ankles caught in the silks. The tattooed angel wings on his back and core flexed as he slowly turned and twisted to whoops and applause. Flipping upright, he spread his legs horizontally and caught his wrists above his head, then tilted his neck seductively from side to side. If there were vampires here, they'd see those pulsating arteries and drool. Returning to vertical, he spun as the silks descended. A dozen feet above the ground, he released the catch on the indigo feathered wings attached to the underside of his arms, so all that could be seen was the raucous wheeling of a giant raven in the spotlight. As the spin slowed, he swept the raven wings across to cover his face and body completely. The spotlight cut to black and *poof!* He was gone.

Dell hit the lights, and the audience gasped as wings and silks fell to the floor. Then the mists mushroomed creating a scarlet scene as intriguing as a Martian landscape.

When he reappeared, standing center stage, bare-chested and beaming, Estrada raised his arms to capture the applause. The lights faded to black, and he climbed back into the silks. Manifesting *fire,* he forced it from his core and down his arms. When the flames burst from his fingertips, he etched a great spiraling *E* in the blackened air, then flung bursts like fireworks high into the crowd and watched them fly. He tucked his hands into his chest, and Dell cut to black. The ohs and ahs spurred him on.

The spotlight flashed gold. As the silks rose, he moved through his aerial act again, with slow precision, and a sheen of sweat formed on his body. He was hanging, arms and legs spread like Vitruvian Man—another vampire ploy—when a flaming arrow sped through the darkness and thwacked him in the shoulder. Then came a second, piercing his opposite thigh. He screamed. He grimaced. But as the third flew, he slipped his wrist free and caught it in his hand. Holding it, he sneered. Stage blood drizzled from the wounds and down his body in deep red rivulets. He flipped the flaming arrow and flung it into the crowd.

Don't fuck with me or I'll fuck with you.

The clamor of screams and scrambles built with the soundtrack as patrons dashed out of the way, and at the height of the cacophony, he spun. Blood and fire wheeling through the darkness like a murderous planet. He swung the silks up to cover his body like a cape, and *poof!* He disappeared again.

The music hushed, the lights dimmed, then *bang!* Dell hit the spot and Estrada stood on top of the bar, blood streaming down his moist skin, but smiling. Triumphant. His eyes scanned the crowd. *There and there. Fangs and hungry faces.* His vampire travesty was a success.

He leapt free just as Michael reached out to grab him, and rushed into the dressing room for a requisite shower and costume change. Michael was too much the celebrity to chase after him.

When Estrada reappeared, he wore a black tux with tails and his shit-kicking boots—the ones stacked with hidden knives. He sauntered to the bar.

"One day you must tell me how you disappear like that," Michael said, and sent a tequila shot careening down the slick surface.

Tossing back his chin, Estrada gulped the shot, then cracked the glass down. Obscenely cocky from the hormonal rush, he glared at Michael. "I thought you didn't like it when

I disappeared." He'd wanted vampiric attention, and now he had it.

A forced laugh, and Michael opened his black silk cape to reveal a petite someone nestled beneath his arm. "Come out, come out, my sassy Jazz. You must meet Estrada."

With shining white contacts obscuring their irises, bleached blond hair standing two inches high, and wearing nothing but a black male G-string and tribal tattoos, Jazz was unlike anyone Michael had introduced him to before. Judging by the flat chest and the distinctive bulge below, one would suspect Jazz to be male, but they had the most beatifically feminine face Estrada had ever seen. A nymph's face forged on the body of a male exotic dancer. With one look, he understood why Mandragora was smitten; though the androgynous angel hadn't got a rise out of the Legendary Estrada and knew it.

Their black lips spread delicately, feigning speech, while their white eyes screamed, *"Fuck you."*

Estrada returned the sentiment with a smirk. He hadn't forgotten Jazz had been in his flat, pawing his stuff.

Michael stood oblivious to the stand-off. "You must join us later, compadre. Jazz was impressed by your act tonight . . . *and* last week."

Last week? Estrada felt the blood rush to his cheeks. He hadn't noticed a camera when they'd had sex but knew Michael often ran personal films to titillate guests at his parties. Fortunately, he hadn't graduated to posting his videos online as he *abhorred* social media. His word.

"Delete it," Estrada growled.

"Already done, compadre. I know how shy you are." He threw back another shot. "But we both appreciated your prowess."

Before anything else could be said, the DJ kicked in with a flurry of staccato beats. Jazz grasped Michael by the belt and dragged him into the throng.

Estrada raised a shot to Dell and threw back another tequila. His eyes scanned the crowd. The cherubic Eliseo would never make it past the sentinels, even with fake ID, but there were others. A few old friends, of the human persuasion, came by to squeeze his shoulder, and a few hopefuls pressed their card into his palm.

Michael and Jazz had disappeared. Gone to the dressing room, no doubt. For a moment, Estrada considered joining them. He wanted to know if Jazz was the source of the vampire blood or just there for the high. If they weren't, who was? And was that knowledge worth what he'd have to do to get it? His gut said no.

A swish of dreads in his periphery drew Estrada's attention back, and he exhaled his angst onto the bar. As the creature turned, he saw the black teardrop tattoos that defined those cold, killer eyes. There was no mistaking Zion. This was the vampire who'd sired Leopold and Michael. Who'd broken Nigel's legs and murdered Ruby Carvello.

Estrada turned to the nearest woman and tickled her under the chin. He was reluctant to use a stranger for subterfuge, but this was a game of knowledge and he couldn't let on what he knew. Who they were. Where they lived. What they intended to do three weeks from now. No doubt Zion had been hiding in plain sight at Pegasus for months before they'd attacked and sailed north on the yacht with Lucy. As Estrada flirted with the woman beside him, he kept one eye on the vampire, who cruised the club like a cat in a freshly cut hay field.

When Zion strutted past, Estrada felt a frigid rush. The eyes glittered black, almost as if he were becoming his corvid self. Perhaps after centuries the two species fused. Estrada's hand reached down, fingers tensing for his knife. One shot between the eyes and the fucker would be dust. But how many others were here, hidden in their midst? Was he willing to reenact *From Dusk Till Dawn*, here and now, at Pegasus?

He signaled Cerise for another shot and leaned his knee against the stool. After the release of adrenalin from his act, the tequila was doubling up, and he was feeling it from his toes to his tattoos like a rush of lust. When the DJ spun a slow clincher, the woman beside him tugged him off the stool and onto the dance floor. He closed his eyes against her shoulder. Her moist skin smelled musky, and he let her fingers dally in his trouser pockets. He was about to press her into some more-secluded corner, where he could perform his own search, when he raised his eyes and saw two men enter the room. He froze. The woman pressed him but he pushed her away.

It was the platinum hair that caught his attention, hanging long and straight like a frozen waterfall. Clad all in white, a button-down shirt and skinny jeans, he was an anomaly in this sea of black. Archangel Gabriel in a midnight graveyard.

Leopold Blosch. And beside him walked *Conall.*

Still wearing *his* leather jacket.

What. The. Fuck.

38

Estrada released the woman in his arms and approached the bard. Staring right into his eyes, he slapped him hard across the face.

"You left me," he said, recreating a scene from their past.

The bard's eyes blazed fire. Then, raising his hand, he returned the slap—a little harder and a little quicker.

"It was you who left me."

Estrada's cheek stung, but shock and relief shoved him back a step. Conall reached out to steady him, pulled him close, and their hot cheeks touched.

Blosch coughed awkwardly.

Estrada turned and glared at Blosch. Had he given the bard what Estrada could not?

Then Dell was in his face.

"If you've got a problem, boys, take it outside."

"No problem," Estrada growled. Several predators circled, drawn by the violence he'd thoughtlessly provoked. The only thing vampires liked better than sex was sport, and even the undead could feel what bubbled between the magician and the bard. Unfortunately, now both Blosch and Conall were on their radar.

Michael and Jazz swaggered from behind the hidden door in the wall that led to the dressing room, him wiping his nose and them licking their lips. Were they tasting Michael then? Maybe they weren't a vampire, just another addict.

Estrada sunk roots into the tile floor to curb his spinning head.

Drawn to the dove in the flock of crows, Michael focused on Leopold Blosch. "Have we met?"

"I've been here before," Blosch said. "Tried your blood clots."

"Aha." Michael nodded to one of the Greek boys, who advanced carrying a fresh tray of deadly erotigens. "Please," he said, gesturing to Blosch. "Be my guest. I'd like to get to know you better."

Blosch waved it away. "Thank you, no. Perhaps another time."

As the boy passed the tray among them, Conall reached out to take one of the ecstatic concoctions. Estrada put a hand over the bard's and shook his head. Of course, Michael saw it, and ignoring both Blosch and Jazz, his eyes surveyed Conall.

"And *you* are vastly new," he said. "Are you and Estrada acquainted?"

Feeling suddenly protective, Estrada draped an arm around the bard's neck. "Conall is an amazing singer. I suggested he come by and check out the club."

"Singer? How fortuitous. You must serenade us, Conall. Beats is building to his blistering peak, and then the stage is yours."

When Conall stared at Michael, just one muscle in his jaw quivered. "I will sing."

Fuck. Estrada wasn't sure why he'd jumped into a pissing match with Michael but now, Conall would be on display to all. "At least let me buy you a beer first," Estrada said, concocting a reason to escape Michael.

The bard followed him to the bar with Blosch in tow.

Conall stared into his eyes. "That is your Michael. Why are you not with him?"

"That's a question I can't answer in the time it takes to drink a beer, or even several. Suffice to say, he's fucking dangerous. Stay away from him and the blood clots. Both of you." Estrada scratched his chin as Cerise set three beers down on the bar. When she held up a shot glass, he shook his head. "Listen, man. You don't have to sing. I just had to tell him something."

"I will sing," the bard said. "I will sing for you."

"For me?" Estrada stared at Conall and then at Blosch. Clearly, something smoldered between the two men. He cocked his head. "So, why are you here?"

Leopold crossed his arms over his chest and shrugged his shoulder. "We didn't know how to find you, then saw the sign outside yesterday and bought tickets." He caught his hair in his hands and tossed it over his shoulder. "A few days ago, Conall came to warn me that the vampires intend to come after me."

Estrada stared at Conall. "How do you know that?"

The bard guzzled his beer, then wiped his lips. "Trees listen."

"And the trees talked to you while you were sitting out in the yard." Suddenly, things were making sense.

The bard nodded. "They are angry Leo did not board the yacht."

"So why are you out in public, especially here, if you know the vampires are after you?"

"No one makes me a prisoner in my own city," Blosch said.

"Don't be a dick. They're everywhere, including here"—his eyes swept the crowd—"and they'll sure as fuck imprison you if they get you to Diego's nest. They'll force you onto a boat to get you there or maybe just pick you up in their talons and fly."

Leopold's face turned as pale as his shirt, and he guzzled his beer.

Estrada signaled to Cerise to bring another round, then turned to Conall. "How did you get from Anmore to downtown Vancouver? How did you even know where to go?" Estrada was pleasantly baffled by this new twist.

"I followed the water west. Then I met people on the road. They asked me where I was going, and I showed them this." From his pocket, Conall pulled the Ecos menu. "When a van stopped, they told me to come with them."

Estrada resisted the impulse to lecture him on the dangers of jumping into vans with strangers.

"Fortunately, he arrived just as I was closing. We had dinner and talked all night." Blosch finished his beer, put it on the bar, and hoisted another. "You should know, I'm in, whatever the plan is to destroy these things."

Estrada ignored him and turned to the bard. "Well, aren't you the persuasive fucker."

Conall beamed. "I told him the truth."

The DJ had stopped spinning, and they lowered their voices in the thrum of conversation.

"Sensara said she saw a vision of you in a garden. Was it the plants at Ecos?"

Conall shook his head. "Gretchen."

"Gretchen is my neighbor," Blosch explained. "When she came for coffee on Monday morning, she and Conall got talking about plants, and she invited him to her garden center."

"She gave me a job." Conall smiled. "I can sleep out back in her greenroom."

"Greenhouse? You're full of surprises." In a matter of days, the bard had acquired friends, a place to stay, and employment. Estrada gestured between the two men. "So, are you two . . .?"

They appraised each other, and Conall's lip curled up in a grin.

"We could be," Blosch said.

Which meant they weren't. Not yet. Estrada felt an unexpected sense of relief. He still had time to finish what he'd started with the bard.

"Zion's here tonight. He's the one who turned you."

"What?" Blosch's eyes scanned the crowd. "Where is he?"

"I don't see him right now but that doesn't mean he's gone. He's tall and muscular, with long dreads and black teardrop tattoos beneath his eyes. Once you see him, you'll never forget him."

"Are there others?"

Estrada was about to voice his suspicions when Michael appeared at his right shoulder. "Mic's on. And there's an electric guitar up there. Do you play? If not, I'm sure we can conjure up a guitarist."

"I play," Conall said, and Estrada remembered their first night back in Ireland—Conall's solstice voice, and long, hungry kisses in the river. He turned to the bard. "Maybe you shouldn't. There'll be other times."

"I want to." Conall followed Michael, and Estrada followed Conall.

Estrada showed him the mic, and as he turned to walk away, the bard reached out and pulled him so close their foreheads touched. "This is your song. It has filled my head since I left. It will not let me go."

Estrada touched the red marks on the bard's cheek. "I will not let you go. I'm sorry I left you."

And when the first sounds burst from the bard's throat, Estrada stood on the dance floor gazing up at Conall and thinking again of that four-hundred-year-old yellow cedar tree that had been split by lightning. Thick as Manuka honey and melodic as his pipes, Conall's voice tossed and turned and evanesced, then spiraled back like Time. Like they were all caught in The Between.

When tears rolled down Estrada's cheeks, he tasted their salt on his tongue.

"Like fucking treacle." Michael's whisper tickled his ear. "I can't wait to taste him."

39

"**D**on't tell me you're gonna walk home." Estrada stared at Blosch. His chest ached, but he was too drunk to care. After a night of tequila shots, dodging Michael, and almosts with Conall—almost making love in the dressing room, almost convincing the bard to come back to his place forever, almost punching him when he refused—the men were arguing out in front of Pegasus. The glaring neon lights on Granville did nothing for the steel grips that pinched the back of his neck, urged on by his rigid shoulders. Nor did the reams of partiers disbursing from every drinking establishment on the entertainment strip at closing time this Friday night—any of whom could be vampires.

"I need to walk," Leopold said. "I'll never sleep after this much stimulation."

Such a sensitive chef, Estrada thought. He cleared his throat and tried to swallow but his mouth was too dry.

"You think *that* was stimulating. You're lucky nobody spiked your drinks."

"They wouldn't do that, would they?"

"You don't get out much, do you?" Estrada had no idea how naïve Leopold Blosch really was. Perhaps he really did nothing but mind his bistro and cook, as he claimed. "You know they're watching and waiting for the right moment to abduct you."

"If what you say is true, they'll be watching, whether we call an uber or walk twenty minutes." Blosch was adamant, and nothing Estrada could say was going to change his mind. "It doesn't make much difference."

"It makes *every* fucking difference." Estrada turned his head and spit. "If you'd seen what I saw."

"I'll be with him." The bard had become Blosch's protector and couldn't be moved.

Estrada grasped Conall's shoulder and lowered his voice to a plea. "This is no tribe like you've ever fought before. There are no rules. They're not human."

Ignoring them, Blosch continued to defend his right to die, or worse. "What can I do? Ecos is my life. I can't just walk away. It's not like calling in sick to a job. I *am* the bistro."

Hello Ego. Estrada was pissed at the pale, arrogant beauty, but not quite pissed enough to feed him to the vampires. "You disappeared for a month when Zion turned you into a vampire, and Ecos was still standing when I brought you back. Is it really worth your life? Your humanity?"

Blosch scoffed. "I'm not the prize you think I am."

"You're more of a prize than I first assumed. I thought it was a coincidence you landed at Le Château, but they *chose* you. Courted your financial manager to get you. That's why Diego only kept you and killed the rest. They want you, Blosch, and they won't stop until they have you."

Blosch shrugged and walked away giving off victim vibes while Conall guarded him like a Doberman.

Estrada shook his head. He never should have introduced Conall to Blosch. He'd underestimated the bard's warrior commitment. He was a protector above all else. That's one of the things he loved about the bard.

He could have walked beside them but refused to leave his Harley parked in the back alley behind Pegasus all night, so went to get it. While the sentinels were active and the club was raving, it was relatively safe, but once everyone left, things changed. Nigel had installed security cameras but the inconvenience of losing his bike wasn't worth the insurance payout. So, he stomped down the side of the building and jammed on his helmet. Already some poor soul was curled up in the shelter of the garbage bins. He stuck a fifty in the guy's pocket, climbed on his Harley, and kicked it up.

There had been more vampires in the club than he'd expected. So many, he'd dug into his trunk for the black leather jacket full of knives and changed out of his tux. He wore the jacket now over his black T-shirt. When he crouched on the Harley, the knife tips jabbed the edge of his hips—small pricks like a woman's nails. Men never hung on like that. Men wrapped their hands around him in different ways.

He revved up the bike and coasted down the alley, then turned with the traffic onto Davie. The glare of the lights did nothing for his headache. He followed them slowly, at a distance, keeping an eye on late night walkers, bodies leaning out of doorways, strange faces frowning from open windows, and casting his gaze upward to scan for silhouetted ravens' wings. He knew vampire eyes were on him too. He could feel them burning holes in his skin.

At Hornby, he turned right and cruised slowly, keeping an eye on the two men. Blosch strutted like a pale peacock. Estrada remembered him saying he was a germaphobe and kept his kitchen spotless. From what he'd seen of the bistro it was true. But he couldn't help but imagine that white shirt spattered with blood.

Conall walked beside Blosch on the street side, hands dangling at-the-ready from his shoulders, fingers twitching nervously. He had a knife hidden somewhere and was itching to use it. Estrada could feel the itch in his own fingers. Perhaps it was a piece he'd picked up from Blosch's kitchen, a cleaver or carving knife, wrapped in a towel, and crammed down his boot—something Blosch used to sculpt carrot blossoms or sliver green onions or toothpick sexy strips of jalapeños. If its point caught the fuckers between the eyes, it didn't much matter.

Just before the Art Gallery, the pair crossed left onto Robson. They were nearly there. Two blocks to Ecos. Stopped by the red light, Estrada sat tapping his toe, every muscle tense. He assessed the people around him through his visor, though no one looked at him. You didn't make eye contact with a guy in black leather driving a Harley at two a.m. unless you wanted a reaction. It was a long light. He glanced up, searching for ravens among pigeons that didn't know the difference between night and day in the city glare.

When the light turned green, he eased around the corner. Where were they? A first wave of panic surged through his core as he searched up and down the street. Was Blosch playing some kind of game? He glanced up side streets as he slowly drove down Robson. *There.* He found them again walking down a dark alley. *For fuck's sake, Blosch. Do you have a death wish?*

He made a sharp left without signaling and sped down the alley, dodging garbage cans, and a few sleepers. He'd almost reached them when he saw the first vampire leap off a fire escape and land on Blosch's back. Registered it in slow motion though it happened in a gasp.

It wasn't Zion or Eliseo, but some hipster with thick ginger hair, buzzed short on the sides and long on top, "Peaky Blinders" style. Conall pulled a butcher knife from his boot.

Estrada was off the bike and charging toward them, opening his jacket as he ran, clutching his first knife.

A second vampire leapt from a doorway and hit Estrada broadside. The force of the two-hundred-pound body sent the knife flying from his hand. It clattered to the pavement as the creature slipped behind him, fangs stroking his neck. This was it. No matter how much he struggled, it had his forearms pinned from behind with steel hands. His muscles and bones melted in a natural habit of escape. Chains. Ropes. Straitjackets. This fucker was no different. When he managed enough flex to grip the tip of a knife, he pulled it up and out, but there was nowhere to stick it.

His eyes rolled back as canines punctured his neck. Then suddenly a warm whoosh hit, and the arms released. He wheeled around wielding the knife, poised to stab and stab, but met Conall, swinging a dripping head by its long black braid.

Instinctively, Estrada reached up and touched the holes in his neck. When he pulled his hand away, it was covered in blood. The rest of the creature was twisting on the ground; not dusted, but writhing like the chickens his abuela butchered when they lived in Mexico.

Was this what they meant by your life flashing before your eyes?

Blosch sat on the ground, his platinum hair matted, his white shirt and pants spattered with blood. There was nothing left of the vampire who'd grabbed him but something resembling a pile of burnt leaves that stunk like a leaky cellar.

"Let's go," Estrada yelled. He turned to Conall, who still stood clutching the vampire's head, "You're not keeping that, are you?" Back in Croghan, trophies were strung down a wall.

Conall looked at it, shrugged, and tossed it, a little too near Blosch who startled but didn't move.

"Blosch, get up," Estrada said in his most commanding voice. "Now." Headlights were coming up the alley. The single bleat of a police siren made him flinch.

Blosch stood, turned, and ran.

Estrada looked at Conall. "Get on."

They sped down the alley on the Harley, following the white speckled streak that was Blosch, and left the cops to solve the headless vampire crime.

Blosch ran full tilt for two blocks, then stopped short in front of Ecos, shaking and panting and jiggling the front doorknob as if he couldn't remember how to get inside.

"Key," Estrada shouted. "Where's the key?"

Blosch slapped his thighs and produced a key from his pants pocket.

Conall slipped off, and Estrada pulled the bike in tight to the wall, turned it off, and locked it up. They trailed Blosch upstairs, where he unlocked a second door that led to his flat.

"Now do you believe me?" Estrada asked.

Blosch didn't answer. Just stood shaking, his eyes wide, his pale skin flushed. Then he spun and hurled in the kitchen sink.

Seeing the bathroom door ajar, Estrada stepped up to the vanity mirror and examined the bloody puncture marks in his neck. They were deep, on his right side, and close to the back. Thank Christ, the thing had missed his artery. Perhaps it was newly fledged and inexperienced. He remembered Michael's body after Diego had drilled a hole through his brain. He'd looked perfect. Undamaged. The longer they lived, the more decrepit they became when finally destroyed. These fuckers were living on borrowed time, and he was going to collect.

Conall stood guard by the door, looking oddly serene, while Blosch leaned over the kitchen sink, running water. The air reeked of sour copper.

"Looks like we're staying here tonight," Estrada said. "And in the morning, we're all getting out of town."

"But I-I . . ."

"Do you still not get it, Blosch? You're the Chosen One. Those fuckers came for *you*." Estrada slipped out of his leather jacket and dampened a white towel to wipe off the blood. "See this?" He held up the bloody towel and showed Blosch the puncture wounds in his neck. "Diego wants you, and he won't stop until he gets you."

"Lorne went-went on the yacht. What will happen to him?"

"This." He pointed again at his bleeding neck.

Blosch turned and puked some more.

Estrada tossed the bloody towel on the counter, then opened the door to the balcony and stepped outside. Like the rest of Blosch's world, it was festooned in greenery. He sat on a lounge chair built of wooden slats, leaned back, and listened to the late-night sounds of the city. Traffic hum. Sirens. Bass and beats. A woman's sexy laughter. A drunken man shouting obscenities.

At least it's real, he thought.

He pulled out his phone. No text from Sensara meant everything was good at the house. He took a deep breath and willed himself to relax. He had to think, and Sensara was right, reptilian brain wasn't capable of thought, only fight, fly, freeze, and fuck. He could use some of that. The men were talking quietly, had bonded over the past few days. He wished he had a joint. Anything to take the edge off. And then he remembered: *Blosch has a full bar downstairs.*

When he came back inside and locked the balcony door, Conall was walking with Blosch toward what he assumed was the bedroom. "Hey, man. Have you got any weed?"

Blosch shook his head.

"Anything to drink?"

His head continued to shake.

"Do you mind if I borrow a bottle from downstairs? I'll pay you for it."

Blosch waved him off with a pale hand. He had more on his mind than a bottle of booze.

Estrada padded back down the stairs still wearing the leather jacket full of knives. Let them come. He'd play carnival games with their heads. *Fuck Fate. Give me enough tequila and I'll make a corpse dance.* And that's all they were. Animated corpses.

He stood behind the bar and stared at all the pretty bottles. It struck him as odd that it was someone's job to sit in a swank office somewhere and design liquor bottles. Probably had to go to school for years and get a degree in fucking graphic design to do it.

Hints of turquoise drew his gaze to the round bottle of Don Julio hidden in the back corner. Silver tequila, one hundred percent *de agave*, it said. From the land of his birth.

Call me cliché, but after almost having my throat ripped out by a novice vampire, I deserve a little homecoming.

He popped the cork and took a deep sniff. If he was going to die tomorrow, he'd drink this tonight.

He chose a tall, crystal glass and filled it, then sank down on the floor behind the bar and sipped. He didn't know the bard was there until he hunkered down beside him.

"Did you tuck him in?" Estrada hadn't spent a lot of time with Leopold Blosch, but he thought the man had a little more backbone than this.

Conall chuckled and took the glass from his hand. He sniffed it once, then chugged it all.

"Hey, man. You drink it, you fill it."

Conall got to his knees and grasped the tequila bottle from the ledge of the bar. After filling the glass, he plunked the bottle on the floor between them. He handed the full glass back to Estrada and smiled.

"It felt good to sing tonight. My voice sounded—"

"In-fucking-credible. You blew us away." Estrada set the glass down and squeezed the bard's fist. "Are you rethinking your career choices? Maybe rock star isn't so bad?"

Conall lifted his fist and pressed Estrada's hand to his lips. "Not if you're there beside me."

"Yeah? Like Estrada & Ceol?" He made air quotes. "The Magician & The Bard. One Night Only."

"Aye, like that."

"Look, I'm sorry about the other night at my place. When Eliseo saw us, I was afraid they'd come after you because—"

"Because you love me."

When Conall grasped Estrada's cheeks and kissed him, it was different than their other kisses. Something had shifted. Sure, Estrada wanted sex. That was pure instinct with a man like Conall. But if they didn't, if they stayed all night locked in each other's arms like this, that would be perfect too.

The crash of breaking glass sent them both skittering sideways in different directions.

Estrada smelled him before he saw him. The stench of decay, last night's copper, and moldering feathers. He glanced up at the shadow in his periphery. Zion stood atop the bar, staring down with a grin that raised the black teardrop tattoos on his cheeks. With a long arm, he reached down, swept up the bottle of tequila, and guzzled.

Estrada pulled a knife from his vest but before he could throw it, an arm came from behind and put him in a headlock. A hand reached out, grasped his wrist, and turned it.

"Drop it, amigo, or I will break your bones."

Eliseo.

Estrada held on until the snap turned his gut. "Motherfucker," he growled over the pain.

"No matter how many times I hear that sound, it still makes me shiver," Eliseo said.

Conall pulled a butcher knife from his boot and lunged at the kid.

But Zion leapt and plucked up Conall in midair. Crushing the bard's back to his chest, he squeezed his wrist. "Father wants to meet your new friend." He sniffed Conall's neck like a dog, then growled and thrust his hips. "Ooohhh. He makes me hungry."

"No. Please. Take me. Not him."

Just then, the upstairs door opened and Blosch scrambled down the stairs pointing a snub-nosed revolver.

Zion cackled. "Bullets? Bullets don't hurt us, chef. We already dead. You pretty, but you stupid."

In a blur of motion, Zion hurled Conall into the bar and grabbed Blosch. The first round sounded before Zion yanked the gun out of his hand. He dropped it and kicked it. Then, he shoved open the door and dragged Blosch outside. All the while, Estrada sat cringing, locked in the vampire-child's embrace.

"No." Conall raced across the room grasping the butcher knife, but Zion had already vanished with Blosch.

When Eliseo leapt to the top of the bar, he lifted Estrada right off the ground. He held him aloft for a moment, then flung him at Conall.

"Enjoy your tequila, amigos," he sang. And then he was gone.

Estrada could hear sirens. "Cops. We gotta get out of here."

"What are we going to do?"

Estrada threw back the rest of the tequila. "Steal something of Diego's. Something I hope he'll want back bad enough to make a trade."

"Magus Dubh. At fucking last." Estrada and Conall had just stumbled through the door of his flat when his phone pinged. He dropped his keys in the turquoise dish and tapped the app on his mobile screen to see Dubh's beaming blue-tattooed face. His swollen left wrist screamed with vengeance and indignation. That little prick, Eliseo, was the first item he'd deal with when he got the chance.

"Always a pleasure, mate. The last time we convened it was to celebrate Dylan's release from prison. I was mad with it. How's the lad now?"

"Good. Happy. Married."

Dubh sat back, mouth open. "Married?"

Estrada laughed. "Yep. Dylan met a sweet Irish girl and fell in love. It's a long story. One we can hopefully share over a few pints soon."

"I can't wait. But I'm curious about your current problem."

"Indeed. We have an escalating situation, but first, how's your aunt, man? When we talked to the bartender at your local pub, he said she was sick."

"Aye, the worst has passed. I left my dear Aunt Jackie sipping sherry. But tell me what brought you all the way to Glasgow?"

"Vampires."

"Vampires?" Dubh's eyes narrowed. "Real or metaphorical?"

Estrada chuckled. "Real. I've met them personally, even been to the nest."

"That's a first."

Not really, Estrada thought. *You've met them too. You just don't know it.* "Diego's a vengeful old Spaniard. He bit Michael last summer while I was in Scotland, and he's been stalking me ever since. Now he's upped his game. That's why we need you."

"I've booked a red-eye, mate."

Estrada released a breath. "I'm glad to hear it. Michael's turning from the bite and needs a hit of your miraculous fey blood."

"You think it will help?"

"I know it will. But that's another story."

"Ach, life's tedious without you, mate."

Estrada huffed. He could use a little tedium. "Michael has an associate I suspect is one of them, perhaps even a spy for Diego. Have you ever heard of binding a vampire?"

"Physically?"

"Yeah."

"Why not just destroy it?"

"I need to trade it. These fuckers abducted a friend of ours."

"Hmmm," Dubh muttered. He cracked the cap on a beer and took a good, long guzzle. "What's coming to mind is a creature in our old Highland myths. A beautiful faerie who charms a man, then stabs him with her long fingernails, and drinks the blood from his wounds."

Estrada thought of the cutting and sipping going on between Michael and Jazz.

"Leannán Sidhe," Conall said.

"Who's that then?"

"Sorry, I should have introduced you two." Estrada held out the phone so Dubh could see the bard standing beside him. "This is my friend, Conall Ceol. He's a Druid like yourself, from Ireland."

"Blessings, mate. What county? I know a few Irish Druids."

"Another long story," Estrada said.

"Delighted to meet you, Conall, and you're correct. Your Leannán Sidhe is an incarnation of our Baobhan Sith."

Baa-van She. Estrada repeated in his head. "In the stories, do they ever bind these things?"

"Iron," Dubh said. "It's in all the fey myths, and it's obtainable."

Estrada remembered being shackled to a huge iron wheel at Le Château. Vampires had pushed it into the center of the room. He shook his head. "I don't think iron hurts this crowd. They seem immune."

"Aye, well. I recollect they trapped the Baobhan Sith in a stone cairn."

"Stone?" Estrada thought of Dylan and his ability to communicate with stones. But how would you trap a creature in stone? Maybe in the U.K. they could seal it in a dolmen, but here they only had caves in the mountains.

"Ach, there's one more thing. The Baobhan Sith can shapeshift."

"Into what?"

"Wolf. Crow. Raven."

Estrada shook his head and snorted.

"I assume you've observed a similar trait in your vampires."

"Hell, yeah. They transform into ravens, and Diego attacked our yacht in the guise of a thunderbird, a prehistoric fucking pterosaur."

"Ach, no way."

"I kid you not." Estrada had missed Dubh's Glaswegian slang and his Scottish lilt. It gave him as much comfort as Conall's and Sorcha's Irish. "How soon can you get here?"

"The best I could do was a midnight departure."

"So, Sunday morning, my time?" The U.K. was eight hours ahead, but it would take Dubh at least twelve hours to make the crossing.

"Aye. Early Sunday morning, six something."

"Good. I'll pick you up."

"Ach, mate. Just text me your address and I'll grab an uber. Six is an obscene hour to be driving to an airport."

"Alright, but text me the info anyway, and if I can pick you up, I will." Knowing Dubh would be there in time for their strategy meeting gave Estrada an immediate sense of relief. "The coven's meeting Sunday afternoon. It'll be good to have you with us, Dubh."

The wee man held up his beer and toasted him. "Sláinte, mate. I was planning to come for your wean's first birthday. I can't wait to meet my goddaughter."

Estrada's heart swelled. He remembered how Dubh had proclaimed himself Lucy's godfather and given her a beautiful charm bracelet for her birthday. "Lucy's gonna love you. Just like her old man. See you soon."

Knowing that Magus Dubh was on his way lightened Estrada's mood considerably. Though Dubh didn't know it, he'd piloted the yacht up the strait when they'd gathered to fight the vampires. Without him, they might never have freed Lucy.

Conall was standing out on the balcony staring into the back alley when he ended the call. Estrada gathered the bard's long, chestnut hair in his hand, moved it to one side, and rested his chin on his shoulder. He loved his musky scent and craved him most raw, the way he'd met him in Croghan. Pressing his face against the back of Conall's neck, he breathed him in. Pheromones were powerful stimulants. He'd experienced a similar draw to Michael when they'd first met, but realized something had changed. Perhaps vampire blood had altered his body chemistry.

"Your Michael seems happy with Jazz," Conall said.

The bard seemed concerned about his relationship with Michael. He obviously knew that's where Estrada had gone when he'd left him at the house. "First of all, he's not *my* Michael, and yeah, of course he's happy. They're both into the blood. Jazz might even be his source."

"How could you tell for sure?"

"Bind Jazz and test them. All I need is one drop of their blood and I'll know." Estrada sighed. "Vampire blood. I can't even describe it to you because you've never taken drugs, and I can't think of anything else that can get you that high." He grasped Conall's shoulder and kneaded the taut muscles with his one good hand, cradling his busted wrist close to his chest. "Think about the happiest moment of your life. Then imagine capturing and reliving that euphoric feeling with just one drop of blood."

"Are the vampires happy then? Will Leo be happy?"

Ah, it wasn't Michael or Jazz that had the bard perturbed. It was Blosch.

"Look. We're gonna get him away from them and cure him."

"And Michael. Will you cure him too? And Jazz?"

"If I can." Estrada's plan had always been to cure Michael, but he wasn't sold on curing Jazz. There was something about them that made his skin crawl. If ever there was a Leannán Sidhe, Jazz was it. He could imagine their long sharp nails slicing through flesh. Their painted lips pressing on the wound and sucking like a Chupacabra. Perhaps, once cured, this feeling of mistrust would dissipate.

Conall leaned back against him as his muscles softened. "But Michael seems happy."

"He's not happy. He's manic." It was late. Estrada was exhausted, his broken wrist hurt like hell, and Michael's moods were too complicated to explain. He didn't understand them himself. All he knew was that Michael and Jazz were into something more sinister than usual. He could sense it.

"Come on. I need to ice my wrist, swallow some painkillers, and go to bed." Nothing was as he expected. Everything had shifted that month he was away. Now, every day things grew stranger and stranger, and he became more and more exhausted. He longed to sleep someplace warm, safe, and soft for a zillion years, preferably beside the bard.

"Go fix it. I need to think."

That was not the response Estrada expected or wanted. Perhaps, more had gone on between Conall and Blosch than they'd let on. What had Blosch implied? We *could* be a thing?

But they had bigger problems, the kind with razor fangs. "You can't stay out here alone. What if they come?"

"They broke through glass tonight. If they want me, being inside won't stop them from taking me."

"True, but it might slow them down. At least, we'll hear them and we can fight. Out here alone, you don't stand a chance. They could swoop in and carry you off, and I wouldn't even know." Voicing that brought a sharp pain to Estrada's chest. "Come on, man. Come to bed with me."

Conall stiffened. "I can't have sex with you while Leo is out there with them."

Ah, so that was it. Conall had developed feelings for Blosch, feelings that lodged in Estrada's chest and squeezed. Estrada didn't care if they had sex. He'd never put sexual restraints on anyone. But feelings were different. Feelings were dangerous.

"Look man, I just want to lie with you, hold you and know you're safe. I've missed you these past few days."

Conall wrapped his arms around Estrada's shoulders, and leaned in so their foreheads touched. They stayed that way a long time, rocking slightly and breathing each other's air.

"Please come to bed with me," Estrada whispered at last.

"I can't." When Estrada stared into Conall's eyes, he saw pain, sadness, and confusion.

"I don't understand."

"I want you. Right here and now. Lying beside you in bed, I won't be able to stop. And I don't deserve such pleasure while Leo is out there being tortured by the Leannán Sidhe."

Estrada grasped his hand. He wanted to ask: *Do you love him?* But was afraid of the answer. "At least, come inside where it's safer."

Finally, Conall relented, and followed him into the living room. Estrada swallowed some painkillers and grabbed a bag of frozen peas, then sat on the end of the leather couch. He motioned for the bard to lie down with his head in his lap. While he iced his broken wrist on the arm of the couch, he stroked Conall's forehead, his temples, his hair.

"Would it help if I told you what Leo experienced when he was with them before? He told me his story, and I don't think he'd mind if I shared it with you. Especially if it gives you comfort."

"You know what's happening to him?"

"I have a pretty good idea." He kissed the bard's forehead. "I don't think they've taken him far. The last time, they had a yacht in the harbor. It takes a few nights to sail up the coast, and I don't think they're ready to leave, so they're probably there."

Conall stiffened. "Let's go get him."

"A, I don't know where the yacht is docked, and B, we need more fighters and better weaponry. We can pop a few heads with knives, but you saw what happened when that goon jumped me from behind. I don't know how many there are, or if Diego is with them." Estrada exhaled. "But, let me tell you about Leo. You saw Zion, the one with the tattoos below his eyes?"

Conall nodded.

"Zion likes blonds. He has a thing for Michael and Leo."

"A thing."

"A penchant. He wants Leo to be his lover. That's why he took him. I'm not sure if that makes you feel better or worse but Zion's not planning to merely feed off Leo and kill him. He wants to make Leo a vampire so they can be together." Estrada took another breath. He wasn't sure how to tell Conall the truth without upsetting him.

"I don't want Leo to die."

"Nor do I, but if Leo dies as a human, Zion will make sure he's reborn as a vampire. And with Dubh's help, once we find him, we can cure him. So, Leo will be Leo again."

"But tonight. What will Zion do to him tonight?"

Estrada reached up and touched the scars on his neck. "When Eliseo bit me it was a shock, and then, as he drank, I felt incredibly sleepy. I closed my eyes and floated. I don't remember anything else until I awoke in Sensara's arms. Dubh had fed me his fey blood."

"And cured you."

"No, I was never a vampire. Eliseo drank much of my blood, but Diego didn't have a chance to feed me *his* blood because Leo destroyed Eliseo and carried me out of there."

"Leo saved your life."

"Yes."

"So we must save his."

"We will. I promise you, Conall. When Dubh comes, we'll find Leo and bring him back."

"Will Zion feed Leo his blood?"

"Yes, and they'll force him to drink more blood, so he becomes addicted. When I met Leopold, he'd been with them for a month. He was starving because he refused to kill. He hated what he'd become, but he was still himself. His spirit hadn't changed." Estrada brushed the scars left by Leopold with his fingers. "He only fed from me because he was starving, and I offered myself. And even after that, we cured him."

"With Dubh's blood."

"Yes. Vampire is a living virus and somehow Dubh's fey blood can kill it. It's stronger. More potent." Estrada ran his thumb along Conall's jaw and across his lips.

"I'm glad Magus Dubh is coming."

"Me too. I'm telling you this, so you don't picture Leo being beaten and tortured in some dungeon. Zion will treat him—" He paused. He was about to say humanely, but realized that word didn't fit in this situation. "He'll treat him like a lover. When Zion says he's hungry, it means he wants sex."

"I understand. I imagined them all feeding off Leo until he died."

"Try not to think like that." Estrada wondered how much to tell Conall. What would make him feel better and what would make him feel worse? Finally, he decided to just tell him the truth. The bard would find out, eventually.

"Leopold told me something else."

Conall stared up at him with wide caramel eyes that were mesmerizing.

Estrada cleared his throat. "The virus arouses them sexually. That's how it replicates in the bloodstream. And why Michael and Jazz are so addicted. I tasted Michael's blood once after Zion turned him, and I know how potent vampire blood is."

"So, Leo will want to have sex with Zion."

"He'll become aroused, yes. I never kiss and tell, but when Leo was feeding from me, we both became aroused. No doubt, we would have had sex if Sensara hadn't come in and caught us."

Conall laughed. "Oh, was she angry? I would not want to anger the Lady."

"Oh yeah. She was pissed. Sensara has never approved of my relationship with Michael or my lifestyle."

"Because you have many lovers."

Estrada sighed. "I like my freedom. Don't you?"

"I do. In our tuath, people are free to have sex if both agree. Children are known by their mother and cared for by everyone."

"A matrilineal tribe. I like that idea." Estrada stifled a yawn.

"I wanted to have sex with Leo," the bard said suddenly.

"Yeah? Did someone come in and catch you too?"

Conall laughed but it was a sad laugh. "No. Leo said we did not know each other well enough." He sniffed back what may have been tears. "I like him."

"That's why we're going to save him." Estrada swallowed and placed a fingertip in the small space between Conall's lips. When the bard took it tenderly into his mouth, Estrada's insides shook. "You can be with anyone you want, and there are lots of men who'll want you. As you told me in Ireland, I'll never hold you back from what you want or need."

Conall caught Estrada's hand. "I need you now. Can I share your bed?"

"*Por favor. Mi cama es tu cama.*" Estrada leaned over and kissed Conall's lips, soft and slow. "That means, yes, please. My bed is your bed for as long as you want it."

41

Estrada awoke feeling loose and easy for the first time in days. He'd been dreaming about his Mayan grandmother, his *abuela*. In the dream, he was a kid running barefoot down the dirt road toward the cenote when he tripped on a rock, threw out his hands, and broke his wrist. His abuela made a stinky poultice from giant leaves and wrapped it like a tamale. He didn't know if this was a shard of memory or if his abuela was reaching out to him psychically. She'd appeared in his dreams before, always when he was hurt or anxious, and always ready to help or reassure him with her own special magic.

He remembered her cozy house of sticks and palm leaves in the Yucatán. She'd fed him chicken tamales with green salsa, and corn tortillas with cochinita pibil and red onions from the pig they slow-roasted underground. His mouth watered thinking of her beautiful food, and then a knot struck his empty belly. She must be getting old, and he hadn't seen her since he was a kid. He was a terrible grandson. The recognition of such irreparable regret kicked him fully into the present, and his swollen wrist screamed.

Fucking Eliseo. That kid enjoyed inflicting pain, especially breaking bones. He'd busted Sensara's finger when he and Zion had abducted her from the fishing lodge. She'd confessed how terrified she'd been when they flew with her clutched in their sharp talons over the sea.

Estrada wondered how Eliseo managed pain. Did vampires even feel pain? They were dead but they reacted to fire. And there were other ways to instill pain. Diego had felt anguish when Christophe had drowned chasing Michael, which meant they had feelings and created bonds. Diego's bonds were with his sons, his saviors. He'd been more and more devastated with each vampire they'd destroyed.

The sound of rustling in the kitchen broke Estrada's revery. The scent of something wonderfully spicy made his stomach growl and he glanced at his phone. *Christ.* It was four p.m. He'd slept the whole day. No wonder he was starving. But first he needed to shower.

He padded into the bathroom, turned on the hot water, and stepped into the tub. Once Conall had accepted that Blosch wasn't being tortured and could be cured, he'd kept Estrada up all night. All his fears of hurting Conall disappeared once they turned to each other in the bed and stared into each other's eyes. They'd made love as naturally as a couple who'd been together for months. No bonds. No drugs. No liquor. No toys. Just pure, gentle love. The joy of watching Conall's face and listening to his body with each pleasing kiss or stroke made Estrada's heart swell. The spiritual had somehow eclipsed the physical, and this, he realized, was the difference between having sex and making love.

Perhaps all the waiting and wanting made a difference. Or perhaps they really were destined for each other. Imagine meeting the love of your life across an ocean two thousand years in the past. It seemed impossible. Yet, one thing Estrada knew. His feelings for Conall grew stronger every day. He cared for the bard with both body and soul. Yet with that awareness came fear. Diego wasn't stupid. He'd come after Conall and hurt him to take his revenge. Estrada must find a way to keep the bard safe without making the warrior feel inadequate. As he soaped and rinsed, he considered how to go about that.

Tonight, he planned to return to Pegasus. He needed to see Michael and unlock the secret of Jazz. His gut told him, they were connected somehow to the vampires. He'd do whatever was needed to discover the truth, especially now that they had Blosch, and he didn't want Conall anywhere near the debauchery that would ensue. He hadn't forgotten Michael's threat. *"Like fucking treacle,"* indeed.

Once dry, he swallowed several pain pills, applied cannabis ointment to his wrist, and wrapped it in an elastic bandage. It wasn't his first rodeo, and he didn't have time to queue at a walk-in clinic. Then he carefully pulled on his black jeggings, and ventured into the living room. Sunlight beamed through the corner kitchen window, hit the minute glass prism on the sill, and was released as a vast rainbow on the far wall. It was a kind of natural magic. After a storm, each spherical raindrop acted as a prism to create an arcing bow of refracted light. It was watching these magical rainbows appear over the Salish Sea that had first attracted Estrada to magic. He ran his fingers through the invisible waves and laughed as they appeared on his hand. This sleight of Nature made him respect her all the more.

Conall had opened the balcony door, and a breeze ruffled the drapes. Estrada peered around the corner into the kitchen and observed the bard as he sat at the wooden table drinking chai. The cinnamon and cloves awakened his senses. Conall's nose and the tops of his cheeks seemed more freckled, perhaps from the sun. His long chestnut hair was damp from showering, parted on the side, and hanging loose around his face. In blue jeans and a sleeveless denim shirt, he made a fine urban cowboy. He remembered how Lucy had wanted to go to the bard after he'd played a lullaby on his pipes.

"*Hola.* What's in there?" A bag of food stood on the counter wafting incredible smells.

Conall's lips rose in a grin. "First, your coffee." He handed Estrada a tall paper cup still wearing its snug lid.

"What did I do to deserve this?" He leaned down and kissed Conall on the lips, then picked up the cup.

Conall flushed. "I went to the Mexican place."

"Which one?" There were several dotting Commercial Drive. That was one reason he'd chosen this neighborhood.

"The red one on the corner."

"The Red Burrito. Great choice." Estrada inhaled the piquant scent as he opened the bag. "Tamales. God, I love tamales. And burritos. Beef or chicken?"

"Both, with green chilis."

"Ah, and tortilla soup. A veritable feast. *Gracias.*"

"This is from your country?"

"*Sí.*" Estrada pulled out cutlery and turquoise dishes from the cupboard. "I just realized that you've probably never eaten corn before. It's the basic ingredient in all these dishes. Dried and ground and made into tamales, tacos, and tortillas."

"I like it," Conall said, as he spread the dishes on the table.

They both dug into the food and ate a while in silence. On a list of amazing mornings, so far this was number one, even though it was late afternoon.

"You know, before I woke up, I was dreaming about *mi abuela,* my grandmother. Maybe it was because I could smell my favorite foods."

"I would like to meet her." Conall's coppery eyes sparkled. Now that they'd finally consummated their relationship, something had shifted between them. That wondering if, and when, and how, had vanished and been replaced by something as warm and substantial as the burrito Estrada clutched in his hand.

"Maybe one day you will." Estrada was suddenly yearning for his mother's Mayan culture; something he knew very little about.

"You miss her. Tell me about her, and your dream."

"Well, mi abuela is my mother's mother. She's Mayan. That's the Indigenous People in the Yucatán. There were Mayans living there when you lived with your Celtic People in Ériú, and they were farmers too. Later, they built huge stone temples that still exist today, though they're in ruins." He sipped his coffee and wiped his lips. No one had ever asked him about his family. Even Sensara. Maybe because she didn't talk about her family either.

"Mi abuela lives in a village near the city of Mérida." He picked up a beef burrito and talked between bites. "I haven't been there since I was a kid, but I remember that Mérida *es hermosa*. Beautiful. In the dream, mi abuela was just as I remember her. She's tiny, you know?" He gestured with his hand that she might reach his armpits. "But powerful. She has kind, brown eyes, and long gray hair swept up in a bun. In my dream, she wore a traditional dress, white with yellow flowers sewn into the neck and hem. I'd broken my wrist, and she boiled these stinky leaves and wrapped them around it."

Conall stopped chewing and his eyes widened. "What leaves?"

"I don't know. They were big like banana or tobacco leaves. She's a healer like Mara."

"She is speaking to you, telling you that plants will heal your bones."

"Yeah. That's what I thought too." Estrada rubbed his wrist. "Daphne's a healer and knows about plants. I can ask her when we go there tomorrow. What did you do when people broke bones in Croghan?"

"The same. The healer used plants and sometimes bound the limb to a stick to keep it from moving."

"Have you ever broken a bone?"

"Here. Here. Here. And here." Conall pointed to his ankle, leg, wrist, and arm.

"Jesus." Cattle raiding, horse racing, and warring had taken its toll on the bard. "Were they all accidents or—?"

Conall laughed. "When I was small, I broke my leg trying to ride a bull. My mother was furious. I could not walk for a long time."

"No way." He really *was* an urban cowboy. "What else?"

"During one cattle raid, I got knocked off my horse and broke my arm."

"Hah, that was karma for knocking me off my horse. Remember that?"

Conall shook his head. "That was your fault for walking down the center of the road."

Estrada punched him in the arm. "Do you think we'd still be sitting here if you hadn't come over the hill that day and hit me? I mean, all these things happen and if we take any one of them out of sequence, does that change the outcome?"

Conall grew suddenly serious. "Druids believe things that are fated cannot be changed. We were destined to meet. If we had not met on the road that day, we would have found each other a different way, but we still would have met. Our souls called to each other, so we were drawn together." He used his hands to show how their hearts made one. "And when Capall galloped through the wormhole, I did not know we were moving into The Between. But now I know my destiny lies here with you."

"That's beautiful." He picked up Conall's fist and kissed his knuckles.

Estrada's phone pinged as he was clearing up the dishes. As he read the text, he smiled. Fate had intervened once again. "Hey. Dylan's inviting you to a special concert tonight at the university to see his pipe band perform. What do you think? Wanna go?"

"Aye. In Scotland, I tried Dermot's bagpipes."

"I'll tell him you're in. I've got some stuff to do downtown tonight and then I have to drive Dubh out to the house tomorrow on my bike. Can you stay with Dylan tonight and go to the coven meeting with him and Sylvia tomorrow?"

Conall eyed him suspiciously. "Are you going after them?"

"No, just doing reconnaissance. I need to know more about Jazz."

"You are going to the club."

"Don't worry. I'll be fine. We have security."

Conall looked doubtful.

"How about we buy you a phone on our way to Dylan's? That way, we can stay connected." Estrada smiled. "You can even send me a video of Dylan playing the bagpipes."

Conall pulled Estrada into his arms and hugged him so hard he felt his bones might break. "Promise me, you will not attack the vampires. If you find out where they are hiding Leo, you will wait for me."

42

Before he went to Pegasus, Estrada cruised by Ecos to see if someone had secured Blosch's bistro. It was a clear, warm, Saturday night on the cusp of a full moon, and the downtown corridor was packed with pedestrians, cars, bicycles, and cabs. He was concerned about the looting of Blosch's well-stocked bar. Fortunately, the police had roped off the area, and the broken picture window had been secured with wooden panels. Knowing that, he breathed easier. Blosch deserved to have everything intact when they brought him home. And they *would* bring him home.

He parked in the back alley at Pegasus and used his key to let himself in through the employee entrance. Saturday was "Masquerade Madness" and a tribute to the goth clubs of the eighties. Most of the patrons weren't born then but they venerated their goth ancestors. The few vintage patrons, who'd remained stuck in the eighties, were treated like celebrities because of their mad stories of concerts and raves and knowing them when.

Bauhaus was blaring through the speakers and the black-draped crowd was immersed in "Bela Lugosi's Dead." *How ironic,* he thought. A tribute to the vampires he was bent on destroying. Bauhaus was the progenitor of goth and never failed to cause a hundred hands to reach out searching for more blood clots. He could practically smell the MDMA coursing through their veins.

When The Cure's "Lullaby" video came up on the big screen, he knew the energy was about to intensify, but not violently. The goth crowd—at least the crowd that frequented Club Pegasus—was imaginative, but relished a slow, dark, creepy crawl, much like the spider man Robert Smith immortalized in his song.

Estrada scanned the room, searching for Michael, Jazz, and anyone else who seemed a little too familiar with Bela Lugosi. The crowd was turning in on itself, heads lolling, shoulder-to-shoulder, hunched and undulating, feet shuffling slowly, an occasional upward glance revealing a lacy mask or a pair of widely-shadowed eyes. He spotted Dell standing guard along the sidelines near the bar and made his way through the shambling bodies.

When he enquired about Michael, he learned through the hushed holes in the tune that he'd stepped out, though Dell didn't know where. That response, he knew, could be a cover. Dell was Michael's guard dog. There was no one more loyal, and nothing Michael could request Dell do that he'd refuse. Where Conall had become Blosch's Doberman, Dell was Michael's Golden Retriever, with one Magnum slung across his chest and another stuck down the back of his belt. His devotion extended to Estrada by way of association. Lately, Dell had been cultivating a bleached David Boreanaz look—a kind of Angel/Spike mashup—and he never went home alone. He was also one hell of a confidant that Estrada could trust with secrets. However, that meant he might not get much out of him regarding anyone else.

He glanced around the crowd and asked Dell if he'd seen Jazz.

"There." When Dell gestured with his dimpled chin, Estrada recalled a couple of nights early on at one of Michael's soirees, when he and Dell had tried each other on for size. The fit wasn't bad, though Estrada got the impression that Dell was a lady's man doing what he must to impress his master.

Estrada could just make out Jazz, snaking through the bodies, in a barely there, black-sequined, evening dress that clung to their flat, naked chest. With their face hidden by a lace mask and feather headdress, they screamed "raven."

"What do you know of them?" he asked.

Dell chewed his bottom lip in a thoughtful kind of way. "Travels frequently. High-end model." He shrugged. "Harmless enough."

"Michael seems rapt."

Dell nodded, then patted Estrada's shoulder. "Don't worry. They never last long."

He gathered Dell was referring to Michael's infatuations. His commiserating could be cloying.

Estrada shuffled through the crowd, a stroke here, a smile there, and rubbed up against Jazz. Brushing his lips along the edge of their chin, he breathed deep and waited for a response. They'd dabbed frankincense on their pulse points, which he appreciated, as the stench of Prada Black was becoming prosaic with this crowd. He stared beneath the false eyelashes into their bright amber eyes and something honest glittered back. Perhaps even harmless, as Dell had said. People who embraced their differences found solace here. He should know. That's how he'd found this place, and Michael. He exposed his neck, hoping to entice them with a throbbing vein and scars that advertised he was into blood. Their tongue ran down his skin, but he felt no urge to puncture, more a curiosity to taste. Michael had already shown them a video of him performing sexually, so there were no secrets in that regard.

Estrada motioned he wanted a drink and danced them off toward the bar. Cerise nodded, and began building his usual: a wooden tray of salt-rimmed, lime-wedged, tequila shots. He passed one to Jazz, picked up his own, and they toasted in a strangely old-fashioned ritual.

"Can I suggest something extravagant to go with your ensemble?"

Jazz nodded, wine-red lips turning down. "Black Magic," they said.

Estrada watched Cerise mix black vodka, cherry juice, syrup, and a pinch of pearl dust in her shaker with a little ice. When she poured it into the long-stemmed glass, the smoking creation resembled Jazz's sparkly dress. It was so bewitching, he waited until Jazz had sipped most of it and set it down before he *accidentally* knocked it off the bar onto the cement floor. They both jumped back as it smashed. Estrada sunk to one knee next to the black stilettos and picked up the shards of glass. In one quick movement, he caught Jazz across the ankle with a razor edge, ran his thumb through the beaded blood, and stuck it in his mouth.

Aghast, Jazz stretched up to their full height. "You cut me, you friggin maniac."

Estrada had yet to be called a maniac and was touched, but apologized profusely. Dell stepped in with a brush and dustpan and swept up the evidence of his crime while Jazz stomped off, their four-inch stiletto heels click-clacking on the cement floor.

The experiment was anti-climatic. He'd felt nothing vampiric at all. Their blood was perfectly normal, which disproved his theory of Jazz being a vampire. They could still be one of Diego's procurers, but he doubted it. Perhaps Jazz was just another human fascinated by Mandragora's flair for orchestrating orgies that could rival Nero.

After all the excitement, he needed to wash up, so headed into the dressing room. It was a shared space where he stored his costumes and props, so he used his own key. When he pushed open the door, he gasped.

Zion sat square in the center of the black leather couch like a great king, naked and sated, with a bleeding wrist resting on either knee. Michael lolled naked in the corner, the vein in his inner thigh punctured and clotted with blood. Clearly, Zion was feeding off Michael, as well as keeping him fed.

Estrada growled. "You bastard." The lining of his leather jacket was studded with stage knives that could dust this motherfucker, and it took all his restraint not to. Blosch was still missing and he wanted him back. Despite their recent interlude, Conall wouldn't fully relax until he knew Blosch was safely home. "What did you do with Leopold Blosch?"

Zion smirked. "The chef? He's sleeping."

"Where?"

"Listen, magician. We just getting started here. Join us or fuck off."

Estrada grasped the tip of his first knife and sent it flying across the room. Zion dodged, and the knife whizzed by, hit the mirror behind him and clattered to the floor.

A second met the same end.

"I thought you were 'The Legendary Estrada' but you feeble. Maybe your wrist aches, eh?"

Indeed, it did. But with the intricacy of sleights he'd practiced over the years, he'd become ambidextrous, and fire didn't need the same amount of force that a knife required.

As he willed the heat from his core down his arms and into the palms of his hands, it surged through his flesh like the fires of hell, and he broke out in a sweat. Raising his arms, he hurled the mass of flames across the room.

Zion's long dreads were the first to catch. The vampire smelled it before he saw it. Howling, he leapt from the couch and danced around, fanning the flames in his fury. Estrada could imagine the alarm sounding and the entire club burning down if he didn't do something fast.

Plucking a knife from his jacket, he rushed in, flipped it in his good fist, and thrust it into Zion's forehead. The eyes, delirious with incredulity, were the last to disappear into the pile of crumbling ash that fell to the floor. He stamped out the remaining flames.

There it was. The creature that had once turned Michael into a vampire and planned to do so again. Now, that could never happen. Unless. Unless that's what he'd interrupted. The blood had been going both ways, and naked and bedraggled, Michael was as pale and silent as the dead. He threw a blanket over him and prayed he'd stay safe until Dubh arrived.

Then, he pulled a broom and dustpan from the closet and swept up what was left of Zion. "Two hundred years, and you gone, man," he said sarcastically. And then it hit him. With Zion dusted, what would Diego do in retribution? What revenge could be harsher than what he'd already inflicted? And what if he thought Michael had killed Zion? Thoughts rushed through his mind like the virus through their blood. Nowhere was safe. Not for him. Not for Michael. Especially in this condition. He had to destroy them all, and that meant taking out Diego.

Estrada walked out of the dressing room and locked the door. He caught Dell's eye and waved him over. The room was throbbing, the bass knocking against the walls like his heart against his ribs.

"Someone sent Michael an anonymous death threat." It had happened before. Some curious wife comes to the club and gets into more than she should. The husband blames Michael. "He's in the dressing room and can't be disturbed.

No one goes in besides me and you. Understand? No Jazz. No one."

There was only one way in and one way out, and this was it.

Dell nodded. "I'll tell the boys."

"And Dell. Michael's not well. Keep him clean. No drugs. No blood. I think you know what I mean. Get food and water into him if you can. He's wasting away. I'll speak with Nigel myself. Keep him here and text me if anything happens."

"Got it."

And what of Leopold Blosch? With Zion gone, what would happen to him? If Blosch was having a long sleep, as Zion claimed, that meant the turning was complete, and when he awoke, he'd be a vampire. Now, he was in stasis. Awaiting rebirth. But, as a vampire would Blosch be safe from the others? Or would this latest fledgling, with no sire to protect him, be regarded as a threat?

43

Dubh was standing outside International Arrivals at Vancouver airport when Estrada pulled up on his Harley at six o'clock the next morning. A blue-tattooed bearded dwarf, wearing a leather kilt and black tank, with his silver hair drawn up in a high ponytail, Magus Dubh was getting more than a few sideways stares. He pulled on his weathered canvas backpack and trotted toward the bike.

"What's happenin' man?" Dubh raised his arms to embrace Estrada, who sat on the bike nose-to-nose with him. The wee man kissed him on each cheek and then gave him one on the lips, just because. They'd saved each other's lives in Scotland last summer and such gestures created lasting bonds.

"Things have escalated since we talked. Climb on. I'll fill you in at the club." The scene Estrada had interrupted last night tormented him.

With Dubh's small hands clutching his waist, he cruised to Pegasus. He'd barely slept and prayed that Dell had followed instructions. The empty club was locked up tight. Estrada let them in the back entrance, and they walked through the hall toward the dressing room; his clunky boot heels slicing the silence, Dubh shuffling in high tops. If anyone was in the club, they'd be alerted to their approach.

As he hadn't heard from Dell, Estrada expected to find Michael still crashed on the couch in the same position he'd left him. But when he unlocked the door, the room was empty. The flush of adrenalin triggered a sweat.

"*Fucking Dell.* He was supposed to text me." Estrada pulled out his phone and called, but the bouncer didn't pick up. At seven a.m. he was either in the throes of his morning entertainment or sleeping it off.

Dubh stared at the blood smears on the black leather couch. "Was Michael critical? Perhaps, he's taken him to hospital."

Estrada growled and tried to think. "He was sick but—*Fuck*, this is my fault. I shouldn't have left him here." Blood pounded in his ears. Seeing the garbage can full of Zion's ashes, he hoofed it across the room.

"What happened to him, mate?"

"I found him here with one of Diego's thugs. The fucker was feeding off him and giving him his blood." Estrada licked his dry lips. "Would that back and forth be enough to turn him?"

Dubh raised his hands and shrugged. "Not a game I play."

The ash hung in the air like a mushroom cloud. "At least, I dusted it."

Dubh raised his eyebrows and touched his mouth when he realized what was floating in the ethers. "How so?"

Estrada stretched out his hands. "I've acquired a new skill. When riled, I can refocus my anger through my core and discharge it through my hands as fire. Watch." He focused his breath and flames burst from his palms.

"Remarkable."

"Last night, after Zion's dreads caught, I put a knife through his brain." He opened his jacket to show Dubh his stash.

"Mercy. Things *have* escalated."

Estrada sighed and closed his jacket. "We need to find Michael." He walked to the door, mind spinning, then paused and stared at Dubh. "Do you think it's possible the vampires are connected telepathically?"

Dubh dropped a bottom lip in thought. "No experience with vampires but you mentioned ravens."

Estrada cocked his head. "Are ravens telepathic?"

"I believe so. Many species use telepathy as a biological survival strategy. How else can they communicate when physically separated? Think of migration, food sourcing, schools of fish who turn as one."

"If that's true, Diego would have felt it when I dusted Zion. And if he knows what that bastard's been up to here with Michael . . ." Estrada pounded the wall. "What if Diego blamed Michael for Zion's death and came for him? He's a vengeful son-of-a-bitch and his progeny mean everything to him. Damn. I have to find him."

Dubh grasped Estrada's arm. "Easy, mate. One thing at a time."

"I hear ya." Estrada took a deep breath. "First, we check Michael's flat. Then, we find these fuckers and exterminate them."

As they drove into the driveway, Estrada felt a tingling sense of déjà vu. The last time, he'd arrived here with Magus Dubh, it had been in the wee hours of the morning and they'd discovered the body of Nigel's mistress on Michael's doorstep. Fortunately, today wasn't nearly so eerie. The bright morning sun beat down on Nigel Stryker's new silver Tesla and etched his Queen Anne home in gold.

Dubh whistled as he jumped from the bike and took in the gray stone house with its gleaming white porches and turreted tower, the tall pines, immaculate gardens, and Grecian statues. "Ach, no way. Who you trying to kid?"

Estrada had to laugh. "The house and car belong to Michael's grandfather. Nigel grew up poor in London and now that he's wealthy, he appreciates the luxuries money can buy. Michael lives up there in the tower flat." He slipped his hand inside his jacket. He'd never noticed just how many corvids there were in Vancouver until now. They careened through the air and fluttered in the tall cedar hedge. He kept his eyes on them and on Dubh, as they walked along the flagstone path toward the back of the house.

When he saw Crimson parked in the lane with the roof up, he felt a sense of relief. Michael never walked anywhere if he could help it. The vintage red BMW was his treasure. So, if Crimson was here, there was a good chance he was too. Maybe he'd just come home to crash after *whatever that was* last night in the dressing room.

Dubh's lip turned up and made a clicking sound when he saw the stained-glass window set in Michael's front door. It was a gothic design of black swords and blood-red teardrops edged in gold.

Estrada shifted a low, loose brick and scooped up the key, then unlocked the heavy oak door, and shoved it wide. Despite the sunlight streaming through the stained glass, the entry hall at the bottom of the stairs felt as bleak as a crypt. Each stair creaked and groaned under their weight as they ascended.

"Mercy. I feel like I'm walking into an Ann Radcliffe novel," Dubh said.

"Not quite an Italian villa but I get the reference." Ann Radcliffe was the godmother of gothic romance novels. Michael read them occasionally.

As he stood on the landing, Estrada took a deep breath and withdrew one of his knives. Then, he turned the brass knob and nudged the door open with the toe of his boot. The dry hinges creaked and goosebumps rose on his skin. Touching a finger to his lips, Estrada signaled silence, and the two men stepped inside.

On first glance, nothing appeared out of place. Estrada scanned the living room, glanced around the kitchen, and headed straight to the bedroom. The door was ajar. With the shades drawn, the room was a gray haze. Seeing something bulge beneath the black satin quilt, he edged closer. Tips of bleached blond hair were just visible against the pillow.

Jazz.

He grasped the quilt and yanked it down. They stirred and fluttered their eyelids, then grasped the quilt to cover their pale, naked body. "What the fuck," they croaked in a raspy voice.

Estrada was not impressed. "What are you doing here? And where's Michael?"

"No idea." As they rubbed their eyes, dark shadows appeared on their fists.

"Get dressed." Estrada said, and walked out. Apparently, the only thing amiss in Michael's flat was Jazz. He walked into the kitchen, filled a glass from Michael's giant bottle, and swallowed it all. Then he refilled it. From what he'd seen last night, Jazz would be dehydrated, and he wanted them talkative.

Dubh stood at the living room window staring out into the backyard. "Are there usually so many corvids around?"

"I hadn't really noticed before but you're right. There are too many for my liking, and there's no way to tell the difference between crows, ravens, and monsters."

When Jazz wandered out wearing one of Michael's black T-shirts, Estrada handed them the glass of water. They gave him a grateful glance, gulped it down, and slunk into the bathroom. When they returned, their makeup was slightly better.

Estrada sat on the couch and leaned one arm along the back. The other, rested close to his knives. "What happened after I saw you last night?"

Shrugging, they sank into the chaise. "Too many blood clots."

Estrada glanced at Dubh. "Ecstasy."

"If I had a good feed of E, I'd be hooking up. It wouldnae matter with who." Dubh raised his eyebrows and waited.

Jazz licked their lips, which did look rather dry and chapped. "I really don't remember."

"Do you remember dancing with me last night?"

"*I'd* remember dancing with you," Dubh said cheekily.

"I bought you a drink," Estrada said. "Black magic."

"Yeah, you cut me, you maniac." Jazz looked down at their ankle, then ran a finger over the thin line. It was barely visible.

"An accident," Estrada said.

"Could their drink have been spiked?" Dubh asked.

"I know the bartender and watched her mix it. Cerise would never drug anyone. But the blood clots . . . There were several trays floating around. It was eighties goth tribute night."

"Sorry I missed that," Dubh said.

"So, you have no idea how you arrived here? Got into Michael's flat? Or into his bed?"

"I have a key." Jazz shuffled back into the bedroom and reappeared holding a small, black, sequined clutch. They unzipped it and held up a shiny gold key. Newly cut.

"I didn't realize—"

"I travel a lot, and I don't have a place in Vancouver, so Michael said I could stay here when I'm in town. He gave me a key in case he wasn't here when I arrived."

Estrada felt a profound heaviness in his chest. Cernunnos was right about changing history. The Butterfly Effect was real. In the month he'd been gone, everything had changed. Michael had made new friends and got into the blood. His personalities were so distinct, he feared the melancholy man he'd met last week had been defeated by the far more dangerous Mandragora. He might never get him back. He leaned against the chaise and stared at the bar. He wanted to crack a bottle of tequila, crawl into a cave in the bush, and stay there. But he couldn't.

The coven was meeting this afternoon to create a strategy to destroy the vampires.

Leopold Blosch, an innocent vegan chef, had been abducted and turned into a vampire.

Michael was gone, and Estrada could only assume he'd been taken by Diego as well.

And Conall . . . He had to make sure nothing happened to Conall.

If Jazz had played any part in this, they were merely a pawn, an addict who craved the highs that Mandragora could produce.

Estrada stood. "We should go. If you see Michael, tell him to call me."

Jazz cocked their head coyly and produced a thin cell phone from the clutch. "Give me your number, just in case."

"Of course." Estrada took their phone and typed his name and number in as a new contact. Then he sent a text to himself, so he had their number as well. "Be careful, Jazz. We're dealing with some very dangerous people, and you might be a person of interest to them because of your connection to Michael. If I were you, I'd leave Vancouver. It's not safe here." He turned and walked toward the door.

"I see why he loves you," Jazz said.

Estrada stopped mid-stride and swung back to look at Jazz. They'd turned away.

"Come on, mate." Dubh opened the door and followed him down the creaking stairs.

Feeling blinded by the sunlight, Estrada pulled his shades from his pannier. Then he proceeded to Nigel's front door. The worst was yet to come.

Dubh stopped in the driveway. "I can wait here while you talk to Michael's grandfather."

"Why would you do that?"

"Well, you know. Some people are bothered by my hue."

Estrada shook his head. "Nigel Stryker is the closest thing I have to a father. He's not *some* people, and *you* are not bothersome in any regard."

"Fair enough, mate."

Estrada rang the doorbell and waited.

Moments later, Nigel opened the door. He was dressed in his Sunday sportswear—a white polo shirt and shorts. Perhaps he had a tennis match.

"Sandolino. This is a pleasant surprise."

"Good morning, sir. Got a minute to talk?"

"Of course. Come in." He nodded to Dubh and offered his hand. "Hello. I'm Nigel Stryker." He'd never lost his British accent or his love of formality.

"Magus Dubh." The Wee Pict grasped Nigel's hand and shook it politely.

Estrada smiled. "Dubh is a good friend who's come from Glasgow to assist with this business I mentioned the other day."

"Ah, yes." Nigel padded down the carpeted hall, then paused at the kitchen door. "Can I offer you a drink? Juice? Coffee? Tea? I was just going to refill my mug. It's a little early for anything else, unless you haven't been to bed yet."

"Coffee sounds good," Estrada said. "Dubh?"

The wee man nodded. "I never turn down a cuppa."

"I heard wonderful things about your new act, Sandolino. Head down to my office, and I'll join you."

As Estrada entered Nigel's wood-paneled den, his gaze settled on the billiard table. The last time he'd walked into this room, he'd been carrying Michael's corpse in his arms. They'd laid him out on the green felt. Dubh had been with him that day too.

Dubh whistled softly and ran his hand along the back of the soft brown leather sofa. "Braw," he said, rolling his r.

"I gather you like it."

"Oh, aye. The man has taste."

Nigel's huge wooden desk dominated one end near the shuttered windows and beside his leather armchair stood an antique table that housed his handmade Briar pipe and imported Cherry Cavendish tobacco. The scents of leather, tobacco, coffee, and Scotch permeated the room.

Nigel arrived with a tray of drinks and biscuits. Tea for Dubh, and coffee for Estrada and himself.

Dubh nodded. "You've a lovely home, Mr. Stryker."

"Nigel, please, and thank you. But you haven't come to banter. What's the news? More problems with these . . ." His voice trailed off before he could name the vampires. Estrada wasn't sure if he truly believed or not.

"It's Michael, sir. I found him with one of them last night, one that's infatuated with him."

Nigel furled his brows.

"I'll speak plainly. Michael's been getting high on vampire blood for a while now. I've only tried it once, and it's the most powerful drug I've ever encountered. But he's addicted. Sick with it. Last night, I found him passed out in the dressing room at the club and this vampire was with him. Zion was letting Michael drink from him." Estrada swallowed. "He was also feeding off Michael."

"Good God." Nigel's tanned face blanched as he covered his mouth.

"You need to know this, sir, or I'd spare you the details."

"Go on."

"I reacted hastily and destroyed the vampire."

"Good. I hope it rots in Hell."

"I instructed Dell to keep Michael locked in the dressing room to sleep it off. But when we returned to Pegasus an hour ago, he was gone. We just checked, and he's not upstairs either. I'm concerned the vampires may have taken Michael in revenge for the one I killed."

"What do you need, Sandolino?"

"Just be on your guard, sir. Is Mrs. Stryker home?" Sunday was the only day Nigel breakfasted with his wife and he seemed to be alone.

"No, Bea's in London with family."

"Good. That extended vacation I suggested you take with Ruby? I think you should go now."

"But what about Michael? How are you going to handle this?"

"The coven's meeting this afternoon to talk strategy. Between us, I'm sure we'll find a way to . . . deal with them. The only thing is, Michael may be among them. I suspect they'll turn him just like they turned another man you know, Leopold Blosch. He owns the Ecos bistro."

"Leopold? Good God. How did *he* get involved in this?"

"Zion wanted him, so he took him. They have no morals."

"But they can be destroyed," Dubh said, "and we know how to do it."

"Yes, and once we get Michael and Leopold back, we can cure them," Estrada added.

Nigel exhaled and seemed to brighten. "I can get whatever you need, Sandolino. Vehicles. Weaponry. An army."

"I think we have it under control, sir, but I wanted you to know the truth of it."

"I appreciate that. You have my private number. Let me know when Michael's safe. If he needs a doctor or rehab, I'll take care of it."

Estrada nodded. "One other thing. Michael has a friend staying upstairs. Someone named Jazz. They have a key. I think they may be in danger too. We just spoke with them, and I suggested they leave town. Could you check before you leave yourself, sir, and make sure they got away?"

"Indeed, I will. And when you find my boy, you'll let me know right away."

"Of course."

When Nigel opened his arms and embraced Estrada, his eyes were brimming with tears. "I know you love him, Sandolino, and I know you'll bring him home."

I wish I were as sure as you are, Estrada thought. Though he was trying to remain positive, his gut told him something was horribly wrong.

45

"Are ye daft, mate? Ye left yer new love back in Ireland with yer old love?" Dubh's blue eyes twinkled. Sorcha had been sending Dylan photographs of Mara, and he was proudly showing them off. "Ach, she's just a bairn. Can't be much older than Lucy." Dylan's blush spread from his cheeks to the tips of his ears, but his grin was wide.

Faced with agenda items so heavy, Estrada was enjoying these light-hearted moments with his family. He'd forgotten what an asset Magus Dubh was to the coven. Wise. Funny. Skilled. Just having him around instilled confidence. And he was the perfect foil for Dylan.

"Ach, they get on like sisters. Sorcha's applied for a permit to dig at Sullivan Stables, and she's going to teach Mara about archaeology."

"Oooff. She'll be diggin' alright. Diggin' into all yer secrets. By the time ye meet again, yer wee bride will be well versed in how to rouse her man to a frenzied peak." With his campy schtick and rolling r's, he was sending the women into fits of giggles. Even Sylvia smiled as she rolled her eyes.

Estrada punched Dylan in the arm. "Hey, that's not a bad thing, man. You just lay back with your hands behind your head and watch her do all the work."

That was too much for the professor, who cleared her throat to rescue her friend. "Enough bathroom banter, boys. Tell us more about this dig."

"Aye. When Sorcha leads a dig, you never know what she'll unearth." Dylan seemed relieved the conversation was turning in a different direction. "Estrada. Conall. Listen up. You'll want to hear this."

Estrada was cruising the brunch buffet on the dining room table. He raised his eyebrows and popped a deviled egg into his mouth, then glanced at Conall, who was relaxing in an armchair with Lucy on his chest. Her baby fingers were curled in his hair. He'd tied it in a half-up man bun, warrior style. Dylan too, was ready for war. He'd arrived wearing his green plaid kilt. Conall gathered Lucy in his arms, stood, and sauntered closer. His proximity sent a shiver through Estrada's limbs.

"Sorcha thinks the back field at Sullivan Stables might be a raised bog covering the trout-filled lake where we met you and Ruairí." Dylan bounced from foot to foot in his navy knee socks.

Conall's eyes narrowed as he straightened. After witnessing Conall's reaction to the bog bodies on display in the National Museum, Estrada knew the bard wouldn't sanction the excavation of the bog, especially since it involved *his* past.

Daphne raised her arms to take Lucy, and he passed her over. Estrada spread grape jelly and goat cheese on a cracker and offered it to the bard as a distraction.

But Conall shook his head and waved it away. "Did you not just tell me you buried Ruairí's head there?"

Daphne blanched and moved toward the living room where Sensara was setting up for the meeting.

"Aye, but it was at Sorcha's request and she's aware. In a large area, the chances of unearthing something like that are minimal, and—"

"Something like that?" Conall let out a low, slow growl that silenced Dylan, whose cheeks burned scarlet. "Ruairí was the Sun God. His flesh should have been burned so he could fly home. I do not mourn him because he is with the Goddess but to disturb his spirit is wrong."

Sylvia raised her eyebrows with interest, and Dylan cowered.

Frankly, Estrada was surprised at Dylan's callous approach. He knew more about Celtic culture than any of them, except for Conall, and maybe Sylvia, and knew the Iron Age Celts took heads as trophies to illustrate their bravery in battle. They'd both seen them hanging from ropes in the big house. When Ana executed Ruairí, she took his head with one swipe of her sword. Estrada would never forget that moment. Dylan hadn't been there for the execution, but Conall had witnessed it.

Perhaps Dylan had forgotten that the bard had been born into a very different culture than any of them. Estrada sometimes forgot himself. The bard seemed to have adapted rapidly, but he'd only been in their world for three weeks. His beliefs and values were different from their own. More visceral. More intense. A lifetime of killing had made him that way. And yet, in moments like this, Estrada was reminded how deeply spiritual Conall was and how coldly scientific Dylan could be.

The bard's lips trembled, and he took several quick breaths. "Because you buried him, his body must remain with the Goddess. It cannot go to *that place*. One day, I will go there, break that glass, and take his body where it can be burned. Then I will plant an oak tree over his ashes."

Estrada wrapped his arms around the bard and held him. He knew Conall had been upset in the Dublin museum but didn't realize just how deeply he'd been affected by seeing Ruairí's torso on display.

A hush fell over them all, and they held the space as they might at a funeral.

Finally, Dylan twisted his watch anxiously, and sniffed. "Ach, well. If breaking into the National Museum of Ireland is our next caper, you can count me in."

"Aye, me too." Dubh said.

"And me." As Estrada released Conall, he touched his cheek. Tears glistened in the bard's eyes, but the tension was fading with the moment. "When we're done here, we'll call Sorcha and make sure she understands how you feel. I'm sure she can do her digging in a good way, so as not to disturb your ancestors or your friends."

Conall blinked slowly and everyone backed off.

Estrada rubbed his wrist. He'd removed the bandage as the swelling had lessened, but his skin was deep purple. The tension had started it aching again.

"What's wrong with your wrist?" He'd been hoping to talk to Daphne privately about an herbal poultice, but Sensara had caught him.

"Altercation with a child vampire who likes the sound of snapping bones."

"Let me see." Sensara examined his wrist, none too gently. "When did this happen?"

"A couple of days ago."

"*Jesus,* Estrada. Why didn't you see a doctor and get it set? It's a fracture. Distal radius. Looks like a clean break but your wrist needs to be stabilized with a splint."

Estrada scoffed. "No time for doctors."

"When I played rugby in Tarbert, I broke lots of bones. Never had one set." Dylan's attempt at rescue was not entirely helpful.

Daphne pursed her lips. "That must be why I've seen you limp from time to time. Could you maybe limp into the kitchen and put the kettle on?" She had Lucy slung on her hip. "We've got comfrey in the herb garden, Estrada. I'll go collect some, and you can soak your wrist while we talk."

"Thanks, Daph. I was hoping you'd doctor it." Estrada's abuela flashed through his mind again and, for a moment, he swore he could feel her presence in the room. He wondered if she could leave her body and travel in spirit. And if she could, why was she coming to him now?

"To be effective, you need to use a poultice three times a day," Daphne said, drawing him back. "I know you won't do that, so I'll give you a tin of comfrey ointment." She handed Lucy to Conall, and said, "Make sure he puts the ointment on regularly until his wrist heals."

Conall nodded.

"Doesn't Raine have a wrist brace with a splint she wears when her carpal tunnel flares up?" Sensara was not about to give up.

"She does, and I'm sure she wouldn't mind if you borrowed it, Estrada. When she comes downstairs, you can ask her yourself."

"I must agree," Sylvia said. "The brace will ease the pain and strengthen your wrist."

"You'll need both hands to fight." Sensara crossed her arms over her chest. "I can't imagine how you managed the last two days."

Painkillers, tequila, and sex, he thought. "Okay, I give." When the women teamed up, there was no point arguing. He'd use the ointment and wear the brace. And when he got an opportune moment, he'd ask Dubh for a shot of healing blood.

Sensara smiled. "Good. It's almost one o'clock. Fill your plates. Once Daphne's dealt with Estrada's wrist, we'll begin."

They helped themselves and found places to sit. Although it was a beautiful day outside, they'd set up a circle in the living room, so they couldn't be overheard by eavesdropping ravens. Conall relaxed in the rocking chair with Lucy and within minutes, she was asleep in the bard's arms. When he kissed her on the cheek, Estrada's heart thumped hard in his chest.

"Let me put her down, so you can get something to eat." Sensara leaned down to take her child. Then Estrada heard her whisper, "But you can have her back later," and a warm sensation spread from his chest to his cheeks.

By the time they'd finished eating and clearing up, Daphne had done her magic. She appeared beside him with a steaming bowl of steeped comfrey leaves and set it on the side table. "Let's slip your hand and wrist right into the tea. Make sure it's completely covered." She ruffled his hair. "Just don't get excited and knock it over. I know how you gesticulate." She dropped a towel in his lap. "Here. Just in case."

Estrada grinned. "I'll try to contain myself. Thanks, Daph."

"Raine just texted to say she's running late, so we should start without her." Sensara had honeyed candles burning in the cardinal directions. Now she lit a sage wand and fanned it with an eagle feather. The pungent smoke spread throughout the room, cleansing the energy. She moved around the circle, offering the smudge to each of them. When she returned to her chair in front of the French doors, she left it burning in a large conch shell on their makeshift altar. The smoking leaves both comforted and energized him.

"The purpose of our meeting today is to discuss a strategy for dealing with this latest threat. Estrada and Dylan, you seem to know the most about the vampires, having been to their . . ."

"Nest," Estrada said. "Diego calls it Le Château des Vampires but it's a nest."

"Can you tell us what you know?"

Estrada closed his eyes to gather his words, and, in that moment, he saw Diego's face as clearly as if the vampire stood before him.

"When Conall, Sorcha, and I returned from Iron Age Ireland, and I realized we were a sabbat ahead of Lucy's abduction, I thought I could make everything right. I thought it would be simple. I had time and foreknowledge. I could right all the wrongs these bastards had done in those days after Lughnasadh." He took a quick breath. "I thought if I knew everything, I could change everything. But I was wrong." He moved, and the water splashed in the bowl beside him. He glanced at Daphne. "Sorry."

She shook her head gently. "Go on, Estrada."

"Cernunnos told us something before we left. Do you remember, Dylan? He said there were rules."

"Aye. 'You can't change history.'"

"I said, *fuck that*. What does it matter if we change history *un poco*." Estrada showed a tiny space between his thumb and finger. "Dylan did too, didn't you?" Dylan pursed his lips and nodded. "But I've come to realize that Cernunnos was right. One thing can change everything. So, that's where I must begin.

"Everything is different than I expected it to be. The vampires are everywhere. Watching us. And they've shown themselves. Eliseo was in my back alley, and Zion walked boldly around Pegasus. Last Friday night, two vampires I've never seen before attacked Conall and Leopold as they were walking home from Pegasus. One of them bit me." He pushed back his hair to show the wound.

Daphne gasped.

"Bastards." Sensara's eyes flashed.

"We destroyed them but within an hour, Zion and Eliseo broke into Leopold's bistro and abducted him. That's when this happened." He pointed to his wrist. "Leopold is innocent, and I can only assume Zion turned him into a vampire."

Conall growled and everyone shivered.

Estrada went on. "Last night, I went to Pegasus to check on Michael and found Zion, not only feeding Michael his blood to get him high, but drinking from him as well. Diego bit Michael last summer, and he's already infected with the virus, so it won't take much to fully turn him. It may have already happened." He raised his hand. "I regret it now but seeing that, I reacted and destroyed Zion."

"Why regret?" Sensara was listening intently to every word.

"Because I don't know what Diego will do in retribution. He's vengeful. This whole thing started because he blamed Michael for the death of one of his agents."

"How did you destroy Zion?" Sensara asked.

"Fire." Estrada closed his eyes, inhaled, and sent flames racing down his arm and out through the fingertips of his free hand to demonstrate.

"How did you do that?" Dylan grinned excitedly. "Another gift from Cernunnos?"

"Perhaps. I also shoved a knife through the bastard's forehead. Fire burns them but a knife through the brain dusts them. And I mean that literally. They turn to dust just like in the movies. At least, the old ones do."

"Take their heads." Conall's jaw was set, his stare intense.

"Yes. Conall saved my life and Leopold's when we were attacked in the alley . . . in that way." He ignored their soft gasps and followed the bard's gaze to the samurai sword framed on the wall. Estrada had seen it before but never asked about it. He gestured to the sword. "Is that real?"

Sensara nodded once. "That katana was forged in the 1700s during the Shinto period. My grandfather gave it to me. My ancestors were samurai."

Estrada felt a flush of adrenaline. "What a perfect weapon to behead a centuries-old vampire. Especially when wielded by a warrior who's an expert swordsman."

Sensara stood and plucked it off the wall. "Conall?"

The bard took the sword from her hands, hefted it, then swept it through the air, the quick swish-swish cutting the silence. Then he carefully put it back on the stand and bowed. "Thank you, Lady. I accept. I will use it honorably in the name of your ancestors."

Sensara smiled. "Any other weaponry?"

"Ach, Dubh. When we fought them before, you carved and enchanted a wooden staff," Dylan said. "It was pure dead brilliant. When Zion broke it in half, I tossed my bit down a fissure and blew up the island."

Dubh puffed up his chest. "I'll get right on that."

"Alright, we have weaponry. Where will this battle take place?"

"We get a boat," Estrada said. "Dylan and Dubh can pilot it to Diego's island in the Broughton Archipelago. We go in quiet and hit them before they know we're there."

Dylan shook his head emphatically. "No, man. Even if they weren't watching us, we were at a disadvantage fighting them on their own island. And out in the boat..." He shivered. "When those ravens attacked it was—"

"Hitchcock," Estrada chewed his lip. "I remember."

"If they're watching us, how will we ever surprise them?" Sylvia shuddered, and they all glanced out the French doors into the backyard.

Estrada turned to Conall. "You told me that the trees heard the ravens talking about abducting Leo. They warned you, and that's why you left last week. Could it work the other way? Could the trees talk so the ravens overhear?"

"Ambush." Dubh winked one bright blue eye.

Estrada raised his free hand. "What do you think, Conall?"

The bard sat quietly considering. Finally, he shrugged his shoulders. "I will ask."

Raine hustled in and sat down next to Daphne, as Sylvia suddenly stood. "Where then? Say we *can* pick our battlefield, where's the best place to make a stand?"

Estrada pulled his hand out of the leafy bowl and wrapped it in the towel. "Somewhere out in the forest. We lure them to a glade—" Daphne shook her head. "Not if you're going to blast them with flames. We can't chance starting a forest fire in this dry heat."

"Where then? On land? On water?" Sylvia was pacing.

"Mountain top," Dylan said. "Fewer trees. Fewer civilians."

"Easy for them. They can fly. But what about us? Are we all going to climb a mountain carrying our weapons? They'll pick us off one by one. No, it must be somewhere close. Somewhere we would choose for a ceremony, so they don't suspect."

Sensara brightened. "What about the beach? We can walk there in our robes. Carry our weapons in packs and pretend we're going for a ritual."

"That's brilliant. Sand beach, lake on one side, trees far enough away not to catch fire when we shoot." Dylan gave the thumbs up sign.

"What about bystanders?" Raine said. "It's hot now, and everyone's going to the beach. The park's open from eight till eight, and the car park's full by noon."

"If the sun rises before six and the gates don't open until eight, we have two hours at dawn. Can we dispatch these fuckers in two hours?" Estrada felt his heartbeat quicken.

"When?" Sylvia asked.

Sensara stood and joined her. "Tonight's a full moon."

"Tonight?" Could they be ready by tonight? Estrada's guts quaked. What if the vampires didn't come? What if they did come, and the coven wasn't prepared enough to destroy them all? Worse still. "What if Diego's not with them? The last time he sent Zion and Eliseo. He might still be on the island."

"You just dusted Zion. If that doesnae bring this fucker out of hiding, nothing will." Dubh bowed to Sensara and Sylvia who stood together backlit by the French doors. "Excuse my language."

"Conall, could you talk to the trees and find out if the ravens are out there right now?" Sylvia asked.

"Of course, Lady."

"As much as I like your idea of interspecies communication, if the ravens are spying on us, all we need to do is go outside and talk about the full moon ritual we're planning for tonight." Sensara glanced around the circle at each of them.

"What about Lucy?" Estrada stared at his daughter sleeping peacefully in her cot.

"Everyone I trust with my daughter is here in this room."

Daphne brightened. "I trust my mom, and Lucy loves visiting her auntie. Raine and I can smuggle her out later tonight."

The room grew hushed as they all considered what they were about to do.

"What if Leo's there?"

When Estrada grasped Conall's hand, he felt the bard's sweat. "When Leo was a vampire, he hated it, and he hated them. If Leo's there, he'll fight with us."

Conall swallowed. "And what if Michael is there?"

46

Later that night, Estrada was between Conall's knees on the upstairs deck when his phone rang. The bard's arms hung loosely around his shoulders, his chin in the crook of his neck. Between the full moon, the comfort of Conall's warm chest against his back, the dose of fey blood Dubh had given him to heal his wrist, and the bottle of Merlot they'd shared, he was inclined not to answer. But caught by habit, he glanced at the screen. *Sorcha.*

"You're up early, Ms. O'Hallorhan. Everything all right?"

"If it was, would I be ringing you at six in the feckin morning?"

"What's up?"

"Is Dylan there with you?"

"Nope. Just Conall." Estrada turned to glance at the bard and felt his soft beard brush his face. It was growing again. Perfectly. His eyes were closed, his breath hushed. He was meditating in some other world. "He says, hey."

"I miss you, Conall. I miss yous both. I wish yous were here."

Estrada heard a tremor in her voice. "Talk to me, Sorcha."

"It's Mara. She just woke up screaming from another nightmare. I've known for days she wasn't sleeping well, and tonight, she finally confessed about these dreams that are plaguing her."

"Dreams?"

"If I didn't know better, I'd say she was possessed."

"By what?"

"Ana."

"Ana?"

"Aye. She's seeing things that only Ana could see. It's as if she's looking through the bitch's eyes."

"Oh, fuck." Had Ana's spirit somehow claimed Mara's body? The girl was nowhere near them when Conall took her head.

"She saw you sitting in a hut across from the bitch."

"Hmmm."

"And she saw you having sex with her in the garden."

"*Jesus.* She saw that?"

"Aye, and likely felt it too. You know how dreams are. Tonight, she watched Criofan die. Ana didn't just poison the old man, she stayed to watch."

"What the hell?"

"Mara told me you gave Manus a gold bangle. Did it belong to Ana?"

"Yeah. I thought the blacksmith could use the gold."

"Aye, he used it alright. Melted it, and forged a gold wedding band for Mara."

Estrada nodded his head. "Can you use psychometry to—?"

"Already did. When I held that ring in my hand, I saw a handful of mushrooms, and then a woman and child. Adamair's first family? They were alive, and then . . ."

"God. She was a serial killer."

"And you slept with her."

Estrada snorted softly. "She wasn't the first. I imagine you've taken it off her."

"Aye, and she's sleeping like a baby. But what do I do with it now? It's the girl's wedding band *and* her father forged it. It's all she's got left of him, poor thing. If that's not sentimental feckin value, nothing is."

Estrada thought for a moment. "Smudge it with sage and stash it somewhere safe. Can you get white sage there? Is there a metaphysical store?"

"I plan to take Mara to Dublin. I'm sure I can find white sage there. So, I just burn it and hold the ring in the smoke?"

"And ask the spirits to cleanse it."

"I'm not really one for talking to the spirits but I'll do what I can for Mara's sake."

Estrada lowered his voice. "Dylan told us you think Sullivan Stables might be sitting over your trout lake and you're planning to dig it up."

"Estrada, it's a field of yellow flowers just like in Ruairí's vision. How can I not dig?"

"I understand your connection to Ruairí and the power of his vision, but keep in mind that Conall has a strong connection to Ruairí too. We're talking cultural differences here. Conall believes that as the Sun King, Ruairí's body should have been ritually burned."

"I know how strongly Conall believes."

"If you find anything, promise me it won't end up in the museum. Conall's already threatening to break in and steal Ruairí's torso from that glass case."

"Is he really?"

"He is. He wants Ruairí properly laid to rest, so if you find . . ." He lowered his voice to barely a whisper. "If you find his head or any other parts, keep them somewhere safe until Conall has a chance to do his thing. Alright?"

"Aye. Mara's of a similar mind."

"Listen. I love you woman. I don't think I've told you that enough."

"Indeed, you haven't. I love you too. And please give Conall a kiss for me."

"You bet. I'll talk to you soon."

As he closed the call, Conall whispered in his ear. "I'll take that kiss now."

Estrada turned and wrapped an arm around the bard's neck. "Did you hear all that?"

"I was resting. I'm not dead."

Estrada caught Conall's mouth with his. When their lips parted, he whistled. "Phew. Sorcha kisses like fire."

Conall's hand strayed and popped the dome on Estrada's jeans.

"Mercy, man. You wanna make love with the ravens watching us from the trees?"

"Let them watch. I want you. I'll always want you. And I'll destroy anyone or anything who tries to take you from me."

When Conall's fingers found their mark, Estrada gasped. "No regrets."

47

W hen Estrada awoke, his arms were still wrapped around the bard. He felt Conall's naked heat beneath the blanket and stirred, wanting more. Brushing his lips against the bard's, he felt him awaken.

"Is it time?" Conall said.

"Soon."

The full dappled face of the silvery moon stared down from a black velvet sky studded with stars. But a thin pink line in the east warned of the coming dawn.

"We always attacked at first light when the Sun God rose to stand beside us."

"What if they don't come?" Estrada said. This thought had been dogging him. Was it a premonition or just anxiety?

"Then we live another day and await another dawn."

"I'm glad you're here with me," Estrada said.

Conall's mouth pressed close to his ear as if he were about to whisper a secret. "Each of these stars is a tiny, yet powerful, Sun God. When I was young, we went raiding and slept out in the fields. At night, I would stare up at the gods and pray for them to send me someone I could love who would love me as I am. When you appeared with wings etched on your back, I knew they had sent you at last. Human or de Danann, it made no difference. You are my gift from the gods. I will honor and cherish you in this life, and for all our lives to come."

Estrada's throat tightened, and he bit his lip to stop the tears. He stared into the bard's deep brown eyes. So many times, he'd thought he was in love. But now, he was beginning to understand what love really meant.

They both flinched at the knock on the door. Then they heard Dubh's voice. "It's time, lads."

Downstairs, everyone was packed and eager to get on with it. The energy was turbulent, ranging between dread and giddiness. They walked through the trails, silently, wearing their weapons concealed beneath their robes. Sensara had given Conall a dark green robe that shimmered like cedar in the moonlight. Dubh wore a white Druid's robe, he'd brought from Scotland. While the others wore their usual colors: Sensara in white, Estrada in black, Dylan in cobalt blue like the western waters, Daphne as gold as the sun, Raine in deep red, and Sylvia in burgundy.

The silvery moon hovered between the dark mountains and streaked down the rippling glacial lake. They set up on the beach by staking out the eight cardinal points. Then, Sensara walked the perimeter, pointing her long quartz wand and chanting:

"I conjure this circle as sacred space
I conjure containment within this place
Thrice do I conjure the Sacred Divine.
Powerful goodness and mystery mine.
From the East to the West
From the South to the North.
I cast this circle and call Magic forth."

She took her place in the North and said, "Our circle is cast. We are between the worlds."

Each of them called on the gods and goddesses of their elemental direction and took an offering into the center of the circle where a small fire blazed banked by round gray stones.

Estrada cast a handful of cedar and sage into the fire and called on Cernunnos to watch over them. Conall called on the spirits of the trees and offered the small horn of holy water he'd brought from Brigid's Well in Ireland. Dubh called on Cerridwen and dropped a handful of ripe salmonberries onto the sand beside the fire.

When all had given their offerings, they joined hands and began the dance. Estrada watched the earth but also the skies, alert for ravens, and the thunderbird that was Diego. As their pace increased, sand flew up, and the energy quickened. Conall was chanting ancient Irish triads, spinning his own enchantments.

Then, just as the sun rose over the edge of the water, Estrada saw a man walk out of the forest.

Michael.

48

Estrada gaped, aware of nothing but Michael. His black silk cape floated from his shoulders like wings and beneath it, his pale, pearly body shone luminescent. Was it a trick of the moon or had he been transformed? His blond hair hung to his elbows in satiny strands, and as he drew closer, Estrada saw that his youth had been restored. Michael was as magnificent as that first night they'd danced.

He's Vampire and he's spectacular. A sudden testosterone spike caught Estrada off guard that his robe couldn't hide.

Michael noticed, and leaning forward, ran a soft pink tongue over his lips. "Miss me, compadre?"

Estrada struggled to remain rooted in the sand, heart fluttering, fingers trembling. *This creature is not Michael,* he reminded himself. *The Michael I love is dead.* Still, the visceral memory of that first night drove his lust and he realized a truth: *I fell for Mandragora that night. There is no separating them.* He squeezed his fists. *I love him in all his madness but I cannot follow him to the dark side. I will not. They'll kill us all if I give in to this.*

Biting his lip, he tasted faerie blood. *But I still might resurrect him if—*

"Do not break the circle." Sensara's command jerked him back.

"Oh, please, empress. You can't hurt me with your *woo woo*."

"What do you want, Mandragora?" Estrada asked.

"Only to talk to you . . . alone."

Estrada caught the slight shake of Sensara's head. He must not break the circle. Whatever power they'd created was contained within it.

"I've never seen one of your woodsy rituals. It's quite impressive. But I thought you danced naked? That would be more stimulating, no?"

"What do you want?" Estrada repeated.

"You, compadre. I want you."

Estrada blinked slowly. The wanting was mutual.

"And I have a onetime offer."

"Make it."

"Can't we talk alone? I've really missed you."

Estrada stood in the southwest quadrant, facing the water, with Sylvia on his left and Dylan on his right. He pointed to the space in front of him on the inside the circle. "Come here then."

Mandragora seemed to float inches off the ground as he moved behind Estrada and crossed into the circle where he hovered, his exquisite face only an arm's length away. Estrada's fingers quivered, itching to brush the sharp blades of his pale cheek. Michael's ivory skin flushed. His green eyes glittered like emeralds, the whites as clear as pearl. Every wrinkle vanished, every muscle hard, every breath a blast of blistering copper. Michael's body was bloated with blood.

Who had he murdered to reclaim his youth?

The thought turned Estrada's stomach, and crossing his arms over his gut, he sucked in a breath to contain his revulsion. This monster was all glam, a mere facsimile of the man he'd once loved.

But is Michael still there, still trapped inside?

"Michael? Are you there? I can save you from this."

The creature leaned in and brushed his cool porcelain cheek against Estrada's. "I don't want to be saved," he whispered. "And I don't want to lose you." His lips brushed the edge of Estrada's ear, sending another rush of lust through his trembling limbs. "Listen carefully, compadre."

Estrada held his breath.

"In return for Zion, Diego wants you."

"No."

"Look at me. I will never grow old or die." He sliced his finger with a razor canine and pressed the beaded blood to Estrada's lips.

Estrada shivered with the rush and swayed on his feet.

"Estrada." He heard his name being called around the circle, a cacophony of voices. "Estrada, stay with us."

Opening his eyes, he glanced from side to side, seeing their terrified faces.

He spit, and jerked back. "No, man. No. I won't. I can't."

"Compadre, we can be young forever. We can have it all."

But Estrada had heard this ploy before and he knew that Vampire was no romance. At Diego's lair, he'd watched Michael kill a man with his nails and teeth while the vampires cheered.

"Is Diego here? Why doesn't he come himself? Is he afraid?"

The manic laugh was clearly Mandragora's. "Oh compadre. Our father is afraid of no one and nothing. Least of all your pack of witches."

Estrada surveyed the coven. The bard was edging forward, gripping the samurai sword he wore belted beneath his robe. Seeing Conall's frantic face reminded him of Blosch. "And Leopold Blosch. Where is he?"

Mandragora made tsking sounds with his tongue. "Come with me and I'll show you. We can all play together."

"There is nothing you can say to make me—"

"Are you sure?" Stepping closer, he grasped Estrada's cheeks in his hands and his flesh burned cold. "You were the best of them. The choicest of lovers. I'd hoped . . ." He dropped his head, voice drifting, and when he raised it again and took a deep breath there were tears in his eyes. One fell. Estrada reached out to touch it, but it turned bloody on his thumb.

"Michael . . ."

Michael turned sharply and stared at Conall. "Very well, compadre. Father also has a craving for Irish treacle here. So, choose. It's you or treacle as recompense for Zion."

The change was so abrupt it caught Estrada off guard. "Or what?"

"Come now, you know the answer to that." As Mandragora spoke, Estrada saw the others lift their gaze to the forest at the edge of the beach, and he knew the vampires had shown themselves. He could feel the darkness deepen behind him opening like a great maw.

When Michael caught his chin with his iron grip and stared into his eyes, a sudden paralysis gripped Estrada's body. Cocking his head, the vampire raised his lip to expose his fangs, then leaned toward the pulsing artery.

The swift woosh of the samurai sword caressed the stubble on Estrada's chin. A rush of chill fluid smacked his face. And the spell broke. Exhaling, he wiped his mouth with the back of his fist.

Michael's eyes deepened in disbelief, and then his head tipped and hit the sand with a dull thunk.

Conall turned to face the woods, raised the bloody sword, and screamed a battle cry.

Estrada turned away from Michael's bloody body. Couldn't feel this loss. Not now. Not when there were so many more to lose.

This was war.

He ripped off his robe to free his arms and opened his leather jacket. The first knife felt hot and he saw flames at the edges of his fingertips. Throwing back his head, Estrada howled. And from somewhere in the black forest came the eerie yips and yowls of a coyote pack echoing his grief.

He turned to face the black woods but the vampires had gone, slipped away leaving Michael headless and bleeding at his feet. His legs gave out then and he fell on his ass.

Conall collapsed beside him. In the aftermath of murder, his trembling hand dropped the bloody sword. They reached for each other and clung.

"I'm sorry. I could not let the Leannán Sidhe have you. I had to stop him."

Estrada glanced into the somber face of a warrior who hated killing. He touched his fingers to the bard's mouth and hushed him. In this moment, words meant nothing.

Sensara was talking. She'd herded the others into the center of the circle, and they huddled around the fire. Fragments filtered through.

"Bury him in the woods . . . shovels and pails."

When he turned, Estrada saw the naked body, half on its side, half on its back, legs askew. Michael's head had rolled and, thank the gods, his face was turned away. The blade had chopped right through his beautiful hair and several inches lay like golden strands across the sand.

Michael was gone, and this time there was no bringing him back. Not even Time could change his destiny. They'd never dance again.

Grasping Michael's black cape, Estrada held it to his face and breathed in the musky scent still embedded in the cloth.

How many nights had Michael swaggered through the club wearing this cape? It was the essence of all he was. And then Estrada envisioned their first night together in the dressing room. Him, lying on his back, wrists bound. Michael naked, on top of him, covering them both with this cape like a giant raven, as he revealed the pleasures a man's body could give for the very first time.

Estrada sighed. Even then, Michael's fate was sealed.

Sensara was walking widdershins around the outside of the circle, closing it. Then Daphne and Raine ran across the beach toward the woods.

"Where are you going?" he yelled.

"Back to the house," Daphne said.

"For shovels and pails," Raine added.

Sensara came then and stood before him. She held out her hand, and he grasped it and let her help him up. When she threw both arms around him, he broke, and sobbed into her shoulder.

"The vampires vanished. They won't come back tonight," she said.

"How do you know?" He wiped the tears and snot from his face with the palms of his hands. There was blood. Michael's tears. Michael's blood.

"If they meant to attack us, don't you think they would have? This was personal."

"Me or Conall, he said. Diego wants either me or Conall."

"He'll have neither." Sensara's authority awed him. Despite all, the high priestess was still in control of her coven and her ritual. "Go clean up in the lake while we take care of this."

This. He suddenly realized what Sensara planned to do.

"I have to take Michael home to his grandfather."

"Not now. It's too risky. We could get caught. We'll bury him in the woods and mark it. Later, if you must, we'll help you get him where he needs to go."

Estrada glanced at the pool of blood that marred the sandy beach. Within hours, kids would be playing here, people sunbathing and picnicking. Sensara was right. They'd never be able to physically move Michael's remains all the way up the hill, through the woods, and into the house without being seen. The gates opened in an hour, and they'd leave a blood trail. They'd get caught, and Conall could be charged with murder.

"We'll take care of everything," she said, reading his mind. "There'll be no evidence on this beach when we're done."

Dubh was suddenly standing beside her. "Come on, lads. Let's get you sorted."

They followed him to the shoreline where Estrada and Conall stripped off and waded into the glacial lake. Estrada washed his hands and splashed water on his face and shoulders. When he wiped his lips, a remnant of Michael's blood caught on his tongue, and he felt another rush of Vampire that left him vibrating.

Conall's sudden dive brought him back. Estrada held his breath, counted the seconds, waiting for him to rise. There was no sign, not even a ripple. Then, the bard's head popped up a hundred yards distant.

Dubh tapped Estrada's thigh and pointed up. Ravens were circling.

Estrada felt a surge of adrenalin amplified by the vampire blood. "Conall, come back!" The bard was too far off, treading water. Naked. Defenseless.

A shadow crossed the clouds and thunder clapped.

"*Motherfucker.* Now he shows up?"

He searched for Conall, but the bard had disappeared beneath the surface of the moss green lake.

Diego cruised the dusky sky, his leathered pterosaur wings catching and holding the thermals, his thick, hooked beak slightly open to reveal a scarlet tongue.

Estrada's hand flew to his forehead as a memory surged. The slash and burn of razored talons in the Underworld. As he ran to retrieve his knives, he willed fire into his palms.

Dubh darted through the sand and grabbed the samurai sword.

Estrada saw bubbles, and then Conall burst from the lake a few yards distant, water streaming from his head and shoulders.

"Catch," Dubh yelled, tossing the sword.

Conall lunged left and caught it, then swept it through the air.

More ravens were circling now, flashing their indigo wings, and diving close to harass the others who huddled backs to the fire, holding flaming sticks they'd borrowed from the blaze.

As the creature bore down, Estrada put all his force into one massive fireball and flung it. It caught the inky tail and the stench of burning flesh filled his senses. The pterosaur screamed and dove into the lake, then emerged in a fountain of spray only inches from Conall. The bard swung the sword and caught the edge of a leathery wing. Then it was hit with another burst of fire. Estrada turned to see Dubh holding his enchanted staff. Swinging it like a Gatling gun, the wee man shot flames at the ravens.

"Hah. You will not win," Estrada screamed, testosterone fueling his bravado.

The creature landed on the beach, lifted its wings, and transformed into its manly form. Standing naked and small, burned and bleeding, Diego looked oddly pathetic. Then his lips curled into a snarl. "I will have you both," he said, with his thick Spanish accent. "If you come with me now, consider it ended. If you do not, I will take one more for each day that passes."

Estrada had heard that threat before. He glanced at the bard, who waded forward through the water shaking his head.

"Fuck off, Diego. I'd like to see you try."

The vampire cackled and spun sand as it shifted back into its avian form. It pushed down with muscular legs and sprung, then flapped its wings and rent the air with an unearthly scream.

"*What the fuck.*" Estrada crashed into the shallow water at the edge of the beach.

Conall hunkered down beside him and wrapped his arm around his shoulders. "We are entwined, friend, and neither of us are destined to live in thrall to this creature, nor die at its hand. Though I do not know about the others."

"We're no farther ahead than when we started this fucking escapade." Estrada stared down at his hands.

"You're wrong, mate." Dubh sank down in front of them on the sand. "We know Diego's here, for one, and we didnae know that when we arrived. We know who he wants and why. And we know he's willing to bargain, which means he's not confident he can take us all on, and win. That's why he sent Michael in alone and didnae come himself until the circle was broken and you two were separated from the group. We also know those cuts and burns hurt him. That scream was one of frustration and pain. He's nae invincible."

"Dubh's right." Sensara was suddenly beside them. "This was a positive first encounter. If we use our knowledge, we'll plan better next time. From now on, we do nothing without thinking, and we do nothing *alone.*" Sensara turned. "Daphne and Raine are coming with the tools. Estrada? What do you want to do?"

"Bury him," he said, and got to his feet. He stood for a moment staring at the mountain, then sent its energy from his crown, down into the ground, to strengthen his wobbly legs. He took Michael's black cape in his hands and placed it with his own. Then he picked up his pale naked body. Glancing at Michael's head, his eyes filled with tears and he turned away.

"I will do it," Conall said, and plucked up Michael's head with both hands.

Estrada took a shuddering breath. "No. Put it here." He gestured with his chin to the dip in Michael's chest. "I'm sorry, amigo. I tried to save you."

Estrada staggered under the weight of Michael's corpse. Now that the adrenalin was subsiding, his strength waned. He followed Sensara's footprints across the beach and into the trees. Sitting with his back to a thick nurse log, he held Michael in his arms as Daphne and Dylan dug the grave.

Conall jumped down into the hole. "Hand him to me, then come down yourself."

Estrada couldn't look at the bard as he passed him Michael's body, but he appreciated the gesture. With his hands free, Estrada lowered himself into the grave, took Michael back, and laid him down with care.

"We'll hide him, but use plants and rocks so it'll be easier for us to move him later," Daphne said.

When Conall began to chant in his ancient language, something in the tones and syllables cracked Estrada's heart wide, and he fell sobbing on top of Michael. Conall continued to sing, moving from deep low tones to ever higher arcs that picked Estrada up and filled and strengthened him. Then the bard offered his hand to help him climb from the grave.

"What did that song mean?" Estrada asked when his feet touched the ground.

"I prayed for him to find peace until his return, and that you find the strength to walk on."

Estrada threw his arm around Conall and they walked back down the beach together to where the two black garments lay together: Michael's silk cape and Estrada's ritual robe.

"You're keeping it," Conall said.

As Estrada plucked it up he inhaled Michael's scent.

"If you could have kept something of Ruairí—"

"I understand," Conall said, shaking his head. "And I am sorry."

"You didn't kill him. *They* killed him. And I'm going to destroy every last one of those fuckers, if it's the last thing I do."

49

It was almost noon by the time Estrada had showered and changed. He found Daphne in the kitchen making another pot of tea.

"How are you, handsome?" she asked.

"I'd really like to talk to my daughter. I need to know she's alright. I don't trust these fuckers."

Daphne pulled out her cell phone. "She's at my parent's cabin and nobody knows they're there. They'll keep her safe." She made a video call, spoke to her mom for a second and handed him the phone.

"Lucita, it's Da Da." She was sitting in a sandbox with a pail of mud and a silver spoon in her hand. There were mud streaks across her cheeks. "Hey, you're not eating that mud, are you."

She giggled. "Ah."

"I'm gonna see you really soon. Te amo, Lucita."

It was a quick call but his heart was full when he gave the phone back to Daphne. "Thank you. I needed that."

"Anytime."

"Where are the others?"

"Resting," she said. "You should too."

He nodded, then strayed out onto the upper deck, confident that they'd seen the last of Diego for today. After staying up all night and the rush of battle, his eyelids sagged. The foam mattress was set up in the shade and covered with a clean sheet. He laid down on his back and covered his eyes with his arms. He had no more tears.

It was Michael's destiny to die a vampire. Twice Estrada had tried to change it, and twice he'd failed. Sometimes a man's destiny could not be changed. Turning to the wall, he let sleep overtake him.

When he awoke, Conall was curled up behind him. He could feel the naked heat of the bard's firm body against his own, his moist breath against his neck. Conall had washed his hair with Daphne's herbal shampoo and some of the damp, scented locks fell across Estrada's shoulder. For a long while, he lay savoring the bard's embrace. Then desire overcame him, and he turned.

Conall's eyelids opened, and he stared so far into Estrada's eyes, he could feel the bard's soul tickling his own.

"Forgive me," he breathed, and Estrada answered with a deep luscious kiss.

"I want you," Estrada said.

"And I want you."

They took each other in a fury, so hard and fast and intense that, in the end Estrada felt he was nothing but a sack of skin, his spirit caught by a thread. He opened his eyes to touch Conall's cheek and spied a shadowy figure in the periphery.

Diego stood on the railing of the deck, watching. Smirking, he raised a finger. "And that is why I will have you both."

Scrambling, they jumped up.

Estrada lunged, fingers surging fire, with Conall at his heels. Diego's fist struck quick like an adder's tongue, catching Estrada by the throat, and yanking him over the railing. In mid-air, the vampire shifted into the pterosaur as Estrada fought for breath.

He saw Conall jump after them, grasp a wing with one hand and slash with his sword at the creature's head. And then Estrada was falling. Pain shattered his senses and he knew no more.

50

DUBLIN

Sunshine beamed through the kitchen window as Sorcha put the kettle on for tea. She'd spent the night alone and woke with a calm tummy for once. She hoped it was a sign her morning sickness had passed.

Mara bounced into the kitchen, bright-eyed and singing, then stood clapping her hands together like a child.

"I gather you slept well last night, Mrs. McBride?" They'd stashed the girl's wedding ring in a box on the fireplace mantle where it could do her no more harm.

"I did, and I can't wait to go to the city. I love all the shops and different people."

"Aye. Me too." Sorcha had told her just before they went to bed that they'd be taking the train to Dublin in the morning. Like most country kids, the city was an adventure. But for a kid raised two hundred years before the birth of Christ, a modern city was like navigating another planet.

Franya stuck her head in the door. "I'm off."

"Oh, hey. Mara and I are taking the train to Dublin. Could you drop us at the station?"

"Sorry, Foxy. Running late." She blew Sorcha a kiss. "Ask Declan." And then she was gone.

This was the Franya she'd known at uni. Vivacious and lightning quick. Up for anything, but oblivious to anyone else's thoughts or feelings. Sorcha had been party to her schemes then—apart from the one that involved sex with Vivian—and was charmed by her mystique. But now? Though Franya still slipped between her sheets when she was in the mood, the rest of the woman's life was entirely her own.

Sorcha wasn't sure how she felt about that. Things were complicated. She was living in the woman's house and about to dig in her field, so Franya had all the power. And the sex, when they had it, was explosive. They weren't in a relationship—it was more of a situation—and she was aware there were terms for it. Roommates hooking up. Friends that fuck. Except they weren't really friends. Still, things were so entangled she couldn't imagine extricating herself. She'd have to take Mara and leave everything behind, including her field of yellow flowers which was her only tangible connection to Ruairí.

"Are you alright, Sorcha?"

Mara was staring, the kettle whistling, and Sorcha still standing, clutching the counter.

She shook her head to bring herself back to the moment. "Aye, I'm fine, love. Let's drink our tea, and head out. We can eat brunch downtown."

Mara's nonstop chatter provided Sorcha with an escape from thoughts of Franya and her secret world. It was a delicious day, so they opted to walk for a while along the River Liffey from Heuston Station. Mara was thrilled with the cobblestone streets, colorful shops, and blaring trad music as they strolled through Temple Bar. By the time they hit Grafton Street, she couldn't contain her smile. Maneuvering through hordes of summer tourists from all over the world, they passed outdoor cafés, buskers, and trendy shops. Not that Mara knew anything about trends. Still, they wandered in and out of shops and Sorcha bought her a new jean jacket, a couple of pairs of skinny jeans, and a hot pink T-shirt. Then they hit a lingerie shop. Sorcha thought it was time the girl learned some seductive tricks. Mara grimaced at the thongs but delighted in the lacy brassieres and sheer nightgowns. By the time they entered the metaphysical store near St. Stephen's Green to buy white sage, they'd slowed down considerably, were loaded down with bags, and dallied in the incense, semi-precious jewelry, and gemstones. Finally, they picked up Asian street food, and sat on the grass on St. Stephens Green to eat.

"This has been the best day of my life, Sorcha. Thank you so much."

"You're welcome, love. But please don't tell Dylan that I'm your best day. He'll be crushed."

"Oh, you know what I mean. I hope we can live here in the city." Mara was a natural with chopsticks. "What's this called again?"

"Pad Thai."

"It's so good. I could eat it every day."

Sorcha giggled. By the time Dylan returned, Mara would be a new woman. She laid back on the grass and stared up at the wispy cirrus clouds. If she closed her eyes long enough, she could fall asleep right here on St. Stephen's Green.

But Mara was still chattering away. "Where are we going next?"

"Someplace more serious. The National Museum of Archaeology."

"Oh, is that where you work?"

"No, but it's the place where I first decided to become an archaeologist. When you've been here longer, and you've learned to read and write, I'm sure you'll find a career that speaks to you the way archaeology spoke to me." During the long days they'd spent together, Sorcha had started teaching Mara to read English, and was surprised how quickly she was picking it up.

"I'm a healer," Mara said. "I've been a healer all my life."

"Aye. There are lots of opportunities for healers in this world. You could be an herbalist who works with plants or a therapist who helps people with their minds or bodies, or both, I suppose. Or you could be a physician or surgeon. This world is about choice. You can explore several careers and decide which one speaks to you.

Sorcha didn't think Mara's eyes could get any wider, but when they entered the National Museum with its Victorian architecture, classical marbled columns, mosaic floors, and glass-encased exhibits, she was so busy gawking, she actually shut her mouth for the first time that day. They began on the ground floor with Prehistoric Ireland, gold exhibits, and the treasury, but Sorcha steered her around the Kingship and Sacrifice exhibit. Remembering Conall's reaction to seeing Ruairí's mummified torso, she'd leave it to last.

Upstairs, Mara was fascinated by Ancient Egypt, which gave Sorcha an opportunity to explain how she and Dylan unearthed the broad collar of Egyptian Princess Meritaten from a holy well in Scotland the previous summer. Mara was curious about the mummification process, so Sorcha explained how the Egyptians believed that the spirit traveled eternally with the Sun God Ra, while the body stayed in the ground entombed with Osiris, the King of the Dead. They mummified the bodies to keep them intact.

"But if their bodies have been taken from the tombs and now live here, how can they be with Osiris?"

And that was the beginning of the philosophical rabbit hole Sorcha didn't fancy going down but knew she must. She'd asked the same basic question of her mother when she was much younger than Mara. *If you dig their bones out of the earth, how can they be at peace?* Sorcha's mother, ever the scientist, couldn't answer the question. And when she told Sorcha about the mummified bog bodies that had been discovered by the peat cutter and collected by archaeologists, Sorcha had a similar reaction. *Shouldn't you leave them in the earth where they were sacrificed to the gods?*

Sorcha's mother explained that peat preserved the flesh, but once unearthed and subjected to air, the body would rapidly decay. She said it was the archaeologist's duty to preserve artifacts so everyone could learn from them and understand the past. Sorcha understood the basic concept of acidic peat bogs and oxidization, but struggled with the concept of duty.

Mara was staring at the elaborate coffin of the Egyptian Lady Tenddinebu with her gold-painted skin, colorful headdress, and massive kohl-lined eyes. "Is she still in there?"

"Her mummified body is inside the coffin, but I like to believe her spirit is with the Sun God Ra." As an archaeologist, Sorcha was a scientist, but she'd come to terms with her own beliefs about the afterlife. She'd never been a Christian who believed in one all-powerful father god who lived in heaven with the spirits of true believers who'd been forgiven their sins by a mortal man. That made no sense when you considered all the people in the world who weren't Christian. But she knew in her heart there was something more than this, and she was starting to believe in the idea of multiple lives. She thought it might even be possible that Ruairí's spirit had been reborn into someone who was alive in this world. She touched her heart. Perhaps, one day, they might meet again as Conall had sung in his song about the Bean Rua.

"When we die, our spirit lives in the Otherworld with our ancestors until we are reborn," Mara said.

"Do you think Ruairí is in the Otherworld?" Sorcha asked wistfully. Whenever she came to this place, he felt so real he could be walking beside her. No other man or woman would ever measure up.

"Ruairí was the Sun King. I do not know the ways of the gods, but if Ruairí has not been reborn, I believe he walks with the gods and goddesses surrounded by light. Don't fret for him Sorcha. He died with honor, and lives through you and in his son."

Sorcha threw her arms around Mara and held on as tears rolled down her cheeks. She'd tried not to cry in front of the girl, but now the dam had broken, there was no containing her grief. Mara, with her youthful wisdom, understood and held her while she sobbed.

"I loved him so much," she said, between gasps. "It's so unfair."

"It is, but Ruairí was avenged by Conall's sword, and I feel him, Sorcha. The gods are everywhere, and his spirit walks beside you. Do you not feel him?"

"I do feel him. I do." Sorcha pulled out a tissue and blew her nose. People were walking by and staring. She wanted to tell them to feck off and mind their own business, but she held her tongue. "His body is here, Mara."

"What do you mean?"

"Several years ago, a man was cutting peat and unearthed Ruairí's body; at least his chest and arms. Archaeologists were called in and they brought him here so what was left could stay preserved."

"Are you saying, Ruairí is here, now, in this building?"

"His remains, aye. I haven't taken you to the Iron Age exhibit yet. I didn't know how you'd react."

The girl tensed. "Are my reactions not my own?"

"They are. I just didn't want to cause you any pain." She took a breath. "Or maybe I was trying to save myself pain if you took offence to the thing I've dedicated my life to."

"What thing?"

"Archaeology."

Mara took Sorcha's hand and held it. "I want to see Ruairí. I've known him my whole life. Of all the nobles, he and Conall were the only ones who accepted my parents as true friends."

"Come on then. I'll show you what archaeologists have discovered about your life."

They walked downstairs through Prehistoric Ireland and into the Kingship and Sacrifice exhibit. As they wandered through the maps and weapons, Mara trailed her fingers along the cases, more enamored by the hard, smooth surface of glass than what lay inside.

"Where is he?" she said, and then stopped when the horizontal case that housed his arms and torso appeared before her. "Ruairí," she breathed. "He's worn this armband since he became a man."

"Is that so?" That braided leather armband with its copper mounts had brought him to life for Sorcha the first time she'd touched it. She stood with her eyes closed and her hand on the glass now, envisioning him the way he'd been that first day during the cattle raid: clean-shaven, nose long and straight, cheekbones high and shadowed. His glittering amber eyes swept up at the corners, both amused and annoyed. The sides of his head shaved close around his ears, but his copper hair gelled up in eight-inch spikes that made him appear over seven feet tall. His chest was smeared with mud and sweat. He was a huge man, broad, muscular, and naked save for a leather loincloth. A man with a heart as large as his hands. A man who'd saved her life, who'd loved her, and given her a child. A man willing to sacrifice his life to the goddess to save his people. No one could ever replace him.

Distracted by Mara, Sorcha shook the thoughts from her head. "Sorry. What did you say?"

"Ruairí's body cannot stay here. It must return to the sun in a burst of flame."

"Aye. Conall's of a similar mind. I don't know what we can do but I understand, and I know how important it is for you both that Ruairí's body is honored in the right way."

"And these sacrifices to the goddess," she said, sweeping her hand toward the bog butter and gold hordes recovered from the earth. "They must be returned."

Sorcha stared from one exhibit to the next in the museum. This was her life, this digging and cataloguing, hypothesizing, and constructing. And yet, having walked in Iron Age Ireland alongside Mara and Ruairí and Conall, she was torn, and that raw wound ached.

"These . . ." Sorcha couldn't call them exhibits or even artifacts anymore. Her whole life, her career, now seemed wrong. "All of this helps people who've never experienced your culture to understand it. We modern people long to learn about our ancestors and this is the only way we can know them and their beliefs. I understand why you want to return these sacrificial offerings to the earth. And I know your beliefs are strong. But think of it so. Your brothers and sisters in Croghan married and had children, and their children had children, and on and on down through time until today. These relics of the past are here so their ancestors can catch a glimpse into the culture from which they came. I know it's not enough, but it's all we've got. That's why I've given my life to archaeology."

"I understand, Sorcha, but I know Conall. He will not rest until Ruairí's body reunites with the Sun God."

Feck, Sorcha thought. *I know him too. I just hope we find the rest of Ruairí in that field of yellow flowers. Maybe that will be enough.*

51

"Sorcha. Wake up." When she didn't immediately open her eyes to Mara's emphatic whisper, a gentle hand clasped her arm.

"What? What is it?" Aroused from a dream, Sorcha still remembered fragments. She'd been stuck in a deep hole. Each time she climbed to the top, she tumbled backwards and crashed at the bottom. She could still feel the terror and smell the damp earth. It felt like climbing from a grave, and she wondered what it could mean.

"Come see." Mara's hand still rested on her arm and the more excited she became, the more it jiggled.

"See what?" Sorcha kept her voice low. Franya was sleeping in the next room. She'd visited earlier but had left immediately after sex without even staying for a cuddle. She said she had another breakfast meeting in the morning and needed her sleep. At least, she hadn't been as drunk this time. Sex with a drunk was not nearly as good when you were sober.

"Kittens." Mara squealed. "This big." She made a circle with her finger and thumb.

Sorcha rubbed her eyes. She forgot sometimes that Mara was still a child—a child with an affinity for all plants and animals. A child who'd grown up on a farm with kind parents and a passel of younger siblings and was now stuck out here alone with her. Sorcha knew Mara wouldn't be satisfied until she'd shared her discovery. And her heart swelled to know she'd been chosen, even though the only other choices were Declan and Franya. Still, it made her feel closer to the girl.

"Please, Sorcha. You'll love them."

"Alright. Hand me my shirt." She'd always slept naked but kept a sleep shirt nearby for nighttime excursions to the kitchen. This one was gray, fell to her knees, and had a grinning orange sloth on the front. "Where are these kittens?"

"In the barn loft."

"Oh, jeez. Way out there? It'll be pitch."

"Please." The girl's pleading awakened Sorcha's maternal instinct.

"Aye, alright." She slipped the shirt over her head and pulled it down as she climbed out of bed. "Let me grab my mobile." A photo of Mara with her kittens would put a smile on Dylan's face.

They tiptoed through the house and stopped at the patio door.

"You'll need those." Mara pointed to Sorcha's flat canvas slip-ons as she shoved her own feet into the hide shoes she'd worn from Croghan.

The waning moon cast enough light for them to thread their way through the backyard. Sorcha noticed that Declan's light was still on and put a finger to her lips to indicate silence. It must be well after midnight. The sounds and silhouettes of nightbirds reminded her how she adored summer nights on a dig. Everyone gathered around the bonfire for music and drinks and the craic was ninety. She couldn't wait to dig again and would soon put out a call for volunteers. She'd invite

Emma when they went to Tarbert to pick up her tent and the rest of her gear later this week. Franya had already agreed to lend her the Land Rover and horse trailer. And once Sorcha had her tent, she'd move herself and Mara out of the house and into the field of yellow flowers. Franya's late night visits felt good in the moment, but Sorcha felt like a sex toy, an object of pleasure but not much else.

The upper half of the barn door was open. Mara quietly flipped the metal latch on the lower door and swung it wide. They walked in. The horses nickered and Mara crooned to each one they passed. Rowan rested with one bent knee but revived when Sorcha paused at the door of her box stall, leaning her velvety nose forward, her horse lips flickering. The pony looked content enough, but Sorcha wished she had an apple to treat her. Declan kept the wood shavings clean and cared for the horses like they were his children.

"There now. I'll bring you a treat tomorrow."

When Rowan blinked her big brown eyes, Sorcha thought of Ruairí and their first horrible ride through the fields to the hut. Ah, but that night had ended sublimely. She touched her belly. That night he'd given her Ronan.

"Up here." Mara stood beside a ladder that led up into the loft. She climbed up first, then leaned down through the hole. "Be careful. The hay's slippery at the top."

Sorcha climbed up the ladder and popped through the hole into the loft. It smelled summer sweet. Moonlight streamed in from the large open double doors, but the rest fell to shadow. She tapped the torch app on her phone and shone the beam around the darkened loft.

They'd piled square bales high on one side, but the other was empty save for loose hay strewn about, and a few stray bales. No doubt they'd be filling it soon. The pasture grass was tall and haying time was coming. She didn't want Declan to cut down her field of yellow flowers, but knew he would, and likely before the dig began. They'd need the winter feed for the horses. Sorcha planned to dig as soon as her permission arrived. Only two more weeks.

"Your eyes will adjust," Mara said. "Come this way."

Sorcha clambered through the hole and stood up. She lowered the beam on the torch but kept it on as they walked across the loft and climbed up through the towering bales.

"How did you ever find these kittens?"

"After one of those dreams I couldn't sleep, so I came to visit the horses. I heard a mewling kitten. He sounded lost, so I followed his cries."

"No mother?"

"She's probably mousing." Mara pointed down between the bails where four tabby kittens slept piled on top of each other in a heap. "Here they are."

Sorcha shone the torch. "Oh, jeez. They can't be very old." Warmth flooded her chest. They were the most adorable creatures she'd seen in a long while.

Mara touched a furry forehead with her finger. The kitten had a black arrow that pointed down to his tan nose. His tiny ears pointed up. When he opened his eyes, Sorcha was surprised to see they were as dark blue as the ocean. His high-pitched squeak woke the others and soon they were all crawling and mewling.

The two women hunkered down in the hay and tucked them in their laps.

"Aren't they grand?" Mara said.

Sorcha was about to agree when she heard footfalls on the ladder. She switched off the torch on her mobile and signaled Mara to hush. She couldn't imagine why anyone would come up here in the middle of the night besides a girl following a lost kitten. She handed the two kittens she held to Mara and tiptoed back through the square bales for a better look. Mara was right. With the light off, her eyes adjusted to the gray tones.

It was Declan, wearing only a pair of pale boxers, and carrying something. A blanket. He walked over to the open double doors and glanced out, then spread the blanket over a pile of loose hay in the moonlight. What was he up to? Perhaps a rendezvous with one of the young women who boarded their horses here. A fair bit of flirting went on whenever they came to ride. Sorcha wanted to announce herself and show him the kittens, but her gut told her to stay quiet and wait.

Soon a head popped up through the hole in the floor. Sorcha strained to see but couldn't tell who it was until the whole body emerged.

Franya. What the hell? She was wearing that white silk slip. *Was this a tryst?* Sorcha's mind spun. *Were they at it the night she'd arrived too?* She remembered how casual he'd been about putting Franya to bed on the couch.

"Mind your step," Declan said.

Franya turned away and padded across the straw-strewn floor in her bare feet. When she reached Declan, she stood and stared at him and then at the blanket. They talked in low tones, but it was so quiet in the loft Sorcha could understand.

"I could use a hand here," Declan said, and stared down at his boxers.

"You know the rules."

I'd like to know the rules, Sorcha thought. Two semi-clad people meeting secretly at night in the hay loft. There was only one thing they could be up to. Sorcha glanced towards Mara who sat cradling the kittens in her lap. After their casual conversation about sex in Croghan, Sorcha didn't think she'd be too surprised, but still.

"Come on, Ms. Rousseau. Help me out." He pulled down his boxers, revealing an arse to be admired, and kicked them away. "At least show me what you and Sorcha do."

"You want to watch do you?"

"Why not? Did you see her tonight?"

"Aye."

"So, show me what you did. Come on. You know I can't go from zero to sixty with nothin'." Franya laid down on the blanket and tugged up her silk slip. Declan watched as she licked her fingers and let them stray. As she played, he played. "Aye. Now your stallion's ready." He sunk to his knees. "Over you go."

Franya turned onto her hands and knees, and when he slid inside, she gasped. Declan held her hips and slowly pumped.

"*Jaysus,*" Sorcha muttered. Even the rear view was titillating.

"Stop. I heard something," Franya said.

Sorcha's heartbeat quickened, and she froze.

"Ah, there's a litter of kittens over there in the hay. The mother's likely returned from mousing."

"Get rid of them," Franya said.

"How?"

"Drown them. Or put them in a sealed box and run exhaust into it. That's what my father always did." She sniffed. "Then get that female fixed."

Sorcha bit her fist. How cold could she be?

Declan started moving again.

"Touch me," Franya said.

"I thought—"

"Just feckin do it."

Sorcha couldn't believe what she was seeing. At uni, Franya's point of pride was that she'd never had sex with one of the "vile creatures" she called men.

Declan spit in his fingers and wound his hand beneath her belly.

"Aye, that's it."

With that encouragement, he soon had them both moaning. When it finally ended in a loud rush, he tumbled into the hay. Franya rolled over and fixed her slip, then laid back and put her knees up. Whether it was an old wives' tale or not, Sorcha knew that's what women did when they were trying to get pregnant.

She's made some kind of deal with Declan. But why would he agree to that? She couldn't imagine him fathering a child, agreeing to keep it secret, and staying out of that child's life. He was too much of a caregiver for that.

"Where are these kittens?" Franya was staring up at the heavy barn beams below the steel roof where swallows had nested in shadowy corners and cracks.

"Over in that far corner." He gestured with a long arm. "Do you want to see them?"

Please. No. Sorcha prayed.

"Feck that. I might take pity on them, and they need to go. As soon as you catch that mother, take her to the vet and get her spayed. Is the other one male?"

He shook his head. "Both females. But there's a big gray tom livin' nearby. Must be his brood. They're all tabbies. Cute as—"

Franya cleared her throat to cut him off. "I don't care how you get rid of them, just do it, and get both females fixed."

"Aye. Alright." He sniffed and rubbed his nose. "Something's worrying me, Ms. Rousseau."

"What's that?"

"What if Sorcha or Mara find out about Ms. Sullivan? Now they're livin' here . . ."

Sorcha straightened and leaned forward.

"There's nothing to find out." Franya stood, brushed off the back of her slip and leaned out the open barn door. She took a breath, then turned to face him. "The coroner declared Vivian's death an accident. It's a done deal, and I have the paperwork to prove it."

"I know but—"

"Don't tell me your testicles have shrunk. It certainly didn't feel like it."

"I just . . . I wish you hadn't buried her out back in the cemetery. I feel like her ghost is watching me."

Franya cackled. "Her ghost? Don't tell me you're one of those superstitious lads who believe in spirits?"

Why would Vivian's ghost be haunting Declan? Or why was Declan so full of guilt, he'd imagine it?

Mara was gesticulating wildly, pointing at her hand and wiggling her fingers. "Mobile," she mouthed.

Ah jeez, what an eejit I am. I should have been recording this whole thing. Sorcha hit the voice memo on her mobile and held it up.

"I took the risk, Miss."

"And the cottage is yours. Are you after something more? Because until Sorcha finds these gold artifacts, there's no more to be had."

"I don't care about the money. I'm worried someone might find out."

"Find out what?" Franya raised her voice. Her patience with Declan's guilt had ended.

"What I did for you," he yelled back.

"And for yourself."

What the feck did you do? Sorcha thought.

As Franya touched his shoulder, her voice dropped. "Look. The coroner is satisfied with his verdict of equestrian accident, and there's no evidence to the contrary. There were no witnesses and no way to tell that you raised that jump."

Declan stiffened. "Or that you talked her into taking off her helmet while I did it."

Feck! Had they conspired to murder Vivian and make it seem like an accident?

"That was her choice. Vivian was a seasoned professional who knew the risks of riding an equestrian circuit without the proper safety gear," Franya said, in her solicitor tone.

"Aye, you're right. I just worry that with people around here all the time, something could slip."

"Then see that it doesn't. I'm not sending Sorcha away because you can't control your guilt. She's a pleasant diversion, and when my baby's born, she can look after both our children while I'm at work."

Sorcha felt her cheeks flush. *Oh, so I'm the feckin nanny. Is that it?*

"I'm sorry, Ms. Rousseau. You're right. No one will ever find out. I just hate going near that cemetery, you know?"

"There are no ghosts, Declan. There is only guilt, and you must purge yours."

"Aye, Miss."

"You know I had no choice. Vivian refused to have a child. And when she found out about the peat, she started divorce proceedings. Then, she listed the property without my consent. What else could I do?"

Jaysus. The manipulating bitch found a way to take it all.

"Come here, Declan. Just to show you how important you are, I'll do something for you, I've never done for any man."

"Miss?"

When Franya got down on her knees and took him in her mouth, he gasped.

Sorcha's eyes widened.

And suddenly Franya was on her back on the blanket, and Declan was madly pumping away his guilt.

Sorcha shut off her phone and slumped against the hay bales. They had to leave. Now. If Franya and Declan had conspired to murder Vivian, what would they do to her and Mara once they discovered they knew the truth? Sorcha stared at her phone. She held the evidence Franya claimed didn't exist right here in the palm of her hand.

52

Sorcha snuck back into the house with Mara and saw the girl safely to her room. Unable to sleep, she packed her bag and sat with her back to the adjoining door to Franya's room. She heard the woman's quiet snores, the boisterous alarm, the bustling as she prepared for her breakfast meeting. She imagined Franya showering and dressing in her fashionable suit. The skinny bitch. This would be her last free morning. Sorcha would not let Vivian's murder go unavenged.

She'd already called the Confidential Garda line to report what she'd overheard. They'd assured her someone would arrive today. She knew she'd have to make a statement and give them a copy of her voice memo. And she'd already left a message for the Kildare SPCA, telling them about the kittens in danger of being slaughtered, and the horses that might be left unattended once the Garda interceded. Now, all she had to do was wait.

When Sorcha heard Franya's tires fade on the long driveway, she walked downstairs, drank a quick cup of tea, and went walking in the field of yellow flowers for one last time. The sun hung low in the eastern sky over the Wicklow

Mountains like it did the day she set off with Ruairí. Walking through the tall grass and buttercups wearing her khakis and canvas shoes, she thought again of his vision. She was leaving and had still not found what she'd lost. Thinking of him, she sank to the ground.

"Oh, Ruairí. I really hoped this dig might bring you back to me. I miss you beyond belief. My heart breaks each time I feel your child flutter inside me." Her throat tightened, and she swallowed her sorrow. But in doing so, she realized her anger still burned hot for Ana. Not only had she executed Ruairí, she'd taken whatever time they might have had together for herself. Tumbling into the buttercups, she sobbed for what never was and never could be.

"*Sow-r-ka.*" The voice was low and breathy and filled her soul. Only two men had ever said her name like that with cadences in ancient Celtic.

When she raised her head, Ruairí hovered before her, a translucent, shimmering being, wrapped in turquoise, his hair gelled high. Wearing the cloak from his inauguration, the Sun King seemed as tall as the sky. Sorcha's hands flew to her mouth.

"Why must you torment yourself? If you would only believe, you would find peace."

"Is it really you?" She leapt to her feet, holding out her arms, wanting to hold him, to crush him to her breasts and never let him go.

"I *am* with you, *Sow-r-ka,* and I always will be. Do you not feel me?"

"I want to feel you. I do. But—"

"You must believe."

The tears rolled down her cheeks. "I want to believe. I wanted to dig here in the lake of *giolla rua* where we first made love. I wanted to find you again."

He touched his heart and then touched hers, and her body tingled right to her toes. "You have found me."

"Please don't leave me. I miss you so much."

"And I you, my fey queen. Come. Hold me."

Sorcha wrapped her arms around his ephemeral body, but as she nuzzled her face into his chest, he suddenly seemed real. She kissed his chest and felt his muscles hard against her. "I'll never love anyone the way I love you, Ruairí Mac Nia. You are my destiny."

"As you are mine. I knew it that first day I found you with the cows."

Time dissolved as Sorcha stood in the field, arms wrapped around her man. But as the sun rose higher in the sky, Ruairí breathed in her ear. "Mara Manus comes. She needs you."

"But I need *you*. Please don't leave me, Ruairí."

"Do you not see? I am here for you, and when you call me, I will come. I do not live in this field. My body means nothing. My spirit encompasses this world, and many others. This field was just a place where I envisioned you standing long ago. Do you remember?"

"Aye. You said I found something that I'd lost."

He looked into her eyes. "And have you found it?"

"Oh, Ruairí. You. I found you."

"Wherever you are, when you call, I will come. Even in your dreams." And then he was gone, and she sank amidst the buttercups and sobbed.

"Sorcha? Are you alright?"

Mara was suddenly standing beside her in the field. Sorcha's heart fluttered, her vision blurred, and everything seemed unreal. Was this the magic Estrada described?

"Oh, Mara. I just saw—"

"Who? Who did you see?"

"Ruairí. I saw Ruairí. He was here."

Mara smiled, sat down beside her and threw her arm around her shoulders. "Oh, I knew he'd come. Was he with the Goddess? Is he the Sun King?"

"Aye. Aye, he is."

"Did he tell you what we must do?"

Sorcha stood and pulled Mara up beside her. "I know what we must do. Are you packed?"

"Aye, but where will we go?"

"First, Dublin. Then we'll board a plane bound for Vancouver. I know the lads wanted us to stay here where it's safe, but clearly, things have changed."

"We're going to see Dylan?"

"Aye, Dylan, Conall, Estrada . . ."

"Oh Sorcha. I can't wait to see them all again." Her face fell. "But what about the kittens?"

"I've already called the animal shelter and told them to intercede. As cute as they are, those wee tabbies will all find good homes. They'll look after the horses too until we can make other arrangements."

"What will happen to Declan and Franya?"

"That'll be up to The Garda. I've already reported what we overheard and told them I have an audio recording. You were a clever girl, Mara, to remind me to turn on my mobile. I think they'll be arriving soon."

"What should we do now?"

"Let's walk, and later, we'll catch the train to Dublin. We can stay at Trinity College while I arrange our flights. It'll give you a chance to experience a college campus."

Mara's eyes shone. "Can I tell Dylan?"

"Let's wait until we're safe in Dublin."

"But what about your dig? You were so looking forward to finding the lake of *giolla rua*."

"It's here," Sorcha said, touching her chest. "You know, I was raised to believe everything had to be seen and proven scientifically." She shrugged. "But some things can't. Some things require faith."

As they walked back through the field of yellow flowers, Mara pointed to a shiny object in the grass. "What's that?"

Sorcha bent down and picked it up. "It's a key." Her eyebrows furled as she stared at it. "This is the house key Franya gave me the day I arrived." The wind caught her hair, and she raised a hand to brush it from her eyes. "I never used it because the house was always unlocked. I didn't even know I'd lost it." She dropped it into the pocket of her khakis.

Mara glanced over at the small cemetery on the hill. "And what about your friend, Vivian? Shouldn't you say goodbye to her?"

"Viv and I said our goodbyes long ago. If she's still here, I imagine she'll find relief when her murderers come to justice."

"Franya will probably talk her way out of it."

"She might, but at least we'll have done our part. We'll tell the truth. That's all we can do."

When they arrived back at the house, three bright yellow vehicles belonging to *An Garda Síochána* were parked in the drive.

"Mara, if they ask why you're here, tell them I was preparing for an archaeology dig and you were assisting."

"Don't worry. I know what to say."

Franya glared from the back seat of the police car.

As their eyes locked, a look of pure hatred passed between them. Sorcha felt her temperature rise. Then Franya tried to raise a hand and realized she was handcuffed.

Sorcha suppressed her glee. *This is only the beginning,* she thought, still not quite believing that Franya and Declan had conspired to murder Vivian and make it seem like an accident. Hopefully, they'd find evidence somewhere and it wouldn't all rest on one audio file of an overheard conversation.

Then Declan walked out of the stable flanked by two gardai, red-faced and babbling. "Murder? She made me do it. I want a solicitor." They put him into the back of another vehicle and shut the door.

Don't call the one in the other cruiser, Sorcha thought. Perhaps an audio file and a confession would suffice.

Sorcha couldn't relax until they were finally free of the Garda and seated on the train enroute to Heuston Station. From there, they bussed to Pearse. When they finally entered their spartan room at Trinity College, Sorcha collapsed on the bed.

Mara was pacing. "Now can I call Dylan?"

"Aye, take my mobile. If you want some privacy, there's a loo across the hall, and the lounge looked vacant."

Sorcha must have fallen asleep because the next thing she knew, Mara was shaking her. "Wake up. Wake up."

"What's wrong?"

"Everything. Dylan said they tried to fight the vampires but Estrada's friend came and Conall cut off his head!"

"*Jaysus.* I hope it wasn't Michael Stryker."

"Michael. Aye, it was Michael."

"Oh my God. Estrada will be devastated."

"Then the vampire grabbed Estrada and Conall and flew into the sky—"

Sorcha held her breath. "Are they gone?"

"No, he dropped them. But Estrada still hasn't woken up."

"*Feck.*" Sorcha reached for her phone.

Naturally, Estrada didn't pick up. She left a long audio message and then started searching for flights from Dublin to Vancouver. When Mara's stomach growled, she realized, what with all the chaos, they hadn't eaten all day.

"There's nothing more I can do from here. Shall we go pick up Asian street food?"

"Aye. Pad Thai."

Sorcha stood and ruffled Mara's hair. When she reached into the pocket of her khakis to stash her wallet, she felt something hard and pulled out the key.

"And what you've lost will not be lost forever," Ruairí had said.

Sorcha dropped it into the metal bin and heard it clang.

Ruairí was the key, and he was exactly where he needed to be.

53

Estrada awoke with a brutal headache, feeling so disoriented he didn't know where he was. His neck burned. His throat ached. His mouth felt dry and sticky. His bladder full. His gut empty. He reached out and placed an open palm on the source of warmth beside him. When he felt flesh, he rubbed his eyes and moaned.

"Ah, there you are." Conall leaned up on one arm and beamed down at him.

"What the fuck happened?"

"Diego plucked you from the deck. You fell and hit your head."

Estrada felt the back of his skull and winced. *Jesus.*

"Aye, but you survived."

"Because you jumped off the deck to save me. I remember now."

"How could I not?" The bard's eyes glowed. "I've been watching you sleep."

"How long?"

"Three days."

"Three days? And the others?"

"All fine."

"And Diego?"

"I hurt him. Cut him. He has not returned."

Estrada glanced around. This was Sensara's room. He remembered the pale blue walls, the jungle of plants and trees standing in pots and hanging amid the landscapes, the canopied bed she'd built herself from fallen sticks and driftwood. He touched the soft white cotton sheets. "Why are we here?"

"The Lady was angry we were sleeping outside where Diego could so easily attack. She's moved everyone around and won't let anyone leave. And there are others here now too." Conall's eyes danced. "Mara and Sorcha."

"What? What are they doing here?"

"It's a long story. I'll get Sorcha and let her tell you herself."

"First, help me into the bathroom. I need to do something with this." He gestured to his body.

When he came out of the shower and glanced in the misty mirror, he noticed Diego's fingermarks still ringed his neck. With them were thin red cuts from when those fingers became talons. Seeing it, he felt the pain intensify. The sick bastard had branded him.

He peeked out the door. Conall was gone, and Sensara was sitting in her armchair, waiting. He pulled his black trunks back on, wondering who'd dressed him before putting him to bed. He always slept naked.

"Good to see you up, Storyman." She handed him a mug of herb tea.

Storyman? She hadn't called him that since their failed tryst almost two years ago. She must have been really worried. He could kill for a shot of espresso but knew if he mentioned that, he might be the one who ended up dead. He smiled and sipped the tea.

"Please don't ever do anything like that again. I don't want to have to tell Lucy that her father died from *hyperstupidity*."

Estrada rolled his eyes. "I'm happy to see you too, and I'm pretty sure you made that word up." He leaned over and kissed her on the cheek. "I feel like we've *gone to the mattresses*."

"Indeed, we have," she said in a terrible *Godfather* accent. "Lucy is still with her aunty, and we have a full house. There are ten of us here now."

"Ten? Where did you put them all? And how are you feeding them?"

"Everyone's pitching in, and we're ordering frequent takeout. I've moved in with Daphne and Raine so you two can sleep *inside* where it's safer." She rolled her eyes at their *hyperstupidity*. "Dubh, that sweet man, asked to sleep here too. He's been worried sick." She pointed to a foamy on the floor in the corner spread with a few blankets. "Your friend Sorcha arrived late last night with Dylan's new wife, Mara. Sorcha and Sylvia became fast friends and they're sleeping in the downstairs living room. And I gave Dylan and Mara a foamy in Lucy's room. They are newlyweds, after all." She smiled. "I haven't seen them yet today."

"Good for Dylan. And you are always so gracious, my high priestess."

"I'm just relieved you're awake and came through this relatively unscathed. I wanted to take you to the hospital, but Conall wouldn't allow it. That man can be almost as stubborn as me. But he's been entertaining us with his music, so I suppose you can keep him." The corner of her lip turned up in a grin.

He was relieved Sensara had accepted his relationship with Conall and included him so easily in the coven. She'd always despised Michael, had never trusted him, and now she'd been proven right.

"So, how are you feeling?"

"Headache, sore neck, and *this* hurts." He touched the lump on the back of his head.

"Best not to touch it then." She shook her head. "You hit a rock in Daphne's garden."

"Ah, that explains it."

"Anything else? Foggy? Dizzy? Any symptoms of concussion?"

Estrada grimaced and lied. "Unfortunately, Nurse Ratched, I remember everything. Diego said he'd take one more of us every day until he had me and Conall. But everyone's here, right? Has anyone disappeared?"

She shook her head. "What does this ceasefire mean?"

"I hope it means that Conall hurt him bad. He cut him with your sword."

"Do you think he might have destroyed him?"

"I doubt it. Conall would have noticed if Diego turned to dust." He touched her hand. "How's Lucy?"

"She's fine, but . . ." She paused, and he felt the hairs on the back of his neck stand on end. "Sylvia is leaving for Wales tomorrow, and she's invited Lucy and me to come with her. I hate being apart from Lucy, but I can't leave you to deal with this alone."

"I'm not alone. You should go, Sara. Take Lucy where it's safe. You two mean more to me than anything in this world."

"I knew you'd say that." She leaned over and kissed him lightly on the lips. "I just needed to know you were alright and . . ." Her voice drifted off.

Get my permission? He was surprised and delighted she'd even included him in the conversation. He stood and pulled her close. "I'll be fine. Like you said, we're not just human. We've got a strong team, and I'll feel better knowing my family is far away from this maniac."

A soft knock on the door made them both flinch. "Come in," Sensara said.

Dubh popped his head in. "Sorry, Lady."

"It's alright, Magus." She touched Estrada's cheek. "I've got things to do."

Dubh darted into the room and Sensara closed the door behind her. "I heard you were awake."

"Get over here, man. I've been thinking about you." Feeling woozy, Estrada fell back on the bed.

"I'm not surprised." Dubh hopped up beside him and held up a cut fingertip.

"Did you?"

"I did. But you were asleep, so I could only put it in your mouth."

"That's probably why I woke up."

"Aye. Are you ready for a full dose of fey juice, mate?"

"Please."

"Stop when I tell you, now," Dubh warned, as he took out a pocketknife and nicked a vein in his wrist.

As soon as Estrada tasted the warm coppery blood, he grasped Dubh's hand and held it to his mouth. Not that he loved the taste of blood, only that he didn't want to miss a drop of the fey wonder drug that had saved his life twice before.

Estrada watched Dubh's eyelids flutter and stopped when the wee man tapped his hand. "There's a first aid kit in the bathroom. I'll get it."

"No, I'm fine. Stay there." Dubh slipped off the bed and returned with a Band-Aid covering the wound. Luckily, not one drop had soiled the sheets.

"Wow." Estrada took a deep breath. "Do you feel this good all the time?" The faerie blood had hit his brain like a long line of coke.

Dubh winked one bright blue eye. "There are perks to having a fey father, even if the bastard didn't stick around."

"What day is it, Dubh?" Estrada chewed the inside of his cheek. His mind was suddenly spinning with scenarios and maybes.

"It's Thursday evening. Why?"

"We need to end this. Have we heard anything about Blosch?"

Dubh shook his head.

"So, they still have him." He flung up his hands. "Somehow, I need to draw Diego out. The ritual didn't work, and I don't think he'll come here again knowing we're so well fortified."

"What are you thinkin', mate?"

"Tomorrow night is my regular Friday gig at the club." He closed his eyes and tried to imagine it. "You, me, Conall—"

"You'll nae get away with that. None of the hens? They'll call you sexist and do as they wish."

"Sensara and Lucy are going to Wales with Sylvia, and I'll talk to Daphne and Raine." They were preparing to have a child, and he was sure they'd be happy to stay somewhere safe. "And Dylan won't want Mara anywhere near Diego."

Dubh grinned. "We haven't seen those two since she arrived. What's the plan?"

"If Diego's hurt, he'll send someone to grab us and take us to him. I destroyed Zion, and Eliseo's too young to get past the sentinels. So, he'll be waiting outside. We go in together holding all the magic we can muster. If Diego does come, we fight him there. If he doesn't, we go with them to wherever he is. The one thing I know for certain is that we must get to Diego and destroy him. He's the key. Once he's gone, they're all gone."

Another knock on the door, and Estrada flinched again. "Yeah?"

Daphne popped her head in. "Sorry to intrude. Sensara said you were awake and feeling good, and I just had to see it with my own eyes."

"I'm good, Daph. Come here." Estrada stood and crushed her in his arms. "I feel like a superhero."

"Really?" She did a little dance. "You know that thing we talked about?"

"Thing?"

"You know."

Dubh snorted. "Later, mate," he said, and slipped out the door.

Daphne grinned. From one pocket of her long dress she pulled a turkey baster and from the other, a jam jar.

Estrada laughed. "Oh, *that* thing."

"I just took my temperature. Right now is perfect and since you're here and feeling so good . . ."

"Oh, jeez. Filling that could be a hardship. You better send in Conall."

Daphne ran to the door. "Right away."

"And tell everyone else, I'll see them later."

It was almost dark by the time Estrada and Conall appeared downstairs, after making a quick delivery to Daphne's room. Dubh was knocking back whiskey shooters and dancing with Sorcha. The music was blaring. Sylvia had obviously left and Sensara was upstairs packing. So, it was just the four of them and Estrada was in the mood to party.

He grabbed a shot and downed it just before Sorcha tackled him. "Hey, it's good to see you too. Dare I ask why you're here?"

"Oh, aye. Declan and Franya murdered Vivian, so I reported them to the Garda. I left you a phone message. Didn't you hear it?"

"Wait." He shook his head. "Murdered?"

"Aye. Plotted it together and made it look like an accident. Mara and I overheard the conversation, and I recorded it."

Estrada glanced at Conall, remembering his warning from the trees. The bard flattened his lips and nodded once.

"Well, I'm glad you're here and you're both safe."

"Me too. It's grand here, and the kids are finally on their honeymoon."

Daphne and Raine walked into the living room holding hands. Estrada winked, and Daphne flushed.

Then, Raine glanced out the window. "Hey, look. There's a deer standing in the backyard just beyond the lights. You can hardly see it but—"

"That's no deer," Sorcha said, and Dubh chuckled.

Estrada glanced out and recognized the antlers. He turned to Conall, "I'll be back. I promise."

Daphne panicked. "What about the vampires?"

"That's the Horned God," Estrada said. "I'd like to see them try."

54

With his eighteen-pronged antlers, Cernunnos easily stood twelve feet tall. His dark eyes were lined in kohl, his lips purple, and a gold serpentine torque circled his neck. Estrada's eyes traveled down his muscled chest to the skin wound round his hips.

He nodded. "Shaman. Are you well?"

"Indeed. I'm honored by your presence. And curious."

The god touched his shoulder, and a shiver rippled through Estrada's body. "Will you walk with me?"

When they came to the path that led through the woods, Estrada stopped. "It's dark in there."

"Can you not light our way?"

"Uh, yeah. Sure." Estrada willed the fire down his palms and into his fingertips. Remembering the forest fires, he kept it as low as a candle and cupped his hand around it.

"Where shall we go? The beach?" The god's voice whispered through Estrada's soul.

"Why not?" Shadows swept through the trees and twigs crackled in the bush with each step.

They followed the switchback down the hill and walked out onto the flat sand. Moonlight struck the lake and played in the ripples, while dark tree-clad mountains surrounded them. It was light enough to see and he let the flame go out.

"Is this where you portray me in your rituals?"

"It is," Estrada said, thinking back to the nights he'd danced in his antler headdress and fern kilt. How empowering it had been to dance as the god.

"And is this where Michael Stryker met his fate?"

"Yes."

"Where?"

Estrada pointed to the sand. There was no blood now but when he closed his eyes, he could see a crimson fog fouled the air.

"Shall we make a fire? Cleanse the beach?" Cernunnos asked.

Estrada brought rocks to make a ring and dried twigs from the woods. He saw the same crimson haze clinging to Michael's grave. Somehow, he'd need to cleanse that too after he'd taken Michael's body to Nigel. He built a small fire and turned to Cernunnos who stood tall with his arms crossed over his chest.

"Will you light it?"

Estrada began to bring the flames down his arms, but Cernunnos came behind him, pinned his arms and held him firm. "Hey!"

"How will you light it now?"

He remembered the night of Ruairí's execution, how they'd all been bound to crosses and he'd breathed fire from his mouth to burn Conall's ropes.

"I was angry then. I don't know if—"

The god leaned forward and whispered in his ear. "Will you not try?"

Estrada stood in mountain pose and focused on his breath. Channeling all his energy into his chest, he stared at the dry twigs, and willed it so. When he opened his mouth, fire blasted forth and the twigs burst into flame. He shut it in surprise.

Cernunnos laughed. "Will you sit with me?"

Estrada hunkered down across the fire from the god and waited. Had he come with a message? All he seemed to be doing was asking questions.

"What other talents do you possess, shaman?"

"I'm a hypnotist, and quick with sleight of hand." He reached up and pulled a stone from behind the god's ear.

Cernunnos cackled.

"I can reposition my bones and escape from pretty much anything, and I can hold my breath underwater for several minutes." He remembered pulling Dylan to safety in Scotland when they'd both been weighted with anchors and dumped into the sea. "Once my spirit flew into the body of a raven, and once I met Diego in the Underworld." Dubh had taken him on a shamanic journey. That's when he'd first seen Diego as a pterosaur.

"What have you learned of this vampire? What is his story?"

Michael had told him that Don Diego sailed with Quadra in the late 1700s and then captained his own ship. "He lost his son in a storm. He keeps trying to replace him with young men." He remembered arguing with Diego. The vampire had said they were the same because they were both good fathers. Estrada refused to be equated with such a villain.

"Where would a sea captain hide?"

"In the harbor, obviously." They'd come by yacht before. Estrada could only assume they'd sailed from the island again.

"Is the creature lonely?"

"Lonely?"

"Do you not think an immortal might become lonely? Crave companionship? Need someone to love?"

Cernunnos leaned forward and gazed into Estrada's eyes as he swept a hand through the fire and played with the flames. It seemed they weren't talking about Diego anymore.

"Are *you* lonely, Cernunnos?"

"If I were, would you care?"

"Of course, I care. That's why I'm asking." What had the god said? *Kisses are crumbs to my hungry heart?*

"Have you come for your loaf?" Estrada asked. The scent of exotic spices filled his senses, and he stared at those plump mulberry lips, lit by the flames of the fire.

"Do you offer it?"

One long fingernail stroked Estrada's chin while another touched his lips. Estrada moved around the fire and knelt before the god. "I don't have three days and nights."

Cernunnos chuckled. "*Sow-r-ka*. She is insatiable."

The antlers had disappeared. The elongated nose shrunk between two high cheekbones and valleys of shadows. His eyes were as black as the night sky but glimmered with stars. Estrada touched his mulberry lips and moved closer as the god rose to his knees, and they were shoulder to shoulder. Man to man.

Estrada laid his palm on the god's heart. "*Are* you lonely, Cernunnos?"

"Like the vampire, I long to take you with me into eternity, to make you mine forever."

"You could do that?"

His bottom lip drooped. "I've never tried, but alas, I feel it's not your destiny. If it was your desire, I'd do my best to make it so, but as you know, we cannot change what is fated. And I would never put you at risk." His face fell.

Estrada leaned forward and caught the god's lips with his own. All his favorite scents and tastes merged into that one kiss. Cinnamon. Coffee. Chocolate. Whiskey. The smells and tastes of Mexico and his abuela's food. They fell on the sand, bodies pressed hard together, hands gripping, pulling tighter. Estrada longed to draw the god into his soul. As the kiss intensified, his body shook and his soul danced with the sheer joy of it. They rolled in the sand, first Cernunnos on top moving his hips to the beat of some far-off drums, and then he pulled Estrada on top of him, and they rolled down the sand into the water.

"I want you shaman. Will you have me? Here? Now?"

Estrada stared into those lonely velvet eyes and saw they glistened with tears. He breathed one word.

"Yes."

55

When Estrada climbed the switchback from the beach to the house, a sliver of sun crested the mountains. He found Conall sitting in the forest near the top of the trail, body nestled into the bulbous roots of a hefty hemlock, back erect, knees tight to his chest. Reluctant to interrupt his conversation, Estrada crouched nearby in the moss and ferns, waited, and watched the handsome bard. It had been a long night, and he was both exhausted and exhilarated. From time to time, Conall moved his ear closer to the bark as he listened to the quiet murmurs of the old tree. When at last his chin fell to his chest, Estrada edged closer, and laid his palm against the bard's thigh.

"What do the trees tell you, friend?"

"The vampires have left this place. Returned to the sea. Leo is among them. That's where we must go." A somber frown had replaced the bard's usual smile. They hadn't spoken of Leopold Blosch since his abduction, but Estrada saw how his situation plagued the bard. The night had painted dark circles under his eyes.

"It's good to know they're gone and we can talk freely. Cernunnos got me thinking of the sea too. Diego is a ship captain and travels by yacht. They'll be harbored in Vancouver."

Conall tensed. Was it the mention of the Horned God or the threat of the vampire?

"I will take his head." It was then Estrada noticed the glint of the samurai sword on the ground near the bard's fingers. "When do we leave this place?"

"Tonight. As soon as Sensara leaves."

"The Lady left with Daphne and Raine. Dylan and Mara went with them. He said to call, and he will join us. All who remain here are Sorcha and Dubh."

"And us." Estrada raked his fingernails through his hair and felt the grit of sand. He felt disheveled after a night of lovemaking on the beach.

"And the Horned God?" Conall's chin tilted high, and Estrada couldn't tell if he was angry or jealous or truly wanted to know if Cernunnos was an ally who would join them in the fight. The grim twist of his lips quickened Estrada's heartbeat. For a moment, he sat in silence, listening to it beat, not knowing what to say. Finally, Conall turned and clutched Estrada's jaw with both hands. "You are troubled. Many things are new for me here, but some things are as old as the Earth." He paused and licked his lips. "Like love and desire. Both come naturally, one to body, one to soul. Sometimes, if Destiny smiles, they come together and dance."

Estrada's lips quivered, but he was loath to speak. Dare he share the rapture he'd felt while making love with the god?

"Do you desire me?" the bard asked.

"Indeed."

"And do you love me?"

"More all the time."

Conall's mouth caught his in a kiss that soothed Estrada's trembling soul but set his blood pounding.

"And you? Who do you desire?"

Leopold Blosch hung in the air like a thundercloud. Estrada was almost afraid to say his name, but knew he must. He'd spent years reveling in polyamory, but now he'd found Conall, a man with the same liberal beliefs as himself, he was afraid to lose him. Afraid the bard might fall in love with someone else and leave him. Was that irony or just karma biting him in the ass?

Estrada took a quick breath. "Leopold? Do you desire Leopold?" He couldn't ask about love.

A slow smile spread across Conall's face as he nodded gently. "I do. And that is why we must find him, and Dubh must heal him with his de Danann blood."

Estrada's face fell under the weight of that confession. Losing Conall now would be far worse than anything Diego could ever inflict upon him.

Conall grasped his chin and turned Estrada's face to meet his own. "Now, we must rest and pray, for tonight we find Leo and end this."

56

Friday Night at Club Pegasus

Friday night, and despite Michael's absence the crowd at Club Pegasus was drowning in Ecstasy. Like a massive jellyfish, it undulated to the slow, pensive beats. Estrada drifted through the weaving feathered, leathered shapes but saw no one he recognized besides the usual talent. Surely, Diego would send an emissary. How else would they find him? There were marinas in False Creek, but also hundreds of boats.

Conall hovered at the bar near Dell, sipping a glass of smoky whiskey. Dell said patrons had been asking for the man with the golden voice, and the bard was eager to sing. He loved the sounds he could produce through the mic. When the track ended, Dell escorted Conall on stage and tested the system while the bard tuned the guitar to his liking. Estrada glanced upstairs. Sorcha and Dubh perched at the manager's table, where they had a full view of the goings-on.

In the dressing room earlier, when Estrada was putting on his makeup, Conall had asked him to paint his face. Estrada had shown him how to apply the smudgy kohl eye liner.

Then, the bard had chosen a dark purple lipstick, close to the mulberry shade Cernunnos wore, to line and fill his lips.

Now, under the spotlights, with his chestnut hair hanging long and loose, and wearing tight brown leather pants with side laces and an open motorcycle vest, the bard oozed rock star. When he approached the mic, the crowd hushed. Then his fingers danced out the first silvery steel riffs. A collective breath exhaled ohs and ahs, spurring him on. Bluesy rock seeped from his pores as if he were the reincarnated soul of Hendrix. When he took it way, way down, the crowd leaned closer wanting to be touched by this god of music. He opened his mouth and a smoky trill poured forth that rivaled Peter Gabriel, then caught fire as it ignited into a shimmering Celtic chant. Estrada glanced up. Sorcha was standing, beaming. "Bean Rua," he said at last, "for the red-haired woman," and lifted a hand to Sorcha, who clapped and howled.

After two more tunes, the crowd was vibrating, caught in his net, and Estrada wondered how he'd ever keep them riveted with his magic act. In the euphoria, he'd forgotten everything but Club Pegasus and his love of live performing. As Conall exited the stage, he was swarmed, and Dell stepped in with the sentinels to make room. Sweating and smiling, the bard nodded in his quiet way and sauntered beside Dell to the back of the club near the bar. Estrada saw a woman hand him her business card. Unable to read it, he simply slipped it into his back pocket and invited the woman to take the vacant stool beside him. Knowing Conall was safely tucked away after his fantastical performance, Estrada crept into the darkened wings and climbed the steps to the fly tower.

The first beats of the soundscape blasted through the speakers. "Ready," he said, and slowly the scarlet silks lowered.

Grasping the fabric, he swung until he'd gained enough momentum to flip up into a handstand. He was grateful that with Dubh's help, his wrist was now completely healed. He wrapped his ankles in the silks and hung upside down, back to the audience, inhaling the applause. Their energy fueled him, and he ran through his sequence in time with the beats, glistening muscles rippling as he pushed each movement to the limit. He'd just finished spinning by his ankles when he felt a whoosh of wings past his head.

He flipped upright as the raven spun around and dove again. Gasped when a second bird slashed his back with its talons. Then the first was on him, squeezing his shoulders and pecking at his neck. He opened his mouth and a rush of fire burst forth. The raven screeched and swooped, wings smoking as a stench filled the air.

By now, they'd lowered the silks, and he clambered out. The crowd, fueled by E, and not knowing if this was part of the act or a real altercation, watched and waited. Then someone spotted his bleeding wounds and panic ensued.

Estrada searched the chaos for ravens, vampires. He found Conall still at the back of the club near Dell. The bard was clutching someone and holding his boot-knife to their throat. Estrada fought his way through the crowd screaming "Stop, Conall. Wait." As he drew nearer, he saw a naked man, arm and shoulder burnt. Finally, he came close enough to recognize the close-cropped platinum hair slicked back from the phantom face.

Jazz.

Dell stood eyes wide.

"Handcuffs?" Estrada asked. Dell shrugged, and Cerise slammed a pair of steel cuffs on the bar.

"You deceitful fucker." Estrada slipped the cuffs on Jazz while Conall continued to hold the knife to their throat. The creature stared with rabid eyes. They still had his blood on their lips.

"That'll do fuck all if they shift back into a raven." Dubh stared up, blue eyes sparkling, lips twisted. Sorcha stood behind him.

"If they *do*, I'll take their head," Conall said. His eyes blazed.

Estrada grimaced, then turned to Dell. "Bring my plexiglass tank from the dressing room." He'd had it especially built for his water act. With the dimensions of a coffin, it could house a full-grown man. Or vampire. Dell and one of the other sentinels fetched it. The patrons who hadn't left the club in the mass panic had gathered, convinced this was still part of the act.

After opening one end, Estrada and Conall lifted Jazz's body and shoved them inside. The curling snake tattoo on their back pressed up against the glass. Estrada locked down the case and stared up into the rafters. The other raven was there somewhere, concealed by the black-beamed ceiling.

Sorcha touched his shoulder. "You need stitches. It sliced right through your tattoo."

Estrada shook his head. "Surgical glue. Come on." He turned to Dell. "Lock down the club. Watch that one and find the other. There's likely a blood trail. And listen man, it may not *be* a raven now." Dell winced. "If you find it, cut off the head or use fire to slow it down until Conall can deal with it." Dell's eyes bulged, but he nodded. "And take someone with you. Conall needs to guard Jazz."

In the dressing room, Sorcha washed the wound with warm water and soap, and then patted it dry. "This might scar your beautiful angel's wings," she said.

"Nah. Dubh gave me a hefty helping of fey blood. I'll heal fast." He touched his neck. It was already cool. He handed her a tube of medical adhesive. "Just push the skin together and apply a thin layer." He winked. "Works like magic." He lit a fat joint and sucked back the smoke as she worked. It'd been too long since he'd ingested cannabis and knew it would bring him to a place where he could think.

"Who's Jazz?" Sorcha asked as she worked.

"Someone who's been partying with Michael for weeks, even living at his flat. They tricked me. I tasted their blood to see if they were infected with the virus and didn't feel it. When I found them sleeping in Michael's bed, I thought they were an innocent victim and let them go."

"Maybe they were. Maybe they weren't turned until later. Maybe himself turned them."

"Michael? I guess it's possible, but I suspected Jazz from the start. I should have relied on my gut and taken them out when I had the chance. Zion and Jazz have been messing with Michael for weeks, the fuckers." The guilt stuck in his throat, and he coughed.

"There now. All done." Sorcha squeezed his shoulder. "Now what?"

Estrada slipped on a T-shirt and wiped off his stage makeup, leaving just a thin black line around his eyes.

"Now? Jazz is either going to lead us to Diego or I'll let Conall take their head. He's itching to do it with that samurai sword."

Sorcha shook her head. The woman was remarkably calm. "You can take the warrior out of the Iron Age . . ."

"Indeed." Conall had a penchant for heads which, in this case, was proving beneficial. Estrada wrapped his arms around Sorcha's shoulders and hugged her close. "I'd appreciate it if you would stay here where it's safe until we return. I don't know what kind of fuckery we're walking into. Knowing Diego, this is a trap, and we need Ruairí Mac Nia's son to grow up so he can fulfill his destiny."

"I know Ronan's destiny. He's to rule Ireland." She touched Estrada's cheek with her palm. "And you know I won't back down from a fight."

Estrada covered her hand with his. "I do. That's why I'm asking you to stay here. Hang behind the bar with Cerise. She's another mama-to-be as kick-ass as yourself." When he'd finished this, Estrada would make sure Cerise got her baby. "If we don't find that other raven before we go, it could cause trouble." He picked up his leather jacket and slipped it on. Then opened it to show her the row of knives inside. "Just make sure you and Cerise always have access to something sharp. Aim for the forehead and drive it into the brain."

When they walked back out into the club, Conall was leaning against the bar, holding the samurai sword in one hand, and cradling a tall glass of Irish whiskey in the other. "It's there," he said, pointing the sword into the shadowed beams.

Estrada squinted. "I don't see it."

"Use your inner sight. Find the wine red shimmer."

"Ah, there you are. But I need a better angle." Estrada walked behind the stage and climbed up into the fly tower. He found the shimmer easily once he knew what to look for. As he relaxed his eyes, the tail feathers appeared. It was faced away, focused on Jazz in the case. There was no way he could hit it with a knife, but what about fire?

Closing his eyes, he deepened his breath and visualized flames bursting from his core. They surged through his shoulders and down his arms into the pointer finger of his right hand. Using a beam to stabilize his wrist, he lined up the sight like he would a gun. When he had it, he pulled the invisible trigger in his brain and sent a shot of flame flying between the beams. The raven shrieked as fire hit its tail. It lit out from the beam and shifted into a man mid-air, then crashed to the floor naked, and rolled, its ass end a mass of burns.

Conall was on it. By the time Estrada reached them, the bard was on his knees with the sword etching the vampire's throat. "It's that kid."

"Hola Eliseo." Estrada stared down at the boy, then turned to Conall. "Take him to the dressing room. There are too many witnesses here." Then he turned to Dell. "Close for tonight, but don't leave until I tell you."

Estrada found Conall kneeling on the floor of the dressing room with his knife at the creature's throat, and joined him.

"How old are you, *el cabrón*?" Estrada asked.

Eliseo stared through dark, narrowed eyes and squeezed his lips tight.

"Thirteen going on two-hundred-and-fifty? It's a shame this life of yours is about to end. Conall here is eager to take your head. So, if you want to keep it, at least until you see *su padre* again, you will comply."

Again, nothing. His silence didn't faze Estrada. He expected such obstinance from the child assassin whose brain had never developed beyond puberty.

"You see, I know you better than you think I do, Eliseo. We've met before, though you have no memory of it." Estrada pulled back his hair to reveal the two scars on his neck left by the boy's teeth. "You did this when you nearly drained me of blood."

The boy's eyes wrinkled in confusion.

"Obviously, you didn't succeed." Estrada caressed the pale cheek. "I know you are the first *El Salvador*. The prototype for Diego's drowned son, and naturally his favorite. I know you're from Lima. And once you stole my baby from her crib and kept her from me for days. And for that, I will turn you to dust."

With his heightened fey senses, Estrada felt the boy's muscles tense and smelled the acrid scent of fear.

"Now you will take us to Diego."

57

In the moonlight, the harbor at False Creek Yacht Club masqueraded like a picture postcard, concealing the evil that lurked within.

Though the plexiglass case was designed for one, they'd crammed both Jazz and Eliseo, head to toe, into the case and wrapped it in chain. Both had immediately shifted into ravens and bashed against the glass. While Estrada and Conall had questioned Eliseo in the dressing room, Sorcha had used her Irish charm and the promise of a cure to elicit one important fact from Jazz who, it seemed, really was newly fledged. After discovering their sire, Michael Stryker, existed no more, they were keen to leave Vampire behind and revealed that Diego's yacht was docked at Berth 77 in False Creek. Since Sorcha and Dubh had borrowed Daphne's pickup truck, they loaded their strange cargo into the bed. Dubh perched between Conall's legs in the passenger seat while Estrada drove.

Though he suspected the vampires shared a telepathic mind, Estrada parked out of view of Berth 77 and stalked through the shadows with Conall and Dubh at his side. Passing party boats blasting tunes, smoke, and sex on this sultry summer night in the harbor city, Estrada wondered what it would be like to live in a world where his life wasn't constantly under threat.

As they approached the million-dollar yacht, Estrada noticed *La Victoria* painted on the side of the cobalt blue hull, and scoffed. Don Diego expected a victory this night as he did every night, but he would not get it. When a dark shape appeared on the aft deck, Estrada recognized the silhouette at once—short, wiry, welterweight. Then as they drew closer, he remembered the face of the creature that had wanted him as a personal sex slave for all eternity. He hadn't known that was to be his function until he'd saved Leopold Blosch and learned the truth. He wondered if that was still Diego's desire or if it had changed.

The vampire's long black hair was tied back from his forehead leaving a distinct widow's peak. Between mustache and pointed goatee were full, rosy lips. He lifted them to reveal his coppery canines. He'd just fed. Estrada wondered who he'd murdered. His deep-set eyes were wizened and whimsical. In short, el *padron* was alarmingly cliché, despite the silver crucifix that dangled around his neck against the black bishop's robe.

Diego's chin rose as his eyes flashed seductively. That desire was still there. "Ah, Estrada, so glad you could join us. I'm pleased you brought Conall. We three will enjoy such sport together." He licked his lips. "And who is this beside the bard? Come into the light, *el enano*, so I can see your face."

Dubh stepped under the overhead light, staff by his side, his blue Pictish tattoos shimmering with sweat.

Estrada narrowed his eyes and stepped in front of Dubh. Magus was their friend and their cure, and he'd protect him at all costs. "Cut the bullshit, Diego. We have something of yours, and you have something of ours. We want to trade."

"Something of yours?" He raised his chin. "Ah, do you mean this?" He grasped Blosch's arm and dragged him out onto the aft deck. Leopold's platinum hair hung in greasy, bloody strings. His eyes were red and hazy. They'd been force-feeding him and he was wasted.

"Leo," Conall whispered. It was the first word he'd uttered since they'd left Pegasus, and it made Estrada's heart skip a beat.

"Come aboard where we can talk like civilized men. A parley, if you will."

There was no way Estrada was boarding that yacht. How many vampires were concealed? Even where they now stood, if they all suddenly turned to ravens, there was no cover. He glanced at Conall. The bard bounced on his toes, a sheen covering his freckled face. Clearly, he seethed beneath the silence. Estrada wondered how long he could hold before he broke.

"The only civilized men are standing beside me." Estrada noticed movement behind the blackened windows.

Diego sneered. "You mentioned trade. Considering you've already destroyed Zion and his lover, Michael Stryker, and you've abducted two of my sons, to be fair, I am owed all three of you. Leopold Blosch will remain mine and—"

Conall lunged.

Diego shifted into the thunderbird before their eyes, pushed off with Blosch's arm in his talon and hovered over them, dangling his limp body in the air. He beat his wings and thunder crashed. Dubh raised his staff and shot fire. And the startled pterosaur dropped Blosch, who hit the gunwale, and tumbled into the water.

Conall dove off the dock and disappeared.

Recovering, the thunderbird flapped its smoldering wings, swooped in, and grasped Estrada in its talons, piercing muscle and sinew between collarbone and shoulder. Unable to raise his arms, Estrada screamed as it plucked him from the deck, his flesh ripping under his weight.

Staring up, open-mouthed, the magician released a first blast of fire. Then, continued blowing flames like an angry dragon, each breath hotter, stronger, more powerful than the last. Ravens were flying beside him now, piercing and pecking his flesh. Finally, one last burst of flame and the creature jackknifed into the creek still clutching him in its talons. One breath, and they hit the surface like stone on glass, and plummeted. Gashes burning from the salt, Estrada writhed in agony.

You will not win, you motherfucker.

As it dragged him along the muddy bottom of False Creek, he stanched his frantic thoughts and reached out to the god. *Cernunnos. Help me.* The flesh ripped at his shoulder, and one arm dangled free. Using all his strength, he plucked a knife from his jacket and stabbed at the other talon. When it wouldn't give, he turned the knife on himself. Silently screaming, he sliced through the remaining skin. Once freed, he shot up through the dark water.

At last, he hit the surface. Gasping and bleeding, he glanced around. *There. Flashes of light. Dubh's staff.* The Wee Pict was still fighting. When a shadow passed over, Estrada dove. The thunderbird was hunting him. He swam underwater as long as possible, then surfaced near the burning yacht. In the distance, he heard sirens. A crowd had gathered.

He swam into a body at the darkened edge below the dock. Blosch clung to the wet wood, head lolling, still breathing. "Hold on, man. I've got you."

"Now will you trade?"

Estrada glanced up. Diego stood behind Conall, his arms locked around the bard's chest, pinning down his sword arm.

"Ah. His heart beats with such passion." Diego licked Conall's back. "I will take him now." When Diego sunk his teeth into the bard's back, Estrada pissed himself. Conall stood in agonized silence as the razor-sharp canines pierced his flesh and the creature guzzled his blood.

"No. Stop. I'll go with you." But still the vampire drank. Estrada watched the bard's eyes roll. His limbs slackened, and when, at last, the creature released him, Conall crashed onto the dock.

Cock stiff, eyes flashing, Diego licked his lips. "Ah, he is exceptional." When the vampire bit into his own wrist, a spray of blood flew, and Estrada's guts squeezed. Diego was going to feed Conall his blood, turn him, and take him right there in front of them.

While Diego was distracted by the orgasm he was about to have amid the chaos, Dubh sprang and thrust his blade into the back of the creature's neck. As he did, Estrada shot out of the water and slammed another knife into Diego's forehead.

Seeing the glint of the samurai sword, Estrada hauled Conall up and put it in his fist. "Take his head, friend."

Conall swung, then tried to grasp the wet black hair as it turned to ash in his hand.

"Fuck. Yeah." All three men stood staring at the pile of dust on the dock.

"Leo? Where's Leo?" Conall said. He was so weak he could barely stand.

"He's here. I'll get him." Estrada slipped back into the water and gathered Blosch in his arms. The man was frail, starved, and emaciated but still breathing. "You saved me once, Blosch. Now we're even."

Dubh had cut into his wrist and was applying his fey blood to the wounds on Conall's back. Then he held it to the bard's mouth while he sipped. "You're next," he said.

Estrada winced. His wet shirt was covered in blood, the flesh ripped on both shoulders deep into the muscles. "I can manage. Take care of him."

When they staggered back to the pickup truck, Eliseo had turned to dust inside the plexiglass case, but Jazz was still a fleshy corpse. Estrada pulled their body out and dumped it in the water. The police might eventually trace Jazz back to Pegasus but by then there'd be no evidence to tie them to the death. It may even go down as a suicide.

"Now what?" Dubh said.

"Now we get the fuck out of here before the cops start asking questions." Estrada helped Conall and Leopold into the bed of the truck and covered them with an old ground sheet.

Dubh climbed into the passenger seat beside him, and Estrada put his foot to the gas. He'd driven onto a side street when he suddenly stopped the truck. He glanced at Dubh lolling on the seat beside him. "If the vampires were all destroyed when we took out Diego, why is Leopold Blosch still alive?"

"I dosed him," Dubh muttered.

Estrada suddenly noticed that the wee man was dripping wet. Had he crawled down below the dock to tend Blosch? "Jeez, man. You've given way too much blood." Taking a knife from his inside jacket pocket, Estrada cut his left wrist and held it to Dubh's mouth. "Drink from me. I'm not going to lose you, Dubh. You're a hero, and heroes don't get to die."

58

When they arrived back at the club, the police were there. Estrada recognized Mowbray, Nigel Stryker's man on the force.

Remembering his bloody shirt, Estrada zipped up his leather jacket. "What's happening?" he asked casually.

"We had some reports of violence, but everything seems quiet now. Have you seen Michael?" Mowbray asked, eyebrows raised.

"Not for a day or two. You know Michael. He's likely holed up with some lovely having the time of his life."

"No doubt," Mowbray said. "Nigel texted to say he was finally taking Ruby for a yachting trip down the California coast."

"He certainly deserves some time away." Estrada glanced around. "Can we go in? We had a private party tonight and things got a little crazy."

Mowbray nodded. He was used to crazy at Club Pegasus. "Sure. Tell Dell, we investigated the complaint and we're moving on."

"Thank you," Estrada said. "I appreciate knowing you're here, sir."

Estrada climbed back into the truck and parked in the alley, then used his key to open the stage entrance. They'd all revived slightly, but it would take some time before they fully recovered. Estrada picked up Blosch and carried him into the dressing room. He laid him on the leather couch, then went back for the others. Dubh was up and moving, and Conall poised to jump off the tailgate.

"Come on, man. You'll be safe here."

By the time they were all collected in the dressing room, Sorcha had arrived with a tray of Irish whiskey shots. "So?" she said. "You're here. They're not. Are we celebrating?"

"We are, but before you disappear could you give me another couple of shots of glue?" He undid his jacket and tugged off his bloody shirt. As the adrenalin decreased, the pain intensified in his shoulders.

"*Jaysus, Mary, and Joseph.* What the feck happened to you?"

"Flying accident."

She warmed a cloth and washed off most of the blood. "This is bad, Estrada. You should go to the hospital."

"Nah, I'll be fine. Just glue it together as best you can." When Dubh had sufficiently recovered, he'd get another shot of his blood, just in case Diego had injected him with the vampire virus. After witnessing what it did to Michael, he was taking no chances. After Sorcha glued his tattered flesh and bandaged it, Estrada found a black dress shirt and dry trousers and slipped them on.

Picking up a shot, he said "Sláinte," and downed it. Then he handed one to Conall who'd been standing silently watching Sorcha doctor his injuries. "Maybe take Leo into a hot shower and see if you can revive him. There are dry clothes here for you both. We've given Leo fey blood and we'll give him more, but I think what he needs now is tender, loving care. Living with vampires has warped his soul. Plus, I don't think he's eaten in days. I'll see if I can find some vegan broth."

Conall threw his arms around Estrada. "I felt Diego's darkness when he drank from me. Thank you for letting me take his head." He rubbed his stubbled cheek against Estrada's. "And thank you for saving Leo."

59

"The usual, please Cerise," Estrada said. The bartender nodded and opened the bottle of tequila, while B.B. King announced "The Thrill is Gone." And, in some ways, it was.

Michael's ghost cruised the club. Estrada sniffed and rubbed his eyes. There'd be no one like him ever again. At least he'd dusted the bastards who'd got him hooked on the blood.

When Estrada squeezed Dubh's shoulders, he could sense that the wee man was finally unwinding.

"You know, that was pure solid, man. I don't know how we did it."

"With a little help from the gods," Estrada said, and gulped another shot. "I can't even go there right now. All I know is, it's finally over."

Dubh raised his glass. "*Sláinte mhath*, Cernunnos."

Conall sauntered out of the dressing room, just as the Mexican takeout arrived. He'd changed out of the brown leather pants into a pair of black stretchy jeans and T-shirt. How sexy could one man be?

"How's your back, man?" Estrada asked.

"The wounds are closing but it will require another kind of magic to cleanse that evil. And your shoulders?"

"I'll heal. How's Blosch?"

"Clean and warm, wrapped in a blanket, and resting on the couch. But it will take time."

Estrada remembered when he'd cured Blosch the last time with his diluted fey blood. He'd fallen into a deep sleep for hours. Things seemed different; perhaps because Dubh had dosed Blosch with so much pure blood. This time the cure was more rapid. "Eat with us, then take him some food. He hasn't eaten in days."

"Aye, and then I will take him home." Conall stared into Estrada's eyes. Did that mean he was spending the night in Blosch's bed?

Estrada's stomach quivered, and he shifted on the stool. No rules. No restrictions. Just love and desire for as long as possible. "Let me know if you need a hand. He may be too sleepy to walk on his own." When Conall touched his cheek another layer of tension faded. "I'm gonna crash here. After a few more shots and a bite to eat, I'll be sleeping myself."

"Thank you for Leo."

"*De nada.* I know how much he means to you." Still, a feather of fear tickled the back of his neck, and he shivered.

Estrada awoke, sprawled on the leather couch in the dressing room. Hearing soft snoring, he glanced down to find Conall, still dressed and curled up on a towel. Estrada tiptoed over him and made his way into the bathroom. He felt suddenly giddy. *Set your lover free and they'll return.* And here he was.

He squeezed cinnamon toothpaste on his brush and cleaned his teeth, then took a long drink of cool water. Today was the beginning of a new era without vampires, and he wanted to cleanse all traces of the past.

After turning on the shower, he tested the temperature, and stepped inside. The warm water felt almost as good as that first shower he'd had with Conall at Doyle's place. Declan Doyle who'd helped that crazy woman Sorcha had once loved murder her wife. He almost couldn't believe it. Only the trees would ever know what really happened to Vivian Sullivan.

The thought faded as he picked up the brown bottle of spicy shower wash and squeezed some into his hand. Cedar, orange, and cinnamon scented the steam and he breathed it in. He'd just washed and rinsed his hair when he heard the shower door open. Conall's caramel eyes flashed, and growling, he moved against him.

Estrada tasted cinnamon on his tongue as Conall's kisses rained over him, their bodies pulsing in the hot steam.

"I thought I'd lost you," the bard whispered.

"And I you. I never want to feel that way again."

Conall squeezed the spicy cedar soap into his hand and lathered Estrada's body. "Reminds me of our first shower together."

Estrada smiled. "You were so innocent then."

"And you were not."

As he entered the dream with Conall, he thought of love and desire, and how sometimes a man was fortunate enough to hold both in his hands.

Turning Conall to rinse his soapy hair, he noticed the marks left by Diego. The wounds had closed but he could see a deep dark shimmer in the bard's aura.

Gently, he kissed the wounds. "We could try more fey blood."

"I have another idea," Conall said.

"What?"

"I want to surprise you. It may take some time, but I will return, and when I do, we will begin again."

"A new life in a new era."

"Without the Leannán Sidhe."

61

Estrada drove the Harley back to Commercial Drive, enjoying his freedom but missing the feel of the bard's chest against his back. Inside, he pulled out his grinder and coffee beans. If this was the first day of a new era, he was going to do everything right. He measured the fresh ground coffee into his French press and added the boiled water. As he let it sit, he opened all the windows and searched his vinyl for *"Moanin' in the Moonlight,"* Chester Barnett's first release from 1959. He couldn't wait to introduce the bard to Howlin' Wolf's brand of blues. The tunes had been playing in his head since he mounted his Harley downtown.

He grabbed his coffee, sat on the Navajo rug, and leaned back against the wall. After a big sip and a bigger breath, he closed his eyes to the blues. Life was good. He'd just soaked in "Smokestack Lightning" when his phone chimed. Someone was using the app, calling from abroad. *Sensara?*

He stood and grabbed his phone from the turquoise bowl where he'd left his keys.

Not Sensara. Sorcha. Of course, she'd brought her phone from Scotland.

"Hey woman. Where did you disappear to last night? I lost track of you and Dubh."

"We stayed the night with Dell, and I finally cleansed my body and soul of that murderous bitch."

"I was not expecting that."

"Neither was I. The Wee Pict is still in the shower beltin' out old Scottish tunes. But listen. How are you and Conall?"

"We're good. I'm back at my flat, and Conall's out on some secret mission to cleanse himself of Diego."

"You did it, man. You rid the world of evil."

"As did you."

"I just read the story online. Declan made some kind of deal and spilled his guts. He and Franya are both locked up."

"What'll happen to the house and the horses?" Conall's white stallion was still there, and Estrada couldn't imagine him just letting go of Capall. Those two were bonded.

"I took care of the animals before I left. They'll be cared for until we can make other arrangements. The house? I can't say, nor do I care. I assume Vivian listed it when she announced she was divorcing Franya. I doubt it will sell now that it's a murder scene."

"So what about your dig?"

"I'm going to leave those yellow flowers just the way they are. I'm sure Viv appreciates gazing down on them from her grave on the hill."

"See if you can find out what happened to Capall. I'm sure Conall will want him back."

"Aye. He'll likely be fostered. I'll give them your number."

"Speaking of studs, what's the plan woman? You two moving in with Dell?" He chuckled. The sentinel's reputation was widespread.

"Well, today, Magus is taking the two of us whale watching."

"Get out."

"He got bletherin' about his Aunt Jackie and the Isle of Mull where he spent his summers as a wean. You know how he goes on. Apparently, there were whales. Dell told him about the whales here and now we're going to see them. They booked us on a boat. I don't mind. It's a grand day to be out on the water."

Estrada glanced at the sun beaming through the open windows. "Indeed, it is." He remembered how the whales had frolicked around their yacht when they'd destroyed Diego before. Would they be celebrating today?

"Oh, and when we get back, Dubh and I are going to grab a hotel room downtown, so you and Conall can have some time alone."

"You don't need to do that. We can sort something out."

"No. I want a big soft bed and if Magus happens to be in it, that's fine too."

Estrada laughed. "I never thought you and Dubh would—"

"*Jaysus.* I'm not going to marry the bugger. We're just sharing a room."

"And a bed."

"Aye." She giggled.

"I'm sure you've made the man's dreams come true, Sorcha. I could see that Dubh was in love with you that first day we walked into his shop in Glasgow."

"Well, it feels good to be loved for who you are and nothing else."

"True enough. It's funny how we came to this moment." Estrada sighed. "If you hadn't gone to Croghan with Cernunnos—"

"I'd never have met Cern if you hadn't conjured him at Ballymeanoch."

"And I'd never have come to Scotland and met either of you if Dylan hadn't been thrown in jail for murdering that journalist."

Sorcha snorted. "*Jaysus, Mary, and Joseph.* It all goes back to that feckin blow job I gave Dylan at Murphy's pub in Oban. One feckin blow job at a festive moment, and look where it's got us. You, in love with an Iron Age Druid. Me, pregnant with his best friend's son, and going whale watching with the Wee Pict and some stud off the West Coast of feckin Canada."

"You're a treasure, Sorcha. I love you."

"And I you, handsome. But now I'm gonna end this call before Magus comes out and grabs the phone. You know how he blethers on."

Estrada laughed. "Later."

The day seemed to drag after that. Estrada hated being alone. He checked in with Sensara and Lucy in Wales and told her the entire story, only slightly exaggerated in parts. Then he phoned Dylan, who was overly-apologetic about not being there to help. After that, he called Daphne to tell her and Raine they'd been victorious, and the vampires were gone. The women were returning from Whistler tomorrow.

Estrada's pack mates were safe and everyone would return for Lucy's first birthday party, three weeks today. He'd done what he set out to do—destroy Diego and his minions and save the lives of everyone who'd been killed the first time around.

Everyone but Michael.

Estrada had one thing left to do. Exhume Michael's body and take him to Nigel for cremation. But maybe not. Maybe he could leave Michael in the beautiful forest at Buntzen Lake, where they held their ceremonies, and each Sabbat, they could pray for his soul and wrap him in love. When Nigel returned, he'd ask what he preferred. Michael was his grandson, after all.

When he heard the doorknob turn, Estrada breathed a sigh of relief and stood as Conall walked through the door. The bard was humming some ancient Celtic chant and carrying a big bag of Mexican takeout.

"Oh wow. Is it dinnertime already?"

"Aye. Open the wine. I have something to show you." He set the bag of food on the kitchen counter, then walked into the bedroom.

Estrada popped a bottle of red, lit the honey candles, and set the table with turquoise dishes and cutlery. When he put Eric Clapton *Unplugged* on the turntable, he nearly dropped the needle, his palms were so sweaty. It was one of Conall's favorite albums and he wanted everything to be perfect tonight.

Conall came out of the bedroom, bare-chested, with a big grin on his face, and his hair up in a man bun.

"You look awfully sly, my friend, and I can see you've got nothing up your sleeve. What's going on?"

Conall turned. His back was freshly tattooed, his pale skin pink around the new ink and covered with a clear bandage. But the tattoo. Twin wolves howled beneath a turquoise crescent moon, their bushy manes wild and ruffled and knotted by the winds of change.

"Wow."

"It's us," Conall said. "You over my heart, and me beside you."

Estrada stood, eyes wide, mouth open, speechless.

Conall took his hand. "Shall we eat?"

"Wait. Wait. When did you decide to do this?"

"When I saw your black angel's wings and that raven on your arm. And then I saw Sorcha's fey butterfly. And then Magus Dubh. When I saw his blue tattoos, I asked him how I could get one of my own. I wanted to surprise you. Sorcha and Dubh helped me find an artist near Pegasus, and now I have my wolves. I have us. And we will howl together. That is what the image says."

"It's incredible, man, and I'm so touched." He grasped the bard's jaw with both hands and their foreheads came together.

"I need to keep the bandage on for a couple of days while it heals," Conall said. "But now Diego's energy is gone from me. I can't feel it at all." He touched his heart. "Now, it's only us."

And as Clapton sang "Running on Faith," Estrada's eyes clouded with tears.

"Us." Standing together on a brand-new day in a brand-new world, where anything was possible.

My Dear Readers,

Using my intuitive process, I wrote this story quicker than any before—even though time-travel messed with my head as much as it did Estrada's. I loved seeing his flat through Conall's eyes, and listened to some lovely old blues while choosing his vinyl. Check out "Estrada's Flat on The Drive" on Spotify if you'd like to hear it too. You can also find "Club Pegasus" there and listen to some old goth.

Many thanks to the following people: Donna Tunney for her developmental edit—her raven eye and storytelling skills helped me fill in holes, smooth, and sculpt this tale. My good friend, author JP McLean for her wonderful endorsement, and for her "beta read on steroids" that looked to me like a copy edit. And to author Sionnach Wintergreen for his beta read, endorsement, and unending support.

If you've read this series from the beginning, you'll know that Estrada's had a challenging time finding his forever partner, what with trying to balance freedom and family along with his polyamorous nature. Even now, as he grieves Michael and celebrates Conall, he fears losing the bard to Leopold Blosch—a man he once desired himself. Writing Estrada, a most complex hero, is one of the joys of my life. I'll soon be calling on him again to see what kind of mood he's in and where he's going to end up. He's left me with unanswered questions.

And in a world gone mad, I'll choose him. Every time.

As always, much gratitude goes to you, my readers. If you enjoyed this story, please leave a review at Goodreads and with your favorite retailer. Reviews help both readers and writers find each other. You can sign up to receive my six-week seasonal newsletter at https://harpercarr.substack.com/and follow me on social media.

g goodreads.com/user/show/183384153-harper-carr

instagram.com/harpers_books/#

tiktok.com/@harperwrites1003

blessings and all good wishes,

Harper
xo

THE MAN IN BLACK SERIES

The Witch Killer

The Conjurer

The Vampire's Game

The Tortured King

The Druid's Tune